PRAISE FOR *HANGMAN*

'Jack Heath's writing grabs you by the throat, gnaws on your bones and washes it all down with a hefty dose of funny. Sick, twisted, violent and oh so good. In Timothy Blake, Heath has created a one-of-a-kind character. I hope.'—Emma Viskic, internationally bestselling author of *And Fire Came Down*

'Blake is a brilliant, complex character . . . this quiet and unassuming figure might just be the most dangerous man in the room. *Hangman* is cinematic and grubby, brimming with pulpy noir.'—Michael Offer, producer, *How to Get Away with Murder* and *Homeland*

'Wild and original, *Hangman* stamps a high and bloodied mark on this dark genre. Hannibal Lecter will be adding Jack Heath to his reading list.'—Ben Sanders, internationally best-selling author of *American Blood*

'Let's cut to the chase: *Hangman* is a great read! Jack Heath's boundless imagination and singular voice have produced a truly unique thriller. By turns psychologically insightful, wonderfully disturbed and even darkly comedic, *Hangman* will keep you coursing through the pages at a lightning pace. Brilliant! (Probably best read with lights on and doors locked. I'm just saying.)'—Jeffery Deaver, No. 1 international best-selling author

'*Hangman* is ghoulish fun, and fills the Dexter- and Hannibal-shaped holes in our lives.'—*Books + Publishing*

'A grisly, efficiently written nail-biter packed with riddles and suspense, *Hangman* has bestseller written all over it. It's a dark book, but one with plenty of humour, and a twisty plot that keeps you guessing to the very end.'—*Sydney Morning Herald*

'Compelling . . . Heath keeps the suspense at a high level through to its stunning conclusion. An addictive and suspenseful thriller that will keep you reading well into the night.'—*Canberra Weekly*

'Blake is a classic kind of hard-boiled hero, mixing cynicism and honour, brutality and sentimentality . . . he's a chivalrous knight of the kind we have never seen before.'—*Weekend Australian Review*

'A cracking read full of well-crafted twists and turns . . . Heath manages to bring Blake out from behind the shadow of his predecessors and stand on his own.'—*Australian Crime Fiction*

'Heath has given the crime world an anti-hero for this century. Gifted and flawed, Blake will horrify and entrance readers, quite often at the same time. An exceptionally taut novel both in action and execution, this sledge-hammer story is sure to entice fans of serial crime fiction, taking readers into the dark and dirty recesses of Blake's mind.'—*Good Reading*

'*Hangman* is a pulpy and perverse delight . . . Heath makes Blake young, rough, streetwise, and precisely the sort of person Dr Lecter would avoid in the street. This is a gobsmackingly (or lip-smackingly) violent tale, but it is also bizarre, hilarious, and a stealthily astute commentary on post-financial crisis America. Give me more.'—Christopher Richardson (blog)

'Richer than Reacher ... *Hangman* literally tingles with tension, and Heath injects a healthy dose of dark humour.'— *Sydney Arts Guide*

'*Hangman* is cheerful in its gore, with a knack for unexpected violence that'll leave even the most jaded crime readers at least a little bit impressed ... It's all the best parts of noir fiction, all the spatter pattern ghoulishness of forensics-focused dramas, and so much fun it might just concern you a little bit.'—Hush Hush Biz (blog)

PRAISE FOR *HIDEOUT*

'Gloriously messed up, with a protagonist who manages to be likeable, reprehensible and totally singular all at once. A crime series like no other.'—Gabriel Bergmoser, author of *The Hunted*

'Thrilling, grisly and inventive: Jack Heath has single-handedly increased my carbon footprint through lights left on.'—Benjamin Stevenson, author of *Either Side of Midnight*

'Heath will make your spine tingle and your fingers flip pages.'—Candice Fox, author of *Crimson Lake*

ABOUT THE AUTHOR

Jack Heath is the award-winning author of more than thirty novels for adults and children. His books have been translated into several languages, adapted for film and optioned for television. He lives on the land of the Ngunnawal people in Canberra, Australia.

Hideout contains scenes readers may find disturbing. It is unsuitable for children, and some adults.

HIDEOUT

JACK HEATH

ALLEN&UNWIN
SYDNEY·MELBOURNE·AUCKLAND·LONDON

First published in 2020

Allen & Unwin
83 Alexander Street
Crows Nest NSW 2065
Australia
Phone: (61 2) 8425 0100
Email: info@allenandunwin.com
Web: www.allenandunwin.com

A catalogue record for this
book is available from the
National Library of Australia

ISBN 978 1 76087 717 0

Set in 12.5/17.5 pt Sabon by Midland Typesetters, Australia
Printed and bound in Australia by Griffin Press, part of Ovato

10 9 8 7 6 5 4 3 2 1

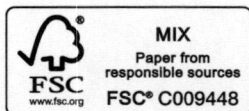

In memory of Peter Jordan

Beware anyone who tries to make you angry.

—Jackie French

CHAPTER 1

Eject my skin so it won't be found.
What am I?

'The other guys?' I say.

'Sure.' Fred smiles. 'You didn't think it was just me out here, did you?'

That's exactly what I thought. The plan was simple: kill Fred, then myself. But my only weapon is the hammer tucked into the back of my pants. If Fred has friends in this house, I'm in a whole world of trouble.

'Great,' I say. 'Can't wait to meet them.'

Fred is looking at the car I arrived in: a midnight-blue sedan, with supple leather seats and a stereo still playing light jazz, even though the engine is off. Blood on the passenger's seat, mud on the driver's. A bullet hole low on one of the doors.

Fred looks at the hole for a strangely long time. A shadow crosses his face.

'Nice ride, Lux,' he says finally.

'Not my car.' Not my name, either.

He nods, unsurprised. 'Anyone looking for it?'

'Maybe. Probably.'

1

'I'll tell Kyle to take care of that.' He holds out a hand for my keys.

If I give them to him, I'm trapped. If I don't, he might realise I'm not Lux.

'You don't need to do that,' I say.

Fred waves this off. 'It's no trouble.'

Hesitating any longer would look suspicious. I pass him the keys. He slides the car key off the ring and tosses the rest back.

'It's fine for tonight, though,' Fred says. 'No one will see it. We're miles from anywhere.'

He's not wrong. The house is in the middle of the woods, at the end of a long driveway off a dirt road. None of my contacts at the FBI know where I am. I don't even have a phone. If I die out here, no one will ever know what happened to me. That was the point.

'Come on,' Fred says. 'You must be freezing.'

'Yeah.' My tattered white shirt, suit jacket and thin socks offer no protection from the night air, and I'm still getting used to having a shaved head. My ears hurt. Hunger burns in my gut, or maybe it's fear. I broke my nose in a car crash two days ago—I can still taste blood pooling at the back of my throat.

Fred locks the car with the key remote. The music and the interior lights fade out, like in a cinema when the movie's about to start. We crunch across the gravel towards the house.

Fred is white, lean and younger than I expected. Late twenties, maybe. Fair skin, scruffy hair, friendly wrinkles at the edges of his brown eyes. He has the voice of a venture capitalist or a junior lawyer. He doesn't look or sound like he runs the most violent porn site on the dark web.

The house is made from many kinds of wood, carefully arranged. Pale slats around the foundations, darker beams up top, with a gradient in between, like a sunrise. Recycled timber, maybe, like in one of those expensive eco homes. The windows on either side look double glazed, the light inside dampened by thick curtains. The second level is smaller than the first, maybe just an attic.

It's a fusion of the Old South and the New. Texans used to march into the wilderness with nothing but a hatchet and build a house to live in. If anyone else settled within a half-mile of them, they'd abandon the house and build another somewhere even more remote. That urge is still there—but now people want their isolated homes to have solar orientation and heated towel rails.

Fred is unlocking the front door, even though he only just walked out of it. 'Automatic locks,' he explains. 'Can't be too careful. There are some bad people out there.'

'Oh?' I say.

He welcomes me into the warmth of a short hallway, two mirrors gleaming on either side, like in an elevator. I can hear a fire crackling somewhere. The downlights are painfully bright, making me feel as though I'm in a dentist's chair, about to be poked with something sharp.

Fred hangs his jacket on an old-fashioned coat stand. The door locks itself behind us with a crisp *beep*.

'Come on.' Fred leads me through the hallway, which opens out into a spacious living area. Two white men in muscle shirts drop their Xbox controllers and get up off a grey sofa. A refined-looking woman in a slinky dress appears at the far end of the room holding a glass of white wine. A young man—maybe a teenager—sits on a beanbag in a hoodie and a baseball cap, looking at his phone. A skinny guy in a suit turns away from the fireplace and looks at me through glassy eyes.

I worked hundreds of cases at the FBI and studied thousands of mugshots, but I don't recognise any of these people. Am I supposed to? Lux never met Fred in person, but he might have met Fred's friends. If he did, I'm screwed. I don't look anything like him.

But everyone is giving me polite smiles. My cover is intact . . . for now.

'Guys,' Fred says, 'this is Lux.'

Heads nod all around. The two muscle men each raise a hand in a small wave. The young guy says, ''Sup?'

'These are the Guards.' Fred points to each person. 'Donnie, Samson, Zara, Kyle and Cedric. Now, repeat all that back to me.'

He's kidding, and everyone laughs.

'Sure.' I point. 'Donnie, Samson, Zara, Kyle, Cedric.'

Fred raises an eyebrow. 'Not bad.'

Memorising names is easy. Sometimes I use celebrities—Donnie, one of the two brawny Xbox players, looks a bit like Mark Wahlberg, and I know Mark has a brother named Donnie, so that's easy. The other player, Samson, has shoulder-length hair. I visualise him as the Samson from the Bible, a servant girl hacking off his locks as he sleeps.

Other associations also work. Zara, the elegant woman in the cocktail dress, has the same name as an upmarket shoe store in Houston. I used to beg for change on a nearby street corner. I imagine this Zara as the owner, shooing me away, threatening to call the cops.

The more emotional the connection is, the better it works. After my parents were shot, I was put in a group home, and one of the other orphans was named Cedric. He wasn't a friend, but no one adopted either of us, so I knew him for longer than most of the other kids. We were both aware that when we turned eighteen, we'd be kicked out. The day before his birthday, Cedric hung himself with the cord of his bathrobe.

That Cedric was a white, heavy-set teenager, while this Cedric is in his mid-thirties, thin and Black. But if I picture a ring of bruises around his throat, the association is there.

I don't know any Kyles, so I go for a rhyme. This Kyle, the teenager on the beanbag, has a Hitler-youth kind of look. Pasty, square-jawed, keen to follow orders. I imagine him at a rally, yelling, 'Sieg Kyle!'

I don't need any memory tricks to remember Fred's name. The human brain has evolved to remember dangerous people.

This isn't the first time I've assumed someone else's identity. Once I dressed as an electrician so I could sneak into a half-constructed house for a shower. Another time I donated sperm for cash using a borrowed ID, because I was too young to do it legally. But now the stakes are higher. If there's one thing rural Texans love, it's guns. I might be the only person in this room who isn't carrying. A single word wrong, and I could get a bullet in my skull.

Donnie, the bulkier of the two gamers, holds out his hand. I shake it. His grip is crushing.

'Cold hands,' he says.

'Cold hands, warm heart,' I say.

Donnie lets go. 'My mom used to say that.'

'What do you bench, bro?' I don't know exactly what this means, but I've heard gym junkies say it to each other like a greeting.

He shrugs modestly. 'Two hundred, back in the day.'

I give a nod that could be interpreted as impressed or encouraging, depending on whether two hundred is high or low.

No one else tries to shake my hand.

Fred is unwinding his scarf. 'Lux made some of our most requested videos.'

There's an awkward round of applause, like after singing 'Happy Birthday' to a work colleague.

'But he has to lie low for a while,' Fred continues, 'so he's gonna stay with us.'

'What happened?' asks Cedric, the skinny guy in the suit. He gestures at his own face to show what he means.

'Car wreck.' I swallow some more blood.

Fred crosses his arms. 'Where's the FBI guy? Timothy Blake?'

It's jarring to hear him use my name. How much did Lux tell him about me?

'It's all right.' Fred has misread my hesitation. 'They're cool. I mean, you know what we do here.'

Some images flash through my head. Blood, chains, screaming.

'I sure do.' I should be mimicking Lux's voice, in case one of these guys has talked to him on the phone. My Texas accent is broader than his was. Too late now.

'So what happened to the cop?'

'Blake's not a cop. He's a civilian consultant.' I clear my throat. 'Was, anyway. I shot him in the head. Left him in Huntsville State Park under six feet of dirt. No one will ever find him.'

The story sounds fake coming out of my mouth. But the people around me are visibly relaxing. If I'm a cop killer, I must be okay.

It's Lux buried in the park, not me. He was a teaching assistant who kidnapped a young woman and sent videos of her torture to Fred. Later, one of his other victims killed him in cold blood. I helped her dispose of the body.

'You hear that, Donnie?' Cedric says. 'Six feet.'

Everyone laughs except Donnie and Samson. I chuckle, pretending to get the joke. Donnie looks about five foot eleven. Maybe Cedric is making fun of him for being short, even though he's the tallest person in the room.

'Blake was trying to shut us down, right?' Donnie asks. He's a bit older than the others—late-thirties—with shaggy hair and a silver chain around his neck. No cross on it.

'He was trying to shut *me* down,' I say. 'Me and Fred. He didn't know the rest of you existed. At least, I don't think he did.'

Fred nods slowly. 'Well, we can get you a driver's licence in a new name. It'll take five, six days.'

I'm not going to last five or six days. These people may not have met Lux, but they communicated with him on the dark web. I don't know enough about him or them to pull this off.

'That's really kind of you,' I say. 'But I can't stay long.'

Fred looks surprised. 'Why not?'

'The cops are searching for me.' I wish this was true. 'I don't want to put the group in danger.'

'You don't need to worry about us,' Samson says.

Fred pats me on the spine, just above the handle of the hammer.

'We got your back,' he says.

Zara speaks for the first time. 'Can I get you a drink, Lux?' Playing the host. Maybe this is her house, not Fred's. Her black hair shines like a grand piano. She has access to expensive shampoo, which might mean regular trips to Houston. Maybe I can join her on one of them. Escape that way.

'No thanks.' For all I know, Lux didn't drink and this is a test. 'But I could use an aspirin.'

She beams. Dazzling white teeth appear between bright red lips. 'Coming right up.'

She walks away, with just enough sway in her hips that I feel like I'm supposed to watch. Her high heels make no sound on the wooden floor, as though she's coated the soles with felt.

'While you're waiting,' Fred says, 'do you want to see where the magic happens?'

The young guy, Kyle, still hasn't opened his mouth. He looks like I did when I aged out of foster care—dishevelled, tense, watchful. He forces a smile at me and then turns back to his phone screen.

'Sure,' I say.

CHAPTER 2

Keep me clean to avoid the police.
Break me and you'll cry. I'm soft on the
outside, hairy on the inside. What am I?

Fred takes me through to the kitchen, which has a stone benchtop so big you could conduct autopsies on it, and the dining area, where someone has already added a seventh chair to the teak table. A bundle of yoga mats lean against a wall in the corner. These criminals do yoga?

A corridor to the right looks like it probably leads to the bedrooms and the stairs, but we go to the back door instead. Another electronic lock clicks and beeps behind us as we walk out into the December air. Fred has a little flashlight on his keys. He shines it at the dead grass as we walk.

No snow yet, but I can feel it on the way. The woods surrounding the house are dense, but the trees look dead, strangled by the frost. I guess Fred is taking me to the server room, where all the videos are stored. Servers need to be kept cool.

I've seen some of the recordings on Lux's hard drive. A woman getting strangled in Tokyo, a man disembowelled in Mexico City, a teenager drowned in a bathtub in Manila, and many others which were far worse. I assume Fred is taking me to see even more.

'I'll get you to keep Abbey's background on the down low.' Fred's breaths come out as plumes of steam. 'The others don't know.'

My mouth is too quick for my brain. 'Her background?'

Fred clicks his fingers and points at me, like he's shooting a pistol. 'Perfect.'

Abbey Chapman was the young woman I rescued from Lux's homemade prison. Lux was making videos of her and submitting them for Fred's site. I have no idea what he thinks I know about her 'background'.

We walk past a small greenhouse. It's dark inside, but I can see red flowers—roses, or maybe poppies—touching the other side of the sweaty glass. There's a vegetable patch here, too. A PVC pipe sticks out of the dirt nearby, maybe part of an underground composting system. On the other side of us, there's a chest-high chain-link fence. Something is breathing heavily from the shadows behind it.

'Back,' Fred commands.

When the dog moves, I see it's a big boxer—short fur and a square black muzzle, with the kind of jaws that clamp down and never let go. Long, muscular forelegs, stubbier hind legs. It sits, little tail flicking back and forth as it watches me. I have enough experience with dogs to know that a wagging tail isn't always a good sign. A second dog slinks through the shadows further away.

'They're friendly . . . once they get to know you,' Fred says.

When the boxer growls, I smell raw meat on its breath.

'You okay?' Fred asks.

I cough. 'Yeah. Just cold.'

'Sorry. I know you've had a rough night. We can do this tomorrow if you want?'

'No, I'm good.' I need to see the whole way around the house. There might be a way to sneak back to the car without anyone noticing.

Fred's expensive hiking shoes leave faint patterns in the dirt. There are plenty of older footprints around in various sizes and facing various directions. Paw prints. Drag marks. Now the markings from my ill-fitting formal shoes are joining the mix. Everywhere you go, everything you say, everything you do leaves a trail. Those inspirational posts clogging up the internet—*You matter! You make a difference!*—are half right. Nothing matters, but everything makes a difference. The wrong person could notice those differences and decode them days or years later.

Which clues might lead the Guards to my real identity? The FBI never paid me with money, so there isn't much of a paper trail to follow. The only agent I was ever close to, Reese Thistle, has quit, and fled from Houston. The Guards are unlikely to find any trace of me there.

But the FBI wasn't my only employer. In addition to selling credit card numbers on Russian web forums and solving riddles for cash, I also worked for crime boss Charlie Warner, disposing of the bodies she left in her wake. Another of her employees might surface and blow my cover.

There are other trails the Guards might follow. The real Lux was a teaching assistant—a profession I know nothing about—in the mathematics department—a subject I know nothing about. I thought I'd only have to impersonate him for thirty seconds before clubbing Fred in the back of the head with a hammer. I didn't think I'd need to fool five other people for hours at a time, maybe days.

Did the Guards know Lux's full name? Maybe not. But if they see 'Shannon Luxford wanted for false imprisonment' on the news, they'll put two and two together. Particularly if Abbey agrees to any TV interviews, taking a network's money in exchange for her tears.

Fifty yards behind the main house, slightly uphill, there's another building. A barn, with metal walls and a huge padlock on the front door. Three big buckets are stacked next to the door, with organic dog food labels on the lids.

When I was homeless, I often broke into buildings like this for shelter overnight. No need to pick the locks; a pair of tin snips would cut right through the wall. But I guess no one is out here looking for computers to steal.

'This place used to be a hobby farm.' Fred pulls on some gloves and searches through a ring of keys as we approach. 'That fenced-off area was the pig pen, and this was the slaughterhouse. But rumours surfaced about cruelty to the animals. Nothing was ever proven, but people stopped buying meat from the farm. Pretty soon the owners were desperate to sell. I got it cheap.' He looks pleased with himself.

'Uh-huh,' I say.

'I renovated the house pretty substantially. But this part has stayed largely the same.'

The back door of the house bangs shut. I turn and see Donnie running up the hill towards us, carrying a SIG Sauer P320.

I freeze, but Fred still seems relaxed. 'No rush,' he tells Donnie. 'They're not going anywhere.'

Donnie catches up to us and claps me on the shoulder with a big hand. 'You excited?'

'Hell yeah.' My heart flutters. Why has he brought a gun?

As we reach the slaughterhouse, I hear something inside. A chorus of cracked voices shrieking, 'Help us! Somebody, please! *Help!*'

I stop dead. Fred's videos come from all over the world. I had wondered if he made some of them himself, but on the long drive here it never occurred to me that he would have live prisoners.

Fred takes a Halloween mask out of his pocket and unfolds it. It's a witch's face, with wrinkled grey skin, a long warty nose and white hair like spider silk.

'I keep telling them that we're miles from anywhere,' he says. 'Nobody can hear them. But they don't believe me.'

'Ha.' I can hardly breathe.

Fred pulls the witch's face on over his own, and hands a second mask to me. A vampire, with arched eyebrows and fake blood dribbling from rubber fangs. 'Put this on.'

'What are we doing?'

The witch stares at me through inscrutable black eye-holes. 'The votes are in.'

I've never seen Fred's website, only the videos on Lux's hard drive. Lux himself told Abbey the site didn't exist. Just the same, I have a sense of what he might be talking about. The dread is like quicksand, slowly swallowing me.

I pull the mask over my face. The eyeholes aren't quite in the right places. My peripheral vision is gone. When I glance at Donnie, I find myself looking at Frankenstein. The square jaw and heavy brows go well with his thick neck.

13

As soon as Fred starts fiddling with the locks, the screaming stops. It's as though the people inside can tell it's him just from the way he unlocks the door.

The door groans as he drags it open and hits a switch. Fluorescent lights flicker on one by one, illuminating a stained concrete floor, rusting steel walls, a small space heater and a hulking machine, with a broad chute bolted to one side and a spout mounted opposite. Inside the chute I can make out jagged shapes designed to shred carcasses. I guess the machine is left over from when this was a functioning farm. Whole pigs go in one end, slop comes out the other.

Fred touches a second switch. Heat lamps come on, lighting up the rest of the slaughterhouse. It's divided into several half-rooms, each with one wall cut away, like a movie set. There's a fake pharmacy. An industrial kitchen. A hotel room. A cinema. A locker room. A church confessional. Some of the sets have foreign power outlets. Through one of the room's phoney windows, I can see the Eiffel Tower.

There are three women and three men, each chained to a separate movie set. They keep their eyes to the floor, trembling as if current is running through their bodies.

I recognise some of the sets from recordings on Lux's hard drive. Fred isn't getting these videos from all over the world at all—he's just making it look like he is.

Donnie walks into the slaughterhouse, hands behind his back. His footfalls are slow and measured, like he's browsing in a furniture shop, trying to decide which sofa to sit on. The soft scuffles echo through the space. Each prisoner looks terrified as he approaches and relieved when he strolls past. Then he reaches the other end of the slaughter-house and turns around. They all tense up again.

'The votes have been counted,' he says, his voice muffled.

Someone whimpers.

My breaths are hot inside the mask. I glance at Fred. He's leaning against the wall, his face hidden behind the witch mask.

'Scammer,' Donnie says finally.

A man in a dirty white coat, middle-aged, Asian American, hunchbacked, starts weeping into his claw-like knuckles. There are sweat patches under his arms, despite the cold. 'Oh, no. Please, God, no . . .'

Donnie walks over and grabs him by his greying hair. The man screams.

'The people have spoken.' Donnie raises his voice to be heard over the sobbing. 'Scammer's time is up.'

He doesn't sound like he's talking to me. I look up. A bundle of cameras and microphones are mounted on the ceiling, nestled in a web of cables. Each lens is pointed at a different set, a little red light glowing underneath.

When I look back down, Donnie has the gun against Scammer's temple.

The chains jingle as the man raises his hands. 'Please! Can you at least just—'

Bang! The muzzle flash lights up a sudden spray of red on the wall. The other prisoners scream. The man goes limp, and Donnie drops him. He hits the concrete floor face first. When a second shot goes through his heart, he doesn't even twitch.

A woman in a tattered evening gown, handcuffed to the door of a priest's confessional, starts weeping.

Fred is watching me closely. This was a test. A cop—or any decent person—would have tried to intervene. At the very least, they would be horrified. But I just stood there and let it happen. I was thinking about how to get myself out of this. It didn't even occur to me to try to save anybody else.

'Cool.' I hold out my hand for the weapon. 'Can I do the next one?'

If I was armed, I could leave. I've never fired a gun before, but the Guards don't know that. I could bluff my way out.

Donnie doesn't give me the P320. He just laughs and looks at Fred. 'Your boy's keen.'

Fred steps away from the wall and stretches. 'After voting closes, sure,' he tells me. He looks around the room at his whimpering prisoners like he's counting them.

A new plan starts to form. One that suits me better.

'Thanks, man. I appreciate it.' I put a hand on Fred's arm and give it a friendly squeeze. It's nice and firm. Fred is one hundred and eighty pounds of lean meat. Donnie is maybe two twenty. What would be the total if I added the others back at the house? A thousand pounds or more?

Without a vehicle or a gun, I can't think of a way to escape.

But maybe I'm right where I need to be.

CHAPTER 3

I cut and cast. You roll with me
even though I'm fatal. Who am I?

'That's what expertise is,' Samson says, throwing some crushed garlic onto the carrots and onions in the frying pan. 'You know more and more about less and less, until eventually you know everything about nothing.'

I nod thoughtfully, as though he's said something profound rather than just spouting nonsense, and hand him the freshly washed spinach. There's no meat in the stir-fry yet, and I'm getting concerned.

'Thanks.' He takes the dripping leaves from me and drops them into the pan with a splash of water.

Samson is about my age—maybe slightly younger, thirty-one or thirty-two. His clear blue eyes and perfectly straight teeth give him a movie star smile. Despite the cold, he's wearing a tank top and shorts. I can smell his sweat from a recent workout. He's pre-salted.

'Got a hand towel?' I ask.

'Over there.'

I volunteered to help with the cooking largely so I could examine the utensils. So far, I've found a cleaver, a carving knife and a nice big freezer.

The hammer is still in the back of my pants. I don't have anywhere safe to hide it.

As I dry my hands, Samson notices that I only have nine fingers. 'What happened to your thumb?'

Just like every time someone asks, I find myself flexing the missing digit. I can still feel it there, as though it's invisible rather than gone. 'I chewed it off to get out of some cuffs,' I say.

He inhales, preparing for a laugh, and then realises I'm not kidding. 'For real?'

I nod.

'That's hardcore. Why didn't you just dislocate it, like the Navy Seals do?'

I frown. 'Huh. Never occurred to me.'

He does laugh now. 'Shit, I wish we had a video of that. It would get into our top ten, for sure.'

'Uh, thanks.'

'I hope you don't mind me saying that?'

A considerate killer. 'It's all good.'

'I saw a lot of dislocated thumbs at the hospital.' Samson crumbles a cube of vegetable stock over the pan. 'Looked painful. Maybe you made the right call.'

Samson—never Sam—used to be a triage nurse, or so he claims. His mother was a pharmacist and his father a physiotherapist, so it was inevitable that he'd end up doing something medical. Even his older sister was a dental receptionist.

At the hospital, Samson sat behind a glass panel from

ten pm to four am six days a week, getting shouted at and spat on by parents who refused to believe that their child wasn't sick enough to need a doctor. During his breaks he'd be on the receiving end of stern reprimands from doctors and administrators about the patients he did let through who had wasted their time.

And then there was that girl with the headache.

'She didn't *tell* me about the nausea,' Samson says. 'She didn't say anything about the loss of appetite. And her parents didn't mention her neck had been sore until much later.'

I don't suggest that it might have been his job to ask those questions. 'Meningitis?'

He looks at me sharply. 'Are you a doctor?'

'What? No. I dropped out of high school.' The response is automatic. Then I remember that Lux had a math degree. 'I mean, I went back, but—'

Samson has already turned back to the stove. 'Yes, it was meningitis.'

'Did she die?'

He ignores the question. 'Hospital made me quit when the parents started talking about a suit. That's what I mean—those lawyers have no idea what it's like on the front line. And can you believe that girl's parents? I mean, take some responsibility.' He snaps his fingers, and I pass him the pepper grinder.

His own parents, he tells me, had been ashamed of him since he was a teenager. He doesn't say why. But after he quit the hospital, the relationship got worse, and they kicked him out. He enrolled for an MBA, then gave up on it. He hasn't spoken to them since.

'So how did you meet Fred?' It's risky asking questions like this, since it might be something I'm supposed to know already. But I figure it's more suspicious to say nothing.

'Well, after I dropped out of college I had a lot of time on my hands. I was on the dark web, and I saw someone posting about the Guards and how horrible they were. I just wanted to take a look. And the first inmate I saw was the stepfather. You know, the video with all the broken glass?'

I don't. 'Sure.'

'And it was great.' Samson takes the lid off a pot of rice and spoons it into some bowls. 'Watching someone like that getting what he deserves. Plus, I'd spent so long trying to heal these bastards, and it had been such a pain in the ass. So watching the opposite, someone getting hurt . . . it was extra satisfying, I guess.' He says this with a frown of introspection, but no shame.

'Right,' I say.

'So I sent a message to Fred to thank him, and he said I could help out if I wanted. I needed to prove I wasn't a cop, obviously. I still had my old ID, so I stole some ketamine from the hospital and mailed it to him. Then he invited me here, and . . . shit, hang on.' Samson opens the enormous oven, where some herb bread is getting scorched. He pulls out the tray and puts it on the bench then starts hastily chopping some spring onion for a garnish.

What he deserves. 'What did the stepfather do, again?'

'He suffocated his kids with cotton balls. You don't remember?'

'Oh, I thought he might have been the guy with the tattoo,' I say, improvising.

'I don't remember any tattoo.'

'Maybe it was just a birthmark.'

'Wait, do you mean the one who broke his girlfriend's neck?'

'Oh, yeah, that's who I meant.' Apparently Fred has made plenty of videos I haven't seen. And it sounds like he doesn't choose his victims at random—he takes killers. Not unlike me.

The thought is uncomfortable. I push it away.

'You know, Donnie cut that dude's foot off.' Samson smiles and shakes his head, amused by Donnie's shenanigans. 'If I hadn't been here to treat the stump, he wouldn't have lasted until—Ow! Fuck!' Samson is sucking on one of his fingers.

'What's up?'

'Just cut myself. Badly. Goddamn it.' He goes to the sink and turns on the water.

I glance over at the chopping board. He's dropped the knife. Next to the blade, I can see a sliver of skin, pink on one side, red on the other.

'Can you grab some paper towel?' Samson asks.

'Huh?' I'm still staring at the chopping board.

'Paper towel. It's right behind you.'

I tear my gaze away from the thin piece of Samson's finger. At my house the paper towel would be stuffed into a cupboard, still half-wrapped in plastic. Here, it's mounted on a neat little rail. I tear off some sheets and hand them to Samson.

'Thanks.' He presses the paper against his hand and it blossoms red immediately, like the flowers I saw in the greenhouse.

'I'll clean up the mess.' I turn back to the bloodied chopping board and the knife.

'Just give it here. I'll wash it.'

'Okay.' I bring them over to the sink.

Samson examines the board, frowning. 'I think I sliced off some skin, but I don't see it anywhere.'

'Huh. Weird,' I say.

His lip curls. 'Sure hope it didn't end up in the food.'

'Yeah.' I clear my throat. 'That would be bad.'

'Lux,' Fred says from behind me.

It takes a second to remember that's my name now, but I turned around as soon as I heard his voice, so he shouldn't have detected any hesitation.

Fred has changed into cargo pants and a sweatshirt with a faded purple logo on the chest. He breathes on his hands and rubs them together.

'Your room is ready,' he says.

CHAPTER 4

Under my crown I'm sometimes
flushed, but I can move any distance
in any direction. Who am I?

An ex-CIA contractor once visited the field office to teach us about undercover work. He wasn't popular. The FBI agents thought the CIA was full of shifty, self-important assholes who refused to follow anyone else's rules. This contempt was envy in disguise—many of them had gone to Quantico only after flaming out at Langley.

I wasn't supposed to be at the presentation, but I had heard there would be food, so I snuck in. The conference room smelled of yesterday morning's coffee and Friday's five o'clock beers. The rumour of food turned out to be false. It may have been a deliberate trick to improve the turnout. This seemed like something the CIA would do.

The contractor's name was Hassan. He was slight and softly spoken, with a crisp grey suit, a tattoo on one side of his neck and an old knife wound on the other. He told us he had been embedded in both Afghanistan and Iraq, and he strongly hinted he had been to other places that he couldn't talk about.

'There are two kinds of cover,' he told us. 'Official and non-official. In an official cover role, you tell everyone you work for the US Government, but you pretend you're in a less interesting organisation than the CIA. The department of transportation, or education. Or perhaps the FBI.' No one laughed. 'You act like a normal bureaucrat, while recruiting local assets to do the real spying for you. If you're caught, you just get sent home. No big deal.

'I did the other kind. Non-official cover, where no one knows you work for Uncle Sam, and you therefore have no diplomatic protection if you're caught. Agents with non-official cover are often executed. Since you'll be going undercover with gangbangers and mobsters, the stakes will be similar.

'To be an effective undercover agent,' Hassan continued, clicking through to the first slide of his PowerPoint presentation, 'the secret is preparation. You need to be able to quickly recall every detail about all the people you'll be embedded with. Make flash cards. Build memory palaces. You need to know your false identity inside out. Not just the biographical details, like your parents' names and when you were supposedly born, but personality traits. How would the person I'm supposed to be walk into a room? How would he greet a stranger? How would he answer this question or that? I recommend spending a few weeks inhabiting this character before you go into the field.'

The surly FBI agents just glared at him. Their budget was pitiful. They didn't have a few weeks to devote to anything. Half of them were supposed to be on vacation right now, and all of them would have to work twice as hard this afternoon to catch up after wasting all morning listening to him.

Undaunted, Hassan clicked through to the next slide. 'Trust your handler and your superiors. They'll do the actual investigating—you're only supposed to be their eyes and ears. You can't focus on your cover *and* bring your own agenda to the mission. There's not enough room in your head.'

'Not in *your* head, maybe,' muttered Richmond. The agent next to him snickered.

Alan Richmond was my handler before Reese Thistle took over. He was equal parts sleazy and lazy. I got away with a lot while he was supposed to be watching.

Hassan looked at Richmond and his buddy for a second, just to let them know he'd heard. Then he moved on.

'All this is easier if you use the role to become the kind of person you always wished you could be. The broad details will be provided by your handlers, but there's wiggle room. Say, deep down, you fantasise about working in a restaurant instead of here.' He waved a hand at the shabby conference room. 'In that case, your cover can be a chef, or you have been a chef at one time, or at least love cooking. Or say you're secretly gay?' He glanced over at Richmond, hoping to get a reaction. It worked. 'Great. While you're in the field, you're *openly* gay. This makes you seem more authentic, so your cover doesn't look like a cover.'

Thistle was there, too, although I didn't know her name at the time. She was in the front row, her spine straight, nails clipped, her wild hair tied up in a bun. She was scribbling on a spiral-bound notepad—but I noticed that she looked at Hassan himself doubtfully, like he was a designer handbag, too cheap to be anything other than a knock-off.

'Why would an agent sign up for such a risky assignment?' Hassan continued. 'This is why. It's not patriotism.

It's not loyalty. It's the desire to be the person society doesn't allow you to be.'

After a bit more rambling and showing of documents that were too redacted to be useful, Hassan asked if there were any questions. It was clear by now that no food was coming, so I stuck up my hand. 'Is the CIA secretly torturing people in Kabul?'

Hassan looked annoyed. 'I'm not here to discuss conspiracy theories.' He glanced at his gleaming watch. 'Actually, I think that's all the time we have.'

Now I'm at Fred's house with a cover so non-official that no one at the FBI even knows I'm here. I wish I'd asked Hassan more practical questions. The tips he gave us are useless. I don't have a handler. I don't have two weeks to prepare. I know next to nothing about the man I'm pretending to be or the people I'm trying to fool.

'Bathroom's just down the hall,' Fred is saying. 'The solar water heater is pretty good, but if a couple of people have had showers right before you, best to wait a half-hour or so. Don't go upstairs, for obvious reasons.'

I don't know what he means by that. Maybe the second floor isn't structurally sound.

The bedroom he's showing me is nicer than any I've ever slept in. A queen-size mattress on an actual bedframe. Clean sheets. A bedside lamp. A window overlooking a grassy slope. Donnie is out there with a flashlight, feeding the dogs. I can see the greenhouse and the compost pipe, but the slaughterhouse is just out of view.

I know the basic layout of the house now. It's L-shaped, with the front door, the living room, the kitchen and the dining room all in a row, followed by a right turn towards the bedrooms, the bathroom and a stairwell.

The window is padlocked shut. Fred doesn't offer me a key. To get outside, I'll have to walk past all the other bedrooms and open the back door.

'There are some clothes in the closet that should fit,' Fred says. 'If not, we can order you some better ones. Money is no problem.'

'Thanks, man.' I sit on the bed, testing the springs. Turns out there are none. It's memory foam, or latex, or something.

As I move, the hammer slips out of my pants and flops onto the bed.

Fred sees it. Frowns.

The blood roars in my ears. I'm sitting down. If I attack him, he'll overpower me easily.

'Did you come here to kill me, Lux?' he asks. He smiles, as though it's a joke.

'No,' I lie. 'But I wasn't sure what kind of reception I was gonna get. Sorry.'

Fred says nothing.

'I figured there was a *chance* you'd decided I knew too much,' I continue. 'Invited me here to tie up a loose end. I figured I should come prepared to defend myself.'

'Well, then.' He crosses his arms. 'Take your best shot.'

I force a laugh. 'It's all good, man. I trust you. If you wanted me dead, you would have shot me when I was getting out of my car.'

'I'm serious.' He nods at the hammer. 'Hit me.'

'I don't want to hurt you. I was just being overcautious.'

He reaches past me, picks up the hammer and presses it into my hands.

'Take a swing,' he says.

My heart rate is through the roof. 'But . . . I don't want to.'

Though maybe I should. Fred and all his friends have to die. Why not start now?

'Stand up,' Fred says.

I do, uneasily.

'Swing.'

School bullies taught me how this game ends. The weaker kid thinks he's getting a free shot at the tougher kid. Then the tougher kid knocks his teeth out.

'You don't need to prove anything,' I say. 'I know you can overpower me.'

'I'm trying to show you something.' Fred holds my gaze. 'You're not making it easy.'

The solution to the schoolyard game is to throw a punch *before* the bully expects you to. Act like you're not going to do it, or you're still thinking about it, then lash out mid-sentence.

I could cave Fred's skull in with this hammer. A fast, silent death. Lead the other Guards into this room one by one and give them the same treatment. Chop up all the bodies, put them in the freezer, put the freezer on the back of the pick-up and drive away. Make an anonymous tip-off to the police so they can come here and let the prisoners go.

Call it an eighty per cent chance of killing Fred quietly. Then another eighty per cent for each of the others. That's about a one in four chance of taking them all out. And I've already left it too late. Fred is expecting it now.

I swing the hammer. Medium speed. Not fast enough to hit him, not slow enough that he can't make his point.

His hand shoots out like a striking snake, and suddenly I'm not holding the hammer anymore.

'Shit.' I'm genuinely impressed.

'See, to get any power from the swing, your opponent needs to hold the hammer close to the base,' Fred says. 'But that leaves plenty of space right under the head. Easy to grab, with a little practice. And the head itself makes it easy to just rip the hammer out of their hand.'

Would he have been able to do that if I'd swung faster, harder? Maybe not. I tell myself there'll be other chances.

'Come with me,' he says.

CHAPTER 5

I have five fingers but I'm not a hand.
I have love in me but I'm not a heart.
What am I?

Fred leads me to a door at the end of the corridor and unlocks it. The room beyond is as cramped and lightless as a basement, even though we're still on the ground floor. It might have been a small study before someone bricked up the window. It smells like the theatre of a bad surgeon— bleach and blood.

The racks on the walls hold swords, railroad spikes, medieval maces, fireplace pokers, giant gardening shears, guillotine blades, rusty hooks, and rolls of barbed wire. Things designed to be sharp, blunt, hot or otherwise painful. There are only four guns, which rounds down to zero by rural Texas standards. But they're big—two Remington shotguns and two Bushmaster XM-15 rifles. The Guards are prepared to defend this house if necessary.

As he walks along the racks, Fred tells me that he once worked at an electronics store. He was a pretty good salesman, always making customers think they needed a bigger screen, a faster processor, an extra warranty.

He even convinced himself, squeezing a giant TV and a virtual reality set-up into his tiny living room. But he preferred working out the back of the store, with all the boxes and pallets and forklifts. Seeing all those shiny, heavy cubes be unloaded from trucks, checked off lists and stickered for sale. Good, honest work, he tells me. Except when he was assembling TV cabinets and computer desks for the displays, the tools often slipped in his sweaty hands.

There are wide gaps in this story. Things Lux would already know. He and Fred had exchanged hundreds of messages. Maybe thousands.

'All this stuff is unnecessary, really.' Fred is rummaging through a crate under the bricked-up window. 'You don't need purpose-built weapons to hurt someone. You can just use an electric kettle, or a screwdriver, or a hockey stick. But it's all about presentation. The subscribers like . . . oh, here you go.'

He pulls out a hammer slightly longer than mine. A work glove is wrapped around the handle, as though the invisible man is clutching it. Fred slides his hand into the empty glove.

'I just Krazy-glued the palm of the glove to the handle,' Fred says. 'Check it out.'

He swings the hammer at my head.

I duck. The hammer clangs against a battleaxe mounted on the wall behind me.

'Dude! You were supposed to grab it, like I showed you.'

Fred swings at me again. This time I lash out and grab the shaft of the hammer.

His invention works well. I can't pull the hammer out of his grip.

'Cool, right?' Fred says. 'Plus, no need to worry about fingerprints.'

'You use this on them?' I jerk my thumb over my shoulder in the direction of the slaughterhouse. I watched all the videos on Lux's hard drive, and I don't remember seeing the hammer.

'Nah, too quick.' Fred slips his hand out of the glove and flexes his fingers. 'Hit someone with this, and they're dead. No screaming, no wriggling around . . . But I thought you'd appreciate it. I know you're all about efficiency.'

Another reminder of how little I know about the guy I'm pretending to be. 'Scammer died pretty fast.'

'Sorry about that, Donnie can be . . . excitable.' Fred sniffs the air. The smell of Samson's cooking has wafted down to this end of the house. 'Let's eat, Lux.'

I didn't, actually. I buried Lux's body, all of it. I was being good.

As I follow Fred up the corridor, I promise myself I won't make that mistake again.

•

It's just as I feared—there's no meat. No beef taken from the fridge and thrown into the stir-fry at the last minute. No side of roast chicken. Not even any bacon bits sprinkled through the salad.

I stare gloomily at all the plant matter on the table. The sharp smell of garlic turns my stomach.

'You okay, bro?' Donnie asks, sitting down opposite me. He's changed from his tank top into a polo shirt, loose enough to hide his muscles. He's wearing a smart watch, and from this angle I can see a stud in one ear.

I force a smile. 'Yeah. Just tired.'

This is true. It's only nine pm, but the drive from Houston took four hours, and I haven't been able to rest since. The hairs on the back of my neck are constantly up, and my mind is whirling like a fairground ride, trying to guess the right answer to every question.

I was supposed to be dead by now. Resting peacefully, having murdered Fred and myself. Plus, my last meal was supposed to be tastier than this.

Not that Samson hasn't done a great job. The food is restaurant quality. The vegetables are crisp, the rice soft, the sauces balanced. Perfect for anyone other than me.

Thistle would adore this, says a voice in my head, one I quickly push away.

Fred sits at one end of the table. He has two bowls in front of him, while everyone else has one. Zara, the elegant brunette, sits at the other end. Kyle, the dour teenager, takes the spot next to Fred. I end up trapped between Samson and Cedric, the thin Black guy in the suit. Everyone starts serving themselves.

Zara has poured me a glass of wine. The fluid makes a prism, splitting the colours into a rainbow. I don't want to touch the drink. I need to stay focused. But I also need to fit in.

'You want to say grace, Lux?' Cedric asks. His mouth is already full.

'Uh . . .' I've visited Lux's house and his childhood home. I do a frantic mental walk through both, looking for signs of religion.

Zara saves me. 'He's messing with you.'

Cedric chuckles, as though the very idea of God is funny.

'It's so great to meet you in person,' Donnie tells me, in a way that implies he's exchanged a lot of messages with Lux.

'You too,' I say. 'Put a face to the name, you know. You're not like I expected.'

'Really?' He looks interested. Most people are interested in themselves.

'Yeah. I pictured you with brown eyes, I don't know why. And your voice is deeper than I heard it in my head.'

I didn't know Donnie existed until two hours ago. But I'm desperate to convince these people that I'm the one they've been messaging for weeks. Or months, or years. I don't even know how long Lux has been part of their online community.

'Thanks.' Donnie looks pleased, as though my comment on his deep voice was a compliment.

Zara scoops some spears of baby corn into my bowl.

'But you're exactly as lovely as I pictured,' I tell her. This seems like the kind of thing Lux would say. I only met him twice, but both times he hit on the women around him.

Zara looks pleased, her hand fluttering over her breast-bone. 'Thank you.'

The others cast a nervous glance at Fred, to see if he'll allow this. Maybe he and Zara are together. He keeps his eyes on his food, shovelling it in like a kid just home from school. He's filled both bowls, but left the second one untouched.

'Do me, do me,' says Cedric. Joking, but not joking.

'Lux would already know what you looked like,' Donnie objects, not in a friendly way. 'You're a celebrity.'

'Our famous writer,' Zara says, tousling Cedric's hair, which is too short to actually tousle.

Cedric looks pleased at the acknowledgement of his fame, but disappointed that there's nothing left to say about him.

'What about me?' I say, trying to head off further questions. 'Am I like y'all expected?'

'I didn't expect any *y'alls* from you,' Samson says, and Donnie laughs. Cedric laughs louder, like they're competing.

'Sorry,' I say. 'My inner redneck momentarily emerged from under my sophisticated exterior.'

I've overcorrected now. Lux's language wasn't that fancy, and I'm still wearing the ill-fitting clothes from the charity bin. But they seem to buy it.

'It's all good, man,' Donnie says.

'Yeah, you don't have to hide here,' Kyle mumbles, his mouth full.

Fred raises his glass of club soda. Everyone else has wine.

'To being ourselves,' he says.

The others all hold up their glasses.

I follow suit. 'Cheers.'

Clink.

The wine burns its way down my throat.

Cedric smacks his lips and sighs. 'So. Who's ready for karaoke?'

•

Everyone helps out with the washing-up. There's a friendly bustle of hands on lower backs, of 'Thank you' and 'Can I just squeeze past?' and 'Here you go'.

After the dishwasher is stacked and the pans scrubbed, there's karaoke. Cedric wasn't kidding.

In the living area, Fred flicks on the TV. It's huge, with a resolution approaching reality and colours exceeding it. Maybe this was where they all watched the videos of Abbey, Lux's prisoner.

Fred brings up YouTube. The others shout requests, mostly on behalf of each other. 'Put on "Call Me When You're Sober" for Donnie!' 'Hey, Zara, are you gonna do "Fergalicious" for us?' 'Anything by Avril Lavigne works for me.'

Fred quickly throws a playlist together while everyone piles onto the sofa.

'What have you got for us, Lux?' Samson asks.

'Yeah, what's your go-to song?'

Cedric answers for me. '"I Try" by Macy Gray.'

He sounds like he's kidding, but I can't admit that I don't know the song, just in case the real Lux was famously fond of it.

'You folks have fun,' I say. 'I'm going to bed.'

'No!' Donnie and Samson both yell.

Zara grabs my hand and drags me down onto the sofa. 'Everyone must sing,' she says, halfway between a threat and a joke.

I laugh nervously. 'Okay, okay.'

'Macy Gray it is,' Fred says, and adds another video to the playlist.

The others can tell I'm anxious. Hopefully they can't tell why. Could the real Lux sing? Would they know?

Samson takes the microphone first. He sings 'Beautiful' by Christina Aguilera. His voice comes out of hidden speakers in the corners of the room. It's not good, but he makes up for it with enthusiasm, hamming it up, closing his eyes as he hits the high notes. Donnie slaps the table in time with the beat. The others applaud wildly. Zara tops up my wine.

Samson passes the microphone to Fred, who is expertly polite—he pretends he doesn't want to perform, but only for a few seconds. He doesn't make the others beg. His chosen song is a cover of 'Uptown Girl', and he sings it more or less in tune, bobbing his head to the thumping bass, glancing at Zara from time to time. She smiles and sips her drink.

'I'm going to bed,' Kyle mutters. He leaves the room, possibly wary of getting dragged into the spotlight.

Zara's Texas accent disappears when she sings. Her chosen song is 'Teenage Dream'—the reference to 'Fergalicious' must have been a joke, or related to something I wasn't present for. She sings without once glancing at the screen to check the lyrics. All her focus is on the audience. It's as though we're on stage rather than her. I shrivel under her scrutiny.

Donnie hands the microphone to me. 'Your turn, Lux.'

I hold up my glass. 'I'm still working up the courage.'

'It's your song,' Donnie insists, his breath smelling strongly of courage. 'Come on.'

Reluctantly, I stand up. I should have pretended that I was already drunk, to explain away not knowing the tune. Too late now. Maybe I'll recognise the song when it starts.

Violins fill the air. On the screen behind me, the singer is geting out of bed. Nothing sounds familiar yet, and the lyrics are already appearing on the screen.

I'm opening my mouth to sing in front of this group of killers who think I'm their friend when Kyle bursts back in. His eyes are wide under his fringe.

'Fred,' he hisses. 'There's someone outside!'

CHAPTER 6

I am a drop, a braid, a kiss.
Where am I from?

Suddenly Donnie's huge hand is on my shoulder, just close enough to my neck to be a threat. I can smell the veins in his wrist. It's hard not to imagine ripping them out.

'You bring anyone with you, Lux?' he asks.

'No.' I try to brush his hand off, but he squeezes tighter.

'I'm serious,' he says. 'Because whoever's out there—'

'They're not with me.'

'No one followed you?' Fred asks.

I think about it. Miles of dark, winding roads, checking and memorising the licence plate of every car I saw. No one I saw twice, and nothing at all for the last few turns.

'No one followed me,' I say.

Fred turns to Kyle. 'Who is it?'

'I don't know. I got a notification—there was movement on one of the cameras.' Kyle holds up his phone. 'I figured it would be an animal, but I checked the feed just in case—'

'Which camera?'

'R3. A hundred yards north of the house.'

'What about the driveway sensor?'

'It didn't go off.'

It takes a moment for this to sink in. The woods surrounding the house are filled with cameras and sensors. My plan to sneak out in the dead of the night would never have worked.

Cedric is checking his phone. Seeing the same notification Kyle received.

'I freeze-framed it downstairs.' Kyle looks nervous but also eager, like he's hoping Fred will scratch him behind the ears and call him a good boy. 'He's about five foot ten, wearing hiking gear.'

'You get many hikers around here?' I ask.

'We do not,' Fred says.

He leads us all back to the corridor where the bedrooms are, and tosses his keys to Donnie, who unlocks the armoury while everyone else goes downstairs.

I hesitate before following. Nothing good ever happens in a basement.

'Lux?' Zara calls.

'Coming.' I force myself to walk down the stairs.

The basement floor is unsealed concrete and the walls are tightly packed dirt, holding up a low ceiling crisscrossed with wooden beams. The cramped space is bathed with light from dozens of screens subdivided into hundreds of rectangles, all showing different parts of the woods. None showing the house itself, I notice. A huge server hums in a corner, protected from the dust by plastic sheeting.

'Welcome to the editing room,' Cedric tells me quietly. 'This is where we cut the subscriber videos. Remove cross-set voices, erase anything incriminating, you know.'

Everything in the videos is criminal, but he doesn't seem to be kidding. He must mean anything that might expose the location of the house.

He seems like the kind of guy who talks too much when he's nervous. Could be useful.

'Where's the intruder?' Fred is looming over one of the desks, the glowing screens reflected in his eyes.

'Hang on, it's gone back to the live feed. Let me bring up the screenshot again.' Kyle grabs a mouse and starts clicking his way through some menus.

'Is R3 one of the cameras we moved this morning?' Fred asks.

'Right. Lucky, otherwise we might have missed him completely.'

I'm scanning the screens, trying to get a sense of the distances between the cameras. But without any recognisable landmarks, it's impossible to tell how the pieces fit together.

'It's probably a hiker,' Zara says.

Fred looks doubtful. 'At this time of night?'

I chew my nails. If it's not a hiker, it could be a cop. The FBI hadn't made much headway investigating this group— we didn't even know it *was* a group—but maybe the county sheriff's office was having better luck. I don't want to be mistaken for one of the bad guys and arrested or shot.

I am a bad guy, of course. But I'm a different kind of bad guy. It feels like the distinction should matter.

'Well, maybe it's Druznetski.' Zara is absent-mindedly tying her hair into a French braid.

Who's Druznetski? I want to ask. But the question might expose me as an impostor.

Fred hesitates. 'Why would he show up?'

Zara shrugs. 'Something he wanted to tell you in person, maybe? No one else knows we're here.'

'He wouldn't be sneaking around in the woods.'

Kyle has found the screenshot. One of the rectangles enlarges—a shadow between two trees. The image is mono-chromatic, and blurry, but it does indeed look like a man in hiking gear.

'Is that Druznetski?' Kyle asks.

Fred stares at the image for a long time. 'No,' he says finally.

'How can you tell?' Zara says. 'That could be anybody.'

The man is still frozen on the screen.

'Well,' Fred says, 'let's get out there and ask him.'

Donnie comes down the stairs carrying the guns, a Bowie knife and six pairs of night-vision goggles.

'I'll take a rifle,' Zara says, holding out a hand.

'Me too,' I say quickly. I don't know how to fire it, but there are only two long-range weapons here; if I have one of them, I'm half as likely to get shot in the back.

Donnie passes the rifles to me and Zara. I keep mine pointed at the floor, trying to look like I know how to hold it. Fred takes the SIG Sauer pistol. Donnie gives one of the Remington shotguns to Kyle and keeps the other for himself. Samson gets the knife.

Cedric holds out his hand for a weapon and realises there are none left. He drops his hand, embarrassed.

'You should stay here and protect the house,' Donnie says.

'With what?' Cedric asks.

The rest of us are already headed back up the stairs. 'Use your imagination.'

'Is there a prize for whoever bags him?' Samson asks.

'The prize is we get to keep doing our work.' Fred pulls a pair of goggles over his head and turns to me. 'Sorry to drop you in the deep end, Lux.'

'I'm good,' I say. An untrue statement in every sense. 'Let's do this.'

•

In the alien light of the night-vision goggles, I can see tree branches bristling with flakes of sleet. The ground is a mixture of rock and muddy slush. If the guy is a hiker, he picked a hell of a night for it. It's the kind of cold that dries out my lips, and leaves my knuckles cracked and bleeding. There's a distant moaning that I hope is the wind but might be wolves. I'm wearing a thick coat from the wardrobe, but it doesn't protect my legs from the frosty air.

We're clustered on the front porch. Fred has switched off the security lamps. He points at each of us in turn, and then jabs his finger towards a different part of the forest. Apparently we're splitting up.

Works for me. If the hiker is a cop, and I have to explain that I'm not a psychopath—just an FBI consultant who eats psychopaths—I'd rather the others weren't within earshot. I just hope I find the guy before anyone else does. And that I see him before he sees me.

'Try to get him alive,' Fred murmurs, then he sneaks off the porch into the darkness of the woods.

I move in the direction he chose for me. There's no trail. I'm wading through thigh-high brush, in shoes that are more suitable for a funeral. With the goggles I have no peripheral vision, but I can see a good distance. Fifty yards away a withered pine leans at a severe angle, threatening to fall. I recognise it from one of the screens inside, so I know there's a camera up ahead, but not the right one. The camera that caught the hiker was pointed at a birch tree with a distinctive wedge taken out of the side, like someone started trying to chop it down and then gave up. I suspect that when Fred was dividing up the search area, he sent me in the direction where the guy was least likely to be.

This is your chance to walk away. I ignore the voice as I creep through the woods.

They don't know who you are. You can sneak back to the house, find a key to one of the cars and drive home.

I rap my knuckles against the side of my head, as though I can dislodge the thought. The goggles flicker for a second. It's not like I can just pretend I never found these guys.

You can call in an anonymous tip. The cops will get them.

And then what?

The voice falls silent. It knows the hunger is already driving me crazy. My supply of cadavers has been cut off. If I go home, I'll eventually hurt someone. If I stay here, at least my victims will have it coming.

I recognise another tree up ahead. It has a straight-out branch supported by one at an angle, like a hangman's gallows. I'm starting to get a feel for the lay of the land. There should be a camera . . . *there*. I see it—a deceptively small white box, nailed to a different tree. No cables, and the foliage is too thick for solar power. Fred and co must use high-quality batteries, and even so, they'd have to change them every few days.

'Hey!' A shout in the distance. A grunt and a splash of

leaves from somewhere to my left. I turn my head so fast I get dizzy. Because of the goggles, the light takes a split second longer to reach my eyes, and it feels like I'm still spinning when I'm not.

Even with the goggles, I can't see the commotion, but I can hear it. A thud. A shallow cry. Someone is fighting for their life, but they're trying to do it quietly.

I head towards the sounds, my head low. The wind picks up, whispering in my ears, and suddenly I can't hear the ruckus anymore. I keep moving. My hands are numb, clutching the gun that I don't even know how to shoot.

Branches whip back and forth up ahead. Someone is running towards me, breathing heavily. I try to move away, but a tree pokes me in the back and snags my jacket.

A figure bursts out of the shrubbery. Not Samson. An older man, Black, maybe forty, with worry lines around his mouth and a wool hat stretched over his head. He's dressed for the weather but not the darkness, his eyes wide and wild. Part of his puffy parka has been sliced open, leaving a dark stain dripping down his arm and onto his khaki trousers.

He crashes right into me. The branch behind me snaps, and we both hit the ground, hard. I cling to the gun as I wrestle him off. He weighs maybe a hundred and seventy pounds. I can smell his blood, hot and sticky.

I shut my eyes for a second. He's a bystander. I can't let myself bite him. I can't.

The man doesn't attack me. He scrambles up, backs off. He doesn't appear to be armed.

'Don't shoot,' he says.

I lower the gun, but not all the way. 'Are you police?'

'No.' He doesn't offer any other explanation for being out here, just gives a little shake of his head.

I have a million questions for this guy, but there's only time for one. 'Druznetski?'

'What?' He looks confused, then his eyes narrow. 'Blake!'

Fear opens its jaws to swallow me. He knows who I am, despite the shaved head and the goggles. How? I'm sure we've never met.

He could expose me to the others. If they catch this guy, I'm screwed.

So either kill him, or get him out of here.

Footsteps crash through the forest towards us. Someone is following his trail.

I point in the direction Fred sent me. Hopefully he won't stray into anyone else's search area. 'Go that way,' I whisper. 'There are five others after you.'

The man hesitates, perhaps wondering if I'm sending him into a trap.

I put the gun down on the dirt and hold up my bare hands. 'Go! Now!'

He gets moving, fighting his way deeper into the woods. I pick up the gun and wait, wondering who his pursuer is. Fred sent Samson that way. But if it's Samson, why isn't he hollering for the others?

Whoever it is, their footfalls soon stop. Maybe they're listening for sounds of the man's escape. I bash through the undergrowth, making as much noise as possible.

Bad idea. I shamble into a clearing only to be attacked with a Bowie knife. A pound and a half of sharp steel sweeps out of the shadows at my chest.

I stagger backwards, swinging the gun just in time to knock the blade sideways into a tree. 'Samson! It's me!'

Samson stops trying to wrench the knife out of the wood. 'Lux,' he says, realising. 'You see which way the guy went? I want to talk to him.'

He seems to have *talk* confused with *stab*. 'He ran back this way.' I point behind Samson. 'Just now. Must have gotten past you.'

Zara emerges from the woods to my left, as silently as a wraith. Her goggles make her expression unreadable. Unlike me, she looks like she knows how to hold her gun. 'What's going on?'

Fred sent Zara in the opposite direction. She must have heard the fight and come running.

'He's around here somewhere,' Samson says. 'Did you see him?' He's favouring one arm, nursing the other close to his chest. The guy must have injured him.

A satchel with a slashed strap lies on the dirt nearby. The fabric is speckled with blood. I reach for the satchel, but Zara grabs it first. She quickly checks inside.

'Nothing,' she says. 'Was this his?'

'Yeah,' Samson says. 'I guess I cut it off him.'

'And it was empty?'

Samson seems to notice the blood on me for the first time. 'What happened to you?'

'I hit him with the butt of my gun,' I say. 'I think maybe I broke his collarbone. But he got away.'

'Shit,' Zara says.

'Which way did he go?' Samson asks.

'Like I said, I thought he went this way, but that turned out to be you.'

The three of us turn around, all scanning different parts of the woods. I'm the only one looking in the right direction, but I can't see him anymore.

Who are you? And how did you know my name?

CHAPTER 7

I steal eggs and cook animals.
Or is it the other way around?

'Kill the prisoners and pack your bags,' Fred says as we walk quickly back towards the house. 'We leave in fifteen minutes.'

I suppress a flinch. 'I only just got here.'

'It's bad timing, I know. Sorry, Lux.'

'You want to leave?' Donnie looks angry. 'Just let the cops run us out of town?'

'We can't stop them,' Fred says.

'Sure we can. We have plenty of weapons. We can hold them off. After two or ten or a hundred dead police, you really think they'll keep trying to get in?'

'Yes,' Fred says bluntly. 'Cops are like mosquitoes. Swat one, and two more will smell the blood and come looking for you.'

Donnie grinds his teeth, but says nothing.

We emerge from the woods and walk up to the porch, where Cedric is waiting. 'What's going on?'

'The guy got away. I'm pushing the button.' Fred gets out his phone and brings up an app I don't recognise. A red circle appears on the screen.

Everyone else tenses up. Whatever this app does, it's serious.

'For real?' Kyle says, eyes wide.

'For real.' Fred taps the red circle with his thumb. A dialogue box appears on the screen. *Are you sure? This action cannot be undone.*

'Wait,' Zara says.

Fred's thumb hovers over the *yes* button. 'The sooner I do this, the more likely it is to work,' he says. 'Right now, that guy will be calling his colleagues. We have thirty minutes tops before they get here.'

Kyle is shifting his weight from foot to foot, his gaze flitting from Fred's phone to all our faces.

'I don't think the guy was a cop,' I say.

Fred looks at me. 'Explain.'

I have no idea if the man told me the truth. But this secret, isolated house is the perfect place to prepare my next six meals. I can't let Fred take the Guards anywhere else.

'He didn't have a weapon or a partner. Police always come in pairs.' I try to sound confident. 'He would have yelled out to his partner if he had one.'

'You're right.' Donnie sounds hopeful. 'They usually wear uniforms, too.'

'A lone police officer, out of uniform,' Cedric says. 'Hmm, seems far-fetched.'

He's calmer than before, his voice flat. Hard to tell if he's being sarcastic.

Zara speaks up. 'He didn't try to call for help with a phone or radio, either.'

'He might be doing it right now,' Fred points out. 'Even if he isn't a cop.'

'Or he might not.' Zara wipes her shoes on the mat. 'A guy out here alone in the middle of the night must be committing some kind of crime. Like poaching.'

'Lux said he didn't have a weapon.'

'I didn't *see* one,' I say.

'Okay, so he's a survivalist or whatever,' Zara says. 'Either way, he doesn't want anyone to know he's out here. He won't call the police.'

'Even a survivalist might take issue with what we're doing.' Fred's thumb is still above the *yes* button. Like Caesar, on the verge of sentencing a gladiator.

'He doesn't know what we're doing,' I say. 'All he knows is that Samson and I were walking through the woods with a gun and a knife.'

'Not suspicious at all,' Cedric says.

'He probably thinks *we're* poachers. If he calls anyone, it'll be Parks and Wildlife, not the police.'

Samson has stayed silent throughout this discussion, even though he was the only other person to see the mystery man. As Fred switches on the porch light, I get a better look at his face. He has a troubled frown and keeps shooting sideways glances at Fred, who doesn't notice.

'I vote we keep looking for him in daylight,' Zara says.

'We're not voting,' Fred says. 'I'm the CEO. It's my decision.'

I wonder if he's actually incorporated his torture porn company. It seems unlikely.

'Of course,' Zara says, with a little bow. 'We can pack some essentials to be ready in case the cops show up in the meantime. If they do, it won't be many. They don't know anything.'

'And if they don't show?'

'Then we get back to work. The subscribers are still waiting for the barbed-wire video.'

I keep my expression neutral.

Eventually Fred nods. 'Okay. We'll wait—for now.'

He closes the app and returns the phone to his pocket.

•

'I can take first watch,' I say. 'I have nothing to pack.'

'It's okay, Lux.' Fred is already pouring coffee into a thermos. 'I got it.'

'You sure? I want to help.'

'No, go to bed. You can help with the search in the morning. You look tired.'

After six panicked hours of improvisation, I've run out of lies. My brain is fried.

'Thanks,' I say. 'See you in the morning.'

Fred trots down the stairs to the basement. I hear the chair creak as he settles in front of the screens. All those rectangles, monitoring the forest outside and the driveway.

It suddenly occurs to me that one of the cameras may have recorded my conversation with the mystery man. Fred could scrub back through the feeds and find it. See us mouthing words at each other instead of fighting. Then he might come and murder me in my bed.

'Sleep well,' he calls.

'Sure.' I leave him to it, a sense of doom falling over me like a heavy blanket.

Samson has disappeared into his room. The other Guards roam the house, packing their belongings. I hang around the kitchen, acting casual. I'm pleased to find an acid-based drain cleaner under the sink.

After two hours, there's still no sign of any police. The others finally go to bed. I'm dirty from my tussle in the forest, so I take a shower.

Under normal circumstances, this bathroom would feel very relaxing. A natural-seeming stone floor, rainforest-green tiles, a huge mirror. A showerhead wide enough for two people to stand under the water at once.

The window is too small to climb through. Ventilation only. Despite this, it's padlocked shut.

I've had some nerve-racking showers in my life. At the group home, the older boys would sometimes sneak into the bathroom and grab me. I never found out what came after the grabbing—they stopped trying when I got a reputation as a biter. But I still showered rarely and anxiously until I turned eighteen and left the home.

Nothing beats this, though. There are six killers in this house. Any of them could walk in and put a bullet through my chest, an axe in my head or chain me up with the rest of their prisoners.

I'm being paranoid. A common problem. Once you've done enough bad things, it's impossible not to imagine them being done to you. But the others think I'm Lux. I'm safe . . . for now.

I lather up with organic shower gel and 'nutrigenic' shampoo, rinse it all off, and pat my body dry with a towel apparently made from bamboo. Someone has left out a toothbrush for me. I scrub my remaining molars and spit, leaving a swirl of pink in the white basin.

The toothbrush isn't one of those rubber ones you get in prison; it's bamboo, too. Snapped in half, it would make a decent shiv. Not enough to win in a fair fight, but if plunged into the neck of a sleeping person . . .

I wrap the towel around my waist and go back into the corridor. All the bedrooms are right here. The weapons are locked up in the armoury. Five killers, defenceless. Could I dispose of them all quietly enough?

A floorboard creaks right behind me.

I spin around. No one there. And it didn't sound like a footstep.

Maybe I imagined it. There's something called 'exploding head syndrome', where the sufferer perceives sudden loud noises, typically right before or right after bed. A kid at the group home had it—he used to fling himself out of bed and scramble away from it, sweaty and disoriented. Apparently the condition is triggered by extreme fatigue and stress.

I don't think I imagined the sound—but that's a symptom, as well. The patient is unable to believe the noise wasn't real. It's a windy night, I tell myself. Maybe the wall studs were just flexing.

I listen at the nearest door. Someone is snoring inside. A helpless sound.

But Fred is awake, and some of the others may be, too. A toothbrush isn't much of a weapon. Even a knife from the kitchen might not be enough. I need a better plan. I go back into my bedroom and shut the door.

In the closet I find some flannel pyjamas in my approximate size. I put them on and wriggle between the smooth, clean bedsheets. There's a reading lamp and some books, mostly about programming. The same kinds of books Lux had on his shelves. Maybe they've been placed here for me.

My coding abilities are rudimentary. I open one of the books, with the half-formed idea that I could master new skills overnight and make a more convincing Lux in the morning. But I'm too tired to absorb the information. I turn out the light.

I think about the hiker, wondering who he was and how he knew my name. Then I find myself thinking about the barbed-wire video, scheduled to be filmed tomorrow. I don't know what's supposed to happen in it, who it's supposed to happen to, or if they will survive it.

Tonight I stood by and let Donnie murder one of the prisoners. Am I going to do the same thing tomorrow?

I didn't come here to save anybody. I just wanted a decent meal before I checked out. According to Samson, the prisoners are killers. *It was great. Watching someone like that getting what he deserves.* I have no obligation to help them.

And yet.

I spend another half-hour lying in the dark, staring at the ceiling. Then I mutter, 'Fuck,' and get up.

CHAPTER 8

What bird do you force
down your throat?

I remember seeing Samson use a can opener on the baby corn spears. He rinsed it straight away and returned it to the third drawer down, on the right-hand side. It was a P-38, the same kind you find in army surplus stores for a dollar: a rectangle of steel with a fin-shaped blade folded against it. Simple, easy to clean, and useful for things other than opening cans. I would have preferred tin snips, but this will do.

Someone has left their phone charging on the sofa, near the fireplace. I don't have the unlock code, but it doesn't matter. I can switch on the flashlight function without it.

A button near the bottom catches my eye: *Emergency call.* I don't need the unlock code for that, either. I could just call the cops.

But then I wouldn't get to eat the Guards. A thousand pounds of meat, wasted.

I clench my jaw, trying to convince myself to make the right choice for once. But I'm so hungry. I might never get another chance like this.

I can always call the police later, I tell myself. Then, as I'm about to pocket the phone, I notice the message up the top of the screen: *No service*. I'm too far from any cell tower. There's wi-fi, but no network signal. Calling the police isn't an option.

I wish I'd tried. Then, when the call didn't connect, I could have pretended to be the kind of person who sometimes does the right thing.

It takes me a minute to work out how to disable the lock on the back door so I don't get trapped outside. Once I'm through, a wall of wind and sleet nearly knocks me off my feet. I pull up the hood of my coat to protect my ears. No moon now, and I don't have my goggles. Donnie locked them away in the armoury with the weapons. Can't risk using the flashlight app yet, not with so many windows facing this way. I try to retrace my steps through the back-yard towards the slaughterhouse.

The dogs growl at me as I pass the fence.

'Back,' I say, imitating Fred's voice.

The dogs aren't fooled. They keep growling until I'm out of sight.

The slaughterhouse is far enough away from the house that I doubt I'll be heard, but it's possible I'll be seen. I circle around towards the back.

No one is screaming inside this time, but I can hear a distant howl from further away. Not the dogs. At first it sounds human, but the longer it goes on, the less sure I am. Could be a bobcat in the woods. Eventually the sound is gone.

When I turn the corner, a red light blinks above me. A surveillance camera. I freeze, my back pressed against the cold sheet metal. I think of Fred, watching all those rectangles. I don't recall any of the feeds showing the slaughterhouse. Hopefully this camera is pointed outwards, towards the woods behind the property. I can't see the lens to make sure.

I fold out the blade of the P-38 and stab it into the wall, about four feet above the ground. It doesn't go through until I thump it with my other hand. The screaming starts from inside. I wiggle the handle back and forth, working the blade towards the ground. The wall is thicker than a can. Cutting through it is slow, hard work.

A woman inside says, 'Shut up!' and the screaming stops. She's realised that the Guards wouldn't be cutting through the back wall of their own dungeon. She thinks this is a rescue mission.

She's right, more or less, although the details might surprise her.

By the time I reach the concrete foundation, my arms are burning. I wrap my sleeves around my hands, grab the sharp edge of the sheet metal, and bend it outwards. It creaks and bangs, but the wind swallows the sound. I don't have a mask, so I pull the hood low over my face, then slip through the triangle of darkness.

Inside, I can hear panicked breaths, and the scuffling of frostbitten heels on cold concrete.

'Who's there?' someone whispers. Maybe the same woman as before.

I don't answer. If I don't succeed in getting the prisoners out, I can't risk any of them exposing me to the Guards.

I get out the phone and use the flashlight app to take a look around. Five shivering people, dazzled by the light, unable to see me behind it. Even with the space heater, their clothes are barely warm enough to keep them alive on a night like this. Sunken cheeks and hollow eyes. Doesn't look very sexy to me. But what would I know?

The time I donated sperm, a tired-looking nurse led me into a small, windowless room with a TV, a chair covered in a giant paper towel and every subcategory of porn movie. I didn't like any of it, and the fact that the nurse knew what I was doing in there made it almost impossible to get the job done. Soon I understood why the law student who loaned me his ID hadn't wanted to do it himself. If I hadn't needed the money so badly, I would have just left.

When I finally gave the sample cup back to the nurse, she told me that prospective couples often asked for her opinion of the donors. The pause after she said this implied that I wasn't going to get any biological children. Fine by me.

But someone else got the ID later. I heard he loved the sterile room, the paper-cocooned chair, the nurse waiting right outside. It was all a turn-on for him.

I guess it's all about taste. The Guards know what their audience likes.

One of the prisoners, an elf-eared woman, her blonde hair falling out, her wrists worn and bleeding, says, 'Who are you?' She has a loud, confident voice that's at odds with her frail, skinny frame.

I shine the light on her restraints. Earlier I got a good look at the cuffs and the chains, but not how they were connected to the walls.

Most of the chains are looped through steel rings embedded in the concrete, or around the beams which hold up the ceiling. The P-38 can cut through the walls, but not the chains and definitely not the beams. Even if I wanted to release the prisoners, I couldn't.

I point the light upwards, looking at the cameras mounted on the ceiling. They look better than the ones outside. Not security—they're for making the videos that the Guards sell. High frame rate, high resolution.

Without those cameras, the Guards have no motive to torture the prisoners.

There's a folding chair next to a stack of bricks in one corner. Some of the bricks are spattered with old bloodstains. None of the prisoners here look like they have matching injuries—the blood must be from a previous prisoner.

Fred's voice in my head: *You don't need all this stuff to hurt someone. You can just use an electric kettle, or a screwdriver, or a hockey stick.* Or a brick, I guess.

I pick it up, grunting with pain and conspicuously favouring one arm, as though the other one is injured. If the prisoners are later interrogated about me, I want them to give the Guards misleading clues. I unfold the chair under the bundle of cameras. One of the prisoners starts sobbing.

'What are you doing?' the woman demands. 'Tell us what you want!'

I climb up onto the chair. I'm no electrical engineer, so this won't be subtle.

I use the can opener to saw through all the cables I can see. It's surprisingly tough, once I get through the rubber to the copper. When I slice through the second cable, a little red power light goes dead. I keep chopping until everything is shredded. I want the damage to be obvious. I crack the camera lenses with the handle, just in case Fred has spare cables back at the house.

'You're not one of them,' the woman says, 'are you?'

'Holy shit,' someone else says. I can't see him well in the shadows, but he looks young, maybe twenty. Dark skin, dressed in tan rags.

'My name's Hailey.' The woman talks slowly, like I'm a special kid. 'What's yours?'

I climb down off the chair and put it back where I found it.

'You have to get us out of here,' Hailey says. 'You hear me? Those guys are gonna kill us.'

'Please,' someone else says.

I know what will happen if I speak up. One of the prisoners will repeat everything I say to the captors, hoping for mercy.

So I head back to the hole in the wall.

'You can't just leave us here!' Hailey shouts.

I slip out, and bend the metal back into place behind me, sealing them in.

CHAPTER 9

I am a card, a loan, a fish.
Who am I?

Scientists used to think sharks didn't sleep, because they swam all day and night. But it turns out they do, at least according to a guy who once sat next to me on a Greyhound bus to Austin. He said one side of their brain sleeps, while the other side swims and hunts and fucks. Then they swap. Left, then right, then left again.

In an unfamiliar environment, humans do something similar. On your first night in a new bed, only half your brain sleeps. The other half stays awake to monitor threats. That's why the scratching of a rat or the compressor in the fridge wakes you up at someone else's place but not at your own.

Several times in the night, I'm woken by more distant howling. Maybe it's human after all—except that I would have thought the slaughterhouse was too far from my window for sound to carry. It's wordless, mindless. I go back to sleep with goosebumps all over my body.

The third or fourth time I wake up, feeble sunlight is coming through the curtains. There's a hollow ache in my belly which could be hunger or anxiety. The noisy twittering of birds is like a lobotomy stick behind my eyeballs. I can hear rushing water, too. There must be a river near here.

I don't feel refreshed. According to the vintage alarm clock on the dresser, I've been in bed for six hours, but I guess only half my brain got any rest.

After meeting that guy on the bus, I used to wonder if the sharks had a dark side and a lighter side, like they only attacked people when the wrong side of their brains had control. Now I think probably both sides are the dark side. Humans too.

I dress in some clothes from the closet. A grey turtleneck, a denim jacket, some thick tan pants. I won't be on the cover of *GQ*, but at least the outfit is warm, and everything's more or less my size. I wonder whose clothes they were. A former prisoner's, maybe.

I emerge into the dining room, where the smell of baking bread is in the air and two yoga mats are unrolled on the floor near the table. Zara and Cedric are stretching, both in skin-tight activewear, black with neon highlights, that shows off their meatiest parts. My stomach burns.

'I know what you're thinking.' Zara smiles between her legs at me, catching me looking. 'Cultural appropriation, right?'

'Exactly what I was thinking,' I say.

'I wasn't sure about it myself.' She rolls her neck from side to side. 'But I did some research. Apparently yoga was mostly a spiritual practice in ancient India—there may not even have been an exercise component. Modern postural yoga has Indian, European and American roots. So I figure it's okay for us to do it.'

'Right.'

'Care to join us?'

'It's a bit early for me,' I say.

Cedric smirks, like he had already guessed my hamstrings wouldn't extend that far. His eyes, which last night seemed glassy, are now bright.

'Suit yourself,' Zara says. 'Three more breaths here, pedal it out and, when you're ready, move into up dog.' She and Cedric both straighten their arms and tilt their faces upwards. I realise that the bird noise and rushing water sounds are fake, coming from a large Bluetooth speaker in the corner.

'Did I miss anything last night?' I ask.

'Don't think so,' Zara says. 'No more activity on the cameras. No cops showed up.'

'I guess it really was just a hiker or a poacher.'

'Hopefully. We'll do another sweep of the forest anyway. Now, open up your hips for lizard—let the earth support you.' Zara and Cedric contort themselves into another painful-looking pose. I wonder why their clothes are so tight. Wouldn't these exercises be easier in loose ones?

Cedric tilts his head towards me. 'Are we gonna put you to work this morning?'

'Sure. Happy to help out any way I can.'

'How much do you know about what we do here?'

Nothing. 'Everything,' I say.

'Great. I could use a hand with some tickets.' Cedric glances at Zara. 'Is Kyle doing a mailout today?'

'Tomorrow, I think,' Zara says. 'Lux, I wouldn't mind your input on some marketing copy, too.'

'Okay with me.' Hopefully I can figure out what all this means when the time comes.

Something dings in the kitchen.

'Bread's done,' Cedric says.

'Great. Let's finish with mountain. Lift your heart to your thumbs.'

The two yogis stand up straight, eyes closed, half-smiles on their faces. The sight is oddly chilling, so I go into the kitchen. Behind the dark glass of the oven, a loaf of bread has risen perfectly. I wrap my hands in a tea towel and take it out.

It feels like I'm dreaming. Yoga and baking with killers.

'Wild-caught yeast,' Zara says from behind me. 'You like?'

I turn around. She has a gym towel draped over one shoulder, like a prop. Her cheeks are flushed and there's a slight sheen of sweat on her throat. The spandex hugs her curves.

'Looks good,' I say.

A coy smile. 'It's not hard to do. Just leave some flour and water out in the open as bait, and you'll snare some. Keep it nice and wet to selectively breed the best strains. I have several secluded spots around the forest where I like to do it. Each place has a slightly different flavour.'

I would have thought yeast was a poor topic for flirting, but she's making it work. 'Can't wait to try it.'

'Help yourself.' She gestures to the knife block behind me.

I pick up a bread knife. It's been years since I used one of these on actual bread. The serrated edge is perfect for sawing through tendons.

I carve off a wedge. Steam spills from inside the loaf.

'Try it.' Zara sounds so insistent that I suddenly wonder if the bread might be poisoned.

I take a bite. It's warm, soft and slightly salty, just like Zara's flesh would be.

'Delicious,' I say.

She beams. 'Plenty more where that came from,' Zara says. 'All you have to do is ask. Hey, how well do you and Fred know each other?'

'We're pretty tight,' I say, instantly on high alert. 'Why?'

Zara must sense my unease. 'No reason,' she says. 'He just never told me how you met.'

'We had a mutual friend.' This seems likely. Safe from contradictions.

'Who?'

'Morning.' Donnie walks in, blinking and yawning. He's wearing a loose white T-shirt which might be his pyjamas, and he hasn't shaved yet. His stubble is remarkably thick and dark.

Zara loses interest in me. 'Morning, Donnie. Coffee?'

Kyle enters next, wearing the same hoodie and sweatpants as yesterday. He looks like he has shaved, even though I'm sure he doesn't need to.

'Hi,' I say.

He just grunts.

Zara and Kyle have toast for breakfast. Cedric eats nothing. Everyone else has Samson's leftover stir-fry from last night, although Samson himself doesn't turn up to eat it.

'He's already out looking for the mystery man,' Fred tells me, when he emerges from the editing room with bags under his eyes. 'I'll join him in a minute.'

Zara spoons the stir-fry into bowls and microwaves them one by one. The men don't offer to help.

'You're a vegetarian, Lux?' Donnie pours himself some coffee.

When I was investigating Lux for murder—a murder it turned out he didn't commit—I quizzed a lunch-lady about his standard order at the college cafeteria. Ham sandwich on sourdough. 'No.'

Everyone around the table looks suddenly uncomfortable. This was a test, and I failed.

'I eat fish,' I add.

The tension in the room eases.

'Oh, that's okay,' Donnie says. 'The environmental impact of fishing isn't nearly as bad as raising cattle or pigs.'

Fred nods thoughtfully. Kyle copies him.

I look around the table at all these killers and torturers. 'Are you all vegetarians?'

'What right-thinking person isn't?' Cedric says, in his hard-to-read way.

If there's no meat in this house—other than the people—I'm going to go crazy.

'Well, here are your cruelty-free vegetables.' Zara has several steaming bowls balanced on the inside of her arm, like a professional waitress. No one thanks her.

'Are you vegans?' I ask, as she puts the bowl in front of me.

'What?' Donnie laughs. 'Not me. I have to drink a pint of milk a day to keep up my muscle mass.'

I watch his muscle mass, trying not to drool.

'And I do love an omelette.' Cedric looks wistful. 'But it's never quite as good here as in Spain.'

'You wound me, Cedric.' Zara tosses a spear of baby corn into her mouth with chopsticks. I try to remember if I put the can opener back in the drawer before I went to bed. I was so tired. But I'm sure I did. Didn't I?

'What's the popularity of the site like these days?' I ask, keen to change the subject.

'About nine hundred people,' Fred mumbles around a mouthful of rice.

'Is that site visits per year?'

Fred laughs. 'No. That's paying subscribers. We get two thousand site visits per *day*.'

I try to sound impressed rather than horrified. 'Wow. People love porn, huh?'

This time, the silence is stony rather than awkward. I've said the wrong thing again.

I backpedal, not quite sure what I'm backpedalling from. 'I mean, you know, it's incredible that you've captured the market so carefully.'

'It's not porn.' Kyle clenches his butter knife like an angry king. 'It's justice. Those nine hundred people are helping us give a voice to victims of crime and show them respect, by punishing perpetrators the system let go.'

It's the first time I've heard Kyle say anything without waiting for Fred to say it first, but he still sounds like he's parroting someone.

'Yeah. We got a Nazi back there.' Donnie jerks a thumb towards the slaughterhouse. 'We got a paedophile. We got a rapist. We got a domestic abuser. We got a paid-up member of the KKK. We got a fucking Isis fighter. That guy I shot yesterday? He stole people's life savings with fake cancer treatments. There's nothing sleazy about giving these people what they deserve.'

He's listed seven people, but I only saw six. Maybe he's killed someone and forgotten about it.

'Sorry, I didn't mean your subscribers were jerking off to

this,' I say, although that's exactly what I meant. 'It's like, you know how people say "food porn"? I meant it like that. You're making high-quality justice porn, you know?'

The tension lingers. Then Fred's face breaks into a smile.

'Justice porn,' he says. 'I like it.'

Everyone relaxes.

Fred wipes his mouth. 'All right. Kyle, you show Lux where to ditch his car. Cedric, get to work on those support tickets. Zara and Donnie, start prepping for the mailout. I'll keep searching for our mystery man, see if I can't pick up his trail. Let's get to work, people.'

As we pack up the dishes, unease gnaws at me. I only eat bad people. It's not much of a moral code, but it's what I have. The Guards have a similar policy. Which puts me in a difficult position, ethically.

It's like one of those recursive logic puzzles that I used to get in the mail. Is it bad to kill people who only kill bad people?

But deep down I know that it doesn't matter. I can agonise and rationalise, but my hunger will eventually pull my conscience into line. The Guards were doomed from the moment Fred let me into their house.

'Don't put those knives in the dishwasher,' I tell Kyle. 'It makes them blunt.'

CHAPTER 10

I eat until I'm fit to burst, and yet
I'm tremendously empty and deep.
What am I?

'Okay, go slow here,' Kyle says. 'It's just up ahead.'

We're in the midnight-blue sedan I stole, bouncing along the dirt. The track isn't designed for cars, and the car isn't designed for off-road. Branches rattle against the under-carriage and scratch the paintwork off the sides. The radio is hissing. Can't get any stations out here.

Kyle has been sent to help me get rid of the car. At first I assumed that meant he was leading me to a chop shop back in Houston, but like a teenage GPS—'Yo, go right. Nah, man, *that* way'—he directed me deeper into the woods rather than back towards civilisation. So I assume we're going to torch it. Hopefully there's a clearing big enough that we can do it without burning the forest to the ground.

Kyle lounges in the passenger seat, chewing his nails. He has none of the obvious signposts of disaffected youth—black clothes, piercings, shaved head. I guess those boys, the ones with dog collars and eyeliner, want you to know how little they care. It's a convoluted way of asking for help. Kyle, with his curly brown hair, pimpled jaw and track pants, looks like a normal kid. Invisible by choice.

'How old are you, Kyle?' I ask.

'Nineteen,' he says, and then glances at me to see if I believe him. I pretend I do. I'm guessing he's more like seventeen, or even sixteen.

'How'd you get involved in this?' I ask him.

'The Guards?' He shrugs. 'I don't know. My friends at school were sharing the videos around. Killers getting beaten up, paedophiles getting buried alive or whatever. I heard they were hiring, and I needed the money.'

'What for?'

'I grew up in Ackerly. You know it?'

I shake my head.

'Of course not. Why would you? It's a town of two hundred people. A meteorite landed in a field once—that's literally the only interesting thing that ever happened in Ackerly. There's a plaque and everything. It wasn't even a good meteorite. Smaller than average and made of chondrite—that's the most common material for space rocks.' Kyle scratches the hair under his baseball cap. 'Anyway, I wanted out of Ackerly. But I needed a car, and gas, and a place to stay. Those things aren't cheap, and no one in town had any cash. My mom spent all her money having me—' the matter-of-fact way Kyle says this makes me think it was something his mother said often '—so I had to get a job.'

'And you just . . . sent in a resume?' *To a dark web torture site?*

'I got lucky. Someone else in Ackerly posted something online about the Guards. She said their site was a hoax. So they gave me a way to prove myself. They told me to put a brick through her window with a message on it. After I did that, I was in. They wired me the money for the fare to Houston, then Fred picked me up from the bus station.'

Kyle wanted money for a car to get out of the middle of nowhere. Now he lives in a house even further from civilisation, and he still doesn't have a car. The irony seems to be lost on him.

I take a risk. 'Who's Druznetski?'

'Oh. He's a private investigator.' Kyle doesn't look suspicious that I don't know this. 'We use him for background checks on potential inmates. Figure out what they did, how they got away with it, if anyone will notice they're missing and so on.'

He discusses abduction with the casual fatalism of a cop nearing retirement age. That ability to simply not give a fuck, I've noticed, is only present is the very old and the very young.

'What's he like?' I ask. 'Druznetski?'

'Dunno. Never met him. He's not one of the Guards.'

'Why are we called the Guards? No one ever told me.'

He looks over. 'You don't remember from your vow?'

What vow? I quickly backtrack. 'I had a little chemical help to memorise the words at the time, you know what I'm saying?'

'Oh.' He glances at my teeth. The missing ones are too far back to see, but he still seems to buy my story that I was a meth head.

'Well, it's named after a group in Finland, I think, or Sweden—one of those countries. They were a small volunteer army who fought off the invading Russians. The actual name was the White Guard, but Fred thought that sounded a bit, you know, Nazi-ish. Whoa, whoa! Stop!'

I hit the brakes just in time to stop the car from going over the edge. There's a gorge here, narrow but deep, and well hidden by the trees on either side of it.

'That was close,' Kyle says. 'Come on. Leave the parking-brake off.'

We get out of the car into the feeble daylight. Kyle's right—it was close. The sedan's hood pokes out over the hundred-foot drop. Down the bottom, a shallow creek flows between boulders, rubble and the skeletons of clumsy cows. I can see the shattered remains of other cars are rusting in the shadows. The Guards have done this before, maybe dozens of times. Some of those steel carcasses probably belong to former prisoners.

'Okay,' Kyle says. 'Make like a pregnant lady and push.'

I hesitate.

'I know,' Kyle says. 'Hurts to do this to such a sexy car, right?' He pats the sedan on the trunk and even gives it a squeeze, as though it's a woman's butt.

I don't care about cars, but I get why some men do. Everyone wants to be beautiful, but men aren't allowed to be. If they use make-up, nail polish or hairspray they get belittled and attacked. So they surround themselves with beautiful things instead. And because their entire concept of beauty comes from advertising, those things tend to be expensive. Luxury sports cars. Guns with high-capacity magazines. Sprawling mansions with swimming pools. And women, which starts the cycle again. Only women are presented as objects of desire, which is why men consider themselves ugly in the first place.

If I'm immune to any of this, it's because I've always been too poor to advertise at. A low-interest demographic. That world of fast cars and big houses has always been so far out of reach that it's not even worth thinking about.

Kyle thinks I care about the car, and I do. If the Guards work out who I am, I'll need a quick escape. Without the car, I'll be stranded at the house in the woods as surely as Kyle was stranded in Ackerly.

'Trust me,' he says, 'the prettier the car, the prettier the crash.'

I put my hands against the trunk. Shoulder to shoulder, Kyle and I push it towards the edge.

The car lurches, and there's a crunch. Kyle and I step back, but it doesn't fall. The front wheels have gone over the edge of the cliff, but now the undercarriage is on the dirt, taking the full weight of the front of the car.

'Damn it,' Kyle says. 'Push harder.'

We do. The lactic acid builds up in my muscles. The wheel is a great invention. On it, a three-thousand-pound car seems weightless. Off it, the thing won't budge at all.

'We'll have to leave it here,' I say. Maybe I can come back later and somehow pull it back.

But Kyle is no quitter. 'Can we lift it? Lever it over the edge?'

We try. The back of the car is too heavy.

'We'll have to start the engine again,' Kyle says. 'Get some power from the back wheels. Drive it off.'

I look at the driver's seat. It's right above the edge of the cliff. A hundred-foot drop onto stone and steel. Plenty of time to panic on the way down.

Kyle isn't about to volunteer. He smirks. 'Go on.'

'It was your idea,' I say.

'I'm a visionary,' he agrees. 'Now over to you for the grunt work.'

Grimacing, I ease closer to the driver's-side door. The icy wind picks up, threatening to hurl me over the edge. I grab the side mirror for support. The car doesn't feel as immovable now as it did ten seconds ago.

Kyle hugs himself. 'Hurry up, man.'

I open the door. No way am I putting my ass on that seat. Instead, I lean in and twist the key in the ignition.

The engine turns over. Kyle coughs as he gets a mouthful of exhaust.

I look around for a rock I can put on the gas pedal. Everything is either too small to hold it down or too big to lift. I'll have to use my hand.

'You ready?' I call out.

'Ready.'

I push my palm down on the gas. The engine roars. The rear wheels spin for a second, then catch. The underside of the sedan grinds along the dirt towards the edge of the cliff. I wrench my right arm out of the cabin just in time. The car overbalances and disappears over the edge.

I crawl towards the cliff and peer over. The vehicle is still falling, the echoes of the idling engine bouncing off the other side of the gorge. Kyle joins me in time to see the impact.

There's a deafening crash. Parts of the car crumple inwards as others fly outwards. The hood is flattened like a cigarette packet under a boot as the car flips onto its roof, which caves in under the impact. Safety glass surrounds the impact zone in thousands of glittering cubes.

The sedan settles on its side, barely recognisable as a car anymore. The last reverberations of the crash die away.

'See?' Kyle says. 'Told you.'

He wasn't wrong. Even though that car was my way out, it was oddly satisfying to see it wrecked, and it wouldn't have been as much fun if the car was a wreck already. The prettier the car, the prettier the crash.

We wait another minute in case the car is going to explode or roll over one more time. Kyle is completely mesmerised. The spectacle, with just the two of us here to see it, creates a strange sense of kinship. I rest my hand on Kyle's back.

I get a vision of myself pushing him over the edge. One Guard down, five to go. It would be so easy.

But how would I retrieve the body?

Kyle looks uncomfortable, but doesn't look confident enough to say so.

I take my hand off him. 'Sorry.'

He gives a half-shrug, like unwanted contact is just part of life.

'Come on,' he says. 'It's a long walk back.'

CHAPTER 11

First I'm a leafy wall, then I'm a dirty,
gluttonous animal.
Touch my back and you'll bleed.
What am I?

When we get back to the house, I let Kyle go on ahead so
I can get a look at Fred's pick-up. Thief's instinct. I can't
walk past a vehicle without wondering how hard it would
be to hotwire.

I peer through the window at the dash. The letters *RF* are
inscribed next to the ignition. That means there's a radio
frequency transmitter inside Fred's key. Even if I took
a hammer and screwdriver to the ignition to make it turn,
the engine wouldn't start unless the key was within three
feet of the onboard computer.

The garage door has small windows built in, slightly
above head height. I stand on tiptoes. There's a white van
inside. I can't tell what model from here. The garage door
looks electric, therefore slow and noisy. At least if any of
the Guards goes anywhere, I'll hear them leaving—

'What are you doing?'

I turn around. Cedric is standing nearby, a bathrobe

billowing around his bare legs. A big triangle of his skinny chest is exposed.

'Aren't you cold?' I ask, avoiding his question.

'Yeah, well, today's an inside day for me.' Cedric sniffs. 'For you too, in theory.'

'It is?'

'Yeah. Time for you to peek behind the curtain.'

His robe flaps suggestively.

'Come on,' he says.

Cedric leads me to what he calls his 'studio', but is clearly just his bedroom. Plenty of bookshelves, a few landscapes printed on frameless canvases. There's a PC and a laptop on a desk. His window is locked with a padlock, just like mine. The room smells like air freshener and spiced cologne.

I've been trying to figure out who the opium addict is ever since I saw those poppies in the greenhouse. Now I'm pretty sure it's Cedric.

'I've made a login for you.' Cedric goes over to the laptop and points to one of the tabs at the top of the screen. He leaves the chair vacant for me. 'Click up there.'

On one of the bookshelves, a slim hardback volume has been placed face out, like he wants people to notice it— *Deciduous*, by Cedric Huxley.

I point. 'Is that your book?'

Cedric tries to look wistful. 'That was a long time ago.'

I open it up. '"The Hedgehog"?'

'Oh, of course you'd pick that one,' he says. 'The publisher said I would struggle to get reviewed if the book seemed too "niche". I knew what they meant, so I tried to write the most over-the-top, British-sounding poem I could think of. You know, something that would appeal to white people.'

He waits for me to read the poem, but it sounds like a trap. I don't know whether I'm supposed to like it or not. So I put the book down and sit in front of the laptop. Click the tab. Type in the login details on the post-it note. An inbox appears on the screen.

'Those are support tickets we've received, sorted by priority,' Cedric says. 'Keywords that already appear on the FAQ page are considered non-urgent, messages about downtime or police activity are urgent, questions from paying subscribers are non-urgent and so on.'

'Shouldn't the paying subscribers be urgent?' I ask.

'No. They're already giving us money, and we're not likely to lose them. The main purpose of support is to convince the free users to become paid users. Similarly, messages that pass certain spelling and grammar checks are prioritised, because that implies a level of education, which is correlated with income. You dig?'

I raise an eyebrow. 'Did you just ask me if I dig?'

He looks embarrassed. 'Sorry. That's my hippie dad coming through. Don't say things like that when you're answering the tickets. Keep it profesh.'

'Sure, I dig.' I scroll through the messages. 'Your dad still around?'

'No. Bowel cancer.'

'I'm sorry.'

'Thank you. I dedicated my first book to him.'

'Oh, you have other books?'

'I'm working on a few ideas,' he says defensively.

Whoops. 'Well, I'll get started.'

'You do that. Make sure you don't respond to any messages about Emmanuel Goldstein.'

'Who?' I say without thinking.

He looks taken aback. 'Fred didn't tell you?'

Too risky to pretend I've just forgotten. Goldstein might not be forgettable. 'No.'

'Goldstein isn't real,' Cedric says. 'We invented him as a kind of anti-mascot, and seeded rumours about him all over the web. We told conservatives that he's a gay child molester who entered the country illegally. We told liberals that he's a racist cop who shot an unarmed Black teenager and doesn't pay his taxes. We told feminists he was a CEO who preyed on young, female employees, we told Jews he's a Nazi, we told Nazis he's a Jewish banker who secretly controls the media—you get the idea. Whatever makes people angry.'

'Why would you do that?'

'Part of our escape plan.' Cedric says this like I'm supposed to know what he means. 'But now we get emails about him all the time. Our subscribers are always begging us to kidnap him, which we obviously can't do. So just ignore those messages, okay?'

'Okay.'

I start opening the emails. Most of them are questions I have no idea how to answer:

—*When will the recording of Scammer's death be mailed out?*

—*How much does it cost to see the full library?*

—*Can I see the criminal records of the inmates?*

A few other messages are simply fan mail:

—*Can't believe that pedo is still squirming.*

—*I want to see what happens to the KKK Queen!*

79

As unsettling as it is to find myself in a house full of killers, this is the more disturbing part. There are thousands of fans out there, all masked by anonymous usernames, Tor browsers and VPNs.

'Who are these people?' I wonder aloud.

Cedric doesn't look up from his computer. 'We've identified most of them. It's not hard, if you have a mailing address. We run an algorithm over the messages they send to guess their age and gender, and there's usually only one person per household who fits. But there's no typical customer. Some are poor people, some are millionaires. Grandads, moms, teenagers. Soldiers, civilians, dental receptionists. Americans, Chinese people, foreign diplomats. The popularity of our product crosses social, cultural and economic borders. Everyone loves seeing bad guys get hurt.'

Eventually I find a useful message. It's a question about billing details, and it features a link to the Guards' actual site on the dark web.

There are descriptions of all the prisoners, detailing their crimes. Their names aren't used—they're referred to only as the Nazi, the Pedo, the Rapist, the Scammer, the Abuser, the KKK Queen and the Terrorist.

Again, seven names for six prisoners, one of whom is already dead. Maybe the site isn't updated very often.

There's also a link to payment plans. When I click it, I finally understand how the Guards make money.

The site has several types of customers. There are free users, who can download some but not all of the videos. There are 'postals', who receive flash drives in the mail with premium videos loaded on to them. The postals can also submit the names of people they'd like to see kidnapped, and vote for a prisoner to get killed every month. There are contributors, like Lux, who make their own violent videos and submit them in return for discounts. I wonder about Abbey, the young woman Lux abducted—what crime did she commit that meant so many people wanted to see her tortured?

There are also gamblers, who pay bitcoin to enter a random lottery. The winners get to visit one of the prisoners and hurt them in person.

Cedric is looking over my shoulder. 'Don't worry about the lottery,' he says. 'It's bullshit—we would never tell anyone where we are.'

The movie sets make sense now. The Guards pretend the prisoners are in several different countries so they can sell lottery tickets in those countries. 'Don't the customers notice that no one ever wins?'

'That's why we wear the masks. The viewers are supposed to think it's a different person each time.'

I wonder how the Guards can trust each other, when so much of what they tell their subscribers isn't true. 'Mailing flash drives is an expensive way to deliver content.'

'Nah.' Cedric sits down next to me. 'Netflix does the same thing, kind of.'

'Really?'

'Sure. They load their most popular shows on to hard drives and mail them to ISPs around the world. So you think you're streaming the show from the other side of the country, but actually the data is coming from your own city. It's cheaper and more reliable. We've just taken it one step further. Look, we have a few layers of protection from the FBI.' Cedric swivels around in his chair and starts counting on his fingers. 'One: using encrypted flash drives helps us conceal just how much traffic there is, and makes this place seem like a normal farmhouse, with hardly any data uploaded via satellite. Two: our customers are less likely to sell us out, because we know where they live. Three: crimes committed via mail are technically the purview of the US Postal Inspection Service, who have less power than the FBI. And four: the users think all our victims are in other countries, so even if one of them informed on us—'

'Don't the users notice that the prisoners all have American accents?'

Cedric smirks. 'You'd think, right? But no, it's never come up. We do a bit of sound editing before we mail out the recordings, but that's mostly just getting rid of noise from the other sets.' He glances at a large plastic clock on the wall. 'Come on, we have to get through these.'

Now that I understand, the questions in the support tickets are easy to answer. I can mostly just copy/paste from the website and hit send.

After doing this for a while, I realise that I'm running customer support for a dark web torture site. This could be the worst thing I've ever done, in a life not short of bad things. But it feels normal—boring, even. Read, copy, paste, click. Read, copy, paste, click. It doesn't seem like a crime.

I pause. 'Are you worried about the guy out there?'

'The underground guy?'

I don't know why Cedric would be refer to him that way. 'The one sneaking around the house last night. The hiker.'

'Oh. No,' Cedric says. 'Are you?'

'A little.' I gesture at the screen. 'You have hundreds of customers. Thousands, even. They can't *all* keep their mouths shut forever. And if the cops ever worked out what was on those flash drives, they wouldn't need to decrypt it. They could plant microdots on them and track them here.'

'Customers only receive flash drives, they don't send them. The drives can't be tracked back to us.'

'The police wouldn't do it that way,' I say. 'They'd start at the other end—put the dots on the flash drives as they roll off the assembly line. Then they'd order some videos from you guys. When a flash drive showed up with micro-dots on it, they'd be able to map out its whole journey, from the factory to them—via here.'

To me, this seems unlikely. It would be a huge opera-tion. But the idea is making Cedric nervous, which is what I want.

'They couldn't dispatch a whole squad to every point on the journey,' I continue. 'They'd send one or two guys in the middle of the night to check out anywhere the flash drive stopped for more than an hour. Don't you think the hiker could have been one of those?'

Cedric looks twitchy now. 'No. Relax.' He looks at his watch. 'I gotta go to the bathroom. You'll be okay here?'

I nod. 'Sure. I hope I haven't worried you?'

He forces a laugh. 'Of course not. Be right back.'

Addicts like him—and me—follow a predictable pattern. They're anxious, so they take drugs. While they're high, their lives deteriorate. Whatever the initial problem was, it's now too big to solve. This makes them even more anxious when the drugs wear off, so they take more. To push an addict off the wagon, just worry him about something.

I wait a few seconds in case Cedric is coming back. Maybe he forgot to take his stash to the bathroom. No—his footsteps recede, and the bathroom door closes and doesn't open again.

I turn back to the computer and type Lux's name into a search engine. Several news stories come up.

TEACHING ASSISTANT SUSPECTED OF RAPE

POLICE MANHUNT FOR TEXAS TEACHER

CAPTIVE FOR MONTHS: ABBEY'S TERRIFYING ORDEAL

I click on an article. It loads slowly, data trickling down from the satellite. Alongside the text there's a picture of Lux, looking handsome, serious and nothing at all like me.

I'm not on social media. I don't have a website. But there is a single photo of me on the internet. A bomb was found under a car, and the FBI closed off the street. A journalist snapped a picture of me standing behind the police tape in the rain, wearing a second-hand leather jacket and muddy jeans, half-turned away from the camera.

Most web browsers have a developer mode. You can go in and change the code so the site looks different. No one but you will be able to see it, but in this case, that's all I need.

I switch on developer mode and type the URL of the photo into the article about Lux. Cropping it with code is fiddly, but I manage. Soon the police tape is gone.

Cedric's footsteps are coming back. I leave the resulting franken-site on the screen, stand up and grab his book off the shelf just as he opens the door.

His pupils are tiny. He looks so relaxed he might forget to breathe. Paramedics call that 'respiratory depression'.

'You okay?' he asks.

'Yeah.' I hold up the book, open to a random page. 'I was just checking out your book.'

'Ah.' He beams. 'I was so young. There was so much I didn't . . .' He trails off.

'This one's my favourite.' I point to the page.

He peers at it. 'Ah! "Mesopotamia". They always asked me about that one in interviews, you know. I had to pretend like it meant something.' He sits down on the bed. 'That's what we're all doing, isn't it? All the time. Pretending like it means something.'

'Interviews?'

'Oh, yes. I was a hot young writer.' His smile turns bitter. 'Years later, I realised no one ever said I was a *good* writer. Just *hot* and *young*. My hair started to turn grey when I was only twenty-four, so I shaved it off. I started moisturising. Exercising. None of it helped. No one wanted my second book. Actually, no one wanted my first book either. My poems were popular on Instagram but not in bookshops. The few copies that sold were given away as gifts to people who never read them . . .'

As he rambles, I feel an unexpected burst of contempt. By the time I was his age, I was homeless and starving. My parents were dead. My dreams were filled with blood. Cedric doesn't know what problems are.

I keep my voice even. 'So you found the site and offered to be one of the Guards.'

'No. I wanted to be one of the prisoners.'

That throws me. 'What? Why?'

'I hated myself,' Cedric says, his voice tinted with something like pride. 'I thought I deserved to be punished.'

He wanted thousands of people to see him suffer. Part of me wonders if this was just a poorly thought-out way to promote his book.

'They wouldn't take me,' he continues. 'The Guards only imprison the worst of the worst. People who can't be redeemed. But Fred saw my potential. He said my words could hack people's brains, make them feel something. That's a valuable skill, he told me.' Cedric's eyes finally focus on the laptop. He sees a picture of me on a major news site, right next to the headline: UNIVERSITY STAFFER SOUGHT ON CHARGES OF FALSE IMPRISONMENT.

'Googling yourself, huh?' He smiles sadly. 'I used to do that all the time.'

'Yeah,' I say. 'At least they caught my good side.'

He stares at the article for a while, but I can tell he's too high to concentrate on it.

'You look tired,' I tell him. 'You want to take a nap while I finish up here?'

'I really shouldn't.' But Cedric is already lying down. 'I have so much work to do.'

As he closes his eyes, I glance down at the open page of his book.

Mesopotamia
Why shouldn't my heart be a stone?
A stone, forged in volcanic fire
Can bear so much
A stone will never be anything
Other than what it appears
A stone will always be here
For you

Doesn't even rhyme. Maybe Cedric *should* be locked up with the other prisoners.

I save a screenshot of the doctored site. It might be useful later. Then I answer a few more support tickets. When I look back at Cedric, he's asleep.

He's thin, but not everywhere. There's some meat on his upper arms, and his calves.

His breaths are shallow. It would be easy to stop them altogether. It would look like an overdose. I could steal the body after the Guards have examined it.

He volunteered to be tortured and killed, says the dark voice in my head. *It wouldn't even be murder. More like assisted suicide.*

I close the door, and kneel next to the bed. I reach under Cedric's robe and squeeze his thigh gently. He doesn't wake up.

My heart is racing. I didn't plan this. I haven't prepared. But it's too good an opportunity to waste.

I reach for the spare pillow—

And the doorbell rings.

CHAPTER 12

I am a hole, yet I'm not empty.
Sometimes you can see right through
me, sometimes you can't. What am I?

I leap to my feet. Cedric stirs, eyelids fluttering, but he doesn't wake up.

I quickly scan the room for signs that I was about to murder its occupant. There's nothing, so I duck out and run towards the living room.

By the time I get there, Zara, Kyle and Donnie are in a panicked huddle.

'Who the fuck is at the door?' Donnie whispers. 'Why didn't our phones go off?'

'I'll check the cameras,' Kyle says, hurrying towards the basement.

'The cameras are all in the woods. This is someone on our goddamn doorstep.'

I share their unease. It's a long driveway off a dirt road off a long-since bypassed highway. No one should be here by accident.

'Where's Fred?' I ask.

'Still out searching for the guy from last night,' Zara says.

'Maybe he locked himself out.'

'He would never ring the bell. None of us would. The bell is a warning system. Someone is here who shouldn't be.'

'Where are Samson and Cedric?' Donnie asks suspiciously.

'Samson's still out with Fred,' Zara says.

'And Cedric's asleep,' I put in.

Donnie and Kyle look incredulous—who could sleep through this noise?—but Zara doesn't seem surprised.

The doorbell rings again. It's not the gentle *bing-bong* that would suit a luxurious house like this; it's a harsh buzz, like you'd hear inside a prison. This is followed by a sharp knock.

Zara has tiptoed over to the front door to check the peephole. Her eyes widen.

'Police,' she mouths at us.

A brief surge of relief. Help has arrived. Then I remember that if the cops arrest the Guards, I'll go hungry.

Donnie turns and heads for the armoury.

'Wait,' I say. 'How many?'

Zara holds up one finger. Not enough to arrest anybody. Donnie will just kill the cop on our doorstep. I can't let that happen.

'Donnie, wait,' I say. 'One cop isn't a raid. We can convince him to go away, but not if you start shooting.'

Kyle comes back up the stairs. His voice is frantic. 'The car came up the drive about two minutes ago.'

'Why didn't we get an alert?' Zara says.

'We probably did. Check your phone.'

'Two minutes is long enough to tell the precinct he made it here,' I say. 'If they don't hear from him again soon, they'll send more.'

'The driver was a woman,' Kyle says.

Donnie returns, holding two shotguns.

'Wait,' I say again. 'I can get rid of her.'

'So can I,' Donnie says, inserting cartridges into his shotgun.

'If you shoot her, more will come.'

'We can be gone by then.'

'Let me talk to her,' Zara says. 'She might be more inclined to trust another woman.'

That sounds like crap to me. 'Why would a woman who looks like you live alone in the middle of nowhere?'

I hoped the flattery would convince her to back off, but it backfires. 'Okay,' she says. 'You can be my husband.'

'What?' I say, but Zara is already walking back towards the door. I run after her.

The doorbell buzzes again.

Zara shakes her hair out and messes it up. 'Unbutton your pants,' she says, and reaches for the doorhandle.

I barely get it done in time. Zara opens the door, revealing a police officer.

She's white, fifties, five-foot-nothing in the black boots and tan uniform of a county sheriff's deputy. She turns back to face us as the door opens, like she'd already given up and started to walk back to her cruiser. It looks like the Guards' problem would have solved itself had Zara not opened the door.

'Sorry,' Zara says. 'We were just—'

'Vacuuming,' I say.

'Washing up,' Zara says at the same moment.

'*I* was vacuuming, she was washing up.' I clear my throat. 'What can we do for you, officer?'

The deputy looks at Zara's dishevelled hair and my unbuttoned pants, and gives a slight nod. 'Sorry to disturb you,' she says. 'I'm Deputy Lewis. Can I come in?'

It's a reasonable request. Snow has started to fall behind her.

I glance back through the doorway. From here, I can see Donnie in the kitchen holding one of the shotguns.

'The place is kind of a mess,' I say, hoping Donnie will take the hint and get out of sight. 'But if you really need to . . .'

'No, it's okay. I won't take up too much of your time.' Lewis watches us closely as she talks. 'A hiker has gone missing in this area. It's been three days since his family heard from him.'

Zara puts her hand on my shoulder. 'Oh God, that's awful!'

'Hiking, at this time of year?' I say. 'He must be nuts.'

A thin smile from Lewis. 'Well, the County Sheriff's Office likes to look after the entire community, not just the sane individuals within it, so we're canvassing the neighbourhood.'

'Not much of a neighbourhood,' Zara says. 'It's just me and David out here.'

I'm David, apparently. My false identities are getting harder to keep track of.

'So you folks haven't seen anything?' Lewis asks.

'We haven't been outside much on account of the weather,' I say.

Lewis glances at my open fly again. 'Right. The weather.'

'Who is he?' Zara asks. 'The hiker.'

'Name of Floyd Harris. He's forty, married, three kids. Walks the Sundress Hills Trail by himself every year, according to his wife, but I guess this time he went off the path. We've walked the whole way along it, looking for him.'

'I've never heard of the Sundress Hills,' I say.

'Me neither, until the missing persons report was filed.' Lewis looks carefully at Zara. 'Is everything okay out here in general?'

She seems to think I might be dangerous. Astute of her.

'We're doing just fine.' Zara threads an arm around my waist and holds me close. Her body is warm, her abdomen soft through her shirt.

'Yup,' I agree.

'Uh-huh.' Lewis offers a card to Zara. 'Well, if you see anything, give me a call.'

Zara takes the card and examines both sides of it. 'Will do.'

Lewis clomps back down the stairs to the driveway, hands clenched into fists against the cold. Strange that she didn't bring a picture of the hiker to show us.

Snow has started to settle on the roof of her patrol car. As she climbs in and takes one last look at us through the windshield, Zara kisses me on the cheek.

'Well done, sweetie,' she says.

'You too.'

I watch as Lewis starts her engine, reverses out and drives away. Another chance to do the right thing, disappearing into the snow.

CHAPTER 13

Which animal keeps track of time?

We find Donnie in the kitchen, still clutching his shotgun. 'Is she gone?'

'She's gone,' I say.

'Did she call for backup?'

'No.' Actually, she didn't touch her radio before driving away. Seems odd that she didn't tell the precinct she'd finished talking to us. If she has a car accident on her way back, a SWAT team might show up here, assuming we're responsible for her disappearance.

'Good news.' Zara straightens her hair. 'The guy last night was just a hiker. His family hasn't heard from him, so the police are just asking around.'

This can't be the whole story—the hiker knew my name somehow. But at least my immediate problem is solved.

'Huh.' Donnie looks relieved, but also annoyed that he won't get to shoot anybody. 'Good job, Lux.'

'Zara was very convincing,' I say.

Zara squeezes my shoulder. 'You make a great husband.'

Kyle clears his throat. 'We all should get back to work then, I guess.'

'Right,' Donnie says. 'Come on, Lux. Let's feed the inmates.'

'Sure.' I try to sound casual. No one has noticed the sabotaged cameras yet, or at least, they haven't mentioned them.

Donnie collects the masks. This time I'm Frankenstein and he's the witch. I can taste his breath from yesterday inside the mask.

Swapping faces probably disorients the prisoners. They can't be sure who's who, or even how many Guards there are.

We go out the back door and up the hill towards the slaughterhouse. I listen for approaching sirens, and hear nothing. Officer Lewis must have been fooled.

Donnie unlocks the door and heaves it open, casting a long rectangle of light on the stained floor. By day, the slaughterhouse looks shabbier. The sets are revealed to be plywood, the props plastic. But looking at the prisoners creates the opposite effect. The bags under their eyes, the scars on their chests and the chains around their wrists and ankles look all too real.

Donnie hands me a stack of plastic bowls and a bucket of dog food. 'I'll be checking on things over there,' he says, gesturing vaguely towards the greenhouse. 'Holler if you need anything.'

None of the prisoners make eye contact as I walk in, but I can feel them watching me as soon as I look away from them. They remind me of zoo animals. Not the cheery ones that run over at feeding time, like monkeys and otters.

Nor the big ones that don't care you're there, like tigers or alpacas. They're like eels, or octopuses. Afraid of visitors, always desperate to get out of sight, cowering in the hidey-holes not quite big enough to conceal them.

I put down the bucket in the centre of the room. I'm hungry. Is there real beef in the dog food? Some vegetarians buy meat for their dogs. I don't know why—the cows are no better off in dog biscuits than in burgers.

'Ironic, right?' One of the prisoners has worked up the courage to talk to me. He's Indian American, forty-something, with deep-set eyes under a heavy brow. He's going both bald and grey. His clothes look like old army fatigues, with leaves and dead grass glued to them.

'What is?' I open the bucket and scoop some dog biscuits into a bowl. The sour smell is sickening. Even I wouldn't eat that—and I once ate my own thumb. Dogs must hate humans.

'It needs to be closer,' the man says. 'I can't reach.'

One of his hands is free, the other is chained to the floor. All the men are secured like that, by one wrist. The women are chained by one ankle instead. This man looks withered and weak, but I don't want to come within reach of his free arm. I nudge the bowl with my foot so it slides over to him, the dog biscuits rattling inside.

'Thank you,' he says. 'You must be the new guy.'

I cock my head. He can't see my face behind the mask. 'New guy?'

He's not fooled. Maybe he recognises my voice from yesterday, or noticed that I only have nine fingers.

'I'm Gerald,' he says.

'Lux.'

'Was it you, last night?'

He's asking if I sabotaged the cameras. I pretend to misunderstand: 'I didn't pull the trigger.'

'Oh.' This time he buys it. I can see him trying not to look disappointed.

'What are you in for, Gerald?'

He swallows. 'Rape.'

I'd read the profile of the Rapist on Cedric's computer. A year ago, he concealed himself among the trees of Memorial Park dressed in a homemade ghillie suit. When the sun went down, he assaulted a court stenographer on her way home from work. She later said it was like the forest had come to life and attacked her. After the rape, he attempted to blind her with a vial of acid so she couldn't identify him. It must have worked, because he was arrested but never charged. The profile included hacked emails and text messages with his attorney, which revealed what he'd done. There were also screenshots of several news articles, complete with photographs of Gerald—looking a lot fatter and happier than he is now.

'It's bad, I know,' Gerald says. 'But this isn't justice.'

I move on to the next prisoner, no longer interested in conversation. This one is dressed in black, with a swastika armband. I guess she's the Nazi. I recognise her from some photos, too.

Looking around, I realise that all the prisoners are in costume. The guy in the brown rags must be the Isis fighter. The woman in white is the KKK Queen.

The Scammer's body is still here, in the early stages of decomposition. He would still be edible, but not for much longer. Now that I'm paying more attention, I realise his dirty jacket is a lab coat. I can see his bare chest underneath it, covered with scars—some from sharp implements, some blunt, some hot. None older than two months or newer than two days. There's a tattoo, hard to read against his dark skin. It's a jagged line, like an ECG, and some heavily stylised text which I think says *RECYCLE ME*.

I've seen similar tatts on bodies in the FBI morgue. Those bodies were usually missing hearts, kidneys, livers— people acquire the tattoo to make sure doctors know that they're organ donors. Or to get themselves laid. Apparently generosity is sexy.

If he's an organ donor, surely he wouldn't mind if—

'We don't deserve this,' Gerald is saying. 'No one deserves this.'

The Nazi holds out a hand for a bowl of dog food. I know what she did, too. She walked up to the tall spiked fence surrounding a Jewish school in Minnesota during recess, dropped a lit cigarette into a milk bottle filled with gasoline and flung it over. No one died, but three children and a teacher were hospitalised with severe burns. In her photos alongside the news coverage, she was smiling. Even before I got here, I knew about this attack. The TV news couldn't use any footage of the children, but they made the most of the screaming teacher being loaded into the ambulance.

I give her the dog food and move along to the Terrorist, who flew to Syria and fought for Isis, taking several wives and trying to bring about the end of the world. He takes his bowl with long, almost skeletal fingers. These people are like the living dead, their tastiest assets starved away to nothing.

I move on to the Abuser. She's Latina, forties, wearing the torn remains of an evening gown. She looks better fed than the others, and has fewer obvious signs of injury, yet she looks more afraid of me than they do. I wonder how the Guards have punished her. I know from her file that she tied up her husband during a sex game and then burned him over and over with a cigarette lighter before skipping town with all his possessions.

There's no sign of the Pedo, who was profiled on Cedric's computer as a priest with exactly the rap sheet you'd expect. Altar boys. Communion wine. A sudden move to a new parish whenever a parent complained. Maybe the Guards killed him before I arrived. There's no way to ask that won't sound suspicious.

Gerald is still talking. 'You know why it's ironic? They feed dog meat to the humans and human meat to the dogs.'

It takes me a minute to realise what he means. Where the food for the watchdogs comes from.

'You see that machine behind you? Do you get what they're gonna do to us?' He's shouting now. 'Do you understand what you're implicit in, Lux?'

'You mean complicit.' I don't turn around, but I know the machine he's referring to. The huge steel box with a chute at one end and a spout at the other. Like a woodchipper, but not designed for wood.

I hand some food to the KKK Queen.

'Shut up, Gerald,' she says as she takes it, ignoring me completely. I recognise her voice from last night, when she introduced herself as Hailey.

'*You* shut up,' Gerald says weakly.

The sixth prisoner doesn't take his bowl. I quickly realise

that he's dead. I've been holding out a bowl for Scammer's corpse.

Everyone stares at me in shocked silence, embarrassed on my behalf, like it's a dinner party and I've just farted. Then the Nazi laughs darkly and throws a dog biscuit into her mouth.

CHAPTER 14

I'm one of a kind, and yet no
matter where you go, I'm always
at your fingertips. What am I?

'This was the spot, right?' Fred asks.

I examine the footprints. The hiker had the same size
feet as me and similar shoes. It's basically impossible to tell
what happened. 'Right.'

The others—Donnie, Cedric, Zara and Kyle—scan the
forest. Branches creak. Birds twitter. Sleet blows through
clearings, settling on leaves. Visibility isn't much better
than it was last night.

'He was just a hiker,' Kyle says. 'Why do we have to
find him?'

'Because Samson attacked him with a knife and Lux
with a gun,' Fred says matter-of-factly. 'If he makes it back
to civilisation, he might tell somebody.' He frowns. 'Has
anyone heard from Samson?'

Blank looks all around.

'Thought he'd come back for something to eat,' Donnie
says.

'Me too,' Fred says. 'He seemed kind of gloomy this
morning. Zara, can you send him a message?'

'On it.' Zara gets out her phone. 'I hope he's okay.'

'Yeah. Everyone else, keep an eye out for him. You see anything, post it in the group chat on your phone. Everyone got push notifications and location sharing switched on?'

Everyone nods. There must be wi-fi repeaters in the forest. Makes sense, otherwise the cameras wouldn't work.

I nudge Fred. 'Can I stay with you? I don't have a phone.'

'What happened to yours?' He looks concerned, probably about my data falling into the wrong hands.

'I swallowed it.'

This might be the first true thing I've said to Fred, but he doesn't look like he believes me. 'Really?'

'Yeah. Police can force you to unlock your phone with a fingerprint, but they can't cut it out of your stomach.'

'How are *you* gonna get it back out?'

'I already did,' I say. 'I figured I had two main options—'

Fred cuts me off with an alarmed wave. 'Jesus, okay. You can stay with me. But we'll have to walk twice as fast to cover the same search area. Let's get moving.'

We all march our separate ways into the forest. I'm the only one without a weapon.

Ferns scrape my arms and legs. Something is crawling over the back of my neck. I swat at it. I'm still hungry. I can eat vegetables until my stomach bursts and still feel empty.

The forest looks different without the night-vision goggles. The constantly shifting shadows on the forest floor create fake holes and conceal real ones. Some blood-red flowers light up the gloom, despite the season. I spot a familiar shrub up ahead, shaped like a giant ribcage. I turn—there's another box camera, nailed to a tree opposite it.

'Do I need to impress upon you the seriousness of this situation?' Fred asks, when we're out of earshot of the others.

I shake my head. 'No, I get it. If this guy tells the cops about us . . .'

'Not that. What you were saying to the others, at breakfast.'

I frantically fast-forward through this morning's conversation. What did I say?

'About the prisoners,' Fred prompts. 'I know you like to play games, Lux. But if you want to stay here, you have to rein it in.'

He thinks I've been feigning ignorance by asking about things Lux would already know. He wouldn't be pleased to hear that my ignorance was genuine.

'Sorry, bro,' I say. 'I wasn't thinking.'

He holds up a hand for silence, scanning the trees around us like a Terminator. Then he says, 'Don't sweat it. Let's keep moving.'

As I trudge through the shallow snow, I try to think of things to say. I want to keep him talking and gather as much information as I can, but there are so many pitfalls. *Are you and Zara a thing?* Lux might be supposed to know that. *Where do you keep the keys for the cars?* Too suspicious. *Does anyone have any blood-borne diseases I might need to worry about?*

'Kyle seems to look up to you,' I say cautiously.

Fred laughs. 'Cute, huh? He never knew his father, and I think for him I've kind of stepped into that role. Ridiculous, right? He's practically our age.'

Actually, I think Fred's about thirteen years older, and I'd be older still. 'But he makes himself useful?'

'Hundred per cent. He cleans and repairs the sets, and he does all the supply trips for us, picking up stuff that keeps us running. He delivers the flash drives to the post office for our mailout subscribers, as well. I don't want anybody else doing that.'

'Why not?'

'Everybody else knows too much. I don't want their faces on camera.'

I get it now. Kyle is expendable.

'The kid knows what we all look like.' I'm trying to keep the conversation going. 'And our names.'

'He won't talk. He loves me and hates cops. I've also made a few transactions in his name, and the police are bound to find something at his old home.'

'Like what?'

'Like whatever. No one's innocent.' Fred says this like a mantra. 'It probably won't be enough to make the police think they've caught the ringleader, but enough that they can pretend they have. They get to arrest someone, we get to walk away, and Kyle gets to sacrifice himself for me. Everyone's happy.'

If he's telling me this, he and Lux must have been even closer than I thought. I need to tread very carefully. 'Do the others know about this plan?'

'No. But they'll go along with it, when the time comes.'

We continue searching for a few more hours. Nothing but dirt and trees. No sign of the hiker.

'I think we've lost him,' Fred says finally. 'You think he'll tell anyone?'

'I don't know.' This is true in every sense. I have no idea what the hiker was doing so far from the trail, how he knew my name or what he might do next.

'It'll be a shame if we have to move on.' Fred turns, cutting back across our winding path towards the house. 'But we've been living in a sandcastle. The tide was always going to come in eventually.'

'Yeah.'

'You're with me? For whatever comes next?'

'Of course.' I think of last night, when Fred was about to push that button on his phone. Compared to the other Guards he seemed so calm, even as he was about to . . . do whatever the button does. Even now, talking about abandoning a business he spent years building, and he still exudes only an air of mild regret. 'I don't know if I've ever met anyone more in control of their emotions.'

'Than me?' Fred looks surprised.

'Yeah.'

He smiles. 'Well, my group leader always said you can't choose what happens to you, but you can choose how to feel about it.'

I think of the moment I realised Thistle was gone forever. What I experienced in that moment didn't seem like an emotion. It was a physical thing, like a flu, making my throat close up, my eyes burn, my stomach twist. No way could I have turned that off.

Fred thinks he's more enlightened than me. I think he's never experienced real pain.

'I'm not sure it's that simple.' I watch a distant crow wrench the innards from a squirrel's carcass.

'Okay,' Fred says, like he knows I'm wrong and will graciously allow me to stay that way.

'How long has it been since you last went to group?' I try to frame the question so if he's still doing the therapy—and if Lux is supposed to know that—he'll think I mean how many days.

'Getting close to three years now,' he says, giving me no clue as to what kind of group it was. Drugs? Anxiety? Grief? 'Before I went, I had a lot of misplaced anger. I thought I was pissed at my wife, but they taught me that those feelings were mostly about my mom. By the time I left, I wasn't mad at anyone.' He glances sideways at me. 'You thinking about joining?'

I wasn't. 'Maybe,' I say. 'You think I should?'

'I think everyone should,' Fred says. 'Life's too short to be unhappy.'

I wonder what kind of man Fred was before group therapy. Sadder, by the sounds of it. Maybe he felt guilty about running a dark web torture site. Now he can choose not to feel bad.

This makes me think I shouldn't go to therapy. Feeling bad about the things I've done is my one redeeming quality.

When we get back to the house, Zara meets us at the door. She's shaking, and there are tears in her eyes.

'Samson is dead,' she says.

CHAPTER 15

Someone hires me to discreetly take
your things, even though they don't
want the things I take. Who am I?

I once worked as a cleaner at a motel in Baytown. I'd push a little cart filled with sheets, bleach and rolls of toilet paper from one room to the next, scrubbing and tidying the things inside. There were only two of us, and a lot of rooms to clean between the hours of ten and two. We didn't have enough time to be thorough, which meant the carpets never got vacuumed and the semen stains on the dressers never got anything more than a cursory wipe.

I did find the time to examine any jewellery guests left in their rooms during the day. Anything simple, like plain gold wedding bands, I could swap for cheaper substitutes later. Diamonds became cubic zirconia. Pearls became plastic.

The other cleaner, Helena, preferred to clean the smoking rooms so she could work with a cigarette pinched in the corner of her mouth. She didn't talk much—each morning she would give me a wary nod and scan me with her hard little eyes—but on my first day, she did warn me that I would eventually come across a suicide.

'Every cleaner finds one eventually,' she said, in a Russian-accented rasp. 'It's part of the job. Don't let it get to you. Just call the manager, and don't touch anything.'

I had never met the manager. He was just a shape behind the venetian blinds in a little office up the back of the lot and the name on the emails that I never bothered to open.

One day I knocked on the door of room twelve, called out, 'Housekeeping,' and unlocked it with the master key. Within ten seconds I knew something was wrong. All the personal belongings were missing—there were no clothes scattered about, no chargers plugged into the wall. It looked like the occupant had already checked out, except that I knew he wasn't supposed to leave until Friday. I soon found a suitcase behind the bed, closed and zipped, as though the occupant had packed all his belongings away in case the cleaners were thieves.

This reminded me to check his desk for jewellery to steal. There was none, but there was a note, written on motel stationery. It said:

Tell Melanie I'm sorry. She deserves better. I hope she finds the man she deserves. Holden

I pushed open the bathroom door and found a man floating in pink bathwater. He was pale, shiny and deflated, like an inside-out football. A steak knife lay on the tiles next to the bath.

If you measure it by years of life lost rather than lives lost, suicide is the leading cause of death in America. Nothing else comes close. And it leaves behind a certain kind of grief among the victim's friends. It's not just the loss of the person, it's the realisation that they were so unhappy.

The way Zara is crying, I feel like I already know what happened to Samson.

'What do you mean?' Fred is asking. His Zen smile is gone; now he just looks worried.

'Did I fucking stutter?' She did, actually. It's like she's choking on the words. 'He's *dead*.'

'Hey, hey.' Fred puts his arms around her. 'Talk to me. Tell me what happened.'

'I just wanted to give him some food,' Zara sobs into his shoulder. 'That's all I wanted.'

Fred kisses her hair and rubs her back, too fast to be relaxing.

'Where is he?' I ask.

Zara points wordlessly, without looking. I walk through the living room, the kitchen and around the corner towards the bedrooms. I don't know which room is Samson's, but one of the doors is ajar. I put my palm against the wood and push.

Samson's room has the same packed-away feel that motel room had. No abandoned clothes, no books. But maybe it's just sparsely decorated. There's an aloe vera plant on the bookshelf and a framed photograph of a bodybuilder on the wall. A ukulele propped up in the corner. A bowl of stir-fry upside down on the carpet in front of the door. The window is padlocked shut.

Samson is lying on the double bed in the middle of the room. His shins are hanging down over the side of the bed, like he was sitting and then flopped backwards. A pistol is still clenched in his hand. There's a small, round hole in his temple.

'Oh, *shit*.' Fred is behind me, his voice muffled, his hands covering his mouth. 'Jesus Christ.'

'I sent him a message, like you said.' Zara's voice wobbles. 'He didn't reply. So when I got back after searching the woods, I sent him another one. I heard his phone go off in here. I realised I hadn't seen him all day, so I thought maybe he was sick and he might like some food. He didn't say anything when I knocked, so I just ...' She sniffles. 'If I'd gotten back earlier, maybe he ...'

A hundred clues assault me at once. Not much blood around the bullet hole, so he probably died instantly. No blood on the walls or the ceiling or the sheets, so the bullet is likely to be still in his skull. When I walk around him, the lack of an exit wound confirms my theory. It's common for low-calibre bullets to stay in the skull. Less common for nine-millimetre rounds, like the P320 in Samson's hand would take.

No smell of gun smoke in the air, so he's been dead at least half an hour. I put my hand in his armpit.

Zara slaps my hand away. 'You really need to check his pulse, Lux?'

'Room temperature, or close to it,' I say. 'He's been dead for hours. Wouldn't have mattered if you came back early.'

Samson must have killed himself at about one-thirty pm, right after we all left to search the woods. Any later and there would still be body heat, any earlier and someone would have heard the gunshot.

'I could have checked on him last night,' Zara sobs. 'I knew he was acting weird. Maybe he wouldn't have done this.'

'What are we gonna do?' Fred's hair is a mess, as if the stress has unravelled it. 'How do we ... oh God.' He bends over, like he's going to hurl. So much for choosing how to feel. He's no stranger to violent death, but when the victim is one of his friends, he doesn't take it well.

I open my mouth to tell him not to puke on my crime scene, and then I remember that's not my life anymore.

Instead, I turn to Zara. 'Where's everyone else?' I ask.

'I don't know. Still out searching, I guess.'

'How long ago did you find him?'

'Right before you got here.'

Makes sense. Otherwise she would have called Fred, I assume. I touch the upturned bowl of stir-fry. Still warm. Consistent with her version of events.

Samson's face is slack and oddly peaceful. I know from experience that people don't look like that when they're about to commit suicide. Death does loosen the facial muscles, at least until rigor mortis, but the expression makes me start looking for other clues. Things that don't fit with the narrative.

Like the gun in his hand. He didn't drop it when he died. Unusual but, again, not unheard of. The bullet hole is neat. No burns around it, meaning he was shot from a distance of at least a foot. Possible, but very unlikely . . . unless he was shot by someone else.

When I was a kid I found an old longboard next to a dumpster. It took me a while to work out how to ride it—you swerve gently left and right to keep your balance and your speed, but eventually it feels like the board is in control, not you. The curves get too wide, too steep, and you know you're going to get thrown off.

This situation feels just like that. Every time I think I understand what's going on, I have to swerve again. And the crash, when it comes, might be the kind you don't walk away from.

'We have to get the others back here.' Zara is texting.

'Right.' Fred visibly pulls himself together. 'And we have to tell his family, I guess. Except we can't, because we don't want the police anywhere near this place. What a mess.'

He takes the gun from Samson's hand and checks the clip. 'The whole house could have gone up. Jesus.'

I guess he means that the bullet might have set fire to the propane tank which powers the fireplace. But that seems unlikely, up this end of the house. Maybe there's something else flammable around that I don't know about.

'Samson hated his parents,' Zara is saying. 'We don't owe them shit.'

'Well, we can't just put him into the grinder like the others.'

'I know. I just can't believe it.'

'Me neither. He seemed so . . .' Fred trails off. Maybe he's just remembered describing Samson as 'gloomy' a few hours ago.

I could tell them not to feel guilty. I'm pretty sure Samson didn't commit suicide. Someone came in here, shot him, and then put the gun in his hand.

But who?

•

When Donnie sees Samson's body, he screams out, 'No!' and punches the open door so hard that we later discover it won't close. His fist leaves a perfect imprint in what looks like plywood—apparently Fred's commitment to bamboo only extends to the unpainted surfaces.

'I'm sorry, pal.' Fred puts a hand on Donnie's shoulder.

Donnie shrugs it off. 'Why the fuck would he do this?'

'I don't know.'

Donnie stares at the bed. His eyes are pink with rage or grief, I'm not sure which. He doesn't bother to pick the splinters out of his knuckles. I watch his blood fall to the carpet. Drip, drip, drip. It's mixing with the fallen stir-fry. Would the others think it strange if I started eating off the floor?

Kyle is next to arrive. He says nothing, looking at the dead body for only a moment before turning to the rest of us. Like he doesn't want to react until he can see how everyone else is responding. It's not until he sees Donnie crying that his own eyes tear up.

'What happened?' he asks.

'Something terrible.' Zara hugs him. If Fred is Kyle's surrogate father, Zara is his mother. 'I'm so, so sorry.'

Kyle hugs her back. His hands are stiff against her spine. They don't slide down to her butt, but I can see them considering it. Zara might see herself as Kyle's mom, but he doesn't think of her that way.

'We should get the body out of here,' I say.

'Are you sure we should move him?' Fred asks.

'Why not?'

Fred looks uncertain. 'I don't know. We just need a plan.'

Cedric appears in the doorway. Looks at Samson. 'Sleeping on the job, huh? Sounds about right.'

Donnie storms out, shoving Cedric out of the way.

'Hey!' Cedric complains.

Donnie doesn't slow down.

Cedric laughs awkwardly. 'What's his problem?'

No one says anything.

Cedric sits next to Samson. 'Hey, wake up, asshole. We've been searching all day.' He slaps Samson's face lightly.

Sees the bullet hole.

'Oh,' he says.

None of the other Guards comforts him in the silence that follows. I scan their sombre faces. None of them looks like they killed Samson.

So was it the hiker? Or is one of them a very good liar?

Fred has noticed the way I'm looking at the others. His eyes narrow.

I turn away. 'I'll take care of the body.'

'You don't have to do that, Lux,' Zara says.

A plan spills out of my mouth while a very different one forms in my head. 'I didn't know Samson as well as the rest of you. I can bury him tomorrow, and everyone can say a few words. A proper goodbye. But we can't leave him in the house. Do you know what happens to a body in the first twenty-four hours after death?'

'We do,' Zara says.

'Right.' I force a smile. 'Forgot who I was talking to. Anyway, you don't want to remember your friend like that. I just need someone to help me carry him to the slaughterhouse.'

'I don't want him out there.' Cedric's voice is soft and measured. 'Not with those animals.'

'If we take him anywhere else, he'll be eaten by literal animals,' I say. 'And the slaughterhouse is cold enough to slow down decomposition. I'll wrap him in a sheet so the prisoners don't see him, okay? It's just for one night, so I have time to dig the grave.' And to figure out how I can butcher him in secret.

Focus. You should be trying to work out who killed him, and why. You don't have time to eat anybody.

Shut up, I tell the annoying voice in my head.

'What did you say?' Fred asks.

I blink. 'What?'

'Did you just say, "Shut up"?'

I sometimes think out loud when I'm hungry. 'No. I said I need help carrying the body.'

When the police came to the motel I worked at, they found the suicide note and matched the handwriting to Holden, the occupant of the room. The devastated widow, Melanie, confirmed that he had attempted suicide once before. But she said she had thought he was doing better.

The police guessed Holden had leaped from the Fred Hartman Bridge, which wasn't far away and was 'popular with jumpers'. They told Melanie that it was likely the body would never be found.

The bathtub was immaculate.

CHAPTER 16

What happened to the cannibal who arrived late to the party?

Donnie is the strongest, but he doesn't volunteer. In the end, it's me and Kyle hauling the body out towards the slaughterhouse. I'm holding the legs, Kyle has the shoulders.

Carrying a body is harder than most people think. It's not just the weight—about two hundred pounds in Samson's case; it's all the joints. Limbs have a way of flopping around, like the corpse is trying to stop you from dragging it away. First-timers often stop to double-check that the person is actually dead.

Kyle doesn't check.

'Has this happened before?' I ask.

'Here? No.'

'Somewhere else?'

'Some asshole brought a gun to my school.' Kyle is panting as we carry the body towards the slaughterhouse. 'He shot six people, but only one died, so it barely made the news.'

'And you ended up carrying a body?'

'The shooter's. He wasted himself with his last bullet.

We weren't a hundred per cent sure he was dead, so we carried his body to the closet and barricaded him in. Didn't matter. He was totally dead.'

'That must have been traumatic.'

'Nah.' Kyle puffs up his chest. 'I didn't even know any of the people who got shot.'

One of Samson's legs jerks unexpectedly. The folded bedsheet over my shoulder slips down. I pause to readjust.

'Offing yourself rather than going to prison, that I get. But this?' Kyle looks down at Samson's cryptic expression.

'He and I were messaging each other a few weeks ago,' I say. 'He sounded a bit beat up about his parents and how they still wanted him to pursue medicine. But he didn't sound, you know, suicidal. Just pissed.'

I don't know if Lux actually exchanged any messages with Samson. But now that both are dead, I can pretend the friendship was strong and use that to infiltrate the group more effectively.

'I guess he was lying to all of us,' Kyle says. 'Figures.'

'Figures?'

Kyle dumps his end of the body next to the slaughter-house door. Samson's skull cracks against the concrete foundations.

'Well, everybody lies, right?' he says, and looks me up and down. I don't think I'm imagining the suspicion in his voice.

'Fred tell you that?'

'Just life experience,' says the seventeen-year-old. 'You reach a certain age and you realise that everything your parents and teachers and the government told you was bullshit.'

I unfold the bedsheet and we roll Samson onto it. There wasn't room to do this on Samson's bedroom floor. The snow and dirt speckles the sheet, like a salt and pepper rub on a chicken breast.

Kyle fishes two masks out of his pocket. A mummy, the bandages made of rubber, and a vampire. He tosses the mummy to me.

'I want to talk to the prisoners,' I say, as I put the mask on. Kyle frowns. 'Why?'

'Someone might have heard the gunshot. They might know what time it happened.'

'Why does it matter what time it happened?'

'I just want to know.' It might help me figure out who killed Samson and why. I can't eat all the Guards if one of them might be on my side.

'Well, okay.' This time Kyle lifts Samson's feet, and I get his cold, stiff shoulders. 'While you're in there, pretend like you won a competition.'

'What?'

'Every month there's a "lottery".' He does air quotes. 'We pretend to select one of the subscribers to come to a secret location and—'

'I know. But why would a subscriber want to know what time the prisoners heard a gunshot?'

'We can edit out the actual question.' I can only see Kyle's eyes through the vampire mask. 'We do a lot of editing. Just pretend with your body language, you know?' He mimes looking around with awe, like he's at the Louvre, then he gets out the keys. I didn't see Fred give them to him.

'I thought you never knew your father,' I say.

'What?'

'You said your parents told you bullshit. But—'

'My *mother* told me a lot of bullshit. Like, for example, that my father was a lawyer.' Kyle unlocks the door. 'On my sixteenth birthday I requested his name. Tracked him down through the donor service.'

'I thought you had to be eighteen.'

Kyle ignores this. 'When I met the guy, he did have a law degree, but he said he wasn't my father. Told me he'd never donated sperm. So either he was lying, or my mother was, or both.'

Kyle drags open the slaughterhouse door. The metal shrieks across the concrete.

I stare at Kyle. 'Your father was a sperm donor?'

He raises a finger to his lips. The prisoners can hear us now.

I follow him inside. Nobody is screaming or crying this time, but everyone seems to be on edge. Last night one of their number died. This morning, a new Guard fed them. In between, they saw someone sneak in here and sabotage the cameras. They don't know it was me, but it was something different, something outside the pattern they've been trapped in for however long, so they're acting different.

Kyle looks around. 'Quiet in here today.'

The silence stretches, like drool beneath a dog's chin. Kyle shrugs. 'Works for me.'

We carry Samson into the corner. The indifferent way Kyle handles the corpse reminds me of myself. It's not a flattering reflection. He might not see it as food, but he sure doesn't see it as a person. Kyle resembles me in other ways, too. His bowed head, his shuffling gait, his life-is-crap attitude.

I tell myself it's impossible. He's the right age, but so are millions of other people. He looks like me, but that's not rare either. And the odds against me meeting my son like this have to be astronomical.

And yet . . .

Kyle glances up at the ceiling through sunken eyes that look eerily like my own.

He stares. 'What the fuck happened to the cameras?'

CHAPTER 17

I have eyes, and a mouth, and a nose,
but I'm not a face. What am I?

'How do you know they were sabotaged?' Fred keeps his voice low. 'They could just not be working.'

Kyle blushes. 'I'm not an idiot. All the cables are cut. Like, chopped in half.'

Me, Zara, Fred and Kyle are huddled around outside the back door of the house, like smokers sheltering a cigarette from the wind.

'How about the feed on the Pedo?' Fred asks.

'I checked. Still working fine.'

I didn't see the Pedo among the other prisoners, but it sounds like he's not dead. Maybe there's a second prison somewhere else—but who is operating it?

'It has to be the hiker,' I say.

'What about Samson?' Kyle suggests. 'He could have damaged the cameras before he offed himself.'

Fred dismisses the idea. 'Samson wouldn't have done that. He was proud of what we're accomplishing here.'

'Did you check the chains?' Zara asks.

Kyle opens his mouth, then closes it again.

'You're thinking one of the prisoners got loose and sabotaged the cameras?' Fred chews his lip. 'Why would they do that?'

'No point hurting them if we can't stream it.' Zara's dark, watchful eyes turn to me. 'And they know that.'

She's wrong about the perpetrator but right about the reason, and that makes me nervous.

'They all looked secure to me,' I say.

Kyle looks baffled. 'Why wouldn't they just escape?'

'If only one of them got loose, they might not have been able to free the others right away,' Zara says. 'We're miles from anywhere, so they couldn't have gone to get help.'

'Well, there's one way to find out.'

Donnie comes back from the armoury. He's carrying a pistol that I didn't realise was in the house—a Taurus PT132. Maybe he didn't want to touch the gun that killed Samson.

'Where's Cedric?' Fred asks.

'Who gives a fuck?' Donnie is already walking towards the slaughterhouse. Fred falls into step behind him.

Kyle follows like a puppy. 'What are you doing?'

'Getting some answers.'

Zara and I hurry after them. 'Freddie,' she says, 'this is a bad idea.'

'Yeah, well, we'll see.' Fred hands out some masks. I get the vampire again. Kyle is the witch, Zara is the mummy, Donnie is a clown.

My heart is racing. I sabotaged the cameras to stop the Guards from hurting the prisoners. It looks like my plan is about to backfire.

Fred pulls on the Frankenstein mask and hauls open the

slaughterhouse door. Donnie walks in first, brandishing the pistol.

'Hello, piglets,' he says. 'Who feels like squealing?'

The prisoners stare at him in silent terror.

Fred examines the shredded cables overhead, then looks around at the prisoners. He doesn't speak, just nods to Donnie.

'I want to know what happened to my cameras,' Donnie says.

He didn't say *our* cameras. Maybe he gets possessive when he's angry.

Hailey, the KKK Queen, speaks up. 'We didn't see anything.'

'Wrong answer!' Donnie takes aim with the pistol, then thinks better of it. He picks up a brick instead and hurls it at her.

Hailey ducks, and the brick crashes through the fake wall behind her. She tries to scramble behind the bed, but her chain goes taut.

Zara and Kyle exchange worried glances. Donnie could easily have killed her.

'The votes aren't in yet,' Zara says.

Ignoring her, Donnie picks up another brick. 'Somebody knows something. How many bones do I have to break to find out what it is?'

I grab Donnie's arm. 'Hey! It's dark enough in here during the day. Even darker at night. She's probably not lying.'

Donnie glares at me for a second, his eyes burning behind the clown mask. 'Okay.' He tosses the brick from one hand to the other. 'I can be nice. How about this? The first person to tell me what happened gets a vacation. One week. No shows.'

Silence.

'No cutting, no beating. Real food,' Donnie continues. 'Aspirin. Toilet paper. Sounds pretty good, right? All you have to do is tell the truth.'

Silence.

'A vacation for one person only. And if you're thinking that I won't hurt the rest of you because the cameras are off, then you've underestimated how much I enjoy it.' He glances at his watch. 'This offer expires in thirty seconds.'

There's a pause. And then:

'We'll tell you.' The voice comes from the middle-aged man—Gerald. The Rapist. He's chained to a water pipe in a fake pharmacy. 'If we *all* get a vacation.'

'Oh, really?' Donnie says.

Gerald's voice wavers. 'Two weeks. All of us. No beatings.'

Donnie hurls the brick at him.

'No!' I shout.

Gerald doesn't duck in time. The brick caves in half his skull and splits the pipe behind him, showering the set with water. The man slackens immediately, ending up as flat on the floor as a chalk outline. His blood turns the water pink.

There were six prisoners when I first arrived. Now only four are left.

I step between Donnie and the others. I keep my voice low. 'You're hurting, I get it. But these people are our livelihood. You have to stop this.'

Three sentences. One appealing to his emotional side, one to his greed and one to his instinct to follow orders.

None of it works. He pushes me aside.

'There will be no negotiation!' he bellows at the prisoners. 'I will kill every single one of you if that's what it takes. There are plenty more rapists and murderers where you assholes came from.'

He picks up another brick. I get ready. He'll pull back his arm to throw it, just like before. When it's all the way back, I can knock the brick out of his hand.

I just don't know what he'll do after that. He still has a gun in his other hand.

Donnie pulls back. I reach out—

'A guy came in last night,' a woman says quickly. The one with the dark hair and the swastika armband.

I drop my hand quickly. Donnie keeps hold of the brick. 'Tell me more.'

'He didn't say anything. He had a flashlight—'

The moustachioed young guy in the rags—the Terrorist—interrupts. 'He was normal height, normal weight. Looked like he was favouring one arm. He was in here for about thirty seconds.' The Terrorist sounds desperate to share in the vacation, or to avoid the punishment everybody else will get.

In the corner, the Abuser starts crying. I watch the blood spread out from Gerald's shattered skull. His brains look like raw pork.

'How'd he get in?' Donnie keeps the brick raised.

'He cut through the wall.' The Terrorist points.

Fred goes over to investigate the hole. I stand still, sweating into my mask, hoping none of the prisoners counted the saboteur's fingers.

'What time was he here?' Donnie asks.

'Eight o'clock,' the Nazi says.

'Eleven,' the Terrorist says, at the same moment.

It was actually about two am. There's a clock in the Parisian set, but it's fake. The hands don't turn.

'Either way, the hiker was in here *before* we spotted him in the woods,' I say, trying to shift blame away from myself.

'Maybe,' Donnie says. He finally lowers his arm.

Zara still seems to doubt that the hiker was responsible. She goes around the room, checking that everyone's chains are secure.

'What about his face?' Fred asks the two prisoners.

'He had a flashlight,' the Nazi says. 'He pointed it at us. We couldn't see.'

'He was wearing a hooded coat,' the Terrorist adds quickly.

I nudge Donnie. 'The guy last night was wearing a coat like that.' He wasn't, but Samson and I are the only ones who met him, and I need to divert suspicion away from myself.

Then I remember that everyone else saw him on the monitor. Hopefully the image was blurry enough that no one can contradict me.

Fred has finished examining the hole. He turns to the prisoners. 'Good work, Emily. You too, Amar. I like your attitude.'

It's the first time I've heard their real names. The Nazi and the Terrorist look pathetically grateful.

'Those chains secure?' Fred asks.

Zara nods reluctantly.

'Okay. We're done here.'

Donnie puts the brick down. I follow the Guards towards the exit.

'The vacation?' asks Emily, the Nazi.

125

Donnie just laughs as he slams the door shut.

'Let's take a look around the back,' Fred says. 'There might be footprints.'

Fear clenches around my heart.

'Good idea,' I say.

As we walk around the side of the slaughterhouse, I make my way to the front of the group. I'm the first one to turn the corner. The hole in the wall is just ahead. My prints weren't obvious last night, but in the daylight they're clearly visible.

I walk right over them, past the hole in the wall. 'Where did he cut through? Over here somewhere?'

'No. Back this way,' Fred says.

I come back, and look down. 'Shit, sorry,' I say. 'I walked all over the prints.'

'Jesus, Lux,' Donnie complains. 'What the fuck is wrong with you?'

Zara frowns at the ground. 'It doesn't matter. I don't see any prints other than yours. The snow must have covered anything from last night.'

'Must have.' I cross my arms in the cold.

Fred looks at me for a long moment. Then he says, 'Kyle, check the security feeds from last night. Zara, find Cedric and get him to work on a message for the site. Something about a planned outage. Order some new cameras, too. Express shipping. Donnie, fix this hole—and calm down, all right?'

Donnie's face twists into a sneer, but he's looking at the wall, not us.

'Lux?' Fred beckons. His gaze is hard. 'Let's take a walk.'

CHAPTER 18

This word has the same meaning as thousands of others, yet it's spelled differently to all of them. What is it?

The sun is setting as Fred and I walk through the forest. Hard to believe it's less than twenty-four hours since I got here. We're looking for the trail of the mystery man—figuring out where he went after he supposedly wrecked the cameras. But I get the feeling Fred has something else on his mind.

'Sometimes you trust somebody,' Fred says, 'but it turns out they're not who you thought they were.'

A chill slithers up my spine. I shorten my stride so Fred isn't behind me, but he slows down, too.

'Even if you've known someone for years,' Fred continues, 'they might actually be completely different beneath the surface.'

I don't have my hammer. No weapons of any kind. My mind is racing, looking for a way out of this.

Fred might not be sure I sabotaged the cameras. If he is, he might not know why. He might not kill me until he finds out. I can stall him.

'Take Gerald, for example.' Fred sidesteps to avoid crushing a crawling insect. 'In all the months he's been here, he always struck me as a coward, but never as an idiot. I was shocked when he stood up for the group like that and got himself killed.'

Fred says 'got himself killed' as though he had no role in the event.

I jam my hands into my pockets. 'What are you getting at?'

'I don't think it was the hiker who wrecked the cameras,' he says.

'You think it was one of the prisoners?'

'No. If they got their chains off, they wouldn't stick around.' He scans the forest around us. 'I think one of the Guards is a traitor.'

A beat, as I realise he doesn't mean me.

'That doesn't make sense.' It would be suspicious if I blamed anyone too soon. 'They all depend on the site. They worked hard for it.'

'That's exactly why it makes sense,' Fred says. 'If they pick us off one by one, they can take this place for themselves. Keep the whole cash cow.'

I'm starting to catch up to him now. 'You think Samson was murdered.'

'I do,' he says. 'And I think *you* think that, too.'

I hesitate.

'When we were in Samson's room, I saw the way you were looking at the others,' Fred continues. 'And at the body. It didn't look like a suicide to you either.'

He's misinterpreted my interest in the body, but I don't say so.

We stop in a clearing. We're a long way from the house. Well out of anyone's earshot.

'Maybe the hiker killed him?'

'I checked the camera feeds from earlier today. Samson got back to the house at one-fifteen pm, while the rest of us were out searching the woods. No sign of the hiker after that.'

'I can't believe any of the Guards are capable of murder,' I say, laying it on a little thick. 'But hypothetically, wouldn't it be easy to work out who was responsible?'

'How?'

The timeline is coming together in my head. 'We know Samson was alive at one-fifteen. He must have been killed soon after that, since his body was room temperature when we found it.' As I speak, I remember that I never asked the prisoners if they heard the gunshot. I was too distracted by the realisation that Kyle might be my son. 'So whoever got back to the house right after Samson must be the killer. You'll see them arrive on the camera feeds. Hypothetically.'

'We don't have enough cameras to cover every part of the woods. That's why we rearrange them from time to time.'

I nod slowly, understanding. 'That's why you think it can't be the hiker. A Guard would know where the gaps were, and could sneak through. The hiker wouldn't.'

'Right. Even if he did, Samson wouldn't have opened the door for him. There are only six keys to the house—all accounted for. I checked. If some random hiker broke in, there would be signs.'

He wasn't just a random hiker. He *knew my name*. But I say nothing.

'Samson was killed by someone he knew.' As usual, there's no anger in Fred's voice, but there's an undercurrent of sorrow. *I'm not angry, I'm just disappointed.*

'I get it,' I say. 'You don't think Samson trusted me enough to be a candidate.'

'I know it wasn't you. We were searching the forest together when Samson died. And you were nowhere near the slaughterhouse when the cameras were sabotaged.'

Fred seems to have connected the two crimes in his mind. Lucky for me. The prisoners' claim that the cameras were wrecked before eleven pm won't withstand much scrutiny. But Fred knows I didn't murder Samson, so he assumes I'm not the saboteur either.

'So what are we gonna do?' I said *we* deliberately. I need Fred to think we're a team.

'Nothing yet,' Fred says, which is a relief. 'Just act normal. But keep your eyes and ears open.' He puts a hand on my shoulder. 'Can I rely on you to tell me anything you notice?'

I try to look offended. 'Of course. You can count on me.'

'Cool. First, though, I've got a little treat for you.'

'Really?'

'We need to replenish our stock. Do you want to help Donnie capture a new prisoner tomorrow night?'

My heart skips a beat. 'I'd love to, obviously. But shouldn't we wait until we know who we can trust and who we can't? I mean, for all we know, Donnie could be—'

'I don't like the thought of Donnie working against us.' Fred looks troubled. 'I don't like the thought of any of them doing that. But every second we're offline costs us money. The new cameras won't arrive until Friday. After that, we need to hit the ground running.'

Today is Tuesday. I have three days before the horror show in the slaughterhouse starts up again.

'I want someone I trust on the expedition,' Fred continues. 'And this is one prisoner you'll want to catch in person.'

'Why?'

'It's a surprise.'

Maybe someone from Lux's personal life. His abusive father, perhaps. Or Abbey Chapman, the woman who only recently escaped from his homemade prison and pressed charges against him. The thought of her getting captured again is horrifying.

I remember what Fred said before: *I'll get you to keep Abbey's background on the down low. The others don't know.* I still have no idea what he meant.

The new prisoner, whoever it is, will know I'm not Lux.

'I want to do an autopsy,' I say, stalling.

'A what?'

'An autopsy. On Samson's body.'

Fred looks horrified. 'You want to cut him open? Jesus!'

'It might help me find the killer.'

'How?'

I shrug. 'I won't know until I do it.'

'Do you have medical training I'm not aware of?'

'Not *training* per se,' I admit. 'But—'

'No,' Fred says. 'Firstly, he was my friend. He's not like those assholes in the slaughterhouse. He's not going to be sliced up. He's getting a proper burial. And secondly, the cause of death is pretty fucking clear. He was shot in the head. You think you're going to find the killer's name written on his organs?'

'What if I found out that he had cancer?' I say. 'Or something else that made it seem like it was a suicide?'

Fred hesitates. 'Do you even know how to tell the difference between a tumour and regular tissue?'

'Sure,' I say. How hard could it be?

Fred doesn't believe me. 'Is there some other reason you want to do this, Lux?'

It had occurred to me that, after the autopsy, no one would notice if not all Samson's organs made it back in.

'No,' I say.

'Then that's your answer,' Fred says. He turns away, shaking his head. The manager of a dark web torture site is horrified by my barbarism.

He seems to take it for granted that I'll follow his orders.

•

Dinner is more vegetables. Zucchini, carrots and potatoes from Cedric's greenhouse, tomatoes and beans from cans. The more I gorge myself, the emptier I feel.

Donnie is bubbling with quiet fury, putting his glass down too hard after every sip of water, and scowling at Cedric for some reason. Cedric, who has finally woken from his opiate-induced stupor, doesn't seem to notice. He stares at his plate as though he can't summon the energy to lift his fork. Kyle is acting like nothing happened, although he was never chipper to begin with. Zara is flighty, topping up drinks and trying to start conversations about neutral topics, like the playoffs and plans for Christmas.

It's like dining alongside the five stages of grief. Kyle represents denial. Donnie is anger. Zara is bargaining. Cedric is depression. Fred, staring wistfully at a blank wall as he chews, resembles acceptance—though I know under-neath the calm exterior he's thinking hard.

A murderer who doesn't want to be caught usually rambles about their victim. They describe their shock and sadness at his or her death and drop casual hints about other suspects, all the while watching you nervously to see if you believe them. But tonight, no one has even said Samson's name out loud.

The Guards' whole business is murder. How can I find a killer hiding among other killers?

After washing the dishes they all go to their rooms, except Fred, who stays up watching CNN. Something's happening in LA. Police are bludgeoning Black protestors with riot shields, while looters smash storefront windows. Fred takes notes in a little leather-bound journal.

'What are you up to?'

Fred looks up. 'Oh, just working on our escape plan.'

'Has it changed?' I ask, with no idea what the old plan was. I remember what Cedric said about Emmanuel Goldstein, the fictional anti-mascot, but I still don't understand.

'Not in any major way. Just tweaking some of the details.'

I nod as though I know what he means. 'Well, goodnight.'

'Goodnight.'

I take a quick shower, go into my room and lie on the bed. After a while I roll over, then back. I flip the pillow. Bunch the sheets around me, then loosen them again. I can't sleep.

Tomorrow night, I'm supposed to pick up a prisoner who probably knows Lux, and who will therefore blow my cover. I should be looking for a way to escape. But I can't leave. Not just because the Guards will start torturing the prisoners again when the new cameras arrive on Friday, but because of Kyle.

The nurse basically told me my sperm would never be used. Even if it was, the chances of me and my progeny ending up at the same house would have to be one in a million. He can't be my son.

What if he is, though?

Logically, there's no reason to care. Kyle is a stranger—worse than that, he's an asshole. So what if he might be related to me? All humans are descended from the same woman, who lived only 150,000 years ago. We all share 99 per cent of our DNA. It shouldn't matter if Kyle has an extra 0.5 per cent of mine.

But I need to find out for sure. I've never been able to accept not knowing something. The compulsion to keep digging at all costs isn't my worst quality, but it's up there.

This problem chases itself around my head for a while. Then I find myself in the kitchen, holding a knife.

It's still night-time. The house is silent. The TV is off, and Fred is gone.

I turn around, disoriented. I'm a sleepwalker, so this happens sometimes. A noise disturbs me and I get out of bed, even though I'm not conscious. If I were in my own house, I'd just walk back to my bedroom, probably without waking up. But here, I've momentarily forgotten where my room is.

I look down at the knife. It's balanced well, the handle exactly as heavy as the blade. A better weapon than the hammer, or the toothbrush shiv. I could slit the Guards' throats as they sleep.

But I can't. Kyle might be my son. And someone else

in the house murdered Samson, for reasons I don't understand yet. That person might not be evil enough to eat. An extra twist on my moral dilemma: Is it bad to kill people who kill people who only kill bad people?

I put the knife back in the block and start to walk towards the bedrooms. But I still have no sense of direction, and I find myself in the living room instead. I rub my eyes, annoyed.

A flicker between the curtains.

I'm suddenly wide awake. I creep over to the curtains and peek through. For a second, I see only darkness. Then there it is again: a flash between the trees. Someone is walking around out there with a flashlight.

I grab one of the coats from the stand at random and pull it on. It's tight. Zara's, maybe. No time to swap it for another. Ditto for the boots I find beside the front door, which are too big. I leave a hat in the jamb so the door doesn't lock itself behind me, then I run out into the snow.

I can't see the light anymore. Desperate, I sprint down the steps, across the gravel and up to the tree line. Still no sign of the flashlight. And without one of my own, I can't follow into the woods. I'd walk right into a tree.

'Hey!' I hiss. 'Who's out there?'

No answer. Branches creak, silver in the moonlight.

All six coats were on the rack, so it's probably not one of the Guards. I take a risk: 'It's me, Blake! I just want to talk to you!'

The icy wind flings the words back in my face.

Frustrated, I walk back towards the house—and then stop.

Footprints in the snow. Some are mine. Some are not.

I bend down, squinting in the dark. The foreign prints are big, bigger even than my oversized boots. At the FBI morgue, there was a pathologist named Dr Norman—a tall blonde with the kind of insight that made me nervous. I once saw her use a complicated equation to estimate a man's height by looking only at his severed foot. 'You know what they say about men with big feet,' she told me. 'Big feet, long corpse.'

I don't remember if the hiker had large feet, but he was tall. I'm guessing these prints are his. It seems unlikely that yet another unknown party is out here.

There's not enough light to follow the tracks into the woods. But I can follow them in the other direction, and see where the guy has been.

I follow the prints up the gravel driveway and around the side of the house. The tracks stay close to the walls, I guess so the guy could duck under the windows and stay out of sight. They go in both directions. He went and came back along the same route.

I feel a chill as I follow the trail. The guy walked halfway around the house. He was right here, while everyone was asleep. And this time he didn't trigger any of the cameras—I assume, since I didn't hear anyone's phone go off and no one else is up. Fred's theory that the hiker wouldn't be able to sneak past the cameras was wrong, or at least outdated. He's learned where the gaps are.

It feels like I'm being watched. I turn to scan the forest. No movement.

The prints go right up to my bedroom window. There's some confusion before they keep going. The guy must have paused here. I look through the window but can't see anything past the curtains and the darkness. Could he have heard me getting up? Could I have heard him, and that's why I got up?

The tracks continue past two more windows without any signs that he slowed down. They stop at the last window along. This was his final destination.

There's a dim light inside, and the curtains haven't been closed all the way. I peer through the gap. There's a blanket draped across an antique reading lamp inside, casting a muted glow across a pile of clothes and part of a bookshelf. Zara is on the bed in a satin nightdress, eyes closed, hair fanned across the pillow, mouth slightly open. An open book has fallen onto her chest.

Around my feet, the tracks fade in the falling snow.

CHAPTER 19

Say a few kind words before you cook me,
spread me and bite me. What am I?

'How'd you sleep, Lux?'

'Yeah. Good. Fine.'

Donnie takes a swig of milk straight from the jug. 'That bad, huh?'

I laugh nervously. 'Right. I guess I'm still getting used to the bed. You?'

'Couldn't sleep. Almost got up and went out back.' He tilts his head in the direction of the slaughterhouse.

I swallow. 'You do that?'

'Sometimes. But Fred wants to wait until the new cameras arrive.'

I don't know why it shocks me that Donnie works out his frustrations on the prisoners. I already know that it's not about the money for these guys. I remember what Fred said about Samson: *He was proud of what we're accomplishing here.*

I sprinkle some salt into my coffee. 'I hope you don't mind me asking, but how much do you get paid?'

Donnie looks confused by the question. 'For what?'

'For, you know, the work you do here.'

Donnie puts the milk back in the fridge. 'I get to live in these beautiful surroundings with great people and make a real difference in the world.'

So, nothing. I wonder if the others all work for free. I sip the salted coffee. Usually I use a drinking straw, like a vein pumping into my mouth, but I couldn't find any in this kitchen.

Kyle enters, bleary-eyed. He doesn't look rested. I wonder if he sleepwalks, like me.

'Morning,' I say.

He just grunts and grabs a Red Bull from the fridge.

I wince. 'There's a lot of sugar in those.'

'Yeah, no shit.' He jams some bread into the toaster. 'Where's Zara?'

'Out collecting yeast with Cedric,' Donnie says. 'Fred's in the editing room.'

'Do the subscribers know about the sabotaged cameras?' I ask.

'No,' Donnie says. 'They think it's a planned outage. But we can only sustain that for a day or two. Rumours are already circulating. Subscribers are saying we've all been arrested. That's why Fred's in there. Gotta cobble together some old footage to make content that seems new.'

'Making a difference in the world,' I say, deadpan.

'Right.'

Kyle's toast pops up, startling me. He opens the fridge and grimaces. 'We're out of eggs.'

'You're doing a supply run this morning, right?' Donnie asks. 'Can I come?'

Kyle shrugs.

Donnie seems to take this as a yes. 'Great. Lux?'

'No thanks,' I say. 'I got a hole to dig.'

Sadness sweeps across Donnie's face, and I find myself wishing I'd been less blunt. 'Right. Okay. See you.'

Fred emerges not long after, stretching a crick out of his neck.

'How'd the editing go?' I ask.

'Ugh. It'll get the job done, but it's like a stew made of offcuts.' He says this with both familiarity and disgust. I wonder how long he's been a vegetarian.

'Will the new cameras be here on Friday?'

'Yes. Zara got the order in on time.' He checks his watch. 'I'm going to change the buckets in the slaughterhouse.'

He disappears out the back door. I put down my coffee, half-drunk. Time for some snooping around. Fred told me not to go upstairs. While he's gone, I want to see what he's storing up there.

I reach the staircase and put my hand on the bannister—then I hear a soft scuffle above.

I freeze. Donnie and Kyle have left, and Fred's in the slaughterhouse, so it must be Zara or Cedric up there. I didn't hear them go up, which probably means they didn't want to be heard. I'm not the only one snooping.

I heard a creaking sound on Monday night, when I was sneaking around with a toothbrush. Could one of the Guards have been searching the attic then, too?

I want to know who it is, but I can't go up there without them spotting me. I'll have to stay close by and see who comes down.

I search Fred's bedroom while I wait. I expect it to be monastic, given his Zen attitude, but it's not. There's a beanbag in the corner and a PlayStation next to a curved screen on his desk. When I wiggle the mouse, the screen lights up. It's locked, but the background image is of a toddler with a gap-toothed grin. A young woman is pushing him on a swing, her face just out of frame. It looks like the photo was taken from a distance.

Under the desk there's a paper shredder. I open it up. Unfortunately, it's a cross-cut mechanism, not strip-cut. The container is full of little diamonds, rather than long strips I could have pieced together.

In the drawers I find some softcore porn and a few sticks of jerky. A guilty pleasure.

I take one. He won't notice, or if he does, he won't complain in front of all the vegetarians. As I unwrap it and stuff it into my mouth, I spot the most important thing in the room—a little wooden bowl on his bookshelf, filled with keys.

I recognise two of them from the front door and the slaughterhouse. There's also a car key, presumably for the van. Donnie and Kyle have taken the pick-up, and apparently Fred's key for it. The rest look like they might be for the padlocks on all the windows.

I chew the jerky thoughtfully. I can't take any of them right now, but it's useful to know where they are. I slip back out into the corridor. Listen for a moment. No one is coming down the stairs yet, so I head for Samson's bedroom.

I've been here before, but this time I'm looking at it differently. A trained investigator learns to search for evidence that contradicts their theory rather than confirming it. When I saw Samson's body, bullet hole in head, gun in hand, an impression formed immediately—suicide. So I started looking for signs of murder instead, and I found them. The look on his face, the lack of burns around the entry point, the absence of an exit wound despite the calibre of the gun.

This time, my theory is murder. So I start looking for signs of a suicide. The null hypothesis.

Samson was tidy, making the room easy to search. First, I look for a note. Nothing on his shelves, in his dresser, or fallen under his bed. I do find a key, though. Looks like it would fit the front and back door. I swipe it.

Most suicides don't leave a note. Many of them think they have no one to write to. I came to this house planning to kill myself, and I didn't leave anything for anybody. Still, it changes the probabilities.

Maybe he left a note on his phone or his computer. I scour the room.

Both are missing. Now *that's* interesting. Could the murderer have taken them? I think I remember seeing a phone on the bedside table last time I was here, but maybe I'm wrong. I haven't slept properly in two days. Haven't eaten properly in a week.

I've always been crazy, but I can usually tell where my imagined world ends and reality begins. Now even that certainty is slipping out of reach.

I start searching for signs that Samson was mentally ill. Most depressed people don't kill themselves, but most people who kill themselves are depressed. Samson has workout gear in his closet, well-worn. A reusable water bottle on his bedside table. The room is generally clean—no crumbs or wrappers or crumpled beer cans. No dust on the ukulele, either. It got a lot of use. All the signs point to Samson having a healthy lifestyle, which usually indicates a healthy mind.

In the dresser I find condoms and lubricant. Again, no dust, and the expiry dates are way into the future. Sexually active people are much less likely to be depressed.

Zara has been flirting with me, but I've seen signs that she and Fred are together. Kyle also seems interested in her. If she was sleeping with Samson as well, she's quite the queen bee. But Samson wasn't necessarily straight. He could have been in a relationship with anyone in this house.

Time to search Zara's room. I slip back out into the corridor, listen at her door for a second, and turn the handle. It's not locked. The door opens without a squeak. I'm reminded again of Zara's footsteps, silent despite the high heels. For someone so eye-catching, she goes out of her way not to be heard.

I only saw a little of Zara's room through the curtains last night—the same part the hiker must have seen, assuming it was him who left those tracks. The rest of it is a junk heap, with clothes piled high on the bed and books on every other flat surface. There's a dressing table, strewn with lotions and concealers and a long pair of tweezers. She's spilled some kind of make-up powder on the floor. Her window is padlocked, like every other one in the house—but unlike the others, there's grey dust all around the padlock. She hasn't cleaned the room in months.

If Samson's computer or phone is in here, it could take me days to find it. And Zara could be back any minute.

A faint scent stops me. It's fruity and feminine, although that's an illusion. Women don't smell like fruit. They smell just like men—sweat and bad breath and farts—until they are doused with chemicals that create the illusion of a fruity odour. Men are instructed to use a different set of chemicals that smell of pepper, smoke or whatever *sandalwood* is.

This particular scent stops me because it's familiar: Reese Thistle's shampoo. The memory is so strong that I turn around, expecting her to be right behind me.

She's not. Just an empty doorway in a house of killers, where I live now, instead of with her. She's gone forever, because of my mistakes.

I shake off the despair and try to focus. If I walk into Zara's room, she might notice my footsteps in the spilled make-up. She could have spilled it deliberately for this reason. It looks like an accident, but is it?

I go to Donnie's bedroom. Despite my theory that there's no such thing as a feminine scent, the air in here is undoubtedly masculine—I can practically taste the testosterone. A couple of thirty-pound dumbbells compress the carpet in one corner, and some magazines about men's health are on the dresser. Under the futon is a pair of running shoes.

I take off my own shoes and pull on Donnie's. A good fit. Small feet for a big guy. Then I go back into Zara's bedroom, leaving Donnie's footprints all over the make-up. The more I can make the Guards suspicious of each other, the less suspicious they'll be of me.

Zara's books have no theme. There's military history, fantasy, biographies of politicians, cookbooks. It looks like she visited a second-hand bookstore with a shopping cart and a blindfold. I open a few books and find receipts tucked into them—painkillers, moisturiser, rump steak. Either the receipt is someone else's, or Zara has only recently converted to vegetarianism.

I get a flash of a big ceremony, Cedric officiating. *Have you accepted cheese and rice as your lord and savoury?*

Even reading the words *rump steak* makes me drool. The jerky is already gone, and it didn't taste real. Too dry, not enough fat. Like eating a belt with a sprinkle of brown sugar.

The backs of the receipts have jumbles of letters and numbers on them, like Zara was trying to solve puzzles. I used to solve riddles for a living, but these are meaningless to me.

When I dig through the clothes on her bed, I find a laptop and a phone wrapped in some leggings and a dress. When I wake up the phone, the background picture is of Donnie, flexing in front of a mirror.

Did Zara steal Donnie's phone? Why? And what will she think when she sees his footprints all over the floor?

I don't know the passcode for the phone, so I open the laptop instead. This time the background is just a beach scene. The username is User73890. No clues there, and no idea what the password might be.

I could take both devices, but I have no realistic way of hacking in and every chance of getting caught. I put the laptop and the phone back where I found them.

At the other end of the house, the front door clicks and beeps.

I race back into Donnie's room as quietly as I can. I kick off his shoes and pull on my own.

Footsteps approach from the direction of the living area. I stuff Donnie's shoes back under the bed, scramble out and close the door.

Looking back, I realise that I left Zara's door open. Too late to close it now—whoever's coming is almost here. Instead, I stand in the doorway of my own room, facing the corridor, as if I'm just coming out.

Cedric appears. His eyes are red-rimmed. From opium or tears? I can't tell. But at least I know it's Zara upstairs.

'Hey,' I say.

Cedric jumps. 'Lux! You startled me.'

'Sorry, man. Heard you were out collecting yeast with Zara?'

'I was. I came back early to, uh, work on something for the funeral.'

'Right.' He doesn't seem to know that Zara came back early, too.

'Would you be willing to read . . .' Cedric seems to change his mind about whatever he was going to say. 'Actually, you want to do some gardening with me?'

'Sure.'

I follow Cedric out to the greenhouse. It isn't very green. Just grubby white glass surrounding glazed brown pots filled with wet dirt. It's winter, I guess. Everything has pretended to die, waiting for the atmosphere to be kinder before they give up their fruit.

But there is fruit, at least according to the labels sticking out of the soil: strawberries, watermelon, grapes, peaches and lemons, along with herbs and vegetables. There's a small apple tree in the corner. I had assumed this place was just Cedric's opium den, but it looks like he's feeding the whole house.

He could poison us all if he wanted to. Apple seeds contain amygdalin, which releases cyanide when digested.

Fred's theory was that the traitor wanted to kill all the Guards and take over the business. If he's right, Cedric isn't the killer. Cedric wouldn't need to stage a suicide—just sprinkle some ground-up seeds into the cooking pot.

'Do the prisoners eat this stuff, too?' I ask.

'No. They get dog food. Soy-based,' he adds hurriedly. 'We don't want to condone cruelty to animals. Did you know a dairy cow can live for twenty years, but they turn them into dog food after six, when the milk starts to dry up?'

'I did not,' I say. 'So what are we doing out here?'

'Oh, if you could just water those two rows, that'd be great. Especially the eggplant. He needs a lot of care.' Cedric smiles, as though this is funny. 'Watering can's over there. Use the worm tea.'

'Worm tea?'

He shows me the worm farm—a big black tub, where earthworms are devouring kitchen scraps. He twists a faucet near the bottom of the tub, and urine-like fluid trickles out.

When the worm tea runs out, I fill the rest of the bucket with rainwater from another tank and start tipping it on the plants. Cedric is doing something with the poppies on the other side of the greenhouse.

I'm hungry, and I don't really have time for this. Tonight I'm supposed to help abduct the new prisoner, who will expose me as an impostor. But maybe I can get some clues from Cedric about the hiker, or who killed Samson.

Almost every case I've ever worked has had a drug angle. 'How do you make the opium?' I ask.

He doesn't turn around, so I can't see the expression on his face, but his arms stop moving and his shoulders tense up. 'Excuse me?'

'You make dope, right?' I say. 'I was just wondering how you do it.'

He looks back at me, like he's trying to read my mind. I find myself thinking neutral thoughts, as though he might really be psychic.

'What makes you think I grow opium?' he asks. A bet-hedging question is as good as a confession.

I cringe. 'Is it a secret? Shit, I'm sorry. I haven't told anyone.'

He stares at me for a long time and then says, 'What the hell—I'll show you. Come over here.'

I put down the watering can and go over to his little field of poppies. They are bigger than they looked at first, the vivid papery flowers almost two inches across, wobbling on foot-long stems.

'You can make lots of things from poppies,' Cedric says. 'Codeine, morphine, heroin. But opium is easiest. Look. This one's ripe.'

He plucks one of the poppies and starts scraping the head with the blade of his gardening shears. The scoured head starts to bleed. 'I'll leave this one overnight so the sap leaks out,' he says as he works. 'After that I'll dry it in the oven on a low heat. Hey presto: opium powder.'

'How did you learn to do this?'

'I read about it in a book, then it was trial and error, basically. I don't know even how most people get drugs. You remember all those lessons in school? Just say no?'

I nod. *'This is your brain, this is your brain on drugs . . .'*

'Ah, you got that one. All kids are told to avoid drugs, but the messaging is subtly different. White kids are told drugs will fuck up their brains. Black kids are told drugs will land them in prison.' Cedric inspects a flower. 'Anyway, the commercials told us to *just say no*. They made it sound like everyone was doing drugs except me. I was desperate to say yes, only I didn't have anyone to say yes to. So I tried this instead. You can buy poppy seeds from anywhere. You don't need to know anybody, like a dealer. You don't need . . .'

He catches himself, but I hear the rest of the sentence anyway. *You don't need to have friends.*

'I can't produce much from a crop this small.' Cedric gives me a sharp look. 'You can try some if you want, but I don't have enough for a second regular user.'

'Is that why you haven't told the others?' I wonder if any of them have already figured it out. Zara didn't look surprised when Cedric slept through the doorbell yesterday.

'No,' Cedric says. 'I don't know why, exactly.'

I can guess. It's easy to convince yourself something is okay. You can come up with all sorts of rationalisations, reshaping the world so you're a hero, or at least not an asshole. But it's much harder to convince yourself that *other* people will think it's okay.

You can take a bite out of a corpse and tell yourself he felt no pain, and that he was a bad guy anyway. But you're not going to tell anyone else you did it, ever. You know they won't see your point of view. Because, deep down, you know your point of view is bullshit.

'They wouldn't understand,' I prompt.

'Or maybe they would understand too well.' Cedric starts scraping another poppy. 'They care about me. They might try to help me.'

I wonder if any of the Guards actually care about Cedric. I haven't seen any sign of that. Killers *can* have emotional connections to other human beings. A group of soldiers might massacre a village and still love their own wives and children. But while the Guards have common enemies—the police, the inmates—that doesn't make them friends.

'And you don't want to be helped,' I say.

Cedric and I make eye contact. For a moment, I feel like he sees me, the real me. It's like he's looking through a powerful telescope that can see the dark, distant edges of my universe, where other people have seen only a scatter of stars.

I can see by the look on his face that he feels the same way. That I understand him more deeply than he wishes to be understood.

'You loved Samson, didn't you?' I say.

It's a shot in the dark. Two-thirds of me expects to be wrong. But Cedric flinches, as though I've hit him.

It was the way he reacted to the body. Just sat next to it, and said, 'Oh.' At the time, the word seemed uncaring, or even flippant. In retrospect, I can hear the sadness in it. *Oh*.

Sadness, but perhaps not enough surprise.

'And he didn't love you back,' I continue. I've heard worse motives for murder.

'He loved me.' Cedric's voice wavers, and he tries to cover it with a cough. 'I know it.'

His knife slips, plunging right through the heart of a poppy he only meant to wound.

'What happened?' I ask. Knowing if Cedric's the killer isn't enough. I need to know if he's my ally or my enemy.

'We'd both been drinking,' he says. 'The others had gone to bed. I was telling him about something that happened at a literary festival in New York—a librarian hitting on me, her daughter getting embarrassed, a publicist trying to get rid of them both. Samson was laughing so hard. And I thought, *See? I can make you happy. Why won't you let me?*'

'When was this?' I ask.

'November nineteen.' It's telling that he knows the date. 'We kept talking. After a while he rested his head on my shoulder. And then . . .' Cedric looks away. Wraps his coat a little tighter around his shoulders. 'Anyway, we stayed on that sofa till sunrise. It was the best night of my life.'

I feel an unexpected trickle of sympathy for Cedric. My situation is different—Thistle fled from me after finding a human head in my freezer—but it's similar, too. She was mine for one night, and now she's gone for good. There are some things no amount of couples therapy will fix.

'But when everyone else got up,' Cedric continues, 'Samson acted like nothing had happened. I spent all day waiting for him to talk about it, but he hardly looked at me. When I confronted him, he said he'd been drinking. Like that explained everything.'

I'm surprised Cedric is telling me this all this. Most men wouldn't talk about it. They'd keep their jaws clenched until they found something to hit. Anger is the only emotion a man is allowed—some would say taught—to feel.

'That must have made you mad,' I say. Mad enough to kill somebody.

'Yes. But not at Samson. At the others, for shaming him.' He looks up at the greenhouse roof, blinking away tears. 'He killed himself over it.'

He sounds like he believes he's telling the truth. I wonder if knowing Samson was murdered would give him any peace.

'I'm sorry,' I say. 'He must have really loved you.'

Cedric kisses me.

It comes out of nowhere. I guess it's been a long time since anyone showed him any kindness, or even listened to him.

His lips, full and soft, are only on mine for a second before I bite him.

'Argh! Fuck!' He pulls free and staggers back.

I lick the blood off my lips. It's electrifying. Like the first salty potato chip out of the packet. Like the first hit of opium after a year sober.

Cedric touches his lips, looks at the blood on his fingers. 'What the hell, man?'

I still don't say anything. I'm frozen, playing tug-of-war with myself. I want more, but I can't have it. That dark voice in my head, saying, *You could eat until you're full and then chop up the rest and bury it in this garden and tell everyone he—*

'Jesus,' Cedric says.

The word, the shock in it, shames me into a moment of decency. 'I'm sorry,' I stammer. And then I run out of the greenhouse without looking back.

CHAPTER 20

Red next to black, safe from attack. Red next
to yellow, you're a dead fellow. What am I?

The urges are worse when I'm stressed or tired. Today
I'm both.

I'm digging like a maniac, trying to avoid the hunger
burning up my guts. The taste of Cedric's blood has awak-
ened something in me. I want more. It's like my stomach is
eating the rest of me in desperation.

Samson's body is nearby, still wrapped in a sheet. He's
going under the vegetable patch. It's fallow at the moment.
No seeds. Plants can turn sunlight into energy, but only if
there's enough nitrogen in the soil. Samson's body is made
partly of nitrogen, so Fred said to bury him here.

*Samson would love the thought that parts of him would
live on*, Donnie told me. I was astonished—and kind of
outraged—to see the tears in his eyes when he said this.
They're going to turn Samson's body into *vegetables*. What
a fucking waste.

But I can't do anything about it. The vegetable patch is
right near the greenhouse. If Cedric walked out and saw me
eating his crush, I don't think I could talk my way out of that.

My plan is to spread the sheet out and lay it on top of Samson, then pile the dirt onto that. Later I can unearth one corner of the sheet, then peel the whole thing back to expose the body.

But there probably won't be a later. Tonight we pick up the new prisoner—one of Lux's enemies. He or she will reveal to everyone that I'm not Lux.

The shovel splits the ground. The dirt has been recently turned, and a square of sackcloth has protected it from snow and frost, but the digging is still hard.

It's not just my life on the line. If I die, or get chained up in that slaughterhouse, those prisoners lose their only hope of salvation. They might be monsters, but the thought still weighs on me. I had the chance to save them, when that sheriff's deputy showed up. Now we're all doomed.

Fear of getting caught is a noose, one that's been around my neck my whole life. Now I can feel it getting tighter and tighter.

The hole is deep enough, but I keep digging. Putting off the moment when all that meat has to go to waste.

There must be a way out of this, a solution to the puzzle— something clever that gets me and all the prisoners out of this alive. But I can't think of it when I'm this hungry.

Samson's foot is sticking out of the sheet. I try not to look at it.

Some days the voice in my head is the sensible one, and I'm the bad guy. Other times, I'm the responsible one.

If you weren't so hungry, you might be able to think of a way out.

'No,' I grunt, still digging.

He's dead. He won't mind.

'No.'

Plus, he was a killer. Who cares what happens to his body?

'No.'

It's not like you'd be destroying evidence. Not any more than you already are.

'No.'

You're a dead man anyway. Why not have a last meal?

The dirt at the bottom of the hole is too compacted to dig through. I throw down the shovel and drag the bundle over. I put the sole of my shoe against the shapeless mass inside and push. The corpse tumbles in, landing with a wet thud and a snap of broken bones.

The foot is still sticking out. I look at it, breathing heavily. I'm so hungry.

The voice is silent. It knows it's won.

I reach down and grab his ankle. Glance back towards the greenhouse. No sign of Cedric.

I put Samson's dirty toe in my mouth. It's bigger than it looked and covered with fine hairs. I'm about to bite down, when—

'What are you doing?' Zara is standing on the other side of me, holding a bag of flour.

Panic. I drop Samson's foot and hastily turn my face away. 'Nothing. Just, uh, saying goodbye.'

I wipe my mouth and glance back at Zara to see if she buys this. A delighted grin is spreading across her face. 'Do you have a foot fetish, Lux?'

'Um . . . yes?'

'Well.' Zara smooths down her skirt and sits on a flat rock next to the vegetable patch. 'Your secret is safe with me.'

'Thanks.' I'm cursing her for showing up at the wrong moment. I really, really wanted that toe.

'Actually, you don't need to keep it a secret,' Zara says. 'We're all very open here. We don't kink-shame anyone.'

She's hasn't mentioned the fact that Samson is dead. That's a bit more than a kink. 'It's . . . kinda hard to be honest about what I'm into.'

'Don't worry. It gets a little easier each time.' Zara kicks off her shoes and starts stretching out her stockinged toes. 'Can I tell you a story?'

'Sure.'

'When I was a kid, I loved drawing. I'd make pictures of dragons and ruined castles and knights on horses. Some were in black and white, some in colour. I got some free illustration software and drew something new every day. I was obsessed.'

'That doesn't sound too kinky.'

Zara gives the comment a more generous laugh than it deserves. 'Well, one day I broke my stepmom's laptop. It was an accident—I tripped over the power cable, and it fell off her desk and cracked. But she wanted to punish me. So she took *my* laptop and she threw it out the window. It was only a ground-floor apartment, but the fall still killed it. All my illustrations were on there. Years of work. This was before cloud backups.' She snorts. 'A wicked stepmother. What a cliché, right?'

She doesn't know how much information she's giving me. If she had her own laptop but used free software, and a ground-floor apartment but a desk for her stepmom, I can pinpoint her household income within a couple of thousand dollars.

'She apologised, of course,' Zara continues. 'She said I'd just made her so angry, and that her work was keeping a roof over our heads. I should be more careful in future, she told me—it was the kind of apology that was really just a list of the things I'd done wrong. So after she and Dad went to sleep, I snuck into their bedroom.'

So far every encounter with Zara has felt like a performance. She's always glancing at the others as she talks, measuring their reactions. Not now, though. Her eyes are trained on the forest, but I don't think she's really seeing it. She's back there, in that bedroom.

'I might have made some noise, but they didn't wake up, or maybe each of them thought it was the other one. I hid under their bed, right under my stepmom's side. I had a needle for sewing badges onto my Girl Scouts uniform. It felt like I sat there for hours with it trembling in my hand, trying to work up the courage. Then I reached up around the side of the bed and pricked her.'

I stare at her. She doesn't appear to be kidding.

'I don't know which body part I got. Her thigh, maybe. I expected her to scream, but she just stopped snoring suddenly, and then there was a little gasp, and she muttered, "What in God's name?" She grabbed around in the bed-clothes like this—' Zara mimes rummaging '—looking for whatever had bitten her. Then she gave up. I waited for her to go to sleep . . . then I stabbed her again.'

Zara's cheeks glow as she describes this. She has one hand resting between her thighs.

I'm distracted by something panting nearby. When I turn to look at the dog run, both dogs are asleep, their heads on their paws. Must be an animal somewhere in the forest—but it sounds close.

'This time she yelped,' Zara continues. 'Ever step on a cat's tail? It sounded like that. She scrambled out of bed and turned on the light. I could see her veiny old feet, right next to my face. I just lay there, my heart pounding. She pulled back the blankets so she could look under the bed. But just as she was bending down, Dad told her to knock it off. "You're imagining things, honey. Go back to sleep." They argued for a while, but eventually she got back into bed.'

I'm strangely uncomfortable hearing this story. Not because of the act—stabbing someone with a needle is nothing compared to the things I've done—but because of the way she describes it. The other Guards see the torture as righteous punishment, a solemn duty. Clearly Zara doesn't.

'It's hard to describe how exciting it was,' she says. 'Having that power to hurt and not get punished for it. Way more fun than drawing. Even after I got my new laptop, I never went back to it.'

'Do the others know this story?'

'Of course. Like I said, no shaming here.' She pats my knee and stands up. 'The sooner you open up to us, the better. You have no idea how good it will feel.'

She's right. I have no idea. I've never told anyone what I am. A couple of people—dead now—found out, but I never *told* them. And even after they knew, my compulsions were only ever discussed obliquely. *Take the body and . . . do what you do*, the old FBI director once said to me. Charlie Warner, the crime lord I used to work for, called it *body disposal*. I didn't want to say the actual words, and they didn't want to hear them.

But I get the feeling that Zara is different. I could tell her: *I eat people.* She wouldn't be disgusted. She might even be excited.

This little group of monsters could be the perfect place for me to settle down. If only I was who they think I am.

'Anyway, I just came back to get some more food for the traps.' Zara holds up a bag of flour. 'Take a walk with me?'

'Sounds good.'

She offers me her hand to help me up. I wipe my dirty palm on my pants before taking it. Then she leads me into the forest, like the fairy-tale creature she is.

The yeast traps are just jelly jars with cheesecloth stretched over the top of them, held on with an elastic band. Through the glass I can see a spongy white mass.

'Here's one I prepared earlier,' says Zara, like a celebrity chef. 'Usually I pour in a cup of milk and wait for it to go sour before I mix in the flour, but this one is a bit of an experiment. I used water instead, because I don't especially like the smell of spoiled milk.'

She shoots me an enigmatic smile, like this is a joke— who likes the smell of spoiled milk?—or a character flaw she's embarrassed to reveal.

'Looks like it's working,' I say, although I really have no idea. I've been hungry my whole life, but I've never had to resort to baking my own bread.

'Hmm,' Zara says, tapping the glass. 'Maybe.'

She lifts off the cheesecloth and adds a little more flour from the bag, along with some water from a steel bottle. She stirs the mixture with a stick from the ground.

Her clothes are loose, leaving her arms and neck exposed. She doesn't seem to feel the cold.

It's like she wants you to taste her, says the voice.

I'm reminded of an old joke about a hungry soldier walking through a jungle. He spots a bacon tree in the distance. As he approaches it, licking his lips, he's shot by an unseen adversary. It wasn't a bacon tree—it was a hambush.

The other kids at the group home thought that was hilarious, but the punchline only made me hungry.

I want to know why Zara was snooping around upstairs, but I don't want to ask directly. 'I was talking to Cedric earlier,' I say instead. 'It sounded like he and Samson were close.'

'Oh?' Zara looks politely interested.

She's not biting. I put some more bait on the hook. 'But it seems they had a falling out.'

If Zara killed Samson, she'll confirm this. Make Cedric look guilty. Divert suspicion. It's what I would do.

But Zara just says, 'Poor Cedric. He has a gentle heart.' She picks up another yeast trap and examines it.

I take a risk. 'Remind me what you did for a living? Before you came here?'

'I never told you,' she says.

Lucky. 'That explains why I can't remember. Were you a baker? A pastry chef?'

'I wish. Just a humble public servant.' She bows. 'I travelled the world, working for the Department of Agriculture.'

I was thinking she might have been a therapist. She has that aura—attentive and non-judgemental.

As we get deeper into the woods, the canopy blocks out more and more of the feeble winter sun. There's barely enough light to see by and every tree looks the same. Zara must have an amazing memory or she'd lose half the yeast traps she hid.

'Is that where you learned this stuff?' I ask.

'God, no. I was working on the language for trade bills. I never met an actual farmer.'

'Why did you leave?'

She shrugs. 'Guess I just got sick of being behind a desk. What about you? You never told me what you did before this.'

She says *before this* as though I'm one of the team. Like now I torture people for a living.

'I was a teaching assistant,' I say, because Lux was. I hope she doesn't ask me any math questions.

'Which school?'

'Braithwaite.'

She holds up a fist. 'Go Panthers?'

'Go Panthers,' I confirm. 'You know your college football.'

'Did you ever play?'

'No.'

'Never?' She squeezes my arm. 'You have the build.'

I don't, and I'm not sure what she expects to gain by flattering me. 'How did you find out about the Guards?' I ask.

She tilts her head. 'Don't you know?'

'Sorry.' I fake a sheepish smile. 'Have you already told me this?'

She waves it off. 'No, I just thought one of the others might have. I was like you: I found the site and liked it. I subscribed to get extra content. Then I started submitting.'

'Submitting?'

'Yeah. Pictures, videos.'

'Of what?'

'Pain,' she says matter-of-factly. 'Other people's. The Guards invited me to join them at HQ because my submissions were popular. You've seen them, right?'

I nod, hoping she doesn't ask what I think.

She flashes a wicked smile. 'Did you like what I did to the Arsonist?'

'Genius,' I say.

She waves off the compliment. 'Well, I had fun. What about you? Do you enjoy submitting?'

'Sure.' I pretend to ignore the double meaning. 'So after that, you were in?'

'Not quite. I had to prove that the videos were original.'

'Your methods, or . . .'

'Oh, my methods were original. But some people try to submit videos they've stolen from other sites.' Zara picks up another trap and peers in at the yeast. The glass distorts her face, shrinking her nose and enlarging her eyes. 'The Guards asked me to make one of my subjects scream my name.'

'Jesus.' The word slips out.

She smiles. 'I've made people scream that, too.'

I want this conversation to be over. I ask straight out: 'Hey, were you upstairs earlier?'

I'm trying to catch her off guard, but she ignores me, staring at a log. 'Want to see something cool?'

I really don't. I'm alone in the deep dark woods with a woman who gets off on hurting people.

'Sure,' I say.

Zara picks up a stick about the length of her arm and presses the tip against the side of the log. 'Don't move, okay?'

'Okay,' I say, trying not to sound wary.

Zara pushes the log hard enough to roll it over. Underneath is a snake, which slowly uncoils as she exposes it.

I step back.

'I said don't move,' Zara says mildly.

The snake stops unravelling, watching us with dull eyes. Its scales are banded in black, red and yellow. There's a lump just behind its head, like it swallowed something big.

'Is it dangerous?' I ask.

'It wasn't,' Zara says. 'But then the company that made the antivenin went bust. So now it is.'

I can't tell if she's kidding. 'How did you know it was there?'

'I saw the tip of its tail.' Zara holds out the stick in front of the snake's face. The snake bares its dripping fangs. 'Look at that. If it bit you, in minutes you'd be slurring your words and seeing double. Pretty soon you wouldn't even be able to explain to anyone what had happened. So even if there was an antivenin, it wouldn't help.'

Is she threatening me? Her face reveals nothing.

'I wouldn't worry, though,' she says. 'This one's dying.'

'It is?'

'Yeah. See that lump in its throat?' Zara points with the stick. 'Snakes can't move when it gets cold, so they have to eat a lot before winter starts. This one left it too late.'

'It looks like it caught something.'

'Yeah, but it didn't leave time to digest it. Digestion takes energy. So the food will just slowly rot inside the oesophagus, while the snake starves to death. Isn't that interesting?' She rolls the log back into place.

I look around at the still, quiet forest. The cold is making it hard for me to move, too.

'I need to finish burying Samson,' I say.

'Right,' she says. '*Burying* him.'

CHAPTER 21

After a fun start, I lead to tears. What am I?

'When I first met Samson,' Fred begins, 'he was kind of a loser.'

Not a great start to the eulogy. Donnie looks up sharply, and Fred holds up a hand. *Calm down, I'm going somewhere with this.*

We're all standing around the vegetable patch. The harsh winter sun has melted the snow, leaving the dirt sodden under my shoes. Zara has collected some wildflowers from the forest and laid them on the dirt. There are tears on everyone's cheeks, except for Kyle's and mine. I've never been able to fake-cry. I like to think it's proof that I'm not a psychopath. I've met plenty of them, and they could all tear up when they needed to.

Maybe Kyle is the same. Or maybe he sees no reason to fake it. He looks kind of bored, staring at the grave, his right hand twitching like he's resisting the urge to pull out his phone.

'He was poor, and lonely,' Fred continues. 'He'd dedicated his life to helping people, and the world just . . . spat on him. But he kept trying.'

This is a more flattering story than Samson himself told me, which in turn was probably more flattering than the truth. The funeral paradox—suddenly the person can no longer take offence, yet no one dares speak ill of them.

'But he found another calling.' Fred's voice wobbles. 'He chose to help us build a better world by punishing those who make it worse. It will be hard for us to continue this work in his absence, but he would tell us not to give up.'

He lets this hang in the air for a moment.

'Samson wasn't religious. He wouldn't want any prayers said over him. But Zara has chosen a song that we think he would have liked.'

Zara steps forwards, clears her throat, and sings:
'*The water is wide*
I can't cross over
But neither have I wings to fly
Give me a boat
That can carry two
And both shall row, my love and I.'

Zara's voice is plain and free of ornamentation. It's as if she's talking rather than singing, except that the words are in tune and in time. I wonder if she knows the rest of the song: *Love be handsome and love be kind, gay as a jewel when first it's new. But love grows old and waxes cold, and fades away like morning dew.*

Donnie's face has crumpled. Tears stream down his face unchecked. Snot bubbles in his nose. I feel a pang in my chest, although I didn't even like Samson. Donnie's grief is contagious—but that doesn't mean it isn't fake.

Zara blows a kiss to the grave.

Cedric pulls a crumpled piece of paper from his pocket. 'I've written a poem.'

Donnie grits his teeth. 'Samson never liked your fucking poetry.'

Cedric looks stricken.

For a moment, the only sound is the growling of the hungry dogs from behind the fence.

'Fine,' Cedric says finally. He neatly folds the poem, crouches down and pushes in into the dirt.

For some reason, this enrages Donnie even more. His legs tense up, like a quarterback getting ready to charge.

Cedric takes a step back.

'Donnie,' Fred warns.

Donnie falters, as though he has a Pavlovian response to Fred's voice. But he's too big, with too much momentum, to actually stop his body moving. Instead, he redirects it back towards the house, his feet trampling the weeds until he barges through the back door and disappears.

Fred shoots Cedric a questioning look. Cedric shrugs but won't meet his eye.

'Ashes to ashes,' Kyle says. 'Dust to dust.'

No emotion in his face. It's impossible to tell if he's trying to contribute and doesn't know how, or if he's making fun of us.

He doesn't look like he needs consoling, but I put my arm around his thin shoulders anyway. He stiffens, but I feel a rush of something hard to describe—longing and grief and joy all mixed together.

He shrugs off my arm. The feeling vanishes as quick as the lights in a blackout.

•

The Scammer and the Rapist don't get a funeral.

The enormous machine in the corner of the slaughter-house functions like a giant woodchipper. Donnie is pushing the Scammer into one end. The machine spits him out the other in a grisly red mist. It sounds like the Scammer is screaming, but I know that's just the mechanisms inside.

Donnie seems to have cheered up. Maybe the funeral helped him purge the grief from his system. Or perhaps he's just one of those people who's most at peace with a job to do.

Or maybe he's Samson's killer, and the grief was never real in the first place.

Gerald, the Rapist, lies on the concrete, limbs twisted, a discarded doll. Waiting his turn. An unposed corpse is hard to look at. My conscious mind understands that Gerald is dead and feels no discomfort, but my subconscious wonders why he doesn't adjust himself into a more comfortable posi-tion. It's like when you see someone else get punched in a bar fight and your own nose stings. Or if you take a bite out of a hamstring, your own leg starts to ache. I've heard the term 'mirror neurons', and I think it might apply.

It's not just sensations; emotions too. The prisoners are all here, eyes squeezed shut or wide with insane terror. I feel their fear as their former—colleague? friend?—is shredded by hidden metal teeth. They must have seen this before. But some things you don't get used to.

Even through his mask, I feel Donnie's satisfaction as he finishes shoving the Scammer into the grinder and scoops up Gerald. I feel Fred's impatience as he waits in the corner. I feel Kyle's gloom as he looks at the giant smear of flesh and sinew on the concrete. Hopefully because he knows this is wrong, and not because it's his job to clean up the mess. I've already started making excuses for him. *He's a good kid, deep down.*

I never slept in gutters when I was homeless—there was always a better option nearby—but I sometimes dreamed that I was asleep in a gutter. I would be lying there on the sun-warmed concrete, and then I'd feel my hair getting wet and sticky. I'd raise my head to find a creek of blood crawling past towards the drain. The storm clouds would be crimson. Then thunder would boom and the sky would come crashing down.

Now my dream has come true. It's literally raining blood, shreds of the Scammer filling the air. I would only have to step forwards, pull off my mask and open my mouth. The Guards wouldn't hold it against me. Their captives wouldn't be any more horrified.

But I don't. Kyle is here. I can't let him see me like that. So I stand in the corner, focus on my breathing and try my hardest not to dream.

After what seems like a long time, the machine shuts down. Dripping sounds echo through the slaughterhouse.

There are two empty spots now. Two chains hanging loose. One for the new prisoner. And one for me, once the new prisoner reveals that I'm not Lux.

Donnie looks around at the prisoners. 'You're all filthy,' he says, like a criticism. 'Who wants a shower?'

•

'I'm Hailey,' the KKK Queen says. She doesn't know she already introduced herself, when I snuck in on that first night.

I don't reply.

'You're Lux, right?'

I don't know how much, if anything, the prisoners know about Lux. I keep my mouth shut as we plod across the damp dirt towards the side of the house.

I'm still wearing the mummy mask. I can feel Hailey looking at me sideways, trying to guess what I'm like underneath, and how best to manipulate me.

Fred says the inmates usually get showers once a week, to stop the spread of disease. Apparently subscribers enjoy watching the inmates get tortured, but don't like watching them get eaten by fungal infections. Seems arbitrary to me.

Today they all need to wash off Gerald's and the Scammer's blood. Fred has given me the job of taking them out, one at a time. He acted like he was doing me a favour.

Hailey isn't restrained in any way. No chains, no rope. But she's barefoot on the cold prickly ground. If she ran, I'd have no trouble catching up.

There's an outdoor shower around the side of the house. The pipe is rusted and the dripping water has left a brown skid mark down the wall. The plastic drain set in the concrete below has weeds sprouting from it like hair from an old man's ears. There's only one tap, which means no hot water.

When this was a working farm, there must have been a water source closer to the pig pen, and therefore the slaughterhouse. I wonder why Fred never got it running again. Maybe he likes getting the prisoners out of earshot from one another.

'You seem like a decent man,' Hailey says. A weak lie, without any evidence. But she speaks with such genuineness that I might have fallen for it, if I actually was a decent man. 'How did you get mixed up in this?'

I can't give her any indication that I'm not Lux. 'How did you?'

'I had a radio show,' Hailey says. 'Well, it started out as a podcast. Just me in my bedroom with a cheap microphone. But I got a lot of subscribers, and when I upgraded my equipment I got even more. After a couple of years a real network took notice.'

I'll bet. I read a description of her show on the dark web site—it was non-stop hate speech. She fawned over her guests, who included Nazis, alt-right trolls and anti-gay preachers. She told her listeners to buy all the guns they could, and to shoot anyone who tried to take them away. She also suggested using sniper rifles on doctors who practised abortions, people who illegally crossed the border and various others.

'Were you already in the KKK?' I ask.

She chews her lip. 'Yes,' she says finally. She offers no further details.

We're standing in front of the shower now. The air is bitterly cold. Hailey starts to get undressed. I turn away, then realise she might run. I turn back, but avert my eyes. Not that there's much meat to be tempted by. She's been starved down to little more than sinew.

'After my show got picked up for broader distribution,' Hailey continues, 'I discovered that not everyone agreed with my politics. I had to stop taking calls on my show because of all the rage. There were death threats in my inbox. Then they started to show up in my physical mailbox as well. These psychos knew where I lived.'

'Did you start to change your views?'

'I doubled down, if anything.' She shoots a quick glance at me. 'I mean, I get it now, though. I did the wrong thing. I'm so ashamed.'

She utters this lie like a deathbed confession. A last-ditch effort to get into heaven.

'One night I woke up to find a man in my bed. He was grinning, like a . . . I don't know, a hyena. I screamed and screamed. He grabbed me. I was sure my husband would come, but he didn't. I don't know if the neighbours could hear—maybe they could and didn't care. Those fuckers.'

I shouldn't feel sorry for Hailey. Her words hurt people. Maybe they even killed people. But there's a line between words and actions, and someone else crossed it. I'm starting to feel like that line is a chasm.

Naked now, Hailey turns the tap. The showerhead gurgles and sputters, then starts dribbling what must be freezing water onto her head. Her eyes scrunched, her shoulders up, she scrubs her body with her hands.

'It was the guy with the freckles.' I guess she means Samson. 'He pushed something into my mouth. Some kind of pill. He pinched my nose and made me swallow it.'

I remember Zara's theory that one of the prisoners may have gotten loose and sabotaged the cameras. If it was Samson who carried out the original abductions, it makes sense that the prisoners would want to kill him. But what would be the reason to lock themselves up again afterwards?

'He dragged me through my living room.' Hailey's teeth sound like they're chattering. 'The last thing I remember seeing before I blacked out was my husband, lying on the floor. I still don't know if he was dead or alive.'

Hailey wants my pity. I can't let her know that she has it already.

'The guy who abducted you is dead now,' I say.

She looks surprised—even disbelieving. 'How?'

'Murdered.' It's dangerous to tell her this, but it might be the only way to shake loose a clue. I watch her for signs of dawning realisation. Like something makes sense to her now.

But she just looks confused. 'I'm sorry,' she says, implausibly. 'I know he was your friend.'

'What time did you hear the gunshot?'

'I didn't hear any gunshot,' she says.

'The house is right there. You didn't hear anything?'

She shakes her head, shivering in the spray.

'That's enough,' I say. 'Turn the water off.'

She turns the faucet off but makes no move to cover her naked body. 'We could just leave,' she says. 'You and me. They'd never find us.'

'Get dressed.'

She forces herself to look at the eyeholes in my mask. 'I could make you happy.'

I shake my head. 'Get dressed.'

Hailey slackens, as though whatever was holding her upright—desperation, hope—has vanished. She starts to cry.

I go to put my arms around her. It's instinctive, not calculated. Hug the cold, wet, crying woman. But she shoves me away. 'Don't you fucking touch me!' She chokes on the words.

I stand back and let her gather her clothes. There's no towel, so she pulls them on over her damp skin. Then she totters, like a drunk in heels, back towards her prison.

CHAPTER 22

Blood colours the water in this sheltered bay.
There's something underneath. What is it?

It's hard not to appreciate the attention to detail. The van is loaded up with everything a kidnapper might need. Rope. Water bottles. Ambien. A black cloth bag. A combat knife. A meal tray, covered with a silver lid. And my hammer, strapped to the wall with duct tape. There are even snacks— what look like homemade granola bars.

'Apple and pumpkin seed,' Donnie says. 'Samson made them.' He blinks away an angry tear and drags the door shut, sealing me and Kyle in the back of the van. The other three Guards aren't coming.

I sit next to Kyle and buckle my seatbelt. Clear my throat. 'How you doing, buddy?'

Kyle looks at me strangely. 'Fine. Why?'

'Just asking.'

Donnie gets into the driver's seat. 'You excited, Lux?'

'You bet.' I grip my knees with my hands, keeping them still.

'Can't wait to see the look on your face,' he says ominously, and starts the engine. The floor vibrates under me.

Little ribbons are tied to the vents. They spring to life like angry snakes as the fan roars. Water drips from the tips of the ribbons.

'DIY evaporative cooling,' Donnie says proudly. 'Just like in ancient Egypt. They used to hang wet reeds in the windows to chill the air as it flowed into the house, or mud hut, or whatever. Aircon puts hydrocarbons into the atmosphere—this is way more sustainable.'

'Pretty cool,' I say, wanting to stay on the muscular psycho's good side.

'Ha, "cool"! I get it.'

'Quit showing off, Donnie,' Kyle grumbles. 'It's already freezing back here.'

Donnie huffs and turns down the fan.

He pushes a button on a remote. The garage door creaks open and the van trundles out into the twilight. The garage closes automatically behind us as we roll through the forest towards the main road. Soon the house is out of view. You'd never know it was there.

Engine rumbling, we head down the long driveway until we hit the dirt road. At the intersection, I can see the motion sensor the others talked about—a little white box with a hole in it, like a small birdhouse, bolted to a tree.

But I can also see something else. A smaller box, painted brown, in another tree further away. Well-hidden. A camera, but not the same design as the others. It's facing the dirt road, so if a vehicle enters the driveway, the driver's face would be momentarily visible to it.

On all those screens in the editing room, I didn't see any feeds which showed the road. This camera is separate. Why?

Kyle is watching me. 'What are you looking at?'

The van turns on to the dirt road, cutting off my view of the hidden camera.

'Nothing,' I say.

Half an hour later we reach the highway and take a right turn towards Houston. We drive through mile after mile of arid flat land. If Texas were a country, it would be the thirty-ninth biggest on Earth, at least according to a library book I read as a kid. It's bigger than France or England.

Outsiders view Texas as simple and homogenous. The reddest of red states. But Texans see it more like several separate nations. People from Houston will swear their town is completely different to Dallas, which is nothing like San Antonio. The only thing these city folks agree on is that the people from the rural areas in between are racist homophobes clutching guns and Bibles. The rural people themselves see the urbanites as corrupt, materialistic degenerates, oblivious to how the real world works.

Neither view is accurate. There are plenty of guns and Bibles in cities, while many rural folks have fought for the rights of their Black or queer neighbours. In a way, the outsiders are right—Texas is more unified than Texans think. But the stereotypes persist, because the city people and country people don't mix.

Ironically, while there is a literal wall between Texas and Mexico, those two cultures have seeped into one another a lot. You'll see cowboy hats in Mexico, sombreros in Texas, and Tex-Mex cuisine in both places. But the wall around the cities is an invisible one called 'cost of living'. It's much harder to cross. Even in the cities, if you become poor—like I was, before I learned how to sell stolen credit card numbers on the dark web—you don't usually get booted out into the darkness beyond the city lights. You stay under the table, stealing scraps from the middle class, who are easier targets than the rich.

As one of those city-dwelling degenerates, I don't feel especially safe out here, where only the occasional farm-house breaks up the flat horizon. But if we're going all the way to Houston, I might have a chance to escape. I run through the steps in my head. One: get out of sight when Donnie and Kyle are distracted, and run like hell. Two: find a phone, call the cops, explain what's going on at Fred's house. Three: go somewhere else before the cops come looking for me, since they'll have questions I can't answer.

But when they realise I'm missing, Donnie and Kyle will call the other Guards, who will clean house. Kill the prisoners, move on, start over. I'll never find out if Kyle was my son.

We're getting closer to the city. Streetlights flash past on the otherwise empty highway. Donnie switches on the radio, drums his fingers on the wheel, humming an old Britney Spears song. Kyle picks up the rope and starts fiddling with it. It looks like he's trying to make it into a noose, but he doesn't quite remember how.

I hold out a hand. 'Here. Let me show you.'

Kyle keeps hold of the rope, frowning. 'I can do it.'

I let my hand fall back into my lap and watch him struggle with it a while longer. His frustration is frustrating.

Trying to distract myself, I take a bite from one of the granola bars. It's dry and crumbly. Apple and pumpkin seed really isn't my thing. I keep stealing glances at Donnie's thick, meaty arms.

We've reached the outskirts of Houston now. Wider roads, a bit of traffic. Familiar buildings on the horizon, the lights blocking out the stars above.

Soon the motel I used to work at appears in the distance. A few of the letters in the VACANCY sign are dead, but SPA ROOM AVAILABLE! is all lit up. There's a truck parking bay out front, empty. It's the kind of place travellers stay if they're using their own money instead of staying on the company's dime.

The van slows down.

'What's going on?' I ask.

'This is it,' Donnie says.

'This motel right here?'

'Yup.'

The unease is like eels in my belly. I thought we were picking up someone connected to Lux. But he didn't live on this side of Houston. Whoever it is, could they be staying at the motel I used to work at? That would be a hell of a coincidence if so. The odds are incalculable.

The alternative is that Fred, or maybe Donnie, has worked out who I really am. But if so, why am I not dead already?

Maybe they're not sure, one way or the other. They're trying to rattle me. See if I recognise this place. My heart is pounding, but I take care to keep my expression even.

'Are we clear on the plan?' Donnie asks.

'Yeah,' Kyle says.

'No,' I say at the same moment.

'According to the reservation database, our target is in room nine.' Donnie shifts into a lower gear. 'Probably alone—it's a single room. She may be armed but won't be expecting us, so we'll be fine if we're quick.'

Room nine is where I found the suicide in the bathtub. The room the police later inspected, finding only a note. This can't be a coincidence.

Maybe they know *everything*. Not just who I am, but what I've done. This could be a ritual. Perhaps the Guards make the condemned face their crimes before they take them prisoner. *See the Cannibal captured in the very hotel room from which he once stole a corpse. Download the video now.*

'You got the card?' Kyle asks.

'Yup.' Donnie keeps his eyes on the road as he produces a key card from his pocket. 'But remember, we shouldn't need it. Plan A is we knock on the door and pretend to be room service. If she opens the door, we grab her. If she refuses, we pretend to go away. I guarantee you she'll get curious and open the door within a minute, *then* we grab her.'

'Maybe we should wait until we're better prepared,' I say. 'Talk it over tonight. I mean, this motel can't be completely empty. What if someone hears her yelling?'

'Don't worry,' Donnie says. 'One hand over the mouth, knife against the throat—I've done it plenty of times. I'll put her in the van, then we're gone. The motel has no recorded CCTV and only two other guests on the register.'

'What did she do?' Kyle asks. 'I mean, why are we taking her?'

'A few reasons,' Donnie says, glancing at me. 'But mostly because she killed a baby.'

'Shit,' Kyle says. 'That'll be popular on the site.'

I keep my eyes on the building as we approach. 'Who is she?'

'You'll see.' Donnie drives into the motel parking lot. It's a two-level place, safety rails around the concrete walkway on the second floor. The van has no windows, but I get a glimpse of room nine through the windshield. It's on level one. The grey curtains are drawn. No cars parked directly out front.

'Okay.' Donnie opens his door. 'Let's do this.'

We all get out of the van. The tarmac is littered with cigarette butts. We're close enough to the highway to smell the diesel from the passing trucks. No other cars in the lot.

Kyle gasps. 'I thought you said no CCTV.'

I don't turn my head. There were no cameras when I worked here. If they've been added since, I don't want my face on the feed.

'I said no *recorded* CCTV,' Donnie says. 'There are no videos in the motel's network, no screenshots, nothing. So either it's a live feed only, or the cameras are fake.'

I sneak a glance. The camera is fake—the cables go directly into the concrete wall, whereas a security company installer would have put them through via the brickwork to one side, and wrapped a steel tube around them to protect them from the elements.

The fact that Kyle spotted the camera at all is impressive, though. It's right up the other end of the motel. He's good at noticing things. Like me.

Donnie gets the meal tray off the passenger seat of the van. Even though I know there's nothing under the lid, the sight of the tray still makes me hungry.

'Come on.' Donnie walks up to the door to room nine, holds the tray up so it's visible through the peephole, and knocks. *Shave and-a-hair cut.* 'Room service.'

Kyle and I press our backs against the walls on either side of the door, so we're not visible from the peephole or through the window.

I was supposed to have a chance to escape, but it's already too late. Now I need to go along with this, whatever it turns out to be.

No one answers the door.

Donnie knocks again. 'Room service. Compliments of the Comfort Inn.'

Silence. If this is a ruse to get me into the room, it's very elaborate.

Donnie places the tray on the ground with a loud *thunk*, and then crouches down, waiting for someone to open the door.

No one does.

After a minute, Donnie stands up. 'Guess she's not in.'

'Makes sense,' Kyle says. 'No vehicles in the lot except ours.'

'Guess we'll have to come back tomorrow.' I try to sound disappointed. 'Or the day after.'

But Donnie is already tapping the key card against the electronic lock. It beeps, a green light flashes, and he pushes the door open.

The motel room has a rattling fridge, a narrow closet and muffin crumbs trapped between the desk and the wall. A ceiling-mounted TV looms over the single bed and its faded sheets. A familiar perfume hangs in the air. I pick up one of the muffin crumbs and put it in my mouth. Blueberry. No more than a day old.

Donnie checks the bathroom. 'Clear.'

Kyle opens the closet, even though no adult could possibly fit in there. 'Clear.'

I check the trash can under the desk. A go-cup, with what looks and smells like milkshake residue stuck to the plastic.

There's a handbag on the nightstand. I search it. No wallet or ID, but there's a can of pepper spray and a box of Tampax Radiant.

I tell myself I'm being paranoid—but I need to get these guys out of here just in case I'm not.

'Damn,' I say. 'She must have checked out already. Let's scram before someone sees us.'

'No,' Donnie says. 'She's paid for another two nights. We can hide in the room, grab her when she comes in.'

'She'll see the van outside,' I say. 'She's not stupid.'

'We can park the van in front of a different room. It's not rocket science.'

'If we do that, we'll be too exposed while we carry her to it. No—we should abort.'

Kyle is giving me a suspicious look. 'How do you know she's not stupid? I thought you didn't know who we were picking up.'

I don't. Not for sure. Lots of women wear that perfume, eat blueberry muffins and drink milkshakes.

'We have to go,' I say.

Then Agent Reese Thistle appears in the doorway.

CHAPTER 23

The lean monarch's mind
races. What is he doing?

It's only been a few days since I saw her last, but Thistle looks years older. There are bags under her eyes and her shoulders are hunched, as though she's been on high-alert for so long that her muscles have started to calcify in that position. She's not wearing make-up, and her hair is frizzy. This is the first time I've seen her in street clothes, her FBI pants suit replaced by a stained Hello Kitty T-shirt and a pair of mom jeans.

Despite all this, she's beautiful, right up until she sees three intruders in her room and her face contorts with alarm and anger.

'What the hell?' She drops the bag of takeout she's holding and reaches behind her back.

Donnie and Kyle lunge at her. Because they both leap forwards at the same moment, they bump shoulders and Kyle trips over Donnie's leg. Thistle pulls out a Glock 17 and points it at them both. Donnie ignores it, still charging forwards.

Thistle looks like she's about to squeeze the trigger, but first she glances over at me, probably checking if I'm armed. I'm not, but she gets a look at my face for the first time.

The anger on her face transforms into fear. 'Holy—'

Donnie crashes into her while she's distracted. She pulls the trigger. *Blam!* A bullet punches through the plaster behind Kyle's head. Everyone in the room ducks. My ears are ringing and the muzzle flash leaves a discoloured spot in my field of vision.

Donnie wrestles the pistol out of Thistle's grip and presses her against the wall. She screams. 'Help! Somebody!'

I'm running forwards, desperate to get him off her before—

Too late. The knife is already at her throat. If I touch Donnie, I might accidentally nudge the blade into her windpipe.

'Make another sound and you're dead,' Donnie snarls. 'Clear?'

Thistle can't move her head enough to nod. She just glares at him.

Kyle is ashen. 'She nearly *shot* me.'

'Leave her,' I say. 'We gotta go.'

'Relax, Lux,' Donnie says.

Thistle looks at me. I can see her thinking, *Lux?*

'Someone will have heard the gunshot,' I say. 'We don't have time to take her.'

'Can't leave her behind,' Donnie says. 'She knows what we look like. She can describe us to the cops.'

'If she's alive,' Kyle adds.

My heart rate accelerates. 'Just grab her driver's licence, so you know where she lives. She won't tell anyone. Will you, lady?'

I silently beg her to play along.

'Fuck you,' Thistle rasps.

'I said no talking,' Donnie says. 'We don't have time to mess around with licences, and we need her alive. Grab her feet, Kyle. Lux, you take her handbag.'

Kyle looks like he's on the verge of fainting, but he helps Donnie carry Thistle out the door. I trail behind, helpless.

Still no one in the parking lot. No one who can save Thistle.

'Give me the gun,' I tell Donnie. 'Otherwise she might grab it.'

I'm willing to shoot him right here. I'd kill Kyle, too, if that's what it takes to save Thistle's life.

'It's fine,' Donnie says.

'I can keep it pointed at her while you're carrying her.'

A light comes on in the back office. The residence of the manager I never met or saw. Another light comes on in one of the other rooms.

Donnie and Kyle stuff Thistle into the back of the van. I climb in after them, feeling sick. Donnie gets into the driver's seat.

Thistle takes in the duct tape, the black bags, the rope. She opens her mouth to scream again.

Kyle brandishes the knife. I hadn't seen him take it from Donnie. I'm getting sloppy. Seeing him threaten her makes me want to rip his throat out.

'We want you alive.' Kyle's teen bravado is back. 'But we don't need you to have a tongue. Got that?'

Thistle shuts her mouth. She's scared, but she's hiding it well.

'I'll tie her up,' I say.

Kyle is already getting out the duct tape. 'I can do it.'

I don't want him to touch her again. 'Don't use that. We'll need to move her soon.'

Thistle looks infuriated as I bind her wrists with a highwayman's hitch. It takes a while because my hands are shaking, and because the last time I tied this knot I had ten fingers. It's the same way I used to strap down my shopping cart, back when I was homeless. It held all my stuff in, nice and firm, but when I pulled on one end the whole thing would come undone, like a magic trick.

Sirens wail on the wind. The sound is common in Houston—it might not be for us.

'We have to go,' Kyle says.

Donnie starts the engine and zooms out of the lot, back onto the highway. I could have threatened them with the pepper spray in Thistle's bag. Too late now. My hammer is still taped to the wall, but against Kyle's knife and Donnie's gun, I don't think it will do much good.

I finish the trick knot. The rope looks tight around Thistle's wrists. It probably feels tight, too. But Thistle is only one careful tug away from escape, if the opportunity arises.

I have no way of communicating that to her, though. I give her a meaningful look. She doesn't get the message. The stare that comes back is hateful.

'You recognise her, Lux?' Donnie asks.

I look at Thistle and pretend to think about it. 'Maybe.'

'That's Reese Thistle. The lady FBI agent who was after you.'

The pieces fall into place. Thistle isn't just connected to me—she's connected to Lux, as well. But why was she in the motel I used to work at?

'Are you sure?' I ask. 'She looks different.' If they think they've got the wrong person, they might let her go.

Thistle squirms against the rope.

'We're sure,' Kyle puts in. 'We hacked her phone. She's taken a leave of absence to run some kind of off-the-books investigation. She may not look like a cop, but she is one.'

'What kind of investigation?' I ask.

The sirens are getting louder. Donnie swerves off the highway onto a side road. Seconds later, a patrol car screams past behind us.

'Kyle,' Donnie says, 'can you get the police off our backs?'

Kyle pulls out his phone. 'On it.'

'What kind of investigation?' I ask again.

'It's complicated,' Donnie says. 'Her partner at the FBI was a guy named Blake. That's the guy you killed, right?'

'Right,' I say.

Thistle looks from me to Donnie and back again, probably thinking fast. Just like me.

'Well, Thistle and Blake were sleeping together,' Donnie continues. I can feel myself blushing, but no one is looking at me. Donnie's watching the road, Kyle is glued to his phone, Thistle is looking at Donnie.

'Thistle stumbles across a dead body hidden in Blake's freezer,' Donnie continues. 'So she tells the FBI, and then skips town. He must have been a scary motherfucker.'

All true so far. I can't meet Thistle's gaze.

'So Thistle's on her way to Mexico when she sees some news on Twitter. The dead man in Blake's freezer? The cops have pinned the murder on someone else. Officially, Blake isn't connected in any way.

'Thistle is sure Blake is guilty. She turns around, comes back to Houston and asks her bosses what's going on. They say the FBI has searched Blake's house. No sign of the body she told them about. No sign of Blake, either.

The place is empty. She reiterates what she saw, but they don't believe her. They think she's having a mental breakdown. And they're not happy about her skipping town in the first place, so she's suspended without pay.

'But does she go to Mexico? No. She spends two days digging through Blake's history unofficially. Calling in every favour she's owed, shaking down every source she can find. And this leads her to a cold case, an apparent suicide at a motel Blake used to work at—'

'Fuck,' I say, out loud.

'—where the body was never found,' Donnie finishes. 'She goes there, rents the exact room, and then we grab her. The end.'

I clear my throat. 'How do you know all this?'

'One of our subscribers works in payroll at the FBI,' Donnie says. 'There's another at a travel agent and another at the phone company. We got all her emails, her reservations, location tracking, her texts . . .'

'Who was she texting?'

'That's the best part! *No one.* She sent the messages to herself, hundreds of them. Keeping a record, in case something happened to her.'

'Prescient.' Kyle sounds like he's proud of knowing the word. 'We deleted them all.'

Thistle keeps her gaze steady, but I can tell this is a blow.

'My name is Michelle Paxton,' she says. 'I don't know who any of you people are, and I don't know who Elise Thistle is.'

'Reese,' Kyle corrects.

'Whoever!' Thistle says. 'I don't want to get dragged into whatever this is. Please just let me go.'

I look at the others. 'She could be telling the truth. Like I said, I don't recognise her.'

'No. It's her,' Donnie says. 'She—shit.'

Through the windshield I see a police car heading towards us.

'Too late to turn,' Donnie mutters. He keeps going straight as the car gets closer and closer.

Just as it's about to pass us, Thistle screams, 'Help!'

Kyle lashes out at her, panicked. I catch his fist just in time.

The police car cruises past us without slowing down.

Kyle shakes his fist loose. 'What the hell are you doing, Lux?'

'We may need to prove she's unharmed,' I say. 'You start hurting hostages, the cops start shooting.'

There are more sirens in the air. 'Kyle!' Donnie yells. 'I need these cops gone!'

'I'm doing it!' Kyle punches some final digits into the phone and puts it to his ear. After a second, he starts yelling: 'He has a bomb! He says he's going to kill us all! Someone help!'

Thistle quickly shouts, 'This is Agent Reese Thistle, I've been abducted by—'

'I already hung up,' Kyle says smugly. 'Hello, *Reese*.'

Thistle glowers at him.

'You spoofed the caller ID?' Donnie asks.

'Yeah. As far as the cops are concerned, that call came from City Hall.'

'Nice.' Donnie turns back the way we came. The sirens in the air fade away. By the time we reach the highway, the only sound is the rumbling of the van's engine.

Kyle nudges me. 'You murdered a serial killer,' he says. 'Holy shit.'

'I don't think that's what Blake was,' I say. 'I got the feeling he was running an off-the-books investigation of his own. That must have been why the body was in his freezer.'

Every person in the van shoots me a sceptical look.

'Either way,' I add, 'Blake didn't seem like Thistle's enemy. In fact, he seemed like he'd do anything to keep her out of harm's way.'

Thistle scoffs. 'He hasn't done a great job so far.'

'He's dead, bitch,' Kyle says.

'How do you know?' she asks. 'He could still be out there, living under a false name.'

She's threatening me. If she tells these guys I'm not Lux, then I'm dead. But if I'm dead, I can't help her. Can't she see that?

'Lux killed him,' Donnie says. 'He's six feet under.'

'Lux did, huh?'

'I can see why you'd want to think he was alive,' I say. 'Without Blake, you're completely on your own.'

I stare at her, trying to make sure she understands.

'You're all making a mistake,' Thistle says. 'You didn't clean the scene at the motel. Prints, DNA, a bullet left in the wall and a casing on the floor—a SWAT team will be breaking down your door within twenty-four hours.'

Kyle looks a little worried by this.

Donnie doesn't. 'I'd like to see them try.'

Thistle has spotted the weak link. 'You really want to spend the rest of your life in prison?' she asks Kyle. 'Assuming you don't get shot during the raid. You could end up quadriplegic, or brain-damaged . . .'

'Don't listen to her, Kyle,' Donnie says. 'Nobody saw us take her. Even if someone heard the gunshot, they probably won't even work out which room it came from, never mind find the bullet hole. And no one's gonna report her missing. You saw her texts and her emails. She's divorced. No kids, no friends, no upcoming appointments and on an *indefinite* leave of absence.'

Thistle chews her lip. She knows he's right. But she keeps trying. 'Kyle, right? I'm Reese. You don't have to do this.'

'Use first names so your captors think of you as human,' Donnie says. 'Try to establish a rapport with your captors. Straight out of the playbook. Anyway, you ever tried to get touch DNA from a cheap motel room? It's useless. There would be evidence of thousands of people and they'd have no way of knowing which samples were relevant.'

Donnie clearly has experience with in-person crime, not just the internet variety. I glance at Thistle—she's realised this, too. It's bad news. Experienced criminals are harder to catch.

'And you Krazy-glued your fingers, right?' Donnie adds.

'Right.' Kyle looks down at his shiny fingertips.

'Well, there you go. No prints, either.'

No one told me to put glue on my fingertips. If anyone does realise Thistle has been abducted, any evidence they find will point to me.

•

Fred, Zara and Cedric are waiting out the front of the house when we get back.

Donnie leaps out of the van, buzzing with leftover adrenaline. 'Honey, I'm home!'

'You caught the Baby Killer?' Fred asks.

'Sure did.' Donnie throws Thistle's handbag into the pick-up, probably so it can be dumped on their next trip to the gorge. If Donnie had a tail, it would be wagging. It's not just Kyle who likes impressing Fred.

I'd forgotten Donnie's claim that Thistle had killed a baby. He seemed to believe it. Why?

It feels like I'm missing something obvious, but I'm too busy trying to save Thistle's life—while also maintaining a false identity and trying to solve a murder—to work out what.

Kyle and I climb out of the van. Fred leans past us and sees Thistle trussed up in the back.

'Nice.' He nudges me. 'You like?'

I don't know if this is a genuine gift or another test. Lux would be thrilled to see Thistle here, while Blake would not.

'Best surprise ever.' I grin. 'Thanks, bro.'

'No sweat.' Fred looks satisfied.

Zara unexpectedly wraps her arms around me and whispers in my ear: 'Does she have nice feet?'

For a second I think I've misheard. Then I remember what she nearly caught me doing to Samson's body.

'I'm looking forward to getting a closer look at them,' I say.

Zara laughs and strokes my chest with a fingernail. Like everything Zara does, it feels like a performance. Maybe for Thistle's benefit.

Thistle clenches her jaw in the back of the van. As far as she can tell, I'm Fred's friend and Zara's boyfriend. My chances of convincing her I'm not one of the bad guys are evaporating. At any moment she could tell them that I'm not Lux.

'I want to make a deal,' she says, as if reading my mind.

Fred raises his eyebrows. 'Oh, really?'

I think of the last person to try to make a deal with the Guards, and the brick that went through his skull.

'Wait.' I climb back into the van. 'No deals. Not before I've had a chance to enjoy her.'

I hear someone chuckling outside.

'I have something to tell you,' Thistle calls.

I clamp a hand over her mouth. Her breath is hot on my palm.

'Talk all you want once you're locked up,' I snarl. Then, as I lean over to untie the ropes, I whisper in her ear: 'I'm trying to help you.'

I release her mouth. She spits on me. 'Like you helped the guy in your freezer?' But she says it too quietly for the others outside the van to hear. Offering me a chance to convince her.

'Please. Trust me.' I tug on the knot, which unravels instantly—showing Thistle that I never properly tied her up in the first place.

As I lean back, Thistle gives me a searching stare. Looking for a killer and not seeing one. Maybe I've convinced her I'm on her side. Or maybe she thinks she'll have more to gain by selling me out later.

'Hurry up, Lux.' Donnie climbs into the van after me. He grabs Thistle and drags her out.

I follow the group as they take her around the side of the house. 'Don't hurt her. I want to draw first blood.'

Donnie laughs. 'You're one creepy motherfucker, Lux.'

193

They carry her past the greenhouse and the fence with the two snarling, snapping dogs all the way to the slaughterhouse.

'Wait,' Kyle says. 'We don't have masks.'

Fred shrugs. 'The cameras are dead.'

'But the inmates will see.'

'So what? They'll all be dead soon.'

'Oh, right.' Kyle laughs nervously.

Thistle stares at the ground, working her jaw.

Fred unlocks the door and slides it open, revealing the machines, the movie sets, the prisoners. I watch Thistle have the same realisation that I did—Fred is making these videos in-house.

'You want her in China or India?' Donnie asks.

'India,' Fred says.

Donnie chains Thistle up in the fake pharmacy, where Gerald was before. No one has bothered to clean up the bloody smear on the ground.

The other prisoners don't say anything. The Terrorist forces an encouraging smile at Thistle. The Nazi avoids her gaze. The Abuser just stares, like a robot.

'Lux.' Fred gestures to Thistle. 'Go nuts.'

Everyone looks at me expectantly.

'But someone sabotaged the cameras,' I say, hoping Thistle will guess it was me.

Donnie frowns. 'So what? This bitch tried to have you arrested. She trashed your reputation so you can't go home.'

'Plus she killed a baby,' Kyle puts in.

Thistle looks shocked.

'Right. Don't you want to hurt her?'

'That's the point,' I say. 'I want it recorded. I want to

be able to watch it over and over. That first moment, you know?'

Thistle retches quietly.

'You sure?' Fred says. 'The new cameras won't be here for another two days.'

'The anticipation is half the fun,' I say.

As we walk out, I can sense every bit of the contempt and fear directed at me. It's not a new feeling. Everyone hated me at the group home, at the fast food place I once worked at, in the homeless shelters, even at the FBI. It was like my aura disgusted people. But the revulsion hurts more coming from Thistle, the one person who used to see what I was like beneath the surface.

Except she never really did, did she?

CHAPTER 24

Feed me and I grow. Starve me and I'll die—
yet I've never been alive. What am I?

It's infuriating, not being able to help Thistle. Knowing she's scared, and angry. As I wash the plates from another meatless dinner, I find myself scrubbing the dishes hard enough to wear away the enamel. Trying to look excited rather than sick with fear.

Cedric is cross-legged on a beanbag in the corner of the dining room, reading a book. He occasionally scribbles notes on the dog-eared pages. He's too absorbed, or perhaps self-absorbed, to notice that I'm acting strangely.

He could have chosen to read in the privacy of his room. Maybe this is for show. *Look how smart I am, with my book and my note-taking.* Or maybe he's out here specifically to keep an eye on me. He hasn't mentioned the kiss, or the bite, but I assume they're on his mind.

As I turn to put a dry blade back in the knife block, I see Zara leaning against the kitchen bench, pouring another glass of wine. She wasn't there a second ago. It's like she's teleported in from another, more glamorous, dimension.

'You okay, Lux?' she asks.

'Yeah. Just, you know, a lot of excess energy.'

'You want to do some yoga before bed?'

I can see Cedric from here. He doesn't look up from his book, but I can tell he's listening.

My enemy's enemy is my friend. The one person who might be able to help me get Thistle out of here is Samson's killer—but I don't know who that is.

'Did Samson used to do yoga with you guys?' I ask, fishing.

'Sometimes.' Zara sips her drink. 'Poor Samson.'

'How long was he living here?' My real question is, why now? Whoever murdered Samson would have had plenty of other opportunities in the past—unless the killer was a recent arrival.

'I'm not sure. He was here when I arrived.'

'When was that?'

Zara considers this. 'Six, no, seven months ago. Samson was so kind to me. He really took me under his wing.'

I remember carrying Samson's body and lying to Kyle about how close we had been. Zara could be doing the same thing.

I lower my voice. 'Were the two of you . . .' I don't really think Samson was sleeping with Zara, but I want to see how she reacts to the suggestion.

A sad smile. 'No. Not like that.'

'Do you think he was interested?'

The pause is long enough for me to realise it might be cruel, suggesting the dead man had unrequited feelings for her.

'In me?' she says at last. 'No. Some men give without wanting anything in return.'

This isn't true in my experience. I especially doubt that it applies to the man who murdered Hailey's husband and slipped into her bed in the dead of the night.

'Did he get on equally well with everyone? Or did he have a special friendship with you?'

'Why are you asking all these questions?' Zara sits on the kitchen bench and crosses her long legs.

'This is such a welcoming, peaceful community out here. I'm trying to understand why he would commit suicide.'

Zara's face darkens. 'You're saying we could have done more.'

'Not at all,' I say quickly. 'I was cooking dinner with him the night before. He seemed perfectly happy. Everyone did, until . . .'

I trail off, thinking. When I arrived, it did seem like a perfectly peaceful community, right up until the proximity alarms went off and we had to search the woods. I don't know the Guards well, but I've met plenty of murderers and people with murderous intentions. No one was acting oddly around Samson, either watching him especially closely or avoiding him altogether. And Samson himself was chatty and friendly, right up until we met the mystery man in the forest. After that he seemed disturbed.

Something changed in that moment. Suddenly someone had a motive to kill Samson, someone who hadn't had anything against him before.

Samson ran into the mystery man before I did. *You see which way the guy went? I want to talk to him.* Did Samson know him somehow?

'You okay, Lux?' Zara is watching me closely.

'What? Yeah.' I clear my throat. 'Just thinking.'

'What about?'

'Just that you never know what's going on in someone else's head.'

'Too true. Samson shouldn't have bottled things up the way he did.' Zara squeezes my hand. 'You know you can talk to me, right? If you need to.'

I look across at Cedric to see if he's watching us. He doesn't glance up from his book.

'You don't need to be ashamed,' Zara continues. 'There's a woman in Congo running an illegal blood bank—she captures people and bleeds them dry. There's a presidential aide in Brazil who sells children as sex slaves. You're one of the good guys.'

I guess I am, if slave-trader is the baseline.

At the FBI field office, there was a fatalistic agent named Ruciani, although everyone called him Pope. Once, when I was waiting out the front for the automatic doors to open, he flicked a burning cigarette butt in my direction.

A younger agent nudged him. 'Knock it off, Pope. Folks around here look up to you.'

'Looking up to people is a waste of time.' Ruciani spoke like he'd already forgotten I was there. 'If you want to be happy, find someone to look down on.'

Zara and her friends seem to have taken that philosophy to its logical conclusion.

'How do you know about those people in other countries?' I ask her.

Zara waves this off. 'I used to travel a lot for work. The point is, don't hide your feelings. I wouldn't want you to end up like Samson.' Is her tone flirtatious, or threatening? It's impossible to tell.

'Right. Thanks.' Talking to her is exhausting, especially with Cedric watching us. I go around the corner into the living room. Music is playing quietly from the hidden speakers—an acoustic version of a Lady Gaga song. I sink into the sofa. The fabric is smooth and the padding soft. It probably cost more than my house.

I close my eyes. I'm so tired. But I already know I won't be able to sleep tonight. Not with Thistle chained up out there in the cold.

The pop and crackle from the fireplace is soothing, although I'm not sure why. Fire is dangerous. My lizard brain shouldn't find it comforting. I don't have a happy childhood filled with campfires to get nostalgic about. It can't be media conditioning. Whenever you see a campfire on TV, something bad is about to come out of the woods right behind the campers.

And now that I think about it, this particular fire smells wrong. There's a sour tang to the wood smoke. Something plastic.

I open my eyes and look over. Just flames. But the smell persists.

I find the remote and turn up the music. The guitar rattles and the cymbals splash. Someone's left a half-full bottle of soda on the coffee table. I tip it onto the flames. There's a loud hiss, but the music covers it. When the cloud of steam dissipates, I crouch next to the fireplace and peer in.

Nestled among the hot, damp coals, there are fragments of paper. Like someone tore up a document and threw it into the fire.

Most of the pieces are too small to be useful, but two

parts are larger. I pluck out the closest one and flatten it beneath my shoe, extinguishing the burning edges. Dense text is printed on both sides. I have the left-hand side of a paragraph on one side, and the right-hand side on the other.

On the other large piece, a transparent film has half-peeled away, like it was printed on photo paper. That must have been the source of the smell. The side I can see is blank.

I reach in and quickly snatch it out. It singes my fingers and I drop it on the floor. It lands on the blank side, revealing the photo.

Most of the photo is taken up by a featureless grey backdrop. I can see the corner of a face—one eye, an ear, some hair.

It's enough to recognise Donnie.

I listen for a second to make sure no one is coming, then I scan the text on the scorched document:

individual, prone to threats and violence. His relationship
emotional as well as sexual, and could be exploited. His
Donald (Snr) and Glenda Walton, do not appear to have
two victims (see appendix B) have both contacted private
leading to the engagement of Lila Preyat.

On the other side:

Subject is unsuitable for direct approach as an
compromise the agent's cover. But a third party
particularly if his parents are unaware of
in the field.

I read both extracts several times. I assume Donnie is the subject. Someone was keeping a file on him. But I'm struggling to fill in the blanks in the text.

So who burned it? Not Fred—he has a paper shredder in his room. And who wrote it?

Normally I would throw the papers back into the fire. Words are easy to remember, since they already have meaning. All I have to do is come up with mental images to remind me of the gaps. For 'relationship . . . emotional', I picture Donnie hugging his girlfriend and sobbing loudly. For 'His . . . Donald' I imagine him taking Trump for a walk on a leash, like a pet he owns. And so on.

But I can't burn this. It's proof of something, although I don't yet know what.

I tuck the papers under my shirt. The hot corners sting my skin. When I walk through the kitchen and dining area, Cedric and Zara aren't there. Maybe they've gone to bed. I sneak back into my room and close the door.

I need to conceal these papers somewhere. But my room could be searched at any time. Perhaps it already has been. A normal hiding place—in a drawer, on a high shelf—isn't going to work. I'd like to smash a hole in a wall, but that would wake up the whole house, and I don't have the materials to patch it up afterwards.

As I walk around the room, looking for ideas, I feel a draft of warm air near my feet. I look under the bed. There's a heating vent down there.

As quietly as I can, I drag the bed sideways to access the vent. I should be able to drop the paper in, then nudge it out of sight around the bend. Safe enough.

But when I lift up the grille covering the vent, I discover

a plastic-wrapped bundle inside. It looks a bit like one of the shrink-wrapped T-shirts you see in tourist traps.

I lift it out. Inside the plastic I can see an ash-grey powder. It's too dark to be heroin or cocaine.

Underneath, I can see a second bag, and maybe another beneath that.

Whose room was this before mine? Do the Guards know this is here?

I sniff the package but can't smell anything through the wrapping. I give it a gentle squeeze and some little white granules come to the surface among the grey.

The realisation comes so suddenly that I almost drop the package.

CHAPTER 25

The more I eat, the fatter you get.
You'll see a picture of me, then we'll meet
in person, and you'll cry. What am I?

Rick Allister married his high school sweetheart, Lynne, and started hitting her as soon as she was pregnant. The first time was when he caught her smoking on the back porch. He slapped her so hard that she fell off her chair.

Rick apologised that night. He said the thought of his baby boy inhaling her smoke made him crazy, although they didn't even know the sex of the baby at that stage.

'When we had the twelve-week sonogram, it turned out he was right,' Lynne Allister told me later. 'I know the odds were fifty–fifty, but it made him seem omniscient. Like anything I did, he would know about.'

We were at a diner around the corner from the FBI field office. Lynne kept watching the windows behind me, scanning every face. She was Asian American, twenties, with arched eyebrows and coffee-stained teeth. Under her hoodie, the tendons in her neck stood out, like she was braced for a car crash.

It was two days after the Hermann Park protests. The

road was still sprinkled with broken glass and scorch marks. No agents had come with me to the diner. Everyone was busy sorting through all the photos and video of the protestors.

The second time Rick hit her, Lynne said, it was because she'd eaten some brie. It could contain listeria, he snapped, which would harm his baby. That time he didn't apologise.

'I asked a maternal health nurse, and apparently getting punched in the head *is* more likely to harm the baby than eating cheese.' Lynne took a thoughtful sip of her coffee. 'But then she said, "Still don't eat any soft cheese, though." Can you believe that?'

As her belly got bigger and bigger, she made more and more excuses for Rick. He was stressed. Their finances weren't great. He was working long hours to support her. She thought he'd stop hitting her when the baby was born.

And he did—for a while.

'That first month, it was as if we were in high school again. We were so in love. Whenever he was home, we just lay in bed together looking at Joey, like he was a beautiful painting we'd paid a lot of money for. Newborns aren't hard. They just sleep all the time. But when he started to get more active, Rick started to have problems with everything I did. If he thought the bathwater was too cold, he'd dump a bucket of it on my head. If he thought I hadn't mashed the baby food up enough, he would throw it at me. "This wouldn't hurt if it was mashed," he'd say. Or one time I put the diaper on too tight, and he came up behind me and grabbed my skull and just squeezed. "You like that? Huh?"'

Whenever Lynne quoted her ex-husband, her voice was a hoarse whisper. I couldn't work out if she was doing an impression of him or was worried about other people in the diner overhearing.

'But I couldn't leave him,' she said. 'Where would I go? My parents were back in Delaware. My friends, too. I couldn't contact them without Rick knowing, because we shared a phone and an email address. I couldn't even write a letter, because he was with me every time I left the house. I tried to talk to a work colleague, but she didn't seem to believe me. Later, I found out that Rick had warned her in advance that I had a history of mental problems. I know, I know.' She held up her hands. 'This is all starting to sound familiar, right?'

I nodded. 'Textbook.'

'I've been doing some research about other women in my position,' she continued. 'Their husbands all did exactly the same things. Exactly. Is there a literal textbook? Required reading for all men—a step-by-step guide to controlling your wife?'

I said nothing.

'Oh, don't give me that *not all men* shit,' she said, as if I had spoken. 'This happens everywhere. Maybe not every man is an abuser, but every man has a responsibility to fix the problem.'

I kept my mouth shut. Boys at the group home had tried to sexually assault me. At school, I'd been beaten up and had my teeth knocked out. As an adult, I'd been threatened at gunpoint.

I knew from the FBI stats that men were three times more likely to be murdered or assaulted than women. But I also knew that ninety per cent of perpetrators were male, so I didn't argue with her.

'When did you decide to go to the police?' I asked.

'Joey was almost one. I woke up one night with Rick's hands around my neck. He said I'd been snoring too loudly and it was disturbing the baby.' For the first time, Lynne wasn't watching the pedestrians outside. She was just staring at the cabinet where all the pies were stored, not seeing it. 'He choked me out. When I woke up, I just knew: the next time he would kill me. There was nothing I could do to make him happy or calm him down. My best behaviour was never going to be good enough.'

'But it took you a couple of weeks, is that correct?' I'd seen the police report already.

'Nine days,' she said, a bit defensively. 'He was on leave. I had to wait until he went back to work. As soon as he left for the day, I started packing a suitcase. Once I had it, I walked to Fulton Street and hailed a cab. Well, four cabs.' She grimaced. 'The first three wouldn't take me. They didn't have a baby seat. The fourth one didn't either, but I begged the driver and he agreed to give me a ride to the police station. I told them the whole story. I got a restraining order. He came to the police station, but I didn't have to see him. I hid in one of the interview rooms while he talked to the police.' She shuddered. 'He didn't yell, or swear. He said he was worried about my mental health, and that I'd talked about hurting Joey. He sounded so reasonable. And I was there on my own, just whispering, "Don't believe him, don't believe him."' She exhaled. 'Luckily, they didn't.'

'Who did you stay with?'

'I spent a few nights in a women's shelter on Waugh before I could get in touch with my parents. After that, they paid for a hotel for me.'

'Here? You couldn't get back to Delaware?'

'Not legally. Joey was Rick's son. I couldn't take him interstate without his permission. Instead, my parents came to Houston to help look after Joey while I talked to a lawyer.'

'Do you think that's why he wanted to have a child?' I asked. 'To control you?'

'No,' she said. 'I get why you're asking, but no. He really loved Joey.'

She was already using the past tense. *Loved.*

'Did you see Rick anytime between then and Monday?'

'No,' she said. 'Not until Monday.'

On Monday, Lynne finished work and took the elevator to the basement parking lot. Joey was with her, having spent all afternoon at the office day-care centre. Her mom had unexpectedly dropped him off at one o'clock that day, so she could take Lynne's father to an appointment he'd forgotten about with an eye specialist. Lynne had found it hard to concentrate after that, knowing Joey was right downstairs, probably screaming because he was surrounded by strangers.

He was fine when she collected him, though. He waved at Lynne's colleagues as they entered and left the elevator. They smiled and waved back but still avoided Lynne's gaze. Thanks to Rick, a few people still thought she was crazy, and those who actually understood her situation were keeping their distance so they wouldn't feel obliged to help.

When she got to the basement, Lynne loaded Joey into the car seat. He was in a squirmy mood. It was hard to buckle him in, but she got it done. She climbed into the driver's seat, started the engine and drove up the ramp towards the boom gate. She swiped her pass and the gate creaked open. She rolled out onto the street. The last of the summer sunshine fell through the windshield, warming her arms. The trees in Hermann Park were beautifully green. She reached into one of the cup holders for her sunglasses.

Then the gunfire started.

She felt the first shot before she heard it—straight through her calf muscle and into the console between the car seats. She thought for a second that she'd been stung by a bee. Her worst nightmare was a bee in the car. It was only when the second shot punched through the car door and tunnelled through the seat beneath her that she realised what was happening. She frantically unbuckled the seatbelt and scrambled away from the door, into the passenger seat. The car rolled forwards across the street, driverless.

Two more shots rang out. Neither one hit the car. Then there was a pause. Police later concluded that the shooter was using a Remington R25 GII, which had only a four-round magazine. He was reloading.

People were screaming on the street. The car hit the kerb and lurched up. The radio babbled, unconcerned. Hot blood trickled down Lynne's leg and into her shoe. She covered her head with her arms, shaking.

'You know what the worst part is?' Lynne told me. 'Actually, the whole thing was the worst part. But here's something I can't stop thinking about: I didn't climb into the back seat and try to shield Joey with my body. I didn't think to do that.'

'You were panicked,' I said.

'No shit. But *I bet he blames me* for not doing that. I bet he still thinks I'm a terrible mother. It—' she rubbed her mouth with one hand, as though wiping away an angry word '—it drives me crazy.'

There was one more shot, and then nothing. Lynne was in the passenger seat, keeping her head below the windows. She pushed the stick into reverse and grabbed the wheel. She steered blind, trying to get the car out of the firing line, but still not sure where the firing line was. Pretty soon she hit something. A car alarm went off. Horns blasted all around. Sirens in the air. Joey was screaming. Lynne couldn't hear herself think.

She shifted the stick into drive again. Rolled forwards. Steered the other way. Hit the same kerb. Screamed every swear word she could think of.

Then a cop banged on her window, scaring the shit out of her.

'Ma'am,' he said. 'It's okay. He's gone.'

Within an hour, the FBI was there, fighting with the Houston PD for jurisdiction. It was a half-hearted argument, because no one actually wanted the case. I was there, too. No reason for me to be, but my handler, Richmond, had been called in, and he wasn't supposed to leave me alone, so he brought me with him.

A photographer with a thin moustache took a snap of me behind the police tape. I told him I'd sue his paper if they used the picture. It was an empty threat and he knew it. The photo ended up on the internet anyway.

By the time Richmond and I arrived, Lynne and Joey had already been loaded into an ambulance. They wouldn't be going far—several medical centres bordered Hermann Park. I watched the ambulance disappear behind the jello mould-shaped spray of the Mecom Fountain.

The beat cops already knew where the shooter had been. A witness had seen him pop out of a manhole, like a prairie dog, at the mouth of an alley next to Lynne's office. After that fifth shot, he disappeared into the labyrinth of maintenance tunnels under Houston. Now the alley was blocked by a police barricade, and Lynne's car was being loaded onto a tow truck. There was blood on the ground where she'd gotten out of the car.

While Richmond and locals cops argued, I stared down at the blood, wondering if anyone would object to me touching it. The rain was slowly sweeping it towards lower ground. I shuffled after it, a twisting red snake in the water, until I found myself standing over the manhole. The bloody water trickled over the edge into the blackness.

My hands in my pockets, I listened to the sloshing and shouting of police below. They were unlikely to get anywhere. Sewer tunnels may be unpleasant, but they do a great job of covering tracks. Prints are quickly washed away and sniffer dogs are useless. I could have climbed down to help, but this wasn't my case.

Still, I found myself wondering why the shooter had picked this spot. It was good for a quick getaway, sure—but not for the actual shooting. The angle was too low. It would have made more sense for him to use the vacant first floor of the building next door. He would have had a perfect view through Lynne's windshield. After shooting her through the heart, he would have had time to jump down and disappear through the same manhole.

Maybe the point wasn't to kill her but to scare her. Though if that was the case, why not stop after the first bullet hit the car? Instead, he fired three more shots, reloaded, and then fired once more before vanishing. It didn't make sense.

I watched the flashing lights on top of the tow truck. Lynne's car had three bullet holes—two at the bottom of the driver's-side door, one in a hubcap. Given the grouping, the two shots that missed had probably gone under the car rather than over it or to either side.

I walked closer and confirmed my theory. There was a chip in the asphalt, where a round might have ricocheted off the car, and a bullet hole at the base of a tree in the public park across the street.

Suddenly I realised what the shooter must have been trying to do.

'Wait,' I called out.

No one paid any attention to me. The driver couldn't hear me over the beeping of his tow truck. The other police were still interviewing witnesses.

I ran towards the truck, but one of the local cops stopped me.

'Move along, sir,' she said, assuming I was homeless.

I dug a worn lanyard out of my pocket. 'I'm a civilian consultant with the FBI.'

'In that case, fuck off.'

'I need to examine the victim's car.'

'Too bad. As I was just explaining to your colleagues, this isn't your case.'

'Blake.' Richmond approached. 'What are you doing?'

While the cop was looking at him, I darted past her and climbed up onto the back of the tow truck.

'Hey!' the driver yelled.

Ignoring him, I lay down on the slowly tilting tray and

peered at the undercarriage of the car. A second later, strong hands grabbed me and dragged me off the tray—but not before I saw it: a lump of white-flecked grey powder, wrapped in plastic, taped underneath the car.

'What the hell are you doing?' Richmond demanded.

'The shooter wasn't trying to hit the victim,' I said. 'He was trying to hit the explosives he'd planted under her car.'

The beat cop looked, and her face went grey. After that, they evacuated the block and called in the bomb squad. The FBI got jurisdiction because the bomb made it a case of domestic terrorism.

Richmond was supremely pissed at me. 'Do you know how many open cases I already have?'

'Next time I spot a bomb, I'll ignore it,' I told him.

As it happened, Richmond didn't have to worry, because two hours later, the Hermann Park protest happened. A local congresswoman got on Facebook and announced a plan to ban semi-automatic weapons. The announcement was shared by the NRA and some far-right groups. Someone else announced that the congresswoman would be making a speech in Hermann Park, and suddenly the park was full of masked, gun-toting protestors. The congresswoman never showed up. She later claimed the initial Facebook post was fake and that she supported the second amendment.

The point is, the FBI's resources were stretched too thin to chase an angry ex-husband who had been misclassified as a terrorist, which was why I was meeting Lynne at the diner. I was supposed to gently lower her expectations, with Richmond's help. Richmond didn't turn up.

'Misclassified?' Lynne said, angry now. 'I survived two years of Rick's *domestic terrorism*.'

The baby, who had been asleep in a carrier next to her chair, started crying. Lynne huffed and began unbuckling the straps.

'I know,' I said. 'But the trail has gone cold.'

'After two days?'

'Yup.' I'm not good at gently lowering expectations.

'Look.' With Joey on her lap, Lynne pulled a brown folder out of her backpack and slid it across the table. 'There's a photo of Rick, and some of his friends. Emails that I managed to print out before he deleted them.'

I opened the folder. There was Rick—thin, hollow-cheeked, with long hair, his face partly obscured by a baseball cap, sunglasses and a huge beard. 'Is this the only picture you have?'

'He took the others with him when he realised I'd gone to the police.'

'I'm sorry.' I pushed the folder back. 'There's nothing we can do.'

Lynne's eyes narrowed. 'Was there a point to this interview?'

Partly I was there because I was told to come. Partly it was my pathological need to know stuff. 'I hoped that hearing the full story would provide context. That's all.'

A beat. 'Fine. I guess you can go.' She took the folder back, exposed one breast, and helped Joey latch on to her nipple.

I was about Joey's age, feeding on my mother when she was shot. Her blood trickled into my mouth and pushed my whole world out of orbit. Watching Joey drink was like seeing the moment it all went wrong. I wanted to tackle Lynne, to save her from the bullet. And to save myself from what I had since become.

But I couldn't change the past. And maybe there was already something wrong with me, even before my mother died. I could have been wrong from the moment of conception.

Joey sucked happily, staring up at his mother. His father was a monster. How much of his destiny was already written in his DNA?

'Do you think Rick will leave me alone now?' Lynne was asking.

'No,' I told her. 'Like you said, he loves Joey.'

She gritted her teeth. 'He tried to blow Joey up.'

'There were four shots, then he reloaded, then he fired one extra shot, then he left. He had three more in the magazine and he hadn't hit the bomb yet. Why do you think he stopped shooting?'

'Maybe he thought someone was about to spot him.'

'Maybe,' I said. 'Or maybe he saw the baby in the back seat. You said Joey wasn't supposed to be with you, right? That it was a last-minute thing.'

She put her face in her hands. 'Oh God. What am I supposed to do?'

'I was told to give you a list of websites that have good advice for managing a violent ex-partner.'

'Websites.'

'Yeah.'

Lynne stared down into her coffee cup. 'So I'm supposed to spend my time on the internet, just waiting for him to show up and ruin my life again.'

Maybe I felt sorry for her. Or maybe I just hadn't eaten lunch yet. But Richmond wasn't there, so I took a risk.

'Do you have a gun?' I asked.

'Yes,' she said cautiously. 'I bought it recently.'

It sounded like we were already thinking along the same lines. 'Are you staying in Texas or going back to Delaware?'

'I haven't decided yet. Delaware might be safer, but I don't want to lose my job.'

'Rick may be less likely to find you in Delaware,' I said. 'But only slightly.'

I pulled out the list of websites and wrote a phone number at the bottom.

'What's that?' she said. 'A helpline?'

'Kind of.' I lowered my voice. 'If you stay in Texas, and Rick shows up, are you willing to kill him?'

She just stared at me.

'You have to decide now,' I said. 'You need to be ready to pull the trigger as soon as you see his face. You can't rely on a self-defence scenario. If you wait for it to be him or you, it might be you.'

There was a pause.

'I'm willing,' she said, committing conspiracy to murder in one breath.

'Well, if he shows up, and you *do* kill him, you can call that number.'

'For a lawyer?'

'You won't need a lawyer,' I said. 'No one will ever know for sure that he's dead.'

•

I gently put the package back in the vent and close the grille. This mixture, known as ammonal, isn't supposed to explode if dropped, or hit with a hammer, or even touched by a lit match. Only a high-velocity bullet will ignite it, according to the pointy-heads at the FBI. But something tells me to be cautious.

The white crystals are ammonium nitrate and the grey powder is aluminium. The two substances are fairly safe unless mixed or stockpiled, which is why it's legal to buy them in small amounts.

This isn't a small amount. The package under my bed would be more than enough to set me on fire as I slept.

Except that can't be the point of it. To set it off, someone would have to crawl under my bed and fire a gun into the vent. They'd die a split second before I did.

So the bomb must be en route to somewhere else. But where? Why?

I think of Fred, taking the gun out of Samson's dead hands. *The whole house could have gone up. Jesus.*

Did he mean the bullet might have tunnelled through two walls and the floor before igniting this small package? Seems unlikely. Unless . . .

With an awful sinking feeling in my chest, I drag the bookcase sideways. A spot high up on the wall has been repaired. Someone made a hole, and then patched it up. Like everyone in it, this house is beautiful until you start looking behind things.

I press my ear to the plaster, and knock gently. It's an interior wall, so it should sound hollow. It doesn't. Something has been packed inside.

I tap a different spot, just in case I was knocking beside the stud. Then I try a different wall. I hear a dull thud each time.

I hope I'm wrong. Because if I'm not, the walls of this house are packed tight with bags of ammonal, mixed and ready to blow. If the cops ever show up, it would be easy to turn the building into a fireball, destroying all the evidence.

I think of Fred, ready to push the red button on his phone. *Are you sure? This action cannot be undone.*

CHAPTER 26

Sometimes I am the ground beneath your feet, sometimes I am the air above your head. I swallow men whole, yet they die without me. What am I?

'You unscrew these two, lever out the battery, put in the new one, and screw those back in. It's not rocket surgery.' Donnie chuckles at his own joke as he inspects his handiwork.

It's Thursday morning. I've volunteered to help change the batteries, mostly so I can learn the position of all the cameras.

I hardly slept last night. It wasn't just the knowledge that I was surrounded by explosives—it was the fear that I wouldn't be able to get Thistle out of here before the Guards resume their torture tomorrow.

'How often do you have to do this?' I ask.

Donnie wipes some sweat off his brow and peers down at the checklist. 'Every four days.'

'You must go through a lot of batteries.'

'We recharge them at a wheel upstream. Hydropower. Disposable batteries are really unethical. Mining of lithium and zinc and cobalt destroys animal habitats. It's the main

219

reason that gorillas are endangered.' He shakes his head sadly. 'But all these assholes keep buying them.'

'Don't the rechargeable ones also require mining?'

Donnie shoots me a suspicious look. 'What's your point?'

'No point.' I follow Donnie downhill through the brush towards a narrow creek. 'How often do you move the cameras?'

'We don't move them, exactly—just point them in different directions. There's no real schedule, but we last did it on Sunday, so there's no need for a while.'

Four days ago. Right before the hiker showed up. 'Why not do it every time you change the batteries?' I regret suggesting this as soon as the words are out of my mouth.

'Planning a new layout is pretty complicated,' Donnie says. 'You can't just point them in random directions. We don't have enough cameras as it is, so we need to make sure we're not doubling up.'

'You don't want two covering the same ground?'

'Exactly.'

'Can I change the next battery?'

'Sure.'

We both jump over the creek. It's shallow and muddy. I see why the Guards don't make the prisoners wash in it. As I look around, I spot two more cameras up ahead. It's not easy to memorise the locations and angles, since all the trees look so similar. Harder still is knowing that I won't spot all of them. Thistle's life depends not only on my memory, but on sheer luck.

'Is this where the water for the house comes from?' I ask, looking back at the creek.

'A little further upstream, yeah.' Donnie looks proud. 'I rigged up the purifier myself.'

'You did? How does it work?'

Donnie explains that he was an apprentice plumber, once upon a time. At first, he was drawn by the money—he'd heard from a friend that plumbers made more than office drones or store clerks—but after going on a few house visits, it started to feel like a calling.

He and his boss would park their pick-up truck in front of a suburban home. A woman in sweat-stained clothes would answer the door, her hair all over the place, a screaming baby in her arms and another two dirty kids yelling on the floor. Everything would smell terrible. After only two hours without water, their lives had fallen apart. Donnie soon realised that every living thing on Earth needed water. It was the world's most important resource.

'What about oxygen?' I ask.

He ignores me. 'Did you know that once the human population hits eight billion, there won't be enough fresh water to keep everyone alive?'

'I did not.'

'Three days without water and you're dead.' He snaps his fingers. 'Like that. Some countries have already started water rationing. We'll all have to do it pretty soon, especially if certain people keep breeding.'

He catches himself. Glances over his shoulder. I guess the other Guards aren't very tolerant of intolerance.

'Which people?' I ask. If I can work out who he's prejudiced against, maybe I can use it to turn him against the rest of the group, or the rest of the group against him.

But he doesn't bite. 'Whichever. You heard of "day zero"? It's when City Hall switches off the water. Then everyone has to go to collection points to get it. Suddenly water isn't just valuable—it's *currency*. People steal it. So other people guard it. Fights break out. Wars start. You know how the Arab Spring got started? All those revolutions in the Middle East?'

'Twitter?' I guess.

'Wrong. Twitter gets the credit, but the real reason was the price of grain got too high. And that's just bread. People don't even need bread.'

'Right. They can just eat cake.'

He ignores me again. 'Imagine what it will be like when it's water. Something you die without. Every population rises up. Every government tries to suppress it. The death toll rises and rises.'

He says all this with increasing fervour, like he's looking forward to the water wars. The veins bulge in his neck and his hands.

I've been thinking about the bullet wound in Samson's skull. If the killer really wanted to make it look like a suicide, they would have forced Samson to hold the gun, then twisted his arm and made him shoot himself. That would minimise the risk of the shot missing, and would also put powder residue on the victim's fingers.

I don't know for sure that the killer did that. But I do know that Donnie is the only person in the house strong enough.

'So how come you're not a plumber anymore?' I ask.

'What's the point?' Donnie finds another camera and starts unscrewing it. 'If everyone's plumbing is gonna get turned off anyhow? So after Fred made the offer—oh, wait. You wanted to do this one.'

He hands me the screwdriver. There are flecks of old blood on the blade. I remember Fred's voice: *You don't need all this stuff to hurt someone. You can just use an electric kettle, or a screwdriver, or a hockey stick.*

I squeeze the grip. Now I'm armed and Donnie's not. I could kill him and hide his body. The others would assume the hiker had done it.

But having the Guards search the woods again won't help me sneak Thistle out of here. The opposite, in fact.

I unscrew the casing for the camera, exposing the battery. 'What offer?'

'I'm just like you.' He claps me on the shoulder. 'I saw a wrong and I tried to right it. The police got all in my face about it, so I came here to lie low.'

Donnie tells me that he saw a busted pipe out the front of someone's house flooding the street. He knocked on their door, but they didn't answer. He tapped on the windows. No answer. He knocked on the doors of some neighbours. One guy—a Black guy, Donnie specifies—opened up, but he didn't know the occupants of the house and certainly didn't have a spare key.

'He just shrugged.' Donnie gives me the new battery. 'Like, "What can you do?" All this water spilling into the street, while half of California is on fire and rivers every-where are drying up. And this son of a bitch just shrugs and closes the door on me.'

I slide the battery into place and seal the casing. 'So what did you do?'

'I went back to the house with the leaking pipe,' Donnie says, 'and I broke in.'

As he describes his method, it's clear that this wasn't Donnie's first attempt at breaking and entering. He casu-ally describes the steps, which include things only an experienced burglar would think of. He moved his pick-up so it wasn't parked too close to the house, broke some branches in the tree out front so they obscured the line of sight between the street and the side gate, then rattled the gate in case a dog came running. He even pulled some condoms on over his shoes so he didn't leave identifiable tracks. 'You'd be amazed how far those things stretch,' he says.

I wonder how many of the homes he visited as a plumber got robbed later.

There was a crawl space under the house, accessible from the backyard. Donnie slid back the bolt and wriggled in. Half of the space was flooded, and the other half was thick with spiderwebs. 'You ever seen spiders trying to escape from a flood?' he asks. 'It's like they go web-crazy. They turn everything above the waterline into cotton candy. I could hardly breathe in there.'

Donnie dragged himself through the mud and cobwebs until he reached the water main, and switched it off. The water stopped. When the occupant returned, they would notice that their faucets didn't work and their toilet didn't flush, and they would call a plumber, who would turn on the main and immediately spot the leak. Problem solved. Maybe Donnie would even get the job.

Then a gun went off above his head.

'Turns out there *was* someone home,' he says. 'Can you believe that? She was too scared to open the door when I knocked. Social anxiety or some bullshit like that. So she saw me out the window climbing over the gate, and when she heard me crawling around under the house, her solution was to go get a gun and start shooting into the fucking floor. I nearly shat my pants, and crawled out of there as fast as I could. But after the second shot, she stops firing and starts screaming. Get this: she literally shot herself in the foot. I mean, not directly, it was a ricochet—but can you imagine?'

Donnie doubles over, laughing too hard to continue the story.

'What happened after that?' I ask.

Donnie wipes some tears from his eyes. 'So the Black guy next door, he hears the gunshots and calls the police. *Now* he cares, right? I was already gone by the time they got there, but he took down my licence plate number, because he thought I was the one shooting. So the cops pick me up later. I tell them the truth, but they decide to press charges for breaking and entering—even though I was only trying to help. I get pulled up in front of a lady judge. I already had a suspended sentence for aggravated assault, so the judge puts me away for eighteen months.'

He glances at me, checking my reaction to the mention of the assault charge. Then he looks pleased, mistaking my complete lack of surprise for approval.

'And this makes the news, right?' he continues. '*Vigilante Plumber Shot At By Anxious Housewife*. So in prison I get a few calls from bloggers, podcasters, whatever. And then, two days after I'm released, I get the call from Fred.'

Donnie's smile fades as he tells me about that phone call. It was confusing at first. He wasn't sure how Fred had gotten his number. They had no mutual contacts. Unlike the podcasters, Fred was interested in the assault as well as the water pipe incident. And unlike them, he seemed to appreciate what Donnie had been trying to do.

'I like a guy who's willing to go above and beyond,' Fred told him. 'To do the right thing, even when the so-called "justice system" says to look the other way. You should be proud, man.'

I'm starting to get a sense of how Fred chooses his staff. He likes practical skills. He likes violence. And he likes crusaders, or at least people inclined to see themselves that way—and inclined to see those with different priorities as enemy combatants.

I give the camera back to Donnie, who reattaches it to the tree.

'That's the last one.' He cracks his knuckles. 'Let's go get some lunch.'

'What happened to the woman whose house you broke into?' I ask.

'Oh, she died,' Donnie says. 'It turns out that shooting yourself in the foot is pretty serious.'

CHAPTER 27

This building has no lock, no door, no guards.
It is easy to enter, yet hard to leave.
What is it?

My eighth-grade math teacher was Mrs Jefferson, a chinless woman with a dry sense of humour who wore huge, bright necklaces and liked to put her feet on her desk while we were working. One time she handed out copies of a maze to the whole class and said she'd give a prize to whoever solved it first.

I took one look at mine and decided it was unsolvable. There were dozens of intersections leading to hundreds of dead ends. Mrs Jefferson had obviously printed out the most complicated maze she could find in the hope of keeping us busy all lesson. Looking around, I saw that most of my classmates had come to the same conclusion and were looking out the window or scratching graffiti into their desks. I flipped the paper over and started sketching an enormously fat man. I had little artistic talent and didn't know why I was doing this. I didn't yet understand that it was a kind of homemade pornography.

I'd hardly finished his enormous round belly when another student called out, 'Done!' and thrust her paper in the air like an Olympic torch. I was suspicious. She must have cheated—there was no way to solve so complex a maze so quickly. It wasn't as though the student was a genius. I'd once seen her ball up a muffin wrapper and swallow it.

But Mrs Jefferson didn't look surprised. She got up, walked over, took the sheet and examined it. 'Well done, Yvette.'

'It was super easy,' Yvette said. 'There were no choices or anything.'

I flipped my sheet over and looked at the maze again. Yvette was right. The correct route was the only route. Starting at either end of the maze lead inexorably to the other, cutting right through the labyrinth of dead ends. None of the intersections were connected to the main path.

'Your prize is the knowledge that some things look impossible until you try them,' Mrs Jefferson said. 'You can share it with the rest of the class.'

She probably thought that was inspiring, but Yvette and the rest of the class just looked annoyed. Most of the kids were like me. Poor, beaten—some literally—and sick of being told that we just had to work harder and believe in ourselves more.

Anyway, that was our introduction to calculus. The way Mrs Jefferson talked, impressed with her own wisdom, reminds me of Cedric a bit.

'People don't always know what they want or why they want it,' Cedric is saying.

We're in the editing room. Cedric is facing the monitors, a few hundred flash drives piled on the desk in front of him. I'm sitting behind him at a table covered in padded envelopes and small cardboard boxes. Every few seconds, he swivels in his chair to hand me a flash drive and an address label. I put the drive in a box, the box in an envelope and the label on top, before dumping it in a tray under the table. We're both wearing latex gloves to keep our prints off the packages.

We've been packing envelopes all afternoon, and Cedric hasn't once mentioned the kiss. The bite. He seems to be pretending it never happened. Just like Samson did, after their tryst.

'We could have more pricing options on the site,' Cedric continues. 'Download the videos for fifty dollars per month. Get it mailed to you in a crappy little bag, fifty-five. Or get it mailed to you in a luxurious gift box, sixty. You know what would happen?'

I don't really care. My mind is on Thistle, chained up in that freezing slaughterhouse waiting for me to save her. Before the new cameras arrive tomorrow.

'Everyone—well, pretty much everyone—would pick the cheapest option,' Cedric says, as if I'd responded. 'Then they'd be unsatisfied, even though they got exactly what they asked for. And sooner or later, they'd unsubscribe. That's what happened when we ran the site on that model.' He passes me another flash drive and an address label. 'But if getting a sexy flash drive in a beautiful box is the *only* option, they're happy to pay through the nose for it forever.'

I don't think Cedric's definitions of sexy or beautiful overlap with my own. The flash drives are white and featureless except for the word *Guards* laser-etched on one side. They look like the headstones at Arlington. The boxes are black cardboard, about the right size for an engagement ring. But inside there's foam rubber, the kind rifle scopes are packed in, with a slot just the right size for the drive.

I suppose they're beautiful in the same way Zara is. Immaculate, but enigmatic. Small but dangerous.

'I guess you have to find a compromise between presentation and price,' I say, still barely paying attention to Cedric.

'Wrong,' Cedric says. 'You have to go with one or the other. No compromise. You see, if everything is beautifully presented, if even opening the box is an experience, people respect that. But if looks homemade, people respect that, too. They like the authenticity of it. Or if it's the cheapest in the market, you'll make plenty of sales that way. But *semi*-professional? Cheap-ish, classy-ish, authentic-ish? That's the danger zone. There's no market for that.'

I seal an envelope and stick on the address label. This one is going to the UK, but I've seen others headed for Germany, China, Brazil, Australia.

'There's no name on this one,' I say.

Cedric waves a hand. 'That's fine. We don't do signature on delivery.'

'How do you stop the drives from going to the wrong people?'

Cedric gives me a funny look. 'The password.'

I'd forgotten that I was supposed to be Lux, a long-time subscriber who would know that the drives are password-protected. I know it, too. I even know what his password was. I'm just distracted.

'I'm not worried about other people finding out what's on them,' I say, thinking quickly. 'I just thought if subscribers didn't get their drives, they'd blame you. Us.'

Cedric shrugs. 'What are they going to do, call the Federal Trade Commission?' Then he looks anxious suddenly. Perhaps for a second he, too, forgot that Lux had been a subscriber. 'Doesn't happen often, though. Even if the subscriber doesn't use their real name, we know who they are, who they vote for, what their religion is . . .'

'How?'

Cedric doesn't answer. He's frowning at something on one of the monitors. 'Goddamn. Look at these numbers.'

While he's distracted, I grab a blank label and a pen, and scribble an address.

Dr Norman
1 Justice Park Drive
Houston, TX 77092

I finish just as Cedric turns back around with the next flash drive and address label.

'What are you writing?' he asks.

'Torture ideas,' I say quickly, covering the address with one hand.

'For the new prisoner?'

'Right.'

'Well, you'd better move fast.'

I don't know what he means by that. As he turns back to face his computer, I peel off one of my latex gloves and stick the label to one of the packages. I squeeze the package so my fingerprints are all over it.

'How long does it take the packages to arrive?' I ask.

Cedric shrugs. 'Depends where they're going. A week? Two?'

My heart sinks. Thistle and I can't survive another week here. The cameras arrive tomorrow. And I don't even know how often Dr Norman checks her mail at the FBI field office, or how long it will take her to figure out what's going on. For all I know, she's away on vacation right now.

Still, I remember Mrs Jefferson. Some things look impossible until you try them. On the back of Norman's envelope, I quickly scribble the GPS coordinates that led me to this place, and my name. Then I bury it among the others, hoping no one will notice.

'See, check this out.' Cedric angles the monitor so I can see it. On the screen is a list of comments from the site:

—*So excited to meet the new inmate! *does happy dance**

—*The baby killer is an FBI agent?? Fucking DESTROY HER.*

—*Cut the FBI bitch's head off.*

—*Rape her with her own gun.*

It feels like I'm falling into a well. Cold stone all around, less and less daylight above.

But the comments aren't even what Cedric is pointing at. Beneath them is a pie chart divided into six uneven slices. One slice, much bigger than the others, is labelled: *Baby Killer*.

I figure out what I'm looking at even as Cedric says the words.

'Polling results.' He hovers over the chart with the mouse. 'The new prisoner is miles ahead of any of the others. Hundreds of votes. We only just got her, and the subscribers want us to kill her already? It's like, learn some patience.'

I crush the arms of my chair in my hands.

'Are you okay?' Cedric says.

I open my mouth to talk, but it's like something is lodged in my throat.

'Lux?'

Just say something. If your cover gets blown, you can't save her.

I fake a cough, which turns into a real coughing fit.

'I get it. It's a shock.' Cedric gestures at the comments on the screen. 'I'm not saying those bastards out in the slaughterhouse don't deserve it. But sometimes the things the subscribers come up with . . .' A shadow passes over his face.

'Yeah.' I look up at him, relieved that he understands. Maybe I have an ally here.

'Oh, well,' Cedric says, like it can't be helped. Then he sits down at the computer and prints out another sheet of address labels.

I try to keep my voice steady. 'When does voting close?'

'Saturday. So if she wins—and it sure looks like she will—we'll kill her on Sunday. Whatever you want to do to her, you'll have to do before then.'

Today is Thursday. I have three days to get Thistle out of here.

Donnie appears in the doorway. He avoids looking at Cedric entirely and lasers right in on me. He's holding a medieval battleaxe.

I try to look calm.

'Lux,' he says.

I clear my throat. 'Yeah?'

'You're up.'

CHAPTER 28

She's sweet, refined and always
full of energy. People love her, but
she kills them. Who is she?

The sun is going down as I follow Donnie to the slaughter-house. He has a spring in his step and he's spinning the battleaxe in his hands.

The old FBI director, Peter Luzhin, used to steal the cadavers of death-row inmates. That was how he rewarded me for solving cases. I sometimes watched the executions. The condemned men would shuffle into the execution chamber as though their shoes were made of lead. Their heads bowed as if before a vengeful God.

Now I understand how they felt.

'Keep up, Lux,' Donnie says. 'It's getting late.'

I force myself to walk a little faster. 'Sorry.'

'Don't kill her, all right? Cuts and bruises are fine, and broken bones aren't a problem, but don't chop off anything that she might bleed out through.'

'We should wait,' I say. 'The cameras are still broken.'

'That's the point,' Donnie says. 'No offence, but it takes skill to do what I do. Think of this as a dry run. An audition.'

'But I wanted the first time to be recorded.'

Donnie holds up his phone. 'Gotcha covered.'

He hauls the slaughterhouse door open. The screaming turns into whimpering when the prisoners see our masks and Donnie's axe. We're not here to save them. We're here to make things worse.

Donnie walks over to Thistle, who is slumped on the floor, unconscious. She must be exhausted after pulling on her chains all day. Her wrists are red and raw. Instead of her Hello Kitty T-shirt, she's wearing a loose suit with a skirt and a fake FBI lanyard. The Guards have given her a costume. The thought that one of them watched her undress, or stripped her, makes me feel sick.

'Wake up, bitch,' Donnie says. 'It's Judgement Day.'

Thistle doesn't move.

Donnie nudges her foot with his own. 'Hey. FBI lady.'

Thistle doesn't react to this.

'Maybe we should come back another time,' I say.

'Screw that.' Donnie leans down and grabs Thistle's hair. 'Wake up, you—'

Thistle drops the act and lashes out at him with her free hand. At the same time, she tries to kick his kneecap inside out.

But Donnie must have been half-expecting this. He lets go of her and darts back, twisting his leg just enough to protect his knee. The punch which should have broken his nose glances harmlessly off the top of his head.

'Whoa!' He laughs. 'She's a fighter. This is gonna be fun.'

Thistle looks warily from him to me. 'What you do right now could be the difference between a prison sentence and a lethal injection.'

Donnie smirks and hands me the axe. The blade is chipped and the wooden handle is rough. It's not as heavy as it looks, but it's still sharp and long enough to do some damage.

'Go to town, Lux,' he says.

'Sure,' I say, thinking fast. 'But not on her.'

Donnie looks puzzled. 'But she's yours. We got her for you.'

One of Thistle's nostrils lifts up, like she's thinking about spitting on me.

If I refuse to torture a prisoner, my cover is blown, and the prisoner will be brutalised by the other Guards. So my plan is to fake it—but it has to be very convincing. That means someone might get hurt for real, and I don't want it to be Thistle.

I lean close to Donnie. 'It's all about the anticipation,' I whisper. 'She has to see someone else take a beating. Let that simmer for a few days.'

Donnie looks impressed. 'That's cold. I like it.'

I point to the woman in the shredded evening gown, chained to a loop in the door of the priest's confessional. The Abuser, who burned her husband with the lighter. She moans.

'I want that one,' I say.

Donnie looks uncertain. 'Ivy? Fred usually does her.'

'Oh. I can choose someone else?'

All the other prisoners tense up. Amar, the Terrorist, mutters a prayer.

'No,' Donnie says. 'It's probably okay.'

I give the axe back to Donnie. 'You can keep that.'

'You sure?'

I flex my hands. 'These are all I need.'

Ivy crawls backwards as I approach, until the chain around her ankle goes taut. Her skin is unblemished, and she's not as thin as the others, even though they're all served the same dog food. Maybe she hasn't been here as long. Or maybe it's metabolic. Some people eat nothing but sugar yet stay thin, while others eat nothing at all and stay fat.

The point is, she has some cushioning. What I'm about to do won't hurt as much.

I tell myself that's the only reason I picked her. Not because, if this doesn't work, I might have to convince Donnie by taking a bite out of her.

'Get up,' I tell her.

She does, slowly, staring at the stained concrete with her large, dark eyes. She's beautiful. Maybe that's why the subscribers picked her. *The prettier the car, the prettier the crash.*

I can't give her any kind of non-verbal signal if she won't make eye contact. 'Look at me.'

She doesn't. She just trembles.

The church confessional is right there. Ivy is the only prisoner with any potential privacy. I wish I could take her inside and explain. But I can't think of a believable pretext. So I grab her by the throat, slam the back of her skull against the wall next to the confessional—or it looks like I do. I kick the tin wall at the same moment, making a convincing boom.

The noise lasts just long enough to cover me as I whisper three syllables in her ear: 'Play along.'

'Don't!' she screams. I don't know if it's because she understood or because she didn't. I pull back my fist, a big, dramatic gesture, and swing it at her. But just before it hits, in the moment when my body is blocking Donnie's view, I open my palm, so the punch turns into a slap. It hits the side of her torso with a thud. Slaps are louder than punches, even if you don't use much force.

She's wearing another layer under the gown—thin thermals, the same colour as her skin. They probably stop her from freezing to death out here, but unfortunately, they also deaden the sound.

Ivy squirms in my grip. 'Help me!' she screeches. Not sure who to.

I hit her again in the same spot. Harder. In Hollywood, making a fight look real takes tricky camera angles, sound effects and hours of rehearsal. I have nothing.

She's sobbing. 'Stop! Please!'

I grab a fistful of her hair. She stands on tiptoes, which makes it look like I'm lifting her up by her scalp. She lets out a squeal of agony. I'm not entirely sure it's fake.

'What's the matter?' I shout. 'Does that hurt?'

Shouting is itself a form of torture. The CIA used it at their secret prisons, along with deafening music played around the clock. But if I can't make this look real, I can at least make it sound real.

I glance back at Donnie to see if he's buying this—and Ivy swipes at me with her free arm, raking her nails down the side of my neck, taking out a shallow gouge. Unlike me, she's not holding back.

I snarl with anger that would be real, if I wasn't so scared. I grab her face and press my thumb into her eyeball—but it's an illusion. That thumb doesn't exist anymore.

It's a trick that will only look real for a second, so I quickly let go and twist her arm behind her back. Police learn the rear wrist lock, because it looks gentle but hurts like hell. In the training manuals it's called *pain compliance*. Right now, I'm trying for the opposite, making it look like agony but keeping it painless. Ivy is shrieking so loudly that I have no idea if I'm doing it right.

Donnie isn't convinced, though. I can feel it, without even looking back at him. I'm going to have to hurt Ivy for real.

I'm not an experienced fighter, but I know anatomy. I don't want to damage her solar plexus or rupture her bladder. I drive my fist into her belly, halfway between the two.

She folds in half with a wrenching cry. Whatever she did to her husband, she doesn't deserve this.

I can't keep up the act. Need to end it somehow. I grab Ivy's throat again, and tense the muscles in my hand and my arm to make it look like I'm squeezing. She takes the hint, going bug-eyed and gurgling in my grip. She's actually very good at this. Maybe she was an actress before she got captured.

I do the wall-kick thing again, and mutter, 'Go limp.' Praying that she obeys.

Ivy gags for a few more seconds and then, to my relief, her eyes flutter closed. I drop her, and she hits the ground like a bag of groceries and lies still.

'Whoops,' I say. 'Must have pressed too hard on the carotid. Sorry, man.'

I crouch next to her. As I pretend to check her pulse, I surreptitiously wipe some of the blood from my neck on her top lip. Now it looks like she has a broken nose.

My blood on someone else's mouth. Not how things usually go.

'Yep,' I say. 'Down for the count. But she has a pulse.'

Finally I turn to Donnie. His expression is hidden by the mask.

I spread my arms wide, breathing heavily. 'So?'

'It's a lot less work with the axe,' he says.

'Not as much fun, though,' I say.

He smirks. 'True. Okay, you get the part. But there's room for improvement—I'll show you over the weekend.'

Only then do I look at Thistle. She's shaking and hugging her legs with her free arm. I convinced her, too.

•

'How'd our boy do?' Fred asks Donnie at dinner.

Donnie raises his beer in my direction. 'Made us proud.'

'And the FBI agent? How did she hold up?'

'Scared shitless,' I say.

Fred raises his eyebrows. 'Just scared?'

'Lux abused the Abuser.' Donnie shovels some rice into his mouth. 'Made the FBI agent watch.'

Fred was reaching across the table for the green beans but his hand stops halfway there. 'You had a turn on Ivy?'

'Yeah.' I try to sound casual.

There's a flicker of something in Fred's expression. Possessiveness?

'Is that a problem?' I ask.

Zara watches this exchange with interest.

Fred shrugs and picks up some beans with the tongs. 'I usually do Ivy.'

'Oh.' I put my water glass down a bit too hard. *Thunk*. 'Sorry. I didn't know.'

Donnie glances at me. I *did* know. He told me.

'It's all good,' Fred says. His face relaxes back into its usual serene smile. 'Just ask next time, okay?'

Now Donnie looks even more uneasy. I did ask, and he said yes.

But I don't rat him out. 'No problem. I will.'

Donnie relaxes. My heart rate settles.

Fred chews on some corn. 'You want to go on the delivery run with Kyle in the morning?'

'I don't need help,' Kyle puts in, looking offended.

'Sure,' I say. My plan is that Thistle and I will be gone by morning. But I still don't know what to do about Kyle.

I wonder if Fred remembers what he told me yesterday— that Kyle does the mail run because he's expendable. Maybe Fred is implying that I'm expendable, too.

•

I lie in bed, listening.

Donnie's footsteps are the heaviest, and he goes to bed first. Someone else has a shower—either Cedric or Kyle, since Fred already had one—then goes into one of the bedrooms and paces around for a while before the bedclothes start rustling. The shower hisses again for someone else. Last to go to bed is Zara, her footsteps lighter and more cautious than the others. No pacing for her. Her footsteps just stop. The bed doesn't squeak either. A good-quality bedframe.

I keep seeing Thistle's face. She already thought I was a monster. Now she's watched me torture another prisoner. At least when she found the head in my freezer, I was able to protest my innocence. This time I couldn't even do that.

After all the movement is over, I wait another four hours. Long enough for everyone to finish reading or watching videos on their phones and fall into a deep sleep. Then I rise and slip out into the corridor.

Remembering the creaking sounds, I keep my feet close to the walls as I walk, reducing the risk of the house giving me away. After turning a corner I'm walking parallel to the boards, so I pick the darkest one—probably the hardest wood—and walk along it, balanced like it's a tightrope, all the way to Fred's bedroom.

No light under his door, so he's not reading or using a laptop. I had hoped he might snore, but there's only silence from inside. I can't tell if he's asleep or just lying there in the darkness.

I touch the handle. Fred is paranoid enough to padlock all his windows closed. Is he paranoid enough to set some kind of trap? It wouldn't take much effort to stretch a trip-wire between the handle and a heavy object, or to lean a broom against the door so it would fall onto something loud when the door was opened.

I'll just have to hope he's not that paranoid.

He's not paranoid at all. You're trying to steal his stuff.

I turn the handle. There's a very soft click. I push the door open slowly. No squeaks from the hinges. No broom, no tripwire. In the darkness, I can see the bed and a shape in it, but I can't tell if the occupant is facing me or not.

He doesn't move, though; I don't think I've woken him.

I can see dim outlines of the furniture in the room. A little red light glows on his phone, charging on the dresser. Some clothes are on the floor, possibly the ones he just took off. Maybe he's planning on wearing them again tomorrow. One of the advantages of making other people clean up the blood—less laundry to do.

The dark makes it impossible to see the key bowl from the doorway. As I enter the room, I bend down and squeeze the clothes, just in case. Nothing in the pockets of his jeans, nothing in his shoes except silicone inserts. The shoes feel like leather—unusual for a vegetarian, though not necessarily for an environmentalist.

This reminds me of the jerky in his desk. I would love some more. But Thistle is depending on me.

So get some for her, the voice in my head suggests. *She's probably hungry, too.*

I ignore the voice and make my way to the key bowl on the bookshelf. Fred's key ring is there. I carefully clench all the keys together so they don't jingle as I lift them up.

It's not enough. The keys make a faint clink. Fred snuffles and rolls towards me. I freeze, my heart hammering, the keys in my hand. I crouch to hide under the bed—

But someone's already down there.

I stifle a yell. Zara is staring at me. She has something clenched in her hand. I'm willing to bet it's a pin.

Fred settles, sighs, and goes still.

Zara and I look at each other for a moment. Long enough for me to realise she isn't going to warn Fred that I'm stealing his stuff. Long enough for her to realise that I'm not going to warn Fred that she's about to stab him.

I slowly rise, back out the door, and close it behind me. I have no idea what Zara thinks I'm trying to do. But it doesn't matter, as long as she keeps her mouth shut until I'm gone.

Escaping isn't going to be easy. I know where most of the cameras are, but not all of them. Plus, once we've stolen Fred's car, the motion sensor on the driveway will go off. Still, with everyone except Zara asleep, we'll have a head start.

I sneak through the backyard, past Cedric's opium farm, past Samson's grave and past the dogs, which make that creepy moaning sound but don't bark, thank God. Soon I reach the slaughterhouse. Some whispering is happening inside, but I can't make out the words.

The whispering dies out as soon as I start unlocking the door. Once it's open, I make my way to where Thistle is chained up. In the darkness I can only see her outline and her teeth. She's slumped against the wall in one corner, one knee up, the other splayed out. At first I think she's playing possum, like with Donnie. Then, for a horrifying moment, I think she might be dead.

'Thistle?' I say.

She flinches. 'You can't kill me.'

'I wasn't planning to.' I was hoping Ivy had told her that my beating was mostly fake, but apparently she hasn't.

'I mean it,' Thistle says. 'The others will tell your pals at the house that you're not really Lux. They all know the truth. Killing me won't help keep your secret.'

'Not unless I kill everyone else, too.'

This is the dumbest thing I could have said. I just wanted to point out the flaw in her plan, as though that would somehow make her trust me, given that her plan was predicated on not trusting me. As usual, my instinct was to be right rather than to be liked.

The other prisoners start whimpering helplessly.

'Relax, goddamn it. I'm not gonna do that.' I reach for Thistle's leg, but she snatches it away. 'Hold still! I'm trying to unlock your chains.'

She hesitates. 'Oh. Sorry. I trust you.'

She's lying, but at this point I don't really care. I just don't want her to die.

I jam Fred's key into the lock. The cuff around Thistle's ankle pops open. 'Now, stay close to me. There—'

She kicks me in the side of the head. A bomb goes off inside my skull. The other side of my head hits the floor. The slaughterhouse is spinning around me like a theme park ride. My guts churn and I fight the urge to puke.

'Hit him again!' someone screams.

'Kill him!' someone else roars.

I never expected a peaceful death—old, in hospital, holding hands with someone who cares about me. Nor could I hope for a meaningful death, like getting killed in a just war, or even a normal death, like a car accident. My demise was always going to be something senseless and bizarre, like getting kerb-stomped to a pulp by the woman I love in an old slaughterhouse.

But Thistle doesn't do that. Instead, I hear her bare feet slap the concrete as she flees.

'Wait!' I stand up and immediately stumble sideways into the shelves of the fake pharmacy. The pill bottles don't fall off—they're glued in place.

Thistle is slipping through the open door. I stagger after her, the ringing in my ears worse than ever. My ear itself feels slightly crushed.

Finally I reach the door. The frame bruises my shoulder as I barge through.

'Thistle?' I hiss. 'Thistle!'

No response. But at least she didn't run towards the house—I can hear her, crunching through the forest to my right. It's only a matter of time before she blunders into the viewing angle of one of the cameras.

I chase after her. I'm still dizzy, but she's barefoot. Soon I can see her in the moonlight up ahead, running between the trees.

'Thistle! Wait!'

She doesn't turn. I catch up. At the last second, she spins around and attacks me with a left hook. It's a hell of a punch—it might have broken my neck if I hadn't tripped on a root at exactly the same moment. I blunder into her with an accidental tackle. We both hit the ground in an explosion of dead leaves.

'No!' Thistle tries to struggle out from under me.

'Stop!' I say. 'There are cameras everywhere. Just stop.'

She pauses. 'Cameras?'

'Right. Plus a motion sensor on the driveway. Plus some fucking scary assholes in that house, one of whom is awake. Please, *please*, just let me help you.'

We're almost face to face in the dark. I can feel her breath on my cheek. Even this close, I can't tell what she's thinking.

'What's your angle?' she says. 'I want the truth.'

'I'm trying to save your life.'

'Why?'

'You know why,' I say.

'I don't. I don't understand you at all, Blake.'

'I'm not with these guys,' I say, gesturing back towards the house. 'I tracked Fred down, but he turned out to have company. I had to pretend to be Lux so they wouldn't kill me.'

'Don't bullshit me,' Thistle snaps. 'I found a human head in your fucking freezer.'

'You did,' I say. 'But I didn't kill him.'

'Oh, yeah? Who did?'

'Nobody. He died of a heart attack.'

'Then what the fuck was he doing in your—'

'I was gonna eat him.'

Finally the words are out. This terrible secret that I've been keeping for my whole life.

Thistle stares at me. She will never love me after this. But if she doesn't understand, she won't do what I say. Telling the truth is the only way to save her.

'Eat him,' she repeats.

'I found his body,' I say. 'I took it home so I could eat it.'

She just stares.

'Look, I'm sick in the head, okay?' I say. 'I admit that. But I'm not gonna kill you. I'm your only hope of getting out of here.'

'Eat him,' she says again.

The idea must be hard to digest. 'I eat people. But I'm not a killer. Well, I have killed people, but only in self-defence. Not for food. Although in some cases I did eat them after-wards, but that's not the reason I—look, can we discuss this on the way?'

CHAPTER 29

What kind of dog has a bark,
but no bite?

Thistle follows me through the forest like a sleepwalker. As if she thinks she might be dreaming.

As we make our way towards the garage—taking a winding route to avoid the cameras—I give her the whole story. What happened to my parents. The abuse at the group home. The would-be mugger who got his throat bitten out. The corrupt FBI director, offering me death-row cadavers in exchange for cases solved. The gangster who offered me the bodies of her enemies. Parts of this Thistle knew already, but I can see on her face that they're starting to make more sense with context.

You'd think it would be a relief to say all this out loud. It's not. Instead of disappearing, the guilt that I've lived with my whole life metastasises into shame. Thistle says nothing, but I can feel her growing horror as she listens.

'Camera just there,' I say. 'Go left.'

She obeys. We walk in silence for a minute. My guts twist as I wonder what she's thinking.

'The severed head,' she says finally.

'You're really stuck on that,' I say.

'It wasn't . . . chewed.'

'I guess I never got around to it.'

She shudders. 'What I mean is, are you sure you're not imagining it?'

'What?'

'I've known you a long time. I never saw any evidence that you were eating people. Are you sure it's not just a delusion?'

This has occurred to me from time to time. It's a drawback of being so good at destroying evidence. Without proof, memory and imagination get all mashed together.

This is an opportunity to take back my confession. To convince her that I'm just crazy and not actually a monster.

I don't take it. 'I'm sure.'

We trudge on. *Someone should put you down.* I can hear her thinking the words.

'You know,' she says instead, 'my life is just as fucked up as yours.'

A dark chuckle bubbles up my throat.

'I mean, I endured the same bad things,' she clarifies. 'My parents died, too. I grew up in the same group home. And I don't feel the urge to . . . do what you do.'

'Lucky you.'

'But . . . why?'

I've thought about this a lot. Bad things happen to everyone, but they seem to make some people stronger and break others. Maybe it depends how strong you were to start off with. Thistle was tough, I was weak.

'Maybe it's genetic,' I say.

'But—'

I hold out my hand, stopping her. There's a camera in one of the dogwood trees up ahead. One I hadn't seen before. It's not pointed at us, but it's facing the direction we need to go.

'We can go around,' Thistle says.

'No time.' The sun will rise soon, along with the early-morning-yoga-loving killers. 'And there are others. Hang on.'

I creep up behind the camera and slowly twist it to face a different patch of forest. Hopefully the gradual movement doesn't trigger an alert on anyone's phone. Or if it does, they won't notice that the camera is now monitoring a different group of trees.

We keep moving.

'Do you want to eat me?' Thistle asks carefully.

The hungry half of my brain interprets this as an offer rather than a question. 'No,' I say. 'Part of my condition—'

'Condition,' she echoes dully.

'I don't see people as people. They're just walking, talking meat. But not you.'

'Why not? I'm trying to understand.'

'Maybe because I knew you from before, or because we've been through so much together.'

'Can't you just . . . stop?'

'I've tried.'

The crickets scream around us as we walk. She's slow, because of her bare feet.

'I can't believe I fucked a cannibal,' she says finally.

'Sorry.'

'My old roommate, Julie—she used to say . . . heh.' Thistle starts to laugh. 'She used to say I had terrible "taste" in men.'

I start laughing, too. I can't help it. Neither of us has slept properly in at least forty-eight hours. It's not the joke itself—it's the whole situation. It's so far from funny that it's somehow hilarious. Like those jokes you hear about dead babies, or about 9/11. Laughter is the worst reaction, so it becomes inevitable.

Thistle speaks in between giggles and gasps: 'Stop! They'll hear us!'

'*You* stop!'

Eventually the guffaws die away.

I wipe the tears out of my eyes. 'Come on, we're almost at the car. Can you drive?'

'Why me?'

'Because you might have given me a concussion.' It's hard to be sure in the darkness, but I think my vision is still blurred.

'Sure, I can drive.'

I toss Thistle Fred's keys. The throw is way too wide. The keys hit a tree nearby.

'Yeah, you should definitely not be driving.' She picks up the keys. Her voice goes serious. 'Blake, when we get to Houston . . .'

'You'll have to arrest me. I know.' Thistle's moral compass might actually be the real reason I don't see her as food.

'I'm not like the old director,' Thistle says. 'I can't let you keep doing this.'

'Reese, it's okay. I'll come quietly.' And I will. As long as she's alive, that's all that matters.

She nods slowly. 'All right. Glad to hear it.' She looks at the lightening sky. 'How long do you think it will take those creeps to realise we've escaped?'

'There's a motion sensor at the end of the driveway,' I say. 'They'll be alerted as soon as we cross it. We'll just have to hope this pick-up can outrun their van.'

'Excuse me?' Thistle lowers her voice—we're not far from the house. 'If that's true, they'll be long gone before I can get a SWAT team back here.'

'I know.'

'They'll just set up shop somewhere else.'

'Probably. I think they already have a second location—the website says they're holding a paedophile there.' I don't like the thought of the Guards escaping justice, but I don't see a way around it.

'And what about the other prisoners?'

'What about them?'

'The perps will kill them as soon as they realise we're missing. How are we supposed to get them out of here?'

I shrug helplessly. 'I don't think we can.'

'We can't just let them die.'

'They're murderers,' I say. 'Terrorists. Klansmen.'

'You *eat* people,' she says.

I throw my hands up. 'What do you want me to do? It's nearly dawn. We don't have time to go back for them. Even if we did, the racist ones won't trust you and none of them will trust me.' *Especially not after what I did to Ivy*, I think. 'As soon as we let them loose, they'll scatter every which way, and we'll all get caught.'

'We can call for backup,' Thistle says.

'I don't have a phone, and there's no cell service out here.'

'The perps are running a website. They must have computers and internet. Send an email to the FBI.'

'They have someone in the FBI, remember? That's how they found you. Plus, I don't know if you heard, but the old FBI director was supplying corpses to a cannibal. We shouldn't trust them.'

'What about the county police?'

'I can't email anybody. I'm sure the Guards track all the data coming in and out. I addressed a package to Dr Norman, but they haven't even mailed it yet—'

'You sent an SOS by mail?' Thistle looks incredulous.

'It was all I could think of, okay?'

'All right.' She chews her lip. 'If they send it today, it'll probably arrive on Monday, or Tuesday at the latest—'

'Thistle, they're going to kill you on Sunday. We need to go, right now.'

'I'm not leaving without the others.' She clenches her fist, like she's willing to beat me unconscious and go back for them by herself.

We stare at each other for a long moment.

'Okay,' I say. 'You take the truck. I'll stay in the slaughter-house and defend the prisoners.'

'That's stupid,' she says. 'You're just one guy, with no weapons.'

'I'll try my best.'

'Your best won't be good enough. The perps will eat you alive.'

Ha ha. 'What, then?'

'We go back,' Thistle says. 'You chain me up again.'

'What?!'

'Just listen. We can try this again tomorrow night. That gives—'

'No,' I say. 'I'm not—'

'It gives you all day to figure out how to turn off the motion sensor in the driveway, and it gives me all day to prep the other prisoners. They'll do as we say if they have some warning.'

'The Guards ordered replacement cameras for the slaughterhouse.' I grab her arm. She shakes it off. 'They're supposed to arrive tomorrow. They're going to torture you.'

Thistle swallows. 'I can handle it.'

'We can't stay any longer,' I insist. 'Three people have died since I got here.'

'Wait. Three?'

Hailey must not have told the others about Samson. Maybe she didn't believe me. I quickly explain about the hiker, Zara finding Samson's body, me concluding that he was murdered, and Fred asking me to investigate.

Thistle chews her lip. 'So we have a potential ally. Whoever killed Samson could be on our side.'

'Maybe. But I don't know who that is.'

'Could it be the hiker?'

'I can't figure him out at all. If he is the killer, he had to know where all the cameras were—except he didn't, because we caught him on one the night before. And Samson had to trust him enough to let him in. If that's the case, who is he? And if it's not the case . . .'

'Then who is he?' Thistle finishes.

'Right. And even if he did know Samson, that wouldn't explain how he knew me.'

'So we've got the perps on one side, us and the prisoners on the other, and either one or two unknown parties, depending on whether the hiker and the killer are the same person.' She frowns at the trees.

I've missed this: working with Thistle. I want to say so, but I'm afraid she'll be repulsed.

'I think identifying the killer has to be our top priority,' she says. 'Getting all the prisoners out will be hard. Having an ally could make all the difference.'

'And if they're not an ally?'

'Then we can still use them. If the perps are turning on each other, they might be too busy to notice a prison break brewing. But you need to work out who the killer is, today.'

'Thistle, you don't have to die for those people back there.' I suck in some air, like a deep drag on a cigarette. 'You can just go. I'm begging you—please, just go.'

'You know I can't do that,' she says. And I do. I want her to leave, because I love her. But I love her because she won't leave.

I rub my face. 'All right. Jesus.'

We make our way cautiously back towards the slaughterhouse. The closer we get, the more anxiety calcifies my lungs.

'You haven't asked me about the baby,' Thistle says.

'What baby?'

'The baby they said I killed.'

I glance over. 'I just assumed that was bullshit. Obviously, you didn't kill a baby.'

'No,' Thistle says. 'But I had an abortion.'

'Oh.' I'm not sure what to say to that. It's like when someone says they're pregnant—you're supposed to congratulate them, unless it was an accident, in which case congratulations are the last thing they want to hear. The context for the appropriate response is missing.

Someone who has had an abortion may want sympathy, or even forgiveness—or they may be deeply offended by the presumption that they need either of those things.

'Nothing to do with you,' Thistle adds. 'But I want to know how they found out.'

'Maybe they didn't. It could be a coincidence.'

'Maybe. Or maybe my doctor is one of their customers. Either way, I need to know. Okay?'

I nod. 'I'll see what I can find out. Was this about four years ago?'

She glances sharply at me. 'How did you know that?'

'Just a guess.' Knowing Thistle, if she was having unprotected sex, it was probably with her husband, and if she got an abortion, it was probably just after they split up. 'But it might help me to work out how Fred got the information.'

'January ten,' Thistle says. 'Four years ago next month.'

I keep my eyes down. 'Got it.'

Soon we're back at the slaughterhouse. Thistle's steps slow down as she approaches. Getting chained up in there again probably seemed like a better idea when the building was out of sight. It's all sheet metal and sharp edges, glinting in the rising sun.

'You sure about this?' I say.

'Yes.' She heads for the door, teeth clenched and shivering. Like she's climbing the ladder towards the highest diving board.

I unlock it and pull it open. Just as we're about to go in, she grabs my arm. 'Tell me again that I can trust you.'

'You can trust me,' I say.

'You're coming back to let us all out tomorrow night. Right?'

'Tonight, technically.' It's almost dawn.

'You're not going to switch sides on me?'

'I've always been on your side.'

'Liar.' A joyless smile. 'You've always been on your own side.'

She has a point. But I just risked my life to save her, and I'll do it again, as many times as it takes. The only good things I've ever done, I did for her.

'I'm coming back for you,' I say.

She nods, and then slips into the dark. I follow.

The other prisoners look surprised to see us coming back together. They thought I was going to kill her. Now they probably assume I raped her in the forest. I don't really care what they believe, as long as Thistle can convince them to keep their mouths shut until our next escape attempt.

She doesn't need me to chain her up. 'I have to get back before they realise I'm gone,' I say.

'Okay. Good luck.' Thistle goes to hug me, and then realises she can't bring herself to hug a cannibal. She pats me on the shoulder instead.

I want to wrap my arms around her, in case we don't make it out of this. But there's a wall between us now. One I'll never be permitted to cross.

'You too.' I walk back out into the morning light.

CHAPTER 30

How do two homes become three,
while acquaintances live inside?

When I get back into the house, it's silent. I slowly open Fred's door. He's still asleep, rolled over so I can't see his face.

A sudden bolt of fear. I forgot that Zara saw me take Fred's keys. It wasn't supposed to matter. I expected to be gone by now.

I peer under the bed. She's gone. What will she tell the others?

I tiptoe across the room, lower Fred's keys into the bowl and sneak back out. I need to shower before anyone sees me. I'm still grimy from rolling around in the dirt with Thistle. I grab a change of clothes and a towel from my room, then creep into the bathroom and shut the door.

A shower is a good substitute for sleep. When I turn it on, the steam clears out my sinuses and opens my pores. I close my eyes and step under the flow, rubbing the scalding water into my scalp, scrubbing my armpits with my hands. Trying not to think about how unfair it is that I get this moment of relief while Thistle is stuck out there in the cold.

The bathroom door opens. Someone else is up.

I clear my throat. 'Occupied.' Which is dumb, because they must know that already. The water is making plenty of noise.

No one replies. The door closes again. Has the person left, or are they inside the room?

I listen. There's a soft rustling sound, possibly from outside the door, possibly not. Then just the hissing of the shower.

I leave the water running, wanting whoever it is to think I assume they're gone. Someone has left a razor in a shower caddy, but it's not much of a weapon. I grab the caddy itself—it's stainless steel and heavy enough to do some damage.

Who's out there? Fred, here to punish me for touching Ivy? Donnie, here to kill me after finding out that I tried to get Thistle out of here?

Zara opens the shower curtain and steps in. She's naked. I have to step back to avoid touching her, my buttocks touching the cold tile.

She reaches forwards, testing the water temperature with an open palm, and then steps right into my personal space, the water trickling down her chest.

'About last night,' she says.

I just stare at her.

'In Fred's room,' she prompts. 'I caught you stealing his keys. Remember?'

I clear my throat. 'I caught you stabbing him in his sleep, that's what I remember.'

When someone has information you don't want them to share, your two options are typically threats or bribery. To threaten someone, you need to know what they're afraid of. To bribe them, you need to know what they want. In Zara's case, I know neither.

She squirts some shampoo into her hand and raises both elbows so she can massage it into her scalp. She waits for me to look down.

I don't. But I can sense all the flesh below my eyeline. My stomach growls.

'Are you threatening me?' She smiles, as though daring me to try.

'No. Are you threatening me?'

'No. You can put that down.'

I lean past her and lower the shower caddy onto the floor. She doesn't give me much space to do it.

'I didn't hurt Fred,' she says. 'But I *could* have. I enjoyed the possibility.' She bows, rinsing the shampoo from her hair. 'So what were *you* up to?'

'I wanted some alone time with the lady FBI agent,' I say. 'Away from the other prisoners. I don't like to be watched.'

'Hmm, a private tryst. I like a man with a sense of romance.' She picks up her razor from the caddy and starts shaving her legs.

She's trying to get a rise out of me, literally. But is she doing it for fun, or is she trying to work out what makes me tick?

'I brought her back after,' I say. 'She's locked up again.'

'Is she? You overpowered a strong woman like that, all by yourself?'

I nod.

'Wow. You must be even stronger.' Zara stops shaving and rests a hand on my chest. She can feel my heart racing, but she's probably wrong about the cause.

I'm starving. She's in danger.

The easiest way for Zara to get into Fred's bedroom would be via his bed. 'Won't Fred be angry if he finds us in here together?' Or if he finds Zara dead and me covered in her blood.

'Fred doesn't get angry. It's a point of pride for him.'

'What kind of relationship do you two have?'

'You mean, is it open?'

'I mean, how long have you been together?'

'We're not together. It's a transaction. He's straight, I'm straight.' Her hand traces down my abdomen. Fondles even lower. 'Nice to know that you are, too.'

You'd think that psychopaths would be better at no-strings-attached sex. No emotional connection, no jealousy. But in my experience, they're actually worse at it. Psychopaths are more inclined to see their partners as their property. Something being stolen.

'But the real transaction isn't what he thinks it is.' I try to ignore what her hand is doing. 'Right?'

'How do you mean?'

'He gets to fuck you, and you get to lie there fantasising about hurting him.'

Zara slashes the razor sideways across my belly.

I cry out and jump backwards, banging my head on the tile. The razor is small, so it's not a deep cut, but it stings.

When I look back at Zara, she has one hand between her legs. The other is still holding the razor.

'I'm not into pain,' I say.

'Perfect.' She swipes at me again. I dart sideways, dodging the razor, but I slip on the soapy floor and crash down on top of the shower caddy. A throbbing warmth spreads across my shoulder blade. The falling water blasts my face.

If I screamed, would the others save me? Or would they just enjoy the show?

Zara puts one foot on my chest, pinning me to the floor, holding up the razor like a hunter posing with a kill. All the air is crushed out of my lungs. Maybe this house had other guests before me. Fred invites someone, they come, the other housemates relax them, then Zara kills them after a few days. I just lost a game I didn't know I was playing.

And without me, Thistle dies.

Zara shifts her foot, and pushes her toes into my mouth.

Water floods up my nose and between my lips, choking me. I almost bite down. Only confusion stops me.

Zara wiggles her toes against my tongue, and then shifts her gaze to my hips. Looking for something, and not seeing it.

'Interesting,' she says. Then she steps back, wraps a towel around herself and slips away.

I roll sideways and cough up a lungful of warm, soapy water. The air rushes back into my lungs.

Getting up will hurt, so I lie there for a minute, thinking. Zara has been looking for a way to manipulate me since I got here. I should have given her a fake vulnerability, something she thought she could exploit. Now I'm considered a threat.

I guess she noticed my lack of a reaction when she shoved her foot in my mouth. Maybe I can pretend to have a foot fetish *and* erectile disfunction. Embarrassing, but better than revealing the truth. If she realises I'm a cannibal, that I was trying to *eat* Samson's foot, she will also realise I'm not Lux.

Then it won't be her coming to join me in the shower with a razor. It'll be Donnie with a baseball bat.

•

Fred is in the kitchen, making coffee.

'Morning, Lux,' he says.

I yawn. 'Morning.' The adrenaline crash after getting slashed in the shower, coupled with a sleepless night, is killing me.

'Coffee?' Fred asks. He has a cup already.

'Sure.'

'Help yourself.' He steps aside.

I put a cup under the nozzle and try to work out what the next step is. I only drink instant coffee at home.

'You called the FBI agent a baby killer,' I say, as I look for some kind of *make coffee* button.

Fred points. 'You have to tip the old grounds out and put more in.'

'Oh. Thanks. I knew that.' I cough. 'Paradox. I'm only mentally capable of making coffee after I've already had coffee.'

'Heh.'

I tamp down the grounds, like I've seen baristas do. 'So did she really kill a baby?'

'Well, a foetus. A few years back.'

Something doesn't fit here. Fred and his team are environmentalists, vegetarians, campaigners against rape and racism. Hailey, the KKK Queen, is here because she advocated the killing of abortion doctors. Imprisoning a Black woman for terminating a pregnancy seems . . . off-brand.

Then again, I noticed that the inmates are mostly women or people of colour. While all the Guards are male except for Zara, and white except for Cedric, who they seem to ignore most of the time. Their commitment to equality is just an excuse for violence, although I doubt they realise it.

'How did you find out?' I ask. It takes me a second to remember the private investigator's name. 'Druznetski?'

Fred chuckles. 'Right. Druznetski.' He sips his coffee, then adds some more cream. 'Medical records. There was a big data breach last year. I bought all the files on the dark web. Hundreds of thousands of patients. Your girl was among them. The company fixed the vulnerability but never notified the patients.' He shakes his head. 'Despicable.'

'Yeah,' I say. 'Goddamn big business.'

'Anyway, breaches like that are super useful. A couple of years ago we got fourteen million Texas voter records. Just recently we got the phone numbers and locations of four hundred and nineteen million Facebook users. There was a law enforcement one just before that, with tens of thousands of cases going back a decade. That was *very* useful.'

'For finding more victims?' I say. 'I mean, inmates?'

Fred smiles. 'I call them "talent". But no, the data is mostly for the riot.'

He starts washing his cup in the sink.

TV shows are full of moments like this, when one person says something deliberately vague and someone else asks for clarification. 'How could you?' one character will demand angrily, just so the other character can say, 'How could I do what?'

In real life, people speak to be understood. Fred isn't waiting for me to ask, 'What riot?' He thinks I already know.

'Oh, right. How is that going?' I ask instead, trying not to sound alarmed.

'Yeah, it's ready to rock,' Fred says. 'But I can always use more material—to make it bigger, more effective.'

At the FBI, I hunted kidnappers and crime bosses and serial killers, but never revolutionaries. I don't know anything about how riots are started or, I now realise, how they are stopped.

'So what did you and Zara talk about?' Fred turns to face me. 'In the shower.'

He's caught me off guard, and he knows it. His gaze is suddenly less friendly.

He must have seen Zara leaving the bathroom, and then me. Or maybe she told him, when I spurned her 'advances'. There are several different ways I could play this, none of them good. Too many angles. Not enough information.

'We talked about boundaries,' I hear myself say. 'I don't know what the rules are here. But I'm not used to people coming into the bathroom while I'm in there.'

Fred takes a step in. Enough that I can sense his physical presence, but not so much that it's definitely a threat. Zara may not be good at boundaries, but he is.

'I don't get angry,' he says, as Zara promised he would. 'Not since group. But that doesn't mean I'm a pushover. Yesterday it was Ivy, today it's Zara. I like you, Lux— but I don't like the idea of you getting naked with my girlfriend.'

'Is your *girlfriend* clear on that?'

He purses his lips, like a chimpanzee about to throw a punch. 'Are we going to have a problem?'

'You and me?' I say. 'Never. Bros before hos.'

Fred barks out a laugh, shattering the tension. 'Cool. Listen, I need a favour.'

Fred has a complicated dance. Friendliness, oblique threats, favours. But I'm starting to learn the steps.

I blow some cool air on my coffee and take a sip. 'What can I do for you?'

'When you go with Kyle to the post office today,' Fred says, 'can you watch him?'

I realise that I never told Thistle that Kyle might be my son. Maybe I forgot. Or maybe I just didn't want her to know he existed. I'll let her arrest me, but I'm not sure I want her to arrest him.

'To make sure he does it right?' I ask.

'No. Well, yes, but I've been thinking.' Fred lowers his voice. 'You know the hiker?'

I see where this is going. 'You think he came here to meet somebody.'

'It makes sense, doesn't it?'

It does, especially after finding the file about Donnie in the fireplace. Maybe the hiker brought the file here and gave it to someone, who read it and burned it. Not Fred, who would have used his paper shredder instead. Not Donnie, who was the subject.

I put the coffee cup down. 'You think it might be Kyle.'

'He has been acting weird lately.' Fred leans over the bench, resting on his knuckles like a general examining a map. 'Will you let me know if he makes contact with anybody at the post office?'

I need to identify the killer before tonight's escape attempt. Kyle and the hiker are two of my suspects. If they're connected . . .

'I'll keep an eye on him,' I say.

CHAPTER 31

What happens at ten o'clock and at again at two o'clock, but simultaneously?

'How does the driveway sensor work?' I ask.

Kyle turns the wheel and the van rumbles out onto the dirt road. 'I don't know. Infrared?'

'Is there just the one?'

'Sensor?'

'Right.'

'Just the one, yeah. Tied to a tree a few feet in. Why?'

I think of the second box I saw, camouflaged, a little deeper in the woods. Is it not a motion sensor—or does it not belong to the Guards?

'Just doesn't seem very secure,' I say. 'What if someone snuck up behind it and turned it off?'

'Can't do that,' Kyle says. 'It would ping all our phones, same as driving past it.'

'Oh. But you can turn it off in the editing room, right?'

He frowns. 'Why do you want to know that?'

'Good point.' I force a chuckle. 'If an intruder broke into the house and turned it off there, we'd have way bigger problems than an unprotected driveway.'

Kyle laughs uncertainly. 'Sure.'

This time the van turns left when it reaches the highway, away from Houston. I guess we're going somewhere smaller. Maybe a town where the post office is so desperate for business that the owner will choose not to be suspicious.

I watch the entrance to the dirt road shrinking in the rear-view mirror. Thistle is back there, with Donnie, Zara, Cedric and Fred. They could do anything to her while I'm gone. I've bitten all my nails down to the quick, so now I start picking at the scabs on my arms.

Kyle drives both proudly and self-consciously. For the first half of the journey he rests one cocky hand on the wheel, leaving the other drumming his leg in time to the music. Then, when he's sick of trying to impress me, he reverts to ten o'clock and two o'clock, his driving lessons only just beneath the surface.

I've been trying to work out how to get Kyle talking about his background. Was he capable of killing Samson? Could it have been a hate crime? And is it really possible that he's my son?

It turns out no subterfuge is necessary. Being a teenager, Kyle rambles about himself throughout the journey with minimal prompting.

'It wasn't a big deal, dropping out of high school,' he says. 'Not like I was learning anything there anyway. I was surrounded by fucking morons. Not just the students, either. I had this one teacher, Mrs Spaniucci? She didn't even know when the Vietnam War ended.' This seventeen-year-old shakes his head in despair at what the world is coming to.

'Was she your history teacher?' I ask.

'No. Math.' Then he catches the implication. 'But she still should have known.'

When people say the world is full of morons, what they really mean is, *I'm smarter than everyone else.* I had that attitude once—and I spent years getting outsmarted by people I had underestimated.

Now I'm not sure idiots exist. Or geniuses, either. A brilliant programmer might make a crappy CEO. A great songwriter might be a hopeless husband.

A skilled FBI consultant might be a terrible father.

'What school did you go to?' I ask.

'Ackerly High. Why?'

I want to know if he was born in Houston, where I donated sperm, or if he and his mom spent their whole lives in Ackerly. 'Just wondering. I had a Mrs Spaniucci at my school, too. But I went to South Houston High.' None of this is true.

'Really? Was she a moron?'

'Not that I could tell. Did you ever live anywhere else? Or your mom?'

He shoots me a suspicious look. 'Why are you asking about my mom?'

'Just making conversation.' I turn back to the window and watch the wasteland flit by. I want to know about the woman with whom I might have fathered a child. But I can tell Kyle will shut down if I ask more questions about her.

'Anyway, she died,' Kyle says eventually. He can't take the silence. Can't retreat into his phone, since he's driving. 'Mrs Spaniucci, I mean. She got shot.'

'At your school?'

'No. Ordering food at a drive-through. The American Civil Liberties Union tried to have it classified as a hate crime, but they couldn't prove the guy who did it had heard her accent. Anyway, it sounded like she was being a total bitch. Holding up the line, you know. Nothing to do with where she came from.'

'Where *did* she come from?'

Kyle shrugs. 'What am I, a geography teacher?'

Two hours later we reach the town. I expected a sign with a name and population size, maybe a corny motto, but there isn't one. This place is too small even for that. It's really just five buildings around a crossing. On one corner, a middle-of-nowhere bar with crumbling wooden walls and dark windows. The sort of place that would go out of business if drink-driving laws were even half-assedly enforced. On the opposite corner, a feed store with a tractor parked out front, and a gas station with rust creeping up the sides of the pumps. Lacy curtains in the window indicate that the gas station is also a cafe. The feed store is closed, even though it's a weekday, heavy shutters over the doors. Next is a general store, with racks of newspapers, potato chip packets and candy bars out the front. *I didn't realise they still made 3 Musketeers*, I think, then I realise they probably don't. These candy bars might have been here since the nineties.

Then there's the post office. A little concrete box, unlike the wood and aluminium structures around it, as though it was built to withstand hurricanes. Some kind of nationwide standardisation, maybe. A faded sign above has both the UPS and FedEx logos.

Kyle parks fifty yards away. 'Not so far that it's suspicious, not so close that the truck will show up on cameras,' he says.

'Smart,' I say, pleased that Kyle has some sense, some critical thinking. There are no morons.

'Yeah, Fred told me to do it that way,' Kyle says.

Oh.

We get out into the frosty air. Even the weak winter sunshine feels painfully bright after all that time in the woods. It wasn't exactly dark in the eco-home, but the downlights only shone on certain parts. The dining table, the kitchen bench and the art on the walls all glowed, leaving the people in the shadows. I remember hearing about a study that showed people behaved less honestly in darkened environments. The Guards want everything exposed except themselves.

Kyle opens the back of the van. He unfolds a trolley, extends the handle on telescopic poles, and starts stacking boxes onto the steel flap at the bottom. He moves quickly and diligently, without asking for help. I'm proud of him for working hard, and then I remember that the work is mailing videos of torture to lunatics.

I pick up a box. Envelopes stuffed with USB sticks jostle inside. 'Let me give you a hand.'

'Sure, whatever.' He steps aside so I can add the box to his stack. He squints into the empty van. 'Not a huge delivery today. Weird that Fred sent you to help me.'

'Maybe he's hoping I'll learn from you,' I suggest.

Kyle brightens. 'Maybe.'

He wheels the trolley along the dirt towards the post office. The dirt becomes sidewalk about ten feet from the door. No graffiti or gum stuck to the concrete. No kids in this 'town'.

We get to the front door of the post office. There's a tub of B-grade romance and C-grade crime novels under the window with a sign that says, *$2.*

'You want to stay behind?' Kyle asks. 'Be the van guard?'

'Ha. That's clever.'

He looks blank.

'Because vanguard means the opposite of "stay behind",' I prompt.

He doesn't seem to understand. 'Are you coming in, or what?'

'I'll come in.'

A bell jingles as Kyle pushes open the door.

There's a security camera right above our heads, another one behind the counter and a third in the corner of the store. With half of rural America now addicted to opioids, this place probably gets robbed from time to time.

I look at the closest camera and give it a meaningful nod. If any of my former colleagues from the FBI ends up watching, I want them to think I'm here undercover and I'm still on their side. Which I am. Sort of.

The store seems to be forty per cent newsagent, fifty per cent gift shop, ten per cent post office. The post office part is right up the back. To get to it, Kyle has to manoeuvre the trolley between two shelves of magazines and past a display of Valentine's Day chocolates that are either two months early or ten months late.

A dapper little Native American woman is behind the counter. Silver chains dangle from her ears and there's an opal pin in her inky hair. Her faded name badge says *Sue.* She looks relieved to see us—we might be her first customers all day. All week, maybe.

'Hello, James,' she says to Kyle. 'How are you today?'

Kyle gives me a smug look. *I'm so clever. I have a false identity.* 'I'm spectacular,' he tells her. 'How are you?'

'You know: busy, busy.' Sue sweeps an ironic glance across the empty store. 'Those chocolates probably need dusting.'

When salespeople joke with customers, it always seems desperate, pleading, no matter how clever the joke or careful the delivery. The customer has money and the salesperson wants it. Knowing that agenda turns the humour sour.

Then again, I'm rarely the customer. When I am, I'm not considered important enough to joke with. Maybe the jokes seem sad to me because I'm not the audience.

Kyle opens the first box and starts passing padded envelopes over the counter. The woman scans them and dumps them straight in a mailbag. The process is quick. Hopefully too quick for Kyle to notice that one package has a handwritten label.

'How's the mouse-trap business?' Sue asks.

'We've expanded,' Kyle says. 'We're getting rid of pantry moths now.'

'Ugh, I have those.'

'Well, now you know who to call.' Kyle holds up one of the packages. 'Stick one of these in your pantry, and they'll be gone within a week.'

'I might just do that. Who's your friend?'

'Timothy Blake, ma'am,' I say. 'Nice to meet you.'

Kyle looks impressed that I came up with the name so quickly.

Sue keeps scanning packages. 'Are you James's new hire?'

'No,' I say. 'Just helping out for the day. I'm his uncle.'

'Oh!' Sue looks us both up and down. 'Yes, I see the resemblance.'

Kyle coughs into his fist. 'Excuse me.' He sounds offended, and now so am I.

'And what do you do, Mr Blake?'

'I'm a civilian consultant for the FBI.'

Kyle kicks me under the counter.

'Really?' Sue asks, eyes wide.

'Off-duty today, though,' I say. 'So if you see any crime, call someone else!' I laugh too loudly.

'Uncle Tim, you're a riot,' Kyle says, through clenched teeth. 'But we gotta get this done.'

'I know, I know.'

The next package Kyle picks up has a handwritten label.

I grab an object at random from the stand next to the counter: a bar of handmade lavender soap. 'Hey, check these out. Should we take one home?'

The distraction doesn't work. Kyle is about to hand the package to Sue, but he hesitates when he notices the label. 'Huh.'

Sue looks curious. 'Something wrong?'

'Oh, that's my fault,' I say. 'I tore the printed label. Had to write a new one. Sorry.'

'Justice Park Drive,' Kyle reads. 'Houston.'

If he flips it over, he'll see the coordinates I wrote under my name.

'Isn't that an FBI office?' Sue asks me. Damn her and her good memory.

'You bet.' I take the package before Kyle can turn it over. My heart is hammering. 'No pantry moths there, not since they started buying these. Right, James?'

'Right.' Kyle looks uneasy. Maybe realising that the Guards do have customers at the FBI, and that it's not smart to chat with Sue about that at length.

I hand over the package, keeping the side with the return coordinates hidden from Kyle. Sue scans it. When it disappears into the bag, I can breathe again.

We unpack the rest of the boxes and Sue scans the last of the packages. She asks if Kyle wants them mailed by air, or wants signature on delivery, and he says no. I know why—he would need to show ID if the parcels were travelling by air, and the Guards' customers would need to show theirs if they were signing for these packages.

Kyle pays in cash. Sue glances at me before accepting, like this might be a sting.

So she hasn't fallen for Kyle's pantry moth ruse. She knows he's breaking the law somehow. But she's pretending she doesn't. I imagine her lying to the police—*I'm shocked. I had no idea he was doing anything illegal.*

'Mind if I have a look at the magazines, son?' I ask. The last word just slips out.

'Sure.' If Kyle's noticed that I called him *son* rather than *nephew*, he doesn't say.

I go and pretend to examine the magazines while he pays. Sue seems happy to take his money while I'm not looking.

One of the tattoo magazines catches my eye. There's a shirtless man on the cover with ink all the way from his jawline to his wrists. Like a beautifully decorated cake.

The novelty is appealing. When I was eating death-row inmates, I rarely got the tattooed ones, because they tended to have blood diseases. I wonder if I could taste the ink in this man's skin.

'Good to go?' Kyle asks.

My gaze snaps up. 'What? Yeah. Let's go.'

I go to put the magazine back. 'Take it,' Sue says. 'It's yours.'

I hesitate. 'You sure?'

'Of course! Take some soap, too. An uncle of James is an uncle of mine.' She laughs, but I can see through it: that desperation no one else ever seems to see or care about.

This is a bribe. The only one she can afford.

'Well, okay,' I say. 'Thank you very much. See you next time.'

'Merry Christmas,' she says, as we walk out. I know it's Friday, but I have no idea what the date is. Is it Christmas? The days have all smeared across each other in a paste of exhaustion and panic.

'What the fuck was that?' Kyle says as we walk back to the van. He's carrying another box, about the size of a milk crate, sealed with packing tape. Supplies for the house, I guess.

'What?'

'Wasn't Timothy Blake the name of the real FBI consultant? I didn't recognise it right away, but—'

'That's the point,' I say. 'When the police go looking for him, his last known whereabouts will be at this post office— not buried out in the woods. It'll throw them off the scent.'

'It'll lead them away from the woods but towards *us*.'

I hope so. 'We're a hundred miles from the house,' I say. 'You gave a false name at the post office. Trust me, for the cops, this lead will be a dead end.'

'What about the cameras at the post office? Do you look anything like the real Timothy Blake?'

'There's a passing resemblance,' I say. 'But Sue probably only keeps the recordings for a week or two. There would be too much data to store otherwise.'

This is probably true, but I hope it isn't. I want Sue to be suspicious enough that she calls the FBI to see if Timothy Blake is a real civilian consultant there. I want my name to ring alarm bells. I want the feds to come here and follow our trail all the way back to the house. If I don't live long enough to save Thistle, I still want her to have a chance.

'What's in the box?' I ask, as Kyle dumps it in the back of the van. It looks heavy.

'The new cameras,' he says.

I find myself taking a step back, as though the box is a time bomb. Today is Friday. The cameras I sabotaged on Monday night have been replaced.

The torture can start again.

In my head I see Donnie, spinning that battleaxe in his hands and whistling.

On the drive back, Kyle glances over at the magazine on my lap. The half-naked man on the cover.

'So,' he says. 'You're queer.'

It's such an old man word, coming out of a young man's mouth, that I'm taken aback. 'Excuse me?'

'I mean you're part of the queer community,' he says. 'Right? I notice you don't have any tatts yourself.'

'Maybe I just like art.'

'Relax. I'm cool with it.' He smiles benevolently, like this makes him a saint.

I'm not sure why I don't want Kyle thinking I'm gay. Maybe it's some latent homophobia on my part. Or maybe he's the only Guard I feel bad about lying to.

'I didn't even want the magazine,' I say, dropping it on the floor between my feet. 'I was just trying to give you some cover.'

'Uh-huh,' he says, not believing me. 'Listen, you're in good company. Donnie's gay. Samson was too.'

'I'm not gay. I . . . Wait, were Donnie and Samson in a relationship?'

'Yeah. You didn't know that?'

'No.' I hope this isn't a dangerous thing to admit. But I certainly didn't see any overt signs that they were together.

It makes sense, though. Cedric's voice in my head: *But when everyone else got up, Samson acted like nothing had happened.* Samson didn't want to own up to his night of passion with Cedric, because he was already in a relationship with Donnie.

Kyle looks wistfully out the window. 'Love at first sight, Donnie always said. But then he'd flex his muscles, like he was talking about how Samson fell in love with him, not the other way around.'

The odds are shifting around in my head. If Donnie found out Samson had slept with Cedric, that might have made him angry.

Maybe angry enough to put a gun to Samson's head and pull the trigger.

'I'll miss Samson,' Kyle continues. 'He was a great cook. He helped out with the inmates. And he didn't try to compete for the only pussy in the house.'

He laughs, as though it's fine to say that as long as you're kidding.

'Don't say things like that,' I say.

He scoffs. 'What are you, my dad? I was joking.'

'No, you weren't.'

Kyle looks annoyed but says nothing. The way young men talk is always grating, but I find it particularly hard to take from Kyle. I want him to be better than the others.

'Zara's dangerous,' I add. 'If I were you, I'd steer clear.'

'Oh, yeah? How about you follow your own advice?'

There's a hint of bitterness in his voice. He's interested in Zara, and he's seen her flirting with me. Fred did say Kyle had been acting strangely—maybe that's why.

Kyle is still talking. I tune in to hear him say: 'Except for the old lady.'

'Old lady?' I say.

'Yeah. The only other pussy in the house. Technically.'

I stare at him. 'An old lady lives in the house?'

Kyle looks at me like I'm an idiot. 'Duh. Who did you think was upstairs?'

CHAPTER 32

A writer from New York realises something
and drops me. What am I?

Back at the house, I stand at the foot of the narrow stairs—
the ones Fred told me not to go up. I think of the creaking
sounds I've been hearing.

An extra person has been here this whole time. A suspect
I hadn't even considered.

Zara's out harvesting yeast. Donnie is servicing the
pick-up. Everyone else is installing the new cameras in
the slaughterhouse. There will never be a better time to see
what's up here. I grip the polished wooden bannister and
climb the stairs.

A sharp bend makes each step narrow on the left and
wide on the right. It's disorienting. Like I'm climbing up
into another dimension, with different laws of geometry.

At the top of the stairs is a flimsy wooden door. There's
no keyhole. Whoever's up here, they're not locked in.

I tap my knuckles on the door. It quivers.

There's silence. For a moment, I wonder if the 'old lady'
is Kyle's alter ego, or a skeleton in a cotton shift and a wig.

Then someone calls out, 'Yes?'

A sharp voice. Female.

I open the door.

The bedroom beyond is lit only by a small window over-looking the driveway. There's an old-fashioned bed with brass fittings. The ceiling is only inches above my head, its weight pressing down.

A woman in her early sixties is sitting at a writing desk, wearing a pale blue robe. Her hair is long and grey. Sunken green eyes in a round face. She swivels in her chair to face me.

'Who are you?' she asks.

I clear my throat. 'I'm Lux.'

'What brings you here, Lux?'

'I arrived on Monday,' I say.

'I know. I saw.' She points her pen out the little window. 'But that doesn't really answer my question, does it?'

'I guess not,' I say. 'Sorry, ma'am.'

The woman lays her pen atop the papers covering her desk. Bowls are stacked on one side. I remember Fred at dinner, eating from one bowl and leaving the other untouched.

'Did Frederick send you?' she asks.

'No,' I say. 'Actually, he said not to come up here.'

'But you did anyway.'

'I did.' She's already set up the rhythm of this conver-sation. Controlling its structure, if not its content. 'You're Fred's mother?'

'Correct. Welcome to my home. Can I get you something to drink?'

'Uh, no, thank you.'

'I was joking.' She gestures at the little room, which has no refrigerator or glassware, although I assume the doorway in the corner leads to an ensuite. 'What do you want?'

I speak carefully. 'Did you know someone was murdered downstairs?'

'My son informed me that there had been a suicide.' She speaks like a school principal, her age creating a sense of authority rather than weakness.

'Fred thinks Samson might have been murdered,' I say. 'He asked me to help him work out who did it, and why.'

I realise my mistake, but too late to stop the words coming out of my mouth. Fred spotted the signs of murder as fast as I did and asked me to investigate almost immediately. There would have been no time to talk to his mother in between. Therefore, when he told her it was a suicide, he already knew it was murder. He lied, and I just exposed him.

But his mother doesn't look surprised. She didn't believe him anyway. 'Is that so?' she says. 'Interesting. How do you two know each other?'

'We met on the internet,' I say. 'Can I ask you some questions?'

'About what?'

'Did you hear any voices before the gunshot on Tuesday?'

'I didn't hear any gunshot.'

I raise my eyebrows. 'Really?'

'I sleep pretty heavily.'

'It was the middle of the day,' I say.

'Time doesn't matter much up here.'

I look down at the floor. Fred's bedroom would be directly below my feet and Samson's was next door. Is it really possible that this old woman didn't hear the shot?

'Do you have trouble with your hearing?' I ask.

The woman avoids the question. 'It's interesting that Fred asked *you* to investigate, rather than any of the other people in the house. He must really trust you. You met on the internet, you say?'

I feel like she's learning more about me than I am about her in this conversation. 'What's your name, ma'am?'

'Oh, I'm Penny,' she says. 'Forgive me, it's been a long time since I've had to introduce myself to anyone.'

'Do the others know you're up here?'

'They know, yes,' Penny says. 'But they may have forgotten. It's surprisingly easy to forget about a woman you never see, even if she lives right above your head.'

She doesn't sound bitter about this. It's as though she prefers to be invisible.

'You never come down?' I ask.

'No. Aren't you going to ask me if I saw anyone approaching the house around the time of Samson's death?'

'*Did* you see anyone?'

'I did not,' she says, and leaves a significant pause. She's trying to tell me that the killer is one of the Guards, which I had already surmised.

'You were looking out the window the whole time?'

She looks pleased. 'That's more like it. No, I was not.'

'How long have you lived up here?' I ask.

She points to some notches carved into the wall. There are hundreds, and I don't know if they measure days or weeks.

'You have paper to write on,' I point out.

'Old habits,' she says. 'Sit down, Lux.' It doesn't sound as if she likes the name.

I approach. The floorboards don't squeak under me, even though I'm heavier than her.

I sit on the bed, which lets out a sick moan and a bad smell. No fancy memory foam up here.

'If you really want to solve this,' Penny says, 'you'll have to pay attention not only to what you hear, but what you don't.'

She clearly knows something. I see no reason not to just ask what it is. 'Do you know who killed Samson?'

Penny raises her eyebrows. 'I haven't left this room in years. How could I know anything?'

So she knows something she doesn't want to share, at least not directly. The best way to find out what it is might just be to let her talk.

'Perhaps you'll save me some counting and tell me the date,' she says.

I've been thinking about it since Sue wished me a Merry Christmas. 'December seventeen.'

'Ah.' Penny looks up at the ceiling. 'Frederick will be twenty-eight soon. If his father and I were still together, last week would have been our thirtieth wedding anniversary.'

'Is Fred's father still alive?'

Penny shrugs and gestures at the room. As if to say again, *How could I know?*

'You're divorced?'

'Neither of us underestimated how hard it would be to raise a child, but both of us overestimated our own strength. Being a man, he felt like he could leave.' She says all this impatiently. It's not what she wants to talk about. 'Anyway, I used to be a police officer. Did my son tell you that?'

'He's told me nothing,' I say, suddenly uneasy.

Penny notices this, and smiles. 'Don't worry. I'm not going to rat you out for coming up here. I appreciate the company.

And as for whatever's going on in the shed, well ... who would I call, and how? You boys have your fun.'

I wonder how much she knows, and how much she's chosen not to.

'Anyway, I have a test case for you,' she says. 'One from my own experience.'

I'm starting to fall behind. 'A test?'

'Obviously, I need to assess your skill as an investigator. To confirm that you're good enough to assist my son.'

I've never seen someone's eye twinkle in real life, but if it were possible, she'd be doing it.

'Okay.' The bed hasn't been made since she last slept in it. The intimacy makes me uncomfortable. I find myself smoothing down the sheets.

'I entered the crime scene at nine thirty-five pm,' Penny begins. 'The bathroom door was locked from the inside. I had to break it down to get in—'

'Wait, what crime scene?' I ask.

'A woman in an adjacent apartment heard shouting,' Penny says. 'A male voice. Then she noticed that the shower had been running for a long time. The pipes went right behind her wall. When she called 911, I was nearby.'

'This is a true story?'

'Yes. There was a thirty-six-year-old male in the shower, deceased. Naked. Blood running down the drain from a head injury. It was concealed by his hair, but the autopsy later confirmed a cracked skull.'

'How much did he weigh?'

'Around two hundred pounds. Why?'

'Just trying to picture it,' I say.

'When my partner arrived at ten oh seven, we found a smudge of blood on a cracked tile, about two feet above the floor. Soap on the floor and on the bottoms of his feet. What does that sound like to you?'

She wants me to say it sounds like the man slipped in the shower. 'Any windows?' I ask instead.

'No.'

'Extractor fan?'

'Switched on.'

Even if the killer—if there was a killer—had climbed up into the vent, they wouldn't have been able to switch on the fan afterwards.

'How big was it?'

She can see what I'm getting at. 'Apparently untouched, and too narrow to crawl through in any case.'

'Who was he? The dead man.'

'Lionel Swaize. Recently released from jail. You ever heard the term "chomo"?'

I nod. It's what they call child molesters in prison.

'Well, that's what he was. You want the details?'

I don't. I'm not even sure what the point of this conversation is. 'Was he married? Living with anyone?'

'No. He didn't seem to have any friends, either.'

'Parents?'

'His father was dead. Cirrhosis. His mother lived in a dementia ward.'

'He sounds isolated,' I say.

'Very.' There's that near-twinkle again.

'Did his victims or their families live nearby?'

'Sounds like you're looking for someone with a motive, Lux,' Penny says. 'Do I need to remind you that the bathroom door was locked from the inside when I arrived?'

'He can't have served much time,' I say, 'if he was only thirty-six.'

'He got off lightly, in my opinion. Seven years, out in five. He got some good character references from friends.'

'You said he didn't have any friends.'

'Maybe they were more like debtors.'

'He was owed money?'

'Not money. Just . . . social capital. He'd been supportive in his community. After providing character references, these people felt like they were square, and they disappeared. No contact with him during his sentence or, as far as I could tell, after his release.'

'The neighbour who heard the shouting,' I say. 'Did she see anybody hanging around beforehand? Listening, waiting for the shower to start?'

'She told my partner she'd seen a woman in the hall, but wasn't sure if she was visiting him or someone else. She couldn't provide much of a description. I quote: "Brown hair, maybe?"'

'What about when she heard the shouting? Did she hear any words?'

'She heard him shout, "What the hell?"'

'Doesn't sound like something you'd say if you just slipped over.'

'Swaize's TV was on quite loud. It's possible that's what she heard.'

'Who takes a shower and leaves the TV on?'

Penny acknowledges this point with a nod.

'How'd you get into the apartment?' I ask.

'Snap gun.'

'But you had to break down the bathroom door?'

'Different kind of lock,' Penny says. 'Just a slide bolt, on the inside.'

'Well, then, it seems pretty obvious what happened,' I say.

She gives me an amused look. 'It does?'

'Sure. After murdering Swaize, the killer put a spring inside the slide-bolt mechanism, then held the bolt in the open position with a credit card. Then they stepped out, closed the door and removed the card so the bolt slid into place, locking the door. The spring fell out and rolled down the drain, disposing of the evidence.' I shrug. 'I hope you didn't waste your whole career on this case.'

There's a pause, and then Penny bursts out laughing. 'Is that really what you think happened?'

'No,' I say. 'I think you killed him.'

This has the desired effect. Penny's composed expression falls away for a split second, and I see the person behind it. I get a sense of loneliness and anger, which soon settles into annoyance. 'Oh. My son already told you.'

'No,' I say. 'But it's the obvious solution, if there really was no other way out. I don't know how you got caught, though.'

We look at each other for a long moment. Penny leans back in her swivel chair.

'How do you know I got caught?' she asks.

I point to the notches on the wall. An old habit from when she was in prison, with the chomos.

'Well, then,' she says, 'let me tell you a story.'

CHAPTER 33

I feed and shelter the living even
as I eat the dead. What am I?

Penny was walking around in circles at one in the morning, rocking the baby, mumbling nonsense under her breath because she had long since run out of songs. His cries occasionally subsided into unhappy little gurgles, but whenever she thought about putting him back in the crib, it was like he could read her mind—the screaming would ramp right up again.

'At eight months old,' she tells me, 'Frederick was already painfully heavy. He would only let me carry him with my left arm. Do you know how hard it is to do everything one-handed? Every day my shoulder blades were a little further apart, my neck a little creakier. I used to limp around like a pterodactyl.'

It wasn't a sudden bathtub-Eureka moment—more like a rising tide. A thought that became a notion that became an idea that became a plan that became an obsession, all in the space of one sleepless night.

She could kill someone.

She wouldn't, of course. But she *could*. Penny had been a police officer for nine years, and a damned good one. She hoped to go back to it, once she worked out what to do with the kid during the day. Mostly the criminals were dumb as rocks. It was almost offensive, how little credit they gave the police. They barely bothered to cover their tracks.

Two years ago she had busted a car thief. Not knowing how to hotwire a car, he'd stolen the driver's keys instead. Then he'd just driven the car around Houston like it was his. He didn't take it to a chop shop. He didn't change the plates. He just rolled down the window and smugly insisted that it wasn't stolen, even when Penny pointed out that the real owner's name and address were on a tag dangling from the keys.

Penny would do much better. If she committed a crime— hypothetically—there would be no evidence at all.

There was no sense risking her career on a petty crime. 'Go big or go home,' her husband always told her. He'd said it when ordering at the steakhouse, back when they could still afford to go to restaurants. He'd said it when they decided to have a baby. Then he'd left her alone with a two-month-old. He went big, then went home.

What would her method be? *If* she did this. Which she wouldn't, of course. Thinking about it was just a way to pass the time.

At seven years old, Penny had started stealing tattered mystery novels out of the cabinet in her mother's study. She had been convinced that her mother would be horrified to learn she was reading them, although when she became an actual police detective she realised how tame the books had been.

Her favourites were the locked-room mysteries. In *Blood and Water*, a man stabbed himself with a knife made of ice, hoping to frame his neighbour for his murder. The ice melted before the police arrived. In *The Squeaking Pulley*, the killer was a child, small enough to escape through the dumb waiter. In *The Black Noose*, the victim appeared to have vanished into thin air, but was later discovered jammed in the chimney—the killer had tried to pull him up using a rope around his neck and he had gotten stuck halfway.

Penny couldn't read, these days. Reading required concentration. Concentration required sleep. The baby had taken even that from her. But she still had fond memories of those locked-room mysteries.

That had to be her method. A dead man in a sealed room, so the police would be forced to conclude accidental death.

It was hard to choose a victim. She knew so many lowlifes who had escaped justice in the corrupt Texas court system. But Penny didn't want to cause any unnecessary suffering. She would pick someone with no dependents, no friends. Someone nobody would miss.

Pretty soon, she had narrowed it down to three men. One had punched his wife and received a reduced sentence after signing up for a twelve-step program and convincing a judge that his wife had attacked him first. Another owned a small building in which hundreds of tenants lived and ate for 'free'—provided they worked with hazardous chemicals for twelve hours a day. The third candidate was a paedophile named Lionel Swaize.

In the end, Penny picked the paedophile, because she hadn't been the lead investigator on that case. She had only

met Swaize once, when raiding his apartment with a bunch
of other officers. She did a mental walkthrough of the place.
Where was the front door? Where was the bedroom? Had
there been a lock on the bathroom door?

There had. She was sure of it. *But none of this is real*,
she reminded herself. These thoughts were just harmless
diversions, while she waited for Frederick to sleep.

Her baby screamed and screamed.

Eight months later, Penny was outside Swaize's second-
storey apartment, waiting for his shower to start. His front
door had been repainted. Hopefully the interior layout was
the same, and the lock on the bathroom hadn't been replaced.

She didn't think anything would have changed. She had
been digging into Swaize's bank records. He was living
month to month. He didn't have the money for substantial
renovations.

She was wearing her workout gear. She'd signed up with
the gym across the street, with the not-untrue excuse that the
police gym was full of sexist, handsy a-holes. Today, she'd
used her key to get into the gym and then slipped out the fire
exit at the back. As far as the security camera out front was
concerned, she was still in there.

This project had remained a game when she researched
Swaize. It had remained a game when she drove past his
building, checking for security cameras. It was a game
when she requisitioned the snap gun for Friday's raid on
the brothel, even though today was only Wednesday. It was
a game when she dropped off Frederick at her mother's
place this morning, not even really seeing him as he waved
goodbye, already thinking about the murder. It was still
a game when she watched Swaize pull into the parking lot,

his hands still dirty from his job at the Texaco. Even now, while she waited outside his door, it could still be a game. She hadn't done anything illegal yet.

A woman was looking at her. A neighbour, unlocking her door with a bag of groceries under one arm. Penny turned her face away, resisting the urge to touch her Mariah Carey wig. She pulled her radio out of her backpack—from a distance it looked like one of those new cellular phones. She started a pretend conversation, affecting a thick Boston accent. 'I'm at thirty-one, but no one's answering. What?' She started walking away. 'You said thirty-one! Yeah, you did. Shoot. Okay, I'll be right down.'

By the time she looked back, the neighbour had disappeared back into her apartment.

And Swaize's shower had started.

After that, it felt like Penny didn't have a choice. She was sure there had been a chance to turn back at some point along the way, but not right now, when she was standing outside a paedophile's door with a snap gun and an alibi. It wasn't a game anymore.

Penny slid the blade of the gun into the lock and pulled the trigger five times. There were five sharp clicks, and the door swung open.

She needn't have worried about renovation. Swaize's apartment was even more of a wreck than when she'd last seen it. People's lives after prison were rarely better than they'd been before it. Empty TV dinners were piled on the floor next to the sofa. The sagging, tattered curtains were closed, but still let in a lot of light through the tears. A cockroach crawled out of a chipped coffee mug, which was on top of a porn magazine, which rested on a cardboard box with a picture of a microwave on the side. A cheap painting of some trees hung crooked on the wall.

As she crept towards the bathroom, the hissing of the shower got louder and louder. She could hear muttering, and a strange slapping sound—like Swaize was patting his belly in there. The oddness of this created a wave of revulsion. Later, Penny reflected that if he hadn't been slapping himself, she wouldn't have been so strangely sickened and she might not have gone through with it. His death was his own fault, in so many ways.

She slowly twisted the handle, so only the little slide bolt held the door closed. She couldn't kick it while holding the handle down. Instead, she took a deep breath, and shoulder-barged the door.

The slide bolt didn't break. The door stayed closed, but there was a loud thud.

Inside the bathroom, Swaize said, 'What the hell?'

Panicked now, Penny barged the door again. This time it burst open. The slide bolt went flying and jingled its way across the tiles into the corner of the room. Swaize was opening the shower curtain. He was white, with skinny limbs but an inflated gut, and hairy nipples on an otherwise bare chest. When he saw her, he instinctively covered his crotch, as though that was what she was after.

Filled with terror instead of righteous rage, Penny charged at him. They were barely a yard apart. Not much of a run-up. It didn't matter. She tackled him, one hand on his shoulder, the other on his face. The hot water got in her eyes, so she didn't see his head hit the wall, but she felt the impact in her palm, and heard the crack. His legs buckled, but didn't go limp the way she had expected. Penny scrambled up and backed away as Swaize crawled around the floor of the tub as slowly as a starfish for a minute that felt like an eternity. He eventually slumped sideways and looked up at her, uncomprehending. Water droplets splashed his eyeballs. When he didn't blink, Penny realised he was dead.

There was a sense of unreality, like this might all be a dream, as Penny went back into the living room, wiping her palms on her spandex pants. She picked up the remote and turned on the TV. She needed something to explain the yelling. There was a documentary on, something about the giant Pacific octopus. A stern-voiced narrator was describing how the octopuses squirt their eggs into the ocean and never meet their young. The narrator got louder and louder, shouting at Penny as she turned the volume up to maximum.

Penny realised she'd just put her fingerprints on the remote. She went to clean them off with a wet wipe from her bag but stopped herself just in time. A remote with no prints on it would be even more suspicious. She'd have to say in her report that she turned it off when she arrived.

She walked back into the bathroom.

Swaize had moved. Or had he? She didn't remember him lying in that position. Perhaps he wasn't dead.

She put a finger to his neck. Couldn't feel a pulse.

She grabbed the cake of soap—it was tiny, like he'd taken it from a hotel—and rubbed it on the soles of his feet. No movement. If he was alive, he wasn't ticklish.

Penny had arrested some killers who shot their victims twenty times, and others who kept hitting them with a baseball bat long after they were dead. She used to think of it as bloodlust. But now she understood. There was an urge, having reached the point of no return, to *make sure*.

She rubbed some soap on the floor, too, making it extra slippery, but avoided the puddle of blood growing under his head. That needed to stay undisturbed. Even a half-decent crime scene investigator would become suspicious if the puddle looked smudged.

Penny didn't have a sense of how long she'd spent in the apartment. It was as though time had stopped along with Swaize's heart.

But then there was a knock at the front door. 'Lionel? You okay?'

The hairs on the back of Penny's neck stood up. Had she locked the front door behind her? She didn't think so. Hadn't thought of it. Planning the perfect crime had been easy in the abstract. Now she was actually here, and it was messy.

Another knock. Probably the neighbour she'd seen before. 'Lionel! I thought I heard yelling.'

Penny tiptoed through the living room and into the kitchen. Dirty dishes were piled high in the sink. Festering paper towels were scattered everywhere. If the busybody came in, perhaps Penny could creep out the door behind her, while she was in the bathroom.

But then it wouldn't be a locked-room mystery. The neighbour would see the broken bathroom door and would immediately suspect murder. *Don't come in*, Penny thought, trying to transmit her thoughts through the wall. *Go away*.

No more knocking. Could the neighbour already be inside? The TV was so loud that Penny wouldn't necessarily have heard the front door open. Or perhaps she had given up and gone away.

Penny eased closer to the kitchen door, preparing to take a peek. She could still hear the shower gushing water onto Swaize's corpse.

The radio in Penny's pack crackled. Her heart leaped into her mouth.

'Officer Randich, this is dispatch, do you copy? Over.'

Penny risked a glance around the corner into the living room. No sign of the neighbour. Just the TV blaring.

'Officer Randich? Over.'

Penny went back into the kitchen, away from the TV, and held up the radio. 'I hear you, dispatch. What's up?'

'Possible domestic disturbance at one twenty-eight Chalmers Street. Apartment thirty-one. You told me you were going somewhere near there, right?'

'I said I was going to the gym on Chalmers. Needed to burn off some energy.' She was talking too much, too fast.

'Oh. If your shift is already over, I can—'

'No. It's fine. I got it. What's the disturbance?'

'A neighbour heard shouting, and the shower has been going for a suspiciously long time. She knocked on the door and no one answered.'

'Is the neighbour still at the scene?'

'She went back to her apartment, number thirty. That's where she made the call. Can you check it out?'

Penny took a deep breath. 'On my way.'

She snuck back out of the apartment. There was no sign of the neighbour in the corridor, but she had to move fast. Someone else might get curious, and the plan would only work if she was first on scene.

Penny hurried downstairs and ran across the street to the gym. She gave the front entrance a wide berth, not wanting to appear on the security tapes. Once she was out of sight around the back, she pulled off the wig and scratched her itchy neck. She pulled open the fire exit and removed the playing card she had taped over the tab to prevent the door from locking.

She had found her rhythm now. No more panicking, like in the bathroom. She was operating as smoothly as an art thief in a movie.

As she walked back towards the door, she took note of everyone in the room, in case she was asked later. A middle-aged woman in yoga pants on the Stairmaster. A purple-faced middle-aged man on the weight bench, with a clean-cut Latino guy spotting him, maybe his trainer. A younger white man on the rowing machine.

Suddenly inspired, she went over to the younger guy. He had long hair, stubble and a nice build. Muscular thighs.

'I've been watching you,' she said.

He looked up. 'You have?'

'Yeah. From over there.' Penny pointed to a spot that wouldn't have been visible to him while he was using the rowing machine.

The man released the handles and wiped his sweaty hands on his tank top.

'You got good technique,' Penny said.

The guy smiled uncertainly. 'Really? Thanks.'

'I'm Penny.'

'Albert.'

He reached up to shake her hand, and Penny pressed her card into it. 'Buy me a coffee sometime, Albert,' she said, and winked. Then she walked away without a backwards glance.

Whether he called her or not, he would remember that she had been here. Penny felt sure that he would tell the police she had been watching him the whole time he was working out. The male ego wouldn't even let him consider the idea that she had noticed him only five seconds before interrupting him. Penny had seen suspects walk away with far shakier alibis.

She walked out the front door, turning her face just enough that the security camera could identify her, but not so much that it would look like she was conscious of it. She had been clumsy at first, but already she was *good* at this.

A few pedestrians were around as she jogged over to her patrol car. A fat old man with Woody Allen glasses watched her unlock the trunk and pull out her police jacket. He looked away as soon as she pulled it on. Didn't mean he had done anything wrong. Being a police officer was like that. Most people avoided eye contact, as though the law couldn't see them if they couldn't see it.

Penny went back up to the apartment. She was about to knock on the neighbour's door, since the neighbour had made the call, but stopped herself just in time. Even if it wasn't protocol, she had to enter the victim's apartment first.

'Police. Open up.' She banged on Swaize's door, like she didn't know what was inside. For a second, she had the strange feeling that he would open the door, looking puzzled and worried. Like she had imagined the whole thing.

He didn't, of course. The neighbour stuck her head out the door just as Penny was getting out the snap gun again.

Penny looked her right in the eye, confident that she wouldn't be recognised. Maybe overconfident.

'Stay inside, ma'am,' Penny told her.

The woman didn't need any further encouragement. She vanished like a cat down a storm drain.

Penny pushed Swaize's door open. The noise of the TV hit her immediately. 'Hello?' she called out, in case the woman from next door could hear.

After a couple of seconds, she turned off the TV. This put her fingerprints on the remote, which was fine. She was supposed to be here this time.

'Hello?' she called out again. She walked to the open bathroom door.

The body was gone.

Penny choked on her own spit. She moved a little further into the room. There it was, thank God. The body had just slumped down a little further into the tub. Softening—rigor mortis wouldn't start for hours yet. The blood had all but washed away.

Penny knocked on the open door and called out, 'Mr Swaize?' She made eye contact with the dead body as she did it. Like she could wake him up. Part of her wanted to undo this. No, that wasn't quite right—part of her wanted to *want* to undo this. To be the kind of person who couldn't kill a stranger in cold blood. *Or tepid blood, at least*, she thought, recalling the surge of panic leading up to his death.

If wishes were horses, her ex would have said.

Penny shoulder-barged the door so the neighbour would hear the thump. Then she pulled out her radio. 'Dispatch? I got a dead body here. Looks accidental, but send forensics. You never know.'

•

Albert, the guy from the gym, did call her in the end. The baby ruined their date by crying pretty much constantly.

Penny couldn't even drink her coffee, because the caffeine would get into her breast milk and keep the baby awake. Albert was talking about his job, and Penny got a sense that all his anecdotes were witty, but because she was distracted by the baby she only really learned that he was a paralegal. *Convenient*, she thought. *I might need an attorney.* All the forensics seemed to think Swaize's death was an accident, but the official ruling hadn't come down yet.

Despite the awful date, Albert still said he wanted to see her again. Penny suggested her place, where she would be better able to keep the baby distracted. There were toys, and a crib.

When he came over, he didn't help feed the baby, change the diaper or put him to bed, but he was patient while Penny did. Far from being annoying, his lack of interest in the baby delighted Penny. When her old friends did call, they would never ask how Penny was—only the baby. Her mother was the same. Her doctor asked how she was doing, but then always added pompously, 'The mother's wellbeing affects the child's, you know.' But Albert was interested in *her*.

Once the baby was asleep, she and Albert had sex. She pushed the clothes, toys and packets of wet wipes aside and rode him, right there on the sofa. She gripped his hair and he squeezed her ass. She thought it might be her last chance to have sex before she went to prison.

She wasn't sure when she had become convinced that she was going to get caught, but a sense of inevitability loomed: the feeling that her days with her baby were numbered. She had driven past the razor wire and hurricane fences of the Gatesville Unit several times, already wondering where in the facility she would be housed.

She waited for someone to notice that she had played a minor role in Swaize's original arrest. No one did. She waited for the neighbour to say that she looked like the woman who had been hanging around Swaize's apartment before his death. The neighbour didn't. She waited for someone to contact the gym and confirm her alibi. Nobody did.

Albert never called again. She left a voicemail for him, and he didn't get back to her. Maybe he was looking for a woman with less baggage. Or maybe the baggage was why he had wanted that second date—he might have thought a single mom would be keen for a commitment-free fuck. He'd gotten what he wanted, and left. *Like they all do.*

She told herself it didn't matter. She'd gotten what she wanted from him, too. And as it turned out, she didn't even need his alibi. Penny's boss called. The death had been ruled an accident.

She was free.

CHAPTER 34

I fill your body as you listen to
music in church. What am I?

'How did you know Swaize would lock his bathroom door while he was showering?' I ask.

'Ex-cons always do,' Penny says.

'But what if he didn't?'

She smirks. 'I guess I would have had to put a spring inside the slide-bolt mechanism, and hold it in the open position with a credit card.'

'So . . . how did you get caught?' I ask.

'I didn't,' she says.

I scan her face. I can usually tell when someone's lying to me, but I don't think she is. Her chin is up, the edges of her lips curled, eyes slightly narrowed, eyebrows raised. Pride, and anticipation.

'You turned yourself in,' I say.

'My, you are a good guesser,' she replies. 'I see why my son picked you.'

'Why would you commit the perfect crime and then confess?'

She looks out the little window. 'Guilt,' she says simply. 'That man's life weighed on me more and more heavily. I couldn't sleep. I couldn't concentrate. I had to make it right.'

'But—' I stop myself. This grinds against everything I know about criminal psychology. People don't turn themselves in out of guilt. They do it out of fear. The fear of getting found out gets bigger and bigger, swallowing up their whole lives like the blob from a horror movie, until eventually they confess just so they won't have to worry about it anymore.

But Penny committed, in her mind, the perfect crime. There was no chance of getting caught. And she doesn't seem to have an anxious disposition—she wasn't going to imagine new evidence that the police might find.

'The Gatesville Unit wasn't so bad,' she muses. 'The library was better stocked than my public library. Two hours outside per day—I never got that at work, or even in high school. And after my accident—'

'What accident?'

She doesn't seem to hear me. 'I got free physiotherapy. Citizens don't have a right to free health care, but prisoners do. The Eighth Amendment—it's considered cruel and unusual punishment to withhold it. Can you believe that? My whole life I worked my ass off for health care. Turns out all I had to do was get myself thrown in jail.'

'What accident?' I ask again.

'Ah.' Penny picks up a pen and starts tapping it on the desk. 'There are rules for prison guards. They can't make you stand up for too long, they can't deprive you of sleep, et cetera. It's in the Geneva Convention. Not so for the other prisoners who, believe it or not, didn't take kindly to having a former cop in their midst. For my own protection I was moved to a segregation unit with the child molesters. They needed protection, too. The other prisoners attack them, to feel righteous. Making themselves into heroes. You know?'

I think of the shed of tortured criminals in the backyard. 'I know.'

'But the paedophiles in seg don't like me much either,' Penny says, 'because I'm there for murdering one of them. So they attack me. Always right after a meal, because there's a lockdown after each fight and no one wants to go hungry. I got stabbed in the kitchen, punched in the shower, and one time someone tripped me at the top of the stairs. I went all the way down.'

Penny hasn't gotten up from her swivel chair the whole time we've been talking. I'm starting to think she can't. That would explain why she never leaves this room—she can't go down the stairs. No wonder such a small woman still makes the floorboards creak.

'You said it was an accident,' I remind her.

'Force of habit. That was how it was recorded in the logbooks. And once it's in there, you can't change it and you shouldn't try. Arguing looks bad to the parole board. I was denied twice.'

You'd think a woman with her experience would know how to manipulate a parole board. Something clicks in my mind. There is another reason criminals turn themselves in. Not for fear, but to escape. A woman beaten by her husband might think she's safer in prison. A man who's made a powerful enemy might find freedom behind bars.

I couldn't sleep. I couldn't concentrate ... They can't make you stand up for too long, they can't deprive you of sleep, et cetera.

'You didn't feel guilty,' I say. 'You just didn't want to look after a kid anymore.'

Penny shoots me a look that could turn people to stone. 'Excuse me?'

'That's why you turned yourself in,' I say. 'That's why you killed Swaize in the first place. Prison was your way out.'

Penny tries to get up, like she's forgotten about her broken spine. She collapses back into the chair and nearly falls off it—grabs the edges just in time.

'I love my son,' she says, so hatefully she's almost spitting.

'Even after he locked you up here?' I say. 'He's punishing you, right? For leaving him.'

Penny is trembling with fury. I must have reached the truth. People who are falsely accused get annoyed. People who are correctly accused get enraged.

'Hey, I get it,' I say, thinking of Kyle. 'No judgement here. Kids can be a real pain in the ass. I—'

Penny flings her pen at me. I duck. The pen cracks against the wall behind me and rolls back under the bed, where she'll never be able to reach it on her own.

'Get out,' she snaps.

'No problem.' I head for the door. I've wasted too much time up here already. She hasn't helped me identify Samson's killer, or told me anything I can use to get Thistle and the other prisoners out.

'Wait. I'm sorry.' Penny rolls her chair after me. Her poise is gone. She still looks pissed, but also afraid of being left alone. No wonder she spent an hour stalling me with a shaggy dog story.

'I haven't told you what happened after I was released,' she says.

'I gotta go. Your son gave me a case to crack.' And Thistle is waiting for me to rescue her. 'So unless you know something about Samson's murder . . .'

Penny's tongue is pinched between her teeth. She desperately wants me to stay, but she has nothing more to give up.

'I'll see you,' I say.

'No! Hang on.'

I pause in the doorway.

'Take a closer look at the body,' she says finally. 'And then come back, so we can talk more.'

'Why?'

She purses her lips, and says nothing.

•

Ten minutes later I'm in the editing room, clicking my way through the security systems. I do want to take another look at Samson's body—but first, I need to work out how to turn off the motion detector on the driveway. If I can't, the Guards will be alerted before Thistle and the other prisoners are half a mile away. They might catch up to us in the van. Even if we get away, the Guards will be long gone before Thistle's colleagues come back to arrest them.

The labels are strings of random numbers. Unsearchable. Every time a rectangle goes dead in front of me, I realise that I've switched off a camera instead of the motion detector, and it takes a few precious seconds to turn it back on. If the

Guards come down here before tonight, I don't want them to notice anything has changed.

On one of the screens, someone has left the voting results from the subscribers open. Baby Killer is still in the lead, with more than two-thirds of the votes now. If I don't get Thistle out of here soon, the Guards will kill her.

I click through the last of the switches. Now the motion detector is off. Theoretically.

As I get up to leave, I glance back at the voting results. All those people, so desperate to watch Thistle die.

When I click on her name, it gives me more details. The usernames of everyone who voted for her, and how many times they voted—users can buy extra votes, apparently. Some of them have spent hundreds of dollars to kill Thistle.

The number of votes per user field looks editable. I click it, and change a one to a zero.

It works. Thistle's section of the pie chart shrinks from 71.22 per cent to 71.13 per cent.

My jaw drops. I can save her right now.

But only if I condemn one of the others.

I look at the chart. Five prisoners. Whose head should I put on the chopping block?

After Thistle, the Pedo has the most votes. But he's not here. And Cedric told me that Emmanuel Goldstein, the fictional anti-mascot, was rumoured to be a child molester. Maybe the Pedo doesn't even exist, in which case the Guards can't kill him on camera.

The Terrorist, Amar, is ranked third. I click through to find the people who voted for him, and I quickly give one of them five hundred extra votes.

It's enough. Now the Terrorist has 63 per cent of the vote, and Thistle's share has shrunk to 28 per cent.

I exit back to the screen I started with and step away from the computer. I tell myself I didn't just kill Amar. I'm going to get him out of here tonight. I'm going to get them all out.

Right?

•

After I unearth the corner of the bedsheet, it takes all my strength to lift the rest of it off Samson's body. Wet dirt is heavy. But it does a great job of preserving the dead.

Exposed to the air, bodies go rotten fast. Decomposition starts four minutes after death. Internal organs begin turning to slush after only a day. The body bloats within three. Bloody foam leaks out the nose and mouth. It's extremely unappetising.

But Samson has been both chilled and compressed. Other than the colourless skin and the clods of dirt in his hair, he looks the same as how we found him in bed on Tuesday.

I look around. Zara went into the house a few minutes ago. Donnie's in the slaughterhouse. No sign of anybody else.

I lift Samson out of the hole and quickly fill it in. Anyone walking past would only think an animal had been scratching around here, if they looked. And no one ever does.

I drag Samson out of sight into the trees, then I strip off his clothes and examine him. He's pissed his pants, but that doesn't necessarily mean he died scared; bladder muscles relax even after a peaceful death. Most people who appear to be in good shape are not, once you get their clothes off. That's the point of clothes—to hide that gut you wish was flatter and those pectoral muscles you don't have. The most beautiful person you know probably looks ridiculous under all that silk and nylon. But Samson is a rare exception. Splayed out on the forest floor in front of me, he looks like da Vinci's drawing of the man in the circle.

I roll him over. There's an extra lump of bone at the back of his skull, probably from looking down at a phone too much while his skeleton was still forming. A couple of childhood scars; nothing recent. If Donnie had crushed Samson's hand around the gun and twisted his arm upwards, forcing him to shoot himself, there would be signs. Squeezing his limbs, I can't feel any broken tendons or dislocated joints. There isn't any bruising, either.

I take the kitchen knife off my belt, but hesitate. If I cut him open, I might lose control. And Thistle is barely a hundred yards from where I'm standing. She can't see me, but knowing she's there makes me want to do better.

Can I really waste all this meat, though? Usually only a few parts are thrown out, like the bones and the brain; eating brains can give you Creutzfeldt-Jakob disease, the human equivalent of mad cow. This time, the whole thing is—

Wait. Back up. The brain.

When I first saw the scene, there were hints that Samson had been shot with something other than the gun in his hand. There was no exit wound, which was unusual for a firearm of that calibre. If I can dig the bullet out of his brain, I can prove my hunch.

I bash the handle of the knife against the side of Samson's head. His skull cracks on the fourth try. I grab his hair and peel away some of his skin to expose the fractured bone, and then pull it apart like an Easter egg. This is not how a real autopsy would go, but it will get the job done.

I unplug Samson's brain from his spinal column with a wet snap. All of Samson's memories and opinions and feelings are stored in this lump of grey flab, inaccessible forever. I can see the little hole where the bullet went in, but other than that, the brain seems largely intact. Not typical. If there's no exit wound, that normally means the bullet ricocheted around and around the inside of the skull, shredding everything. Maybe Samson's brain was unusually dense.

I peel the two hemispheres apart, stretching the membranes until they pop. There's the hole again, where the shot exited the right hemisphere and entered the left. I pull apart the left hemisphere, looking for the bullet.

It's gone.

Someone got here first. Someone with more finesse than me—and probably a long pair of tweezers. They removed the bullet. If I hadn't smashed the skull, I might have seen scrape marks around the edges of the entry wound.

A bullet that didn't match the gun would prove Samson was murdered. But a missing bullet also suggests murder, or at least foul play. So what was the point of removing it?

The type of bullet must identify the killer. Maybe it would match another gun in the house. A small one, since there was no exit wound. Maybe the kind of gun that would fit in a woman's hand. A hand that could manipulate tweezers delicately enough to get the bullet out the same way it came in.

Zara had a long pair of tweezers in her room. And on Monday night, when we were out looking for the hiker, she strayed from her search area. She ended up near me and Samson, where the hiker actually turned out to be. Later, his footprints led right up to her window.

I remember the way she grabbed the satchel with the slashed strap. The way she searched it. The way Samson was favouring one arm, acting strangely. It all fits.

I leave Samson's corpse in the woods and run back to the house. Time is short. The sun's going down.

My hands are covered with gore. I keep them in my pockets so they won't stray near my mouth. For Thistle. As soon as I'm inside, I force myself to wash them. The blood spirals down the sink.

I find Zara on the couch in the living room. She's reading one of the dusty paperbacks from her room. It's called *1984*—I guess it's a history book. A glass of wine is on the table beside her, as usual. But she's not drinking it. It's a prop. So is the paperback. Everything Zara does is an illusion.

'Good book?' I ask.

She looks up. 'One of Fred's favourites. It has lots of useful ideas. How's your belly?'

I don't need the reminder that she's dangerous. She killed Samson. But if I'm right about why, she won't kill me.

'Where are the others?' I ask.

'Cedric and Kyle are in the greenhouse.' She appears not to notice the grubby cuffs of my sleeves. 'Fred's showering Ivy. Donnie's making a new video with the Terrorist.'

I cough. 'He is?'

'Yes. Apparently there was a sudden influx of votes. We have to make the most of our friend from Isis before we kill

312

him on Sunday.' She puts the book down on her lap. 'What can I do for you?'

'I want to talk to you.'

'Sure.' She smiles and swings her legs out of the way, making room on the couch. She pats the cushions. 'I came on too strong this morning, didn't I?'

I'm sick of her games. 'Somewhere private.'

Her smile grows wider. 'Okay.' She stands up, smooths down her dress. 'Let's *talk* in my room.'

I follow her swaying hips up the corridor. This is a risk. I don't know how she'll react when I confront her. But the indirect approach won't save Thistle. I'm out of time.

She enters her bedroom. Before I've even closed the door, she's undressing, letting the straps of her dress fall from her shoulders. There are freckles on her back.

When she turns to face me, she's holding a gun.

'So,' she says, the flirtatious act gone, 'what do you want to talk about, Blake?'

I put my hands up. It's just the kind of gun I expected to see: small, lightweight. Medical tape dangles from one side—she must have had it stuck to her chest, just below her bra, where the folds of her dress would cover it.

It takes me a moment to realise she just used my real name. I guess that means I'm right. But this isn't going how I thought it would.

'We're on the same side,' I say.

She doesn't lower the gun. 'You're FBI.'

I nod slowly. 'And you're CIA.'

CHAPTER 35

You fill me with time, then mail me away.
What am I?

'I should have figured it out the second you told me about all the travel you'd done with the Department of Agriculture,' I say. 'That was official cover, with diplomatic immunity. You sat in an embassy, waiting for local assets to bring in secrets for you to send home. But you got bored.'

Zara keeps the gun trained on my heart. She doesn't say anything, but she doesn't have to. She gave me the truth yesterday: *I just got sick of being stuck behind a desk.*

'So you asked to be reassigned. You wanted a non-official cover role, with more opportunities for . . . excitement.' Opportunities to hurt people. I remember the consultant's words: *Why would an agent volunteer for such a risky assignment? This is why. It's not patriotism. It's not loyalty. It's the desire to be the person society doesn't allow you to be.* 'This little group was easy to infiltrate. You just had to submit a few videos to prove you weren't a cop. As luck would have it, they wanted exactly the kind of content the CIA specialises in.'

The look on her face is unreadable. I don't know how

long we have. I need to prove that I've figured it all out, so she doesn't waste time denying it. I keep talking, fast.

'The hiker wasn't a hiker,' I continue. 'He was your handler. Right? He came here to give you a dossier about Donnie. But his timing was bad. The Guards had re-arranged the cameras that day and you hadn't had a chance to warn him. He walked right past one of them. You tried to convince us all he was Druznetski, the private investigator, who none of us had met. When that didn't work, you suggested that he was a hiker. A fake cop showed up the following day to reinforce your story—and to check that your cover was intact.'

I think of the way the sheriff's deputy looked at Zara as she spoke: *Is everything okay out here in general?*

Zara keeps the gun trained on me. 'Lift up your shirt.'

'We're on the same side,' I say again.

'Do it.'

I untuck my shirt and lift it up, exposing the cut Zara made this morning.

'Turn around,' she says.

I do, letting her pat me down, checking for weapons or listening devices.

'That first night,' I say, 'you knew more or less where your handler would be. You were desperate to warn him that he'd been spotted. But Samson found him first. He cut the bag off his shoulder. Suddenly Samson had the dossier about Donnie, not you.'

As I'm talking, I'm picturing her expression when she found the bag empty. *Was this his? And it was empty? Shit.* And the look on Samson's face. *You see which way the guy went? I want to talk to him.*

'And he'd opened it,' I continue. 'He wouldn't have had time to read it, but he saw the pictures. Proof that someone in the house was a spy. And he didn't know who.'

Zara finishes searching me. Steps back.

I turn around again. 'He was acting weird that night, and he didn't come out of his room the next morning. So when we all went out to search for the mystery man, you came back. You shot Samson in the head and put one of the guns from the armoury in his hand to make it look like a suicide. You took his phone and laptop, so you could figure out if he had told anyone else what he knew. You threw the dossier into the fireplace, just in case someone searched your room—you could maybe explain away the phone or the laptop, but not that. But then you realised Fred was getting suspicious. He had asked me to investigate, and I was getting closer. There was one more piece of evidence which could sink you—the bullet.'

'Wow. You really are with the FBI,' Zara says, looking amused.

'You dug up Samson's corpse,' I say. 'You used tweezers to—'

'I'll stop you there.' Zara sits down on her bed, suddenly relaxed. 'You're way off, Mr Blake. I didn't kill Samson.'

This isn't the kind of denial I expected, nor the point at which I expected one. 'Why should I believe you?'

'Why would I lie?' She spreads her arms wide. For the first time, the gun isn't pointed at me. I could pounce, try to get it off her. I don't. With her training at Camp Peary, her hand-to-hand skills would greatly outclass mine—and anyway, we're supposed to be allies.

'Exactly,' I say. 'Don't play dumb. We can help each other.'

I can see her deciding how much to tell me. At last she says, 'The CIA doesn't kill people.'

'No?'

'No. We recruit assets.'

We. An admission, finally.

'Patrice Lumumba might disagree,' I say.

Zara ignores this. 'I'm here to gather intelligence. If my cover was blown, I would have left. I wouldn't have killed Samson, staged a suicide and then stayed for the fallout.'

She's talking like a normal person now. The breathy, sex-kitten voice is gone. It's a relief.

I keep pushing. 'If Samson read the file—'

'That dossier wasn't just about Donnie. It was an update on the operation as a whole—and it included a fake file on me, so I wouldn't be compromised if it fell into the wrong hands. Which it did, because of you.'

'Me?'

'Fred's not the only one with cameras,' Zara says. 'The station clocked you turning into the drive on that first night.'

I remember the camera I saw near the mouth of the driveway. Better hidden. More powerful.

'Within minutes they matched your face to the FBI database,' Zara continues. 'My handler brought the dossier ahead of schedule, so he could tell me in person that some bumbling FBI guy had turned up. But I hadn't had a chance to warn him that the cameras had been moved.' She adjusts her hair and leans back on the bed. 'So, yes, this is all your fault.'

'What are you even doing here?' I ask. 'The CIA isn't supposed to operate on US soil.'

'The FBI isn't supposed to recruit cannibals, either.'

A chill crawls up my spine. *She knows.*

'Cannibals?' I echo.

A twitch of her lips. 'Now who's playing dumb?'

When her handler came back the following night, he must have brought a second dossier—this time with a section about me. The CIA unearthed my terrible secret less than thirty-six hours after taking my picture.

Either that, or they had a file on me already.

'I don't know what you're talking about,' I say. If she confronts me with more evidence, maybe I can identify her source.

But she's not so easily manipulated. 'What do you want from me, Mr Blake?'

'I want you to help me get the prisoners out.'

'Why would I do that?'

I frown. 'Why wouldn't you?' I know Zara gets off on hurting people—I don't think that's just part of her cover—but it's also her job to protect US citizens.

Zara toys with her gun, saying nothing.

'You've been here for months,' I add. 'Your people should have moved on this place ages ago.'

'Like you said, the CIA isn't supposed to operate on US soil.'

'You could notify one of the other agencies.'

'We're not going to do that.'

'Why not?'

'Counter-offer,' Zara says. 'I help *you* get out of here. The prisoners stay.'

It takes me a second to think my way into the head of a CIA agent, but I get there. 'You don't care about the

Guards,' I say. 'You care about their international customers. If you find out that a Chinese delivery driver likes torture porn, you can blackmail him into transporting packages for you. If you find out that the vice-president of Turkey is a subscriber, you can force him to go through his boss's filing cabinets. This place is an intelligence goldmine.'

'Are you going to take the deal or not?' Zara says.

The scope of this is alarming, even for me. The CIA is letting Americans be tortured and killed in order to steal classified data from foreign leaders.

I had expected Zara to be on my side, but our goals don't line up at all.

'Just Agent Thistle, then,' I say. 'Help me get her out of here. I don't care about the others.' I don't know how I'll convince Thistle to leave them behind, but it sounds like my only choice.

'What's in it for me?' Zara asks.

I rack my brain for something I can offer her. 'I don't tell the Guards who you're working for.'

'You can't,' Zara points out. 'You're a single Google image search away from being exposed. After that, they won't believe a word you say.'

'How about I help you figure out who really killed Samson. If it really wasn't you, don't you want to know?'

'Samson killed himself,' Zara says. 'Sorry, but it's that simple. Gay men in Samson's age group are five times more likely to attempt suicide than straight men.'

'Are they also likely to remove the bullets from their own heads afterwards?'

There's curiosity in Zara's eyes now. 'The bullet is really gone?'

Before I can work out what to say next, footsteps thump up the corridor towards us.

Zara and I look at each other. What's our excuse for being in here together?

A different bedroom door flings open. Mine. Someone is looking for me.

Another door opens. Whoever it is, they're searching the whole house.

Zara quickly tucks the gun under her blankets. Then she grabs my hand, pulls me down onto the bed with her, and kisses me. Her lips are smooth and warm. She tastes of mint. I try to struggle free, in case it's Fred in the corridor, but she doesn't let me go.

At that moment, the door bursts open. Donnie storms in. He sees us both on the bed, my shirt untucked, Zara's arms around my neck, her dress open to the waist. His expression darkens.

'Get up,' he snarls.

Zara releases me. 'Donnie—'

Donnie grabs me by the ear and pulls me off the bed. Pain explodes across the side of my jaw and scalp.

'Wait,' I say.

'How much have you told him?' Donnie snaps. Not what I expected him to say.

'We weren't *talking*,' Zara says pointedly.

'Good.' Donnie kicks me in the ribs with a steel-capped boot, leaving me wheezing. 'Because he's a fucking FBI agent.'

No.

No.

This is exactly what I've been dreading.

'What? That doesn't make sense.' Zara sounds genuinely shocked. She's a hell of an actress.

'Maybe not, but it's true.' Donnie hauls me by the collar out the back door, past the greenhouse and the vegetable garden. The dogs snap and snarl as we pass.

'Donnie, listen,' I say. 'Someone is lying to you—'

He punches me in the eye socket. Sparks fill my vision and my brain wobbles like jello.

Fred emerges from around the side of the house.

'Found him,' Donnie says.

Cedric looks up—he's been scraping food scraps into the composting pipe. 'What's going on?' he asks as Kyle runs out of the greenhouse.

'Lux is a fucking fed,' Donnie says.

Kyle's eyes go wide.

'I'm not!' I scream. But I can't come up with anything to support the lie.

Donnie kicks me in the back. Something cracks. Hopefully not my spine. He loses his grip on my collar and grabs my throat instead. I can't speak anymore. I can hardly breathe.

Fred is already unlocking the slaughterhouse. He doesn't look as surprised as the others. Donnie must have told him already, before he started looking for me.

Zara is right behind us. 'I can't believe it,' she says, but that's all. She doesn't try to defend me.

'How do you know?' Cedric demands.

'I just got a message from Druznetski,' Fred says.

The private investigator. My heart sinks. I hadn't even considered him as a threat.

'This guy isn't Lux,' Fred continues. 'It's the FBI agent he killed—the one he *claimed* to have killed. Blake.'

I was never an agent, I was a civilian consultant. I don't think they'll care about the distinction.

It's not true, I try to say, but Donnie's hand is still squeezing my throat. All that comes out is a choked gasp.

'Holy *shit*,' Kyle says. A look of betrayal has washed away his faux-nihilism.

'But—but I saw a picture,' Cedric stammers.

Fred opens the slaughterhouse door, ignoring him. The other prisoners stare as Donnie drags me in. I try to get a look at Thistle, but my head is twisted the wrong way.

I can't rescue her if I get chained up in here. I kick and squirm, but I can't loosen Donnie's grip.

The shiny new cameras watch us from above, red lights blinking. Whatever is about to happen to me will be recorded for thousands of greedy psychos.

'Help me chain him up,' Donnie tells Kyle. 'I'll beat some answers out of him.'

'No,' Fred says sadly. 'Druznetski gave me all the information I need. Switch on the grinder.'

CHAPTER 36

A sickness rearranges
the gale—it's a crime!

The motor growls and the blades clatter, louder and louder as the machine warms up.

The prisoners shrink back against the walls of the slaughterhouse, preparing for the rain of blood. Thistle's the only one who doesn't close her eyes. She hasn't seen this before. She doesn't know what's coming. But she knows it's bad.

Sweat glitters on her forehead. It would be nice to imagine that she's scared on my behalf, but really, she knows that if I die, she and the others have no hope of escape.

'Wait,' she says.

The Guards ignore her.

Donnie takes his hand off my throat so he and Fred can load me into the chute. I try to struggle free, but they're too strong.

'If I was a cop, I would have arrested you all by now,' I rasp. Talking is my only option. 'You've done plenty of illegal things. I helped with some of them. I'm just like you.'

'Don't listen to him,' Fred says. 'He's done nothing but lie since he got here.' He and Donnie lift me up, feeding me headfirst into the chute.

It's barely wider than my shoulders and made of slippery steel with a cheap shimmer. Just enough light to see what lies ahead.

I cut my own hair, so I've seen electric clippers up close: two serrated blades, one lying flat on top of the other. The bottom one slides back and forth while the top one doesn't, opening dozens of little gaps and then shutting them over and over, slicing the hairs in two. The inside of the grinder is like that writ large. Enormous jagged blades whirl in the shadows, row after row of them. Like huge teeth, designed to shred me for easy digestion by the finer gears below. The square chute amplifies the racket, funnelling it into my brain.

I brace my arms against the walls, trying to stay clear of the sharp edges further down. Fred and Donnie push me in. It must be hard work. This disposal method is designed for the dead, who don't struggle.

'Druznetski is lying!' I shout. 'Think about it! How would he even know what I look like?'

Four strong hands are holding my torso and legs. I don't know whose is whose, but I feel two of them hesitate.

'I sent him a photo,' Fred says to someone. 'Snapped it while Lux—Blake—was asleep. I felt bad at the time for invading his privacy. Now I'm glad I did.'

I've been sleeping so little and so lightly that I'm amazed Fred pulled this off.

The hesitant hands—they must have been Donnie's— become firm once more, pushing me deeper into the grinder. The swirling blades get closer. The noise is stabbing me in the eardrums. The wind blasts my hair. My hands are slippery against the walls. I can't hold on.

At least my head will go in first. There will only be a moment of pain before I'm pulped.

'He will have called for backup,' Donnie says.

'Yeah.' Fred sounds disappointed. 'We have to shut this place down and move on.'

Shut this place down. He's talking about killing the prisoners. Thistle will go through the grinder, right after me. I can't let that happen. But I don't know how to stop it.

Hands crush my calf muscles, thrusting me deeper into the chute. The blades are deafening, only inches away now.

'I know who killed Samson!' I scream.

I don't. I'm not sure where the words come from. But in my desperation to save Thistle, it's like I'm slamming against the walls of my own brain, and a half-formed idea is shaken loose.

One of the Guards killed Samson. And the other four will want to know who.

I keep yelling the same sentence over and over. 'I know who killed Samson! I know who killed Samson!'

Someone loosens their grip on my leg again. But this makes one of my hands slip off the wall. My arm disappears into the spinning blades. Hot blood splashes my eyes. There's a split second of agony—

And I snatch my arm back out again, just in time. I can't see it, but I can still move all my fingers.

I'm getting dizzy. My blood pressure is dropping.

An argument is happening outside the grinder. I can only hear bits and pieces of it, echoing down the chute.

'. . . thought Samson committed suicide?'

'How would he know?'

'Maybe he did it.'

'. . . doesn't make sense . . .'

Then Zara says the words that save my life: 'You know, I saw him eating a human foot the other day.'

'Eating?' someone else says incredulously.

'Yeah.' I can practically hear Zara shrugging. 'It just doesn't seem like something an FBI agent would do.'

Finally convinced, Donnie drags me back out of the grinder. Maybe he was just sick of holding onto my legs. I fall to the concrete floor with a wet splat. I try to protect my head with my arm, but I miss somehow and my skull hits the floor. The world starts to spin and fade.

Donnie looms over me, boots ready to kick. 'Who killed Samson?' he snaps.

I'm too nauseated to respond. His gaze shifts to my arm, and his expression changes.

I look down. I can still feel my fingers—but they're not there. There's just a bloody stump where my elbow used to be.

'Oh,' someone says.

Then I'm gone.

•

I'm on a bed/the ground/a table. The sun/moon/kitchen lights burn my eyes. Chills ripple across my flesh. I'm cold/hot. My arm is here/gone.

Pressure. A tightening/loosening around my bicep. Someone/something is squeezing it like a frosting tube.

A demon/angel looms over me.

'Do you know what you're doing?' he/she whispers/shouts.

My lips move/are frozen. Doesn't matter. The creature isn't talking to me.

'Remember when Donnie cut that guy's foot off?' another voice says. 'I helped Samson keep him alive.'

'For about two weeks, sure. Then he died of infection.'

'Two weeks is plenty. It won't take long to find out what Lux knows.'

'He's not Lux.'

'You sure about that?'

I try to look at my arm, but my head doesn't turn. The world spins instead. Nausea floods up my throat like wasps.

'What if he's not a cop?'

'He is.'

'But what if he's not? We can't just let him die. Not if he hasn't done anything wrong.'

'Everyone's done something wrong. No one's innocent.'

My head finally turns. I'm on the kitchen bench. The room is full of people. Samson is here, watching me, his mouth a straight line. The real Lux is right behind him. The Scammer is here, too, and Gerald, and Charlie Warner, and the old FBI director. They're all waiting for me.

The voices are starting to fade. The lights in my eyes don't seem so bright now. I can't feel my arm anymore. Can't feel anything else, either.

'Oh, shit,' one of the monsters says. 'You're losing him.'

'I know! Shut up. Grab that, will you?'

Something plastic/iron covers my mouth. Air/poison is forced into my lungs.

'Just breathe, you fucker,' someone says.

The world goes dark and quiet once again.

•

'Blake. Blake. Blake.'

The voice is like a recorded distress call: once urgent but now automatic, and probably irrelevant. No sense coming late to an urgent problem. They solve themselves, depending on your outlook. Yes, they do.

'Blake. Blake.'

I try to stay asleep. Whatever they want, it can wait a few minutes. I need to get back to the nightmare I was having. Gotta finish it. If I don't finish it, the nightmare will still be there when I wake up. It will escape into real life and exist forever.

'Blake.'

It's the determination that makes me finally recognise the voice. Anyone else would have given up fifty Blakes ago. Only Reese Thistle would keep going, trying to wake me up.

I blink and try to rub my eyes with a hand that isn't there. My other hand is cuffed to something. So my eyes go unrubbed. I blink them instead. I'm in an industrial kitchen. No—I'm on a movie set rigged up to look like an industrial kitchen. My wrist is chained to the door of a fake oven. The door is welded shut and the inset window is just a sticker.

I lean sideways, peering between the ingredients on some metal shelves. Thistle is right where I left her, handcuffed to a table leg in a replica of a pharmacy.

'Thank God,' she says. 'Are you okay?'

I swallow a tickle of laughter.

'Sorry,' she says, looking at my arm.

A bandage is wound tightly around the stump. Some asshole has drawn a smiley face on it with magic marker.

No blood is visible, but I can smell it beneath. And there's a hot throbbing, which probably isn't good news. Without antibiotics, I'll be dead in days.

Of course, depending on what the Guards decide, I could be dead in hours.

Two weeks is plenty. I recognise the voice now. Donnie. He was trying to save me, at least temporarily. Therefore, he's not Samson's killer. The killer would want me dead before I could expose them.

Zara tried to save me, too. And I know the killer isn't Fred, because I was with him when Samson was shot. That only leaves Cedric and Penny.

And Kyle. I don't want to believe it was him. But I have to accept that it's possible.

When the Guards realise I don't actually know who murdered Samson, they'll put the rest of me through the grinder, followed by the other prisoners. Even if I somehow figure out who the killer is, they'll still puree us after I tell them.

I touch the bandage gingerly. A flash of pain, and I can feel something pointy underneath. A curved shard of exposed bone. They haven't filed it off, like a surgeon would, or stitched anything up. They're not interested in helping it heal properly. Just doing the bare minimum to keep me alive.

How much did my arm weigh? I've never wondered before. Ten pounds, maybe? I don't know why it matters, but I can't stop thinking about it.

My voice comes out as a croak. 'How long was I out?'

Thistle gestures at the dark slaughterhouse and the fake clock. 'Impossible to know. A day, maybe? They fed us. The rest of us.'

I look at my hand, the one I still have. The cuff is too tight to slip off. Almost too tight for circulation. My fingers are swollen and going purple. A few days here and I could lose that hand as well.

It's the one with the missing thumb. Those sons of bitches didn't even leave me with my good hand. I'm down to only four digits.

'Do you have a key?' The hope in Thistle's eyes breaks my heart.

'No,' I rasp. Samson's key may still be in my pocket—I can't reach down to check—but it was for the house, not the cuffs.

'A hairpin? Anything?'

'There's nothing we can do. This is the end.'

'I get that you've been through a traumatic experience,' she says. 'So have I, believe it or not. But we don't have time for you to sit there feeling sorry for yourself.'

'As opposed to what? I have nothing. I have *less* than nothing. My arm is gone, I'm probably dying of infection, unless those assholes inside decide to kill me early—'

'You still have your brain,' Thistle says. 'Use it.'

I think, long and hard. Only one solution comes to me.

'We can kill ourselves,' I say.

Her eyes are hard. 'I'm serious.'

'So am I.' I swallow the hard lump in my throat and keep talking. 'It's our only option. Find something sharp. Cut the radial artery. Bleed out. It'll be better than going through the grinder alive.'

Thistle looks disgusted. 'If I had something sharp I'd pick the lock in these fucking cuffs,' she says. 'And if that didn't work, I'd keep it close and stab the next one of those motherfuckers who comes within reach. I'm not giving up.'

The utter helplessness makes me feel sick. My face gets hot, and I turn my face away from Thistle, not wanting her to see me cry. But the tears don't come. Maybe I'm dehydrated after losing so much blood.

Or maybe it's a sign that things could still get worse.

CHAPTER 37

The people of this nation shine.
Who are we?

Hours pass. Maybe days. I find myself thinking of Abbey Chapman, the young woman I rescued from Lux's home-made prison. She described to me the sense of hopelessness that came from being so totally at someone else's mercy. I thought I understood, at the time. Now I realise that I understood nothing.

The cameras above us blink, blink, blink. They're not transmitting anything—just recording our fear and pain for the later enjoyment of strangers. Knowing that doesn't lessen the feeling of being watched.

Thistle has given up on talking to me. She's interrogating the other prisoners instead about the movements of the Guards, the weapons they carry, the meal and shower schedules. She must have asked them about all this before, but she's doing it again, hoping to stumble upon a secret solution that none of them has thought of in all the months they've been here. I've reached despair, but she's stuck all the way back at denial.

'Which ones don't always do what the others tell them?'

Thistle is asking. 'Any sign that one of them has a conscience? Or a rebellious streak?'

She's not getting far. The prisoners are more interested in condemning me than helping themselves.

Hailey, who only days ago suggested she and I could run away together, is throwing granules of concrete in my direction. It wasn't a problem at first, but her aim is getting better. The granules are blunt and nearly weightless. They don't hurt, but the impacts are stopping me from sleeping.

'Will you cut that out?' I snap.

She leers, satisfied to finally get a reaction. 'Nope.' She tosses another stone at me. I raise my hand to block it, but the hand isn't there anymore. The stone bounces off my hair.

'Explain to me how this helps you.'

'You kept me prisoner. You fed my friends into a meat grinder. You watched me shower. That's how it helps.'

This time, the rock hits me in the eye. 'Ow! Fuck.'

Hailey cackles.

I doubt it would help to tell her that it was the other Guards who put her friends through the grinder. I try a different tactic.

'You know what it's like inside?' I ask.

'In the house?'

'No. The grinder.'

She throws another rock. I twist my head far enough to dodge it.

'We're all going in there eventually,' I tell her. 'Thought you might appreciate some advance warning. I can describe it. Vividly.'

'Shut up,' she says. Clenched jaw, eyes averted. Trying to block out anything else I might say.

You can't ignore someone and throw stones at them at the same time. The rocks stop. I close my eyes.

Thistle hasn't given up, though. 'Hey, Amar.'

A grunt from elsewhere in the room. 'What?'

Amar, the Terrorist, has a swollen eye and a mangled ear. The skin of his legs bears dozens of puncture wounds. If I had to guess, I'd say he'd been whipped with barbed wire. My fault, for rigging the election. No regrets. That could have been Thistle's eye. Thistle's ear. Thistle's legs.

'That nail sticking out of the wall behind you,' Thistle is saying. 'Can you get it out?'

A pause. I can hear groaning and puffing. 'No.'

'Keep trying.'

'Trust me, it's not going anywhere.'

'Okay. Maybe it doesn't have to. Hold up your hands. Can you get the nail into the lock in the cuffs?'

Some jingling. 'Now what?'

'Are they single-lock handcuffs or double?'

'How should I know?'

'They didn't teach you that in Syria?'

'I've never been to Syria.'

'I thought you were—'

'I didn't run off to join Isis, okay? It's all bullshit. The Guards made it up to get subscribers.'

My eyes pop open. I need to look at Amar as he says this.

Thistle doesn't believe him. 'I'm not here to judge you, okay?'

'It's all bullshit,' Amar repeats. 'I was born on Long Island. I moved to Texas when I was six. I've never been any place else. I'm not a fucking terrorist.'

In the dim light, it's hard to see his face clearly, but I can see his eyes, glowing with frustration and anger.

'You confessed,' I say.

'Stay out of this, Blake,' Thistle says.

Amar is looking at me now. 'Yeah, no shit. Whatever the Guards say you did, you have to pretend to be sorry. The things they hurt you with are so much worse if you tell them you didn't do it.'

'You stood up for a terrorist online,' Hailey points out.

'I said he had a right to a trial,' Amar says. It sounds like they've had this argument before. 'Do you not get how that's different?'

I look around at the other prisoners. 'What about the rest of you?'

'Oh, so *now* you care?' Hailey snaps. 'You get yourself chained up so you can't help us and suddenly you care that we're innocent?' She throws another rock at me. 'I was just a podcaster. It was a conservative show, sure, but I was never in the KKK.'

Her contrition seemed insincere before—perhaps this is why.

'Did you really tell people to murder doctors on your show?'

'Being pro-life is not the same as being pro-murder, asshole. The opposite, in fact.'

I let that one go. 'How about Gerald?'

The Nazi, Emily, speaks up. 'He told us he didn't attack that woman. But really, how are we supposed to know? He sure seemed like a creep.'

'Are you really a Nazi?'

'No.'

'Not exactly,' Amar adds, eyebrows raised.

'*No*,' Emily repeats. 'I shared a meme, okay? It was just a joke.'

'What was the joke?'

Emily rolls her eyes. 'Does it matter?'

Thistle is watching her closely. 'It might.'

Emily sighs. 'There was a woman removing her nail polish with chemicals. And then it said, "But when Hitler removed Polish with chemicals, people lost their minds."'

Silence falls.

'I didn't make the meme,' she says defensively. 'I just shared it. Anyway, that's what I thought they were talking about when they kidnapped me. I didn't hear about the attack at the Jewish school until I'd been here for weeks.'

The attack at the school really happened—I knew about it before I got here. But she looks and sounds like she's telling the truth. She's not the perpetrator.

I glance over at Ivy. 'And you?'

She just turns her face away. Maybe she's still scared of me, and rightly so. I'm the only guilty person in here.

I've been an idiot. Right after I fooled Cedric by adding a photograph of myself to a news article about Lux, I read profiles on all the prisoners, complete with photos and articles. I fell for my own trick.

I've misunderstood the Guards' business model. They lock up innocent people and blame them for real crimes, finding their victims via relevant social media posts to make the illusion more convincing. A right-wing podcaster becomes a Klansman, an anti-war type is turned into an Isis fighter, a shitposter is turned into a Nazi.

Except . . .

The Guards really seem to think these people are guilty.

Donnie's voice in my head, full of pride: *We got a Nazi*

back there. We got a paedophile. We got a rapist. We got a domestic abuser. We got a paid-up member of the KKK. We got a fucking Isis fighter. There's nothing sleazy about giving these people what they deserve.

Kyle told me that Druznetski, the private investigator, does background checks on all the inmates. Making sure they're guilty. It sounds like Druznetski is lying to the rest of the Guards. Why?

A loose thread tickles something in my brain, but I can't quite catch it.

'Now isn't the time for this,' Thistle says. 'Amar—try to tighten the handcuff.'

'*Tighten* it?'

'Yeah. Just one notch.'

Snick. 'Ow.'

'Okay, it's a single-lock. That's good news.'

'It doesn't feel like good news,' Amar grumbles.

'It's easier to pick. I've done it plenty of times. I'd do it right now if I had something sharp. Can you bend the nail?'

'No.'

'Try. Bang the cuffs against it.'

'I'm likely to stab myself in the wrist.'

'Do you want to get out of here or not?' Thistle's voice is hard. 'There's a spring-loaded bar inside the mechanism. You need a bent nail to push it back. Or you could always chew your own thumb off instead. Worked for this asshole.'

'Don't,' I advise Amar. 'Not now that you've tightened the cuff. You'll still be stuck, and you'll bleed out.'

Amar looks from me to Thistle and back, horrified. He's no Isis fighter, that's for sure.

'What is wrong with you two?' he demands.

I open my mouth to defend Thistle—there's nothing wrong with her—but she's already talking: 'Just try, okay? There's a flat plate on the opposite side of the cuff from the keyhole. Bang that part on the tip of the nail. Gently.'

Tap, tap.

'It's not bending.'

'Harder,' Thistle says.

Tap, tap, tap.

'Stop,' I say.

Because the lock outside is rattling. The big door creaks open.

Kyle enters. He's wearing dirty trainers, faded jeans and a ripped sweater. Under his baseball cap, I can tell that his hair is a mess. I resist the urge to tell him to comb it.

He comes straight over to me, carrying a bottle of water and a steaming bowl of food. More of Samson's stir-fry. A dead man's leftovers now a week old.

Kyle puts the bowl and the bottle on the floor. 'Eat up.'

I reach for the food with a hand that isn't there, and then another one which turns out to be cuffed to the wall.

Kyle smirks. Somehow, this hurts more than the look of betrayal he wore before. He's learned the same lesson I did at about his age—people can't hurt you if you don't care about them.

'I'm not a cop,' I say. Technically true.

'He is,' Hailey says unhelpfully.

'Zip it, bitch.' Kyle picks up a spoonful of defrosted rice and beans and holds it out for me. My stomach growls. I lean forwards to take a bite, but he eats it instead.

'So,' he mumbles through the food, 'who killed Samson?'

I don't know, and I won't get far pretending I do. 'Zara sent you, didn't she?'

His nostril twitches.

'She stopped Donnie from killing me because she wanted to know what I knew,' I continue. 'But she didn't want to come in here and ask. You know why?'

Kyle scoops up another spoonful and holds it up. He's made a mistake. The spoon is out of reach, but his foot isn't. I could kick his ankle, snap it like a chicken bone. I can feel all the other prisoners waiting for me to do just that.

I don't.

'Tell me who did it,' he says.

'One of the Guards.' I rest my head against the wall. 'Whoever it is, they want me dead: to hide their secret. So anyone who talks to me is a target, too. Zara didn't want that to be her. She sacrificed you, instead. She's like a coal-miner and you're like her canary.'

'I'm what?' I've lost him.

'She's not the only one trying to throw you under the bus. Ever wonder why Fred makes you do all the trips to the post office? You're on the cameras there. The staff know you. Your fingerprints are on the packages. Fred's even used your real name on some paperwork. If the Guards ever get caught, you're going to look like the mastermind.'

Kyle refuses to be distracted. 'Who killed Samson?'

'Listen to me. You can't trust the Guards. You should take one of the cars and get out of here. Go home to Ackerly before—'

'You're not ready to talk? Fine.' Kyle turns to leave.

The prisoners wait for me to kick him in the back of the leg. Knock him down, get his keys somehow. I don't.

'Samson's killer.' I raise my voice. 'I've narrowed it down. It's not Donnie or Zara, because they didn't let me die. It's not Fred, because I was with him when Samson got shot.' I force myself to ask: 'Was it you?'

Kyle's eyes widen. 'Me?'

He sounds so shocked that I feel a pang of guilt for suspecting him.

'You haven't got a clue,' he says. 'You've been bluffing this whole time.'

'Kyle—'

He kicks me in the face.

My head snaps back and bangs against the wall. The slaughterhouse swings around me and suddenly I'm on the floor, one arm up in the air, still suspended from the cuff, like I want permission to ask a question.

Sideways, I watch Kyle storm back out. He slams the door.

He's forgotten to lock it. It creaks back and forth in the cold breeze. A slice of freedom is visible, but none of us can get to it.

Can't get to the stir-fry, either. Kyle left the bowl just out of reach.

'Hey, push that over here with your foot,' Amar says.

'Kyle's a piece of shit,' Hailey says, maybe trying to endear herself to me and get the food for herself.

'Goddamn it, Blake.' Thistle shifts on the floor, her chains jingling. 'He was within range. You could have knocked him over. He had the keys.'

I work my jaw from side to side. Kyle's kick has loosened it. I think of the snake in the woods, opening wide to swallow a rat—and nevertheless starving to death.

'He might be my son,' I say.

Thistle stares at me, baffled. 'What?'

I'm still dizzy. Blinking like I'm high. 'I think I'm Kyle's father.'

Thistle's mouth falls open. 'I thought you were a virgin. Before.'

'From a sperm donation. He's about the right age, and he looks just like me. Acts like me, too.' I spit some blood on the floor and look out the half-open door, where Kyle disappeared. Silence outside. 'Is it possible to love someone you don't even like?'

Thistle doesn't respond.

'That's deep,' Amar says. 'Now pass the fucking food already.'

I stretch out with my foot, but I can't reach it. I try to prop myself up on my elbow, forgetting that my elbow is gone. For a split second my weight is on the bandaged stump. I collapse, groaning with agony.

'Cry me a river,' Hailey says. 'You don't know what hurting is.'

'Your son.' Thistle coughs, and then the cough turns into a laugh. A demented chuckle, bouncing around the walls in the gloom.

I feel my stump. It's bleeding again. The sharp edge of bone isn't tender anymore. It's like the nerves around it have died.

The sharp edge of bone.

The sharp edge.

Sharp.

Thistle gives up on me. 'Amar? How are you going with that nail?'

I rest my stump on the concrete, deliberately this time, and roll onto it. The pain is like lava, not just in the stump but everywhere, flowing up from my stomach towards my oesophagus. I stifle a sick moan.

'What the hell are you doing?' someone says. Could be Hailey, could be Amar. Could be me.

'Grrargh!' For a second, all my weight is on the stump. It's agony. And then—

Snap! The curved piece of bone splinters off. I gasp through chattering teeth. I'm suddenly freezing.

'Jesus,' someone says.

Can't black out. It's all for nothing if I do.

The broken shard of bone is in a puddle of blood on the floor. I can't reach it with my cuffed hand. Instead I wriggle around on the floor like a fish, using my chest to push the shard up towards my head. It leaves deep scratches all over my torso. At least it's sharp enough.

I rest my face in the puddle of blood for a second, and pick up the bone shard with my lips.

I'll only get one shot at this. *Don't fuck up, Timothy.*

I take a deep breath and spit the bone towards Thistle. It lands right next to her hips.

'Can you pick the lock with that?' I wheeze.

Maybe she says something back. Maybe not. The world goes grey and fluid, and I collapse back into the puddle.

Some time later, I feel Thistle grabbing my four-fingered hand. Fiddling with the lock and finally popping it open with my homemade skeleton key. My arm flops to the floor. The blood pumps in and out of it. It feels like I'm holding a beating heart in my fist.

'Leave me behind,' I mumble. 'You can come back and arrest me later.'

'Shut up. Drink this.' Thistle pushes something into my mouth. The water bottle. I slurp greedily at it, and choke.

'Quiet,' she says. 'We don't know how far away they are. We have to go—now.'

I swallow. Some of the nausea eases. The dark fog recedes, leaving a moment of clarity. Just long enough for me to realise something.

'Don't unlock Ivy,' I say.

Thistle frowns. 'What?'

I turn my head and see that she's already freed the others. All of them. Ivy looks at me, eyes wide.

I meet her gaze. 'She's been spying on you all. For Fred.'

CHAPTER 38

Smoke us, play us, fill us with water—what are we?

The other prisoners all just frown. No one believes me—until Ivy bolts towards the open door.

'Grab her!' Thistle hisses.

Amar manages to snatch Ivy's wrist. She trips, and they both hit the concrete floor. She screams, 'Help!'

Thistle slaps a hand over her mouth, muffling the sound. She and Amar keep Ivy pinned to the floor. Thistle's knee is on her back.

We all wait. The dogs moan and wail outside. No one comes out of the house. Hopefully the Guards didn't hear us.

Thistle looks at me. 'Start talking.'

'She didn't have visible injuries like everyone else.' I try to stand. My legs shake. It's not just exhaustion, or blood loss—having only one arm has thrown off my balance. 'Someone gave her thermal underwear. She looked like she had been eating better, too. Fred doesn't let the other Guards touch her. And when I pretended to torture her, she played along too well. She was used to it.'

Ivy makes angry noises, maybe objecting to the word *pretended*. She would still be sore from that final punch. I remember her screaming, *Help me!* Not to the other prisoners—to the Guards.

'Druznetski didn't tell Fred who I was.' I stagger over to them. 'That was bullshit. It was Ivy. Fred took her away for a shower and then came back knowing. You told Ivy, she told him. Look in the confessional, near where she was chained up. Dollars to doughnuts you'll find something you didn't know she had.'

Emily is already opening the door. 'Motherfucker!' She holds up a tube of antiseptic lotion.

Hailey aims a kick at Ivy, who shrinks back in terror. 'You goddamn treacherous—'

Thistle shoves Hailey away. 'Back off.'

'Leave her chained up here,' I say.

'No.' Thistle is still holding Ivy against the floor. 'We don't know what the Guards will do to her.'

'Who gives a shit?' Emily demands. 'She's working with them.'

'We're not leaving her behind.' Thistle takes her hand off Ivy's mouth.

'I'm sorry,' Ivy croaks. 'I couldn't take it anymore.'

'Fucking bitch,' Hailey says.

Thistle ignores this. 'Hey. Look at me.'

Ivy does, with big, wet eyes.

'You want to come with us?' Thistle asks.

'Yes.'

'And you'll be quiet?'

Ivy nods desperately.

'Okay. Let's go, before that kid realises he forgot to lock the door.'

'This is bullshit,' Amar says.

'We can't just walk to the nearest town.' I cough and wipe my mouth. 'They could notice we're missing any minute. They'll catch us long before we get anywhere safe.'

'We don't have a choice,' Thistle says.

'We need the car keys,' I say. 'I'll go get them.'

'You can barely stand. *I'll* get the keys.'

'I know where Fred keeps them.' I swallow, and stagger towards the door. 'I know the layout of the house. Every squeaking floorboard. It has to be me.'

'Blake, they'll kill you—and not just you. If they see you in the house, the first thing they'll do is check on the rest of us. We won't get half a mile away.'

'Then I'd better make sure they don't see me.'

Thistle doesn't look convinced.

'Look,' I say. 'Go to the pick-up. Wait for me. Plan A is I come out of the house with the keys and we drive. We'll be back in Houston before the Guards even realise we're gone. But if I'm not at the pick-up within ten minutes, or if you hear yelling from inside, let the air out of the tyres and then run like hell. That's plan B. Okay?'

Thistle exhales through her teeth. 'Okay. Just try to make plan A work.'

'Yeah, no kidding.'

The door is still open a crack. Hailey has her eye pressed to the gap. 'All quiet out there,' she says.

'Can you take the same path through the forest we took last time?' I ask Thistle. 'To avoid the cameras?'

Thistle nods. 'I remember.'

'Okay. Go.'

Hailey pushes the door open. We all flood out into the

night, like roaches fleeing when a box is lifted up. I head for the house while everyone else runs for the woods. Thistle tries to keep them in line, away from the cameras, but in their panic it doesn't look like they're paying much attention. I don't know how much time I have.

Halfway to the house, I can hear that howling on the breeze again. I look at the dogs, but they're sleeping. The sound seems close but far away at the same time. Hopefully it's nowhere near where Thistle and the others are.

The windows on this side of the house are dark, but I can hear conversation. Too far away to tell who is talking, or what they are saying. It doesn't matter. Sounds like they're in the living area, which is a long way from Fred's room.

Miracle of miracles, Samson's house key is still in my pocket. The Guards must not have thought to search me, or maybe the key is so small that they missed it. I pinch the key between my knuckles and unlock the door as quietly as I can, then I push it open, fast enough that it doesn't creak.

The lights are off in the kitchen and dining area, but there's a reflected glow from the living room around the corner. Donnie is at the stove, working in the semi-darkness. I'm looking at his back, at the apron tied around his waist and neck, as he fries something on a hissing skillet.

The kitchen bench is between us. A large cleaver rests on a bamboo chopping board. How quietly could I snatch it up and dispose of Donnie?

I tiptoe further into the room, willing him not to turn around.

He turns—but not towards me. He faces the oven, leaning down to check something inside. He's out of reach now. I'd have to go around the bench, or throw the cleaver.

I do neither. I sneak past and slip into the corridor, heading towards the bedrooms. Once I'm out of sight I listen for a moment. Donnie is humming quietly, oblivious.

I creep up the corridor towards Fred's room, trying to work out how much time has passed since I left the slaughterhouse. One minute, maybe. Distracted, I nearly step on a squeaky board. At the last second I put my bare foot somewhere else, and reach for the wall to steady myself. But that hand doesn't exist anymore, so I overbalance. Hit the wall with my shoulder, my bandage leaving a red smear.

The humming in the kitchen stops.

I hold my breath, heart racing.

'Zara?' Donnie calls. 'That you?'

'What?' Zara calls, from the living area.

I open Fred's door, slip through and close it again, just in time. Donnie's footsteps thump out of the kitchen, past the dining table and around the corner into the corridor.

I scan Fred's room for somewhere to hide. Under the bed might work. But crawling would make a noise. I stay frozen.

Several agonising seconds tick past. I picture Thistle and the prisoners, picking their way through the woods towards the car. They're taking the long way so they're not visible through the windows. I'll have to do that, too.

Thump, thump, thump. Donnie goes back to the kitchen.

I exhale and look at the bowl where I last saw Fred's keys. They're gone.

I mouth a bunch of swearwords, pinching my lower lip between my teeth on the Fs, almost hard enough to make it bleed.

I quickly rummage through the discarded clothes on the

floor. The pockets of his jeans are empty. His puffy synthetic jacket has two zippered pockets. I check them. Nothing.

But when I drop the jacket, something jingles.

I pick it up again. There's a secret pocket on the inside. I unzip it and dig out the car keys. Bingo.

Seven minutes, give or take, until Thistle and the others leave. Plenty of time.

But when I emerge back into the corridor, I can hear voices. Closer this time. More people are in the kitchen.

'Who was the subscriber?' Zara is asking.

'Username PrincessChalk,' Fred says. 'Real name Matilda Glasset.'

'How did she even know where he was?'

I can hear the clattering of plates, the gurgling of glasses being filled.

'So you saw the suggestion—'

'And lost my shit, yeah.'

They're setting the table for dinner. There's no way I can get to the back door without them seeing me. I'll have to wait until after dinner, by which time Thistle and the others will be long gone, hiking through the freezing forest on foot.

I retreat into Fred's room. It's hard to think with a ticking clock. An unfortunate paradox—the less time you have, the longer it takes to solve a problem.

Cedric's voice: 'You really think Lux is FBI?'

'I don't know. He's been acting like a cop, investigating all of us,' says Fred, who told me to do exactly that. 'And we never saw his face on any of the Abbey Chapman videos, did we?'

'You're saying he didn't even make them?'

'I'm saying the rest of him needs to go into the grinder.'

Zara doesn't speak up for me. I guess Kyle already told her that I don't know anything useful. Now I'm nothing more than a threat, because I know she's CIA. If I don't die soon, it'll be her having to make a quick escape—

And suddenly I know what to do.

I open Fred's door. To get to Zara's room, I'll have to cross the corridor. I'll be visible for a second from one corner of the dining table. Usually Kyle sits there.

I wait for Fred to speak again, since Kyle always looks at Fred when he's talking.

The seconds tick away.

'PrincessChalk is right, you know,' Cedric muses. 'He *is* a good candidate.'

'I don't care,' Fred says. 'It's too dangerous to keep him.'

I dart across the corridor, slip into Zara's room and shut the door almost all the way. I don't turn on the light.

I'm now convinced that Zara's mess isn't mess. She knows exactly where everything is. An intruder in a tidy room can easily put things back the way he or she found them. That's much harder in a messy room, and the intruder may not think it necessary.

I don't have time to cover my tracks. I wade through outfits and books and make-up power to get to the window. Hoping the silver dust I noticed around the padlock wasn't dust.

Until now, I never wondered how Zara's handler intended to give her the dossier. She was inside with us, and Fred had padlocked her window shut. But the handler went right up to it the following night. I followed his footsteps.

An undercover CIA agent would want a secret escape route. A window is ideal. So Zara would have sabotaged the padlock, just in case. She could have cracked the tumblers with a hammer and chisel, or—more likely, given the metal shavings I mistook for dust—she could have stolen his keys, opened the padlock, filed off just a little from the tip of the curved bar, and then 'locked' it again before returning the keys. Fred would assume she was still locked in, but she was free.

Praying that I'm right, I rattle the padlock.

It doesn't budge.

Grimacing, I pull with as much force as I can—which isn't much, given that I only have four fingers and eight pints of blood left.

The lock clicks. Zara was amazingly precise, shaving off just enough metal that the lock could be forced open but not so much that it wouldn't latch closed.

I don't pause to admire the craftsmanship. I drop the lock into my pocket just in case I need to hit someone with it, then I lift the window and scramble out into the night.

Five minutes to go. As long as I don't blunder into the sightlines of any cameras, I should be okay.

As I stagger through the backyard towards the safety of the woods, a sound stops me. This time it's more like a moan than a howl. It seems closer than the woods, but that's impossible. I spin around and around, scanning the darkness. There's no one here. Am I losing my mind?

Then I look down. I'm right near the PVC pipe that I nearly tripped over on my first night here. The one I assumed was part of an underground compost system. Suddenly the shape, curving around and down, doesn't seem so inexplicable. It's not for letting water out. It's for letting air in.

Seven prisoners on the website. Only six in the slaughterhouse.

How about the feed on the Pedo?

I checked. Still working fine.

Is it possible that someone is buried alive, right beneath my feet? That they've been here this whole time?

I crouch down next to the pipe. I twist it up to face my mouth, and whisper into it: 'Hello?'

There's a pause. Then a shriek of madness and terror from below.

CHAPTER 39

I'm joy on your tongue, tears in your eyes.
Freeze me to keep me hot. What am I?

I rip off my shirt and stuff it into the pipe, muting the sound. I shoot a glance towards the house.

For a second, there's no sign that anyone heard or cares. But then the back door creaks open.

I flatten myself against the dead grass. I'm so filthy that from fifty yards away, I hopefully look like just a rise in the dirt.

A flashlight clicks on and sweeps across the yard. It tickles the tips of the grass blades above my head.

The light clicks off.

Someone says something from inside.

'No,' says the person in the doorway. Sounds like Cedric. 'The Pedo must have had a nightmare.'

Laughter from inside. The door shuts again.

I rise slowly, wondering what to do. Four minutes before Thistle gives up on me and sabotages the tyres of our getaway vehicle. I should just go. Leave this guy to his fate.

But Thistle wouldn't do that.

'Goddamn it,' I mutter, and grab the shovel from the vegetable patch.

No time to wonder who's down there. No time to feel bad for not figuring it out sooner. I frantically stab at the ground. With one arm, I can't lift the dirt—I can only drag it aside. This is going to take hours that I can't spare.

But I get lucky. The shovel gets tangled in a sackcloth sheet. Apparently I'm not the only one who buries things this way.

I grab the sheet and pull it aside. Dirt cascades onto a coffin, buried barely a foot down. I guess Donnie was too lazy to dig any further.

Left him in Huntsville State Park under six feet of dirt. No one will ever find him.

You hear that, Donnie? Six feet.

I expected an old-fashioned pine coffin, but it's steel. No expense spared. No way to punch through it from the inside. Wires trail out one side to a battery pack in a Ziploc bag. I don't touch them. Cutting off the feed may trigger an alert.

The muffled screaming continues unabated. If whoever is in there keeps this up, I'll have to knock them out with the shovel and drag them to the car.

I wedge the side of the shovel into the seam and lever the coffin open. A foul smell sends me reeling. Inside, a gaunt man in priest's robes is surrounded by granola bar wrappers, empty water bottles and a puddle of his own shit. He's as bald as a skeleton, with sallow skin, yellow fingernails and scratch marks all over his throat. Now that the coffin is open, I can see the fish-eye lens cameras built into the lid.

When the fresh air hits him, the man stops screaming and starts gasping. It sounds like a paddling pool being pumped up.

'Stay quiet,' I say.

He looks up at me, his one-armed saviour. His voice is hoarse. 'Are you real?'

'I'm real. Get up.'

'I didn't hurt those kids.' His bloodshot eyes meet mine. 'Never, never.'

'I don't care.' I grab his hand and pull him out of the hole. 'Come on.'

He's very weak, staggering around like a newborn calf. His muscles have atrophied.

'Hurry,' I say, even though it probably doesn't matter. We're already two minutes late. Thistle and the others will be gone, marching on a doomed mission through the woods. This asshole has cost us our chance of escape. But I keep dragging him towards the woods, because I don't know what else to do.

He's whimpering and gibbering, trying to tell me something, but half the words sound made-up. He could be protesting his innocence or confessing his sins. I wonder if he's a real priest, or if the Guards just dressed him like that for the subscribers.

The dogs behind the fence see us and go crazy, scream-barking and running around in circles, their collars jingling. I keep pulling the priest along, desperate to get him out of sight.

As we reach the safety of the trees, he collapses.

'Get up,' I snap.

He tries, but his limbs quiver and he hits the dirt.

I heave him up. Put his arm around my neck. The smell is horrifying. Holding him leaves me without a free arm to keep branches out of my face. Scratches accumulate on my cheeks.

When we're barely ten yards into the woods, I hear the back door open again. Someone has come to investigate the barking.

The priest is half limp. 'Keep moving,' I whisper, 'or we're dead. You understand?'

He doesn't seem to hear me. He's dead weight. But I can't leave him. Not now.

'They'll put you back in the ground,' I say.

That gets his attention. He looks at me with wide, yellow-rimmed eyes. 'Oh, please, God, no! Don't!'

'Not me, them. Shut up and run.'

Cedric's voice from the backyard behind us: 'Shit!' Then, louder: 'Hey! Come quick! The Pedo's loose!'

I hobble faster through the shrubbery, twigs lacerating my feet. The priest stumbles along as best he can. We're maybe a hundred yards from the car, but it's slow going.

The door bangs again.

'I fucking told you to bury him deeper,' Cedric is saying.

Donnie's voice: 'This isn't my fault. He must have had help.'

Fred, grimly: 'Check the slaughterhouse.'

Eighty yards to go. My teeth are clenched so hard they're on the verge of cracking. Flashlights sweep around behind us. I think we're out of their range, for now. I try to move quietly, but the priest's breathing sounds like a hacksaw. I want to cover his mouth, but he seems so sickly that he might suffocate.

'Shh,' I whisper.

Donnie is back: 'Shit—they're gone!'

Fred: 'Who is?'

'All of them. Goddamn it!'

'How?'

Kyle: 'I . . . I must not have locked the door.'

In real life, a punch doesn't sound like in Hollywood. You don't get that deep, baseball-bat-into-a-phonebook thud. With knuckles on cheekbone, you only hear a sharp tap. Just the same, the sound stops me in my tracks. I'm trembling, like my voltage has been turned up.

I've wanted to eat people before, but this might be the first time I've wanted to kill someone.

The priest squirms, his arm around my neck like a python. 'What?'

Somewhere behind us, keys are jingling. Why are they locking the slaughterhouse *now*, after the prisoners have escaped?

'What?' the priest says again.

The rusty gate squeals, and I realise my mistake: the Guards aren't locking the slaughterhouse. They're *un*locking the dog run.

Fred sounds suddenly friendly. 'Go, girls! Go get 'em! Go!'

The two boxers bark hungrily.

'Run!' I whisper.

We stumble through the dark, the priest still wrapped in his soiled robes, me half naked and half the man I used to be. Fast, heavy breaths and the pounding of paws on dirt echo through the forest. The dogs aren't after us yet—it's like they're doing a perimeter check or a victory lap around the house. But the sound is getting closer.

I'm ignoring the cameras now, just blundering right past them. It doesn't matter if they see us. What matters is getting as far away from those dogs as possible.

But if we escape, the dogs might find Thistle and her group instead.

I falter, missing a step, and the priest almost falls off my back. Maybe I should be letting them find us, so she survives.

Or maybe I should abandon the priest. Let the dogs tear him apart, while Thistle and I both escape.

I take a second to wonder how Thistle would feel about sacrificing a stranger to save her own life. Then I keep carrying the priest through the forest.

Excited barking from somewhere behind us. The dogs have found our trail. It wouldn't be hard, given the smell the priest has left in his wake. The dogs will be on us any second.

But I can see the pick-up through the trees. No sign of the other prisoners, but even if they've punctured the tyres like I told them to, the priest and I can hide inside the cabin for protection from the dogs.

I can hear whispers. The Guards must be catching up to us.

I let go of the priest, dig the keys out of my pocket and push the button on the remote. The lights in the pick-up come on as it unlocks.

The other prisoners scramble out from behind it. Thistle is with them, her handbag over one shoulder and a phone in her hand. The bag must still have been in the tray of the pick-up, where Donnie dumped it. I told Thistle there was no phone service out here, but she would have tried anyway.

Seeing her gives me a surge of energy—desperation and relief all mixed together. I drag the priest out of the woods. 'What are you still doing here?'

'Finally! She wouldn't let us leave without you,' Hailey snaps. Then she sees the priest. 'Who the hell is that?'

'One more prisoner,' I say. 'He was buried in the back-yard. Had to dig him up.'

Thistle looks at me, shirtless and weak, then at the priest and his soiled robes. 'Holy shit.'

I laugh, and then realise the joke wasn't intentional. I toss her the keys. 'Dogs are after us. Get in quick.'

Everyone piles into the tray, except Thistle, who gets in the passenger side and slides over to the driver's seat. She leaves the door open for me and starts the engine.

'I'm not coming,' I say.

She stares at me. 'What?!'

'I have to get Kyle out of here,' I say.

I don't know why I can't abandon him. He's committed abduction, false imprisonment, torture, assault, mail fraud and probably a whole host of other crimes.

But Thistle seems to understand immediately. 'What about the dogs? And the Guards?'

'I'll think of something. Just go.'

'You heard him!' Hailey yells from the back. 'Go!'

Thistle doesn't. She rummages through her handbag, pulls out the can of pepper spray and throws it to me. 'Use this.'

I love you, I want to say. But, 'Thanks,' is all I have the courage for.

'You too,' she says, which doesn't make sense unless she's telepathic. Then she stamps on the gas and screeches away down the gravel driveway.

I turn back to face the woods. I can't see the dogs yet, but I can hear their paws, their snapping jaws, their ragged breaths.

I look down at the pepper spray. I've never used this stuff. The can is no bigger than a deodorant stick, black, with an orange button on top. It feels light. Almost empty, maybe.

But a little should be enough. After the FBI developed pepper spray in the eighties, US Army scientists determined that it was too toxic to use on civilians. The FBI approved it anyway, which paved the way for other agencies to use it. It turned out that the head of the FBI less-than-lethal weapons program was taking bribes from pepper spray manufacturers. He was jailed, but the damage was done. Pepper spray was already being used by hundreds of other agencies.

When I look back up, the dogs are already here, racing out of the darkness towards me, teeth bared for the kill. I raise the spray can. It's hard to hold it with only four fingers.

The faster of the two dogs streaks across the dirt, crossing the last six feet in a terrifying leap. I take aim with the spray can and push the button, just as the dog's huge paws hit my chest, knocking me over backwards.

I hit the dirt so hard that the air explodes out of my lungs. The first blast from the spray can shoots uselessly up into the air, but the dog takes the second one right in its slavering jaws. It makes a sound like a whinnying horse and scrambles backwards, sneezing and whimpering. Eyes shut, it frantically rubs its snout with its paws, trying to get the spray off.

The other dog snaps at my leg. It misses my flesh but grabs my pants. The fabric rips as the dog wrenches its head sideways, like a gator trying to break a deer's neck.

I spray it with the last of the can's contents. The dog yelps and backs off immediately. The first one is still freaking out a few feet away.

I have a split second to feel triumphant before the cloud from my first blast, the one that missed, comes back down and settles all over me.

It's like being set on fire. My eyelids clamp shut as though someone else is controlling them, and even so, my eyeballs burn. The skin all over my face seems to bubble and boil. I can't breathe. I suddenly feel sorry for the dogs.

I rub my face, but that just seems to make it worse. My palm stings where I touched the chemical.

I'm too dizzy from the lack of air to stand, so I throw the can away and crawl back up the gravel driveway, towards the house. I need water. I can't think while my whole body is burning. That freezing shower I made Hailey stand in would be perfect, if I can find it.

It's hard to crawl on one arm. My hand has to jump quickly from one spot to another while my abdominal muscles strain to hold up my torso. How fast can a human being crawl? One mile per hour? Less? It'll take me hours even to circle the house.

Soon I can't hear the dogs anymore. I must have crawled out of earshot. Or maybe they ran away. It's impossible to know.

Grass under my hand, not gravel. I've gone off-road. I back up, find the driveway again. But then I hesitate, not sure which way leads to the house. Right or left? The longer I wait, the harder it is to work out which way I came.

Before I can decide, engine noise fills the air. Tyres crunch on gravel towards me. I can see headlights behind my closed eyelids. Has Thistle come back for me?

A car door opens. I can hear dinging from the dash—a *door open* alert.

Shakily, I stand up. My hopes are crushed when the driver speaks.

'What the hell?' Donnie says.

'Donnie.' My voice breaks. 'Thank God.'

'How the fuck did you get out?'

'Hailey had a key to her cuffs.' I spit a glob of peppery saliva onto the ground. 'Don't know how she got it. She started letting all the other prisoners go. I waited until she freed me, and then I started screaming for you guys. You didn't hear me?'

I'm still blind. I have no way of knowing if Donnie is buying any of this.

More footsteps. The other Guards are here.

'When they ran, I chased them,' I continue. 'But Hailey had a key to Fred's truck, too. I tried to stop them getting away, but the FBI agent pepper-sprayed me. I guess the can must still have been in the pick-up. But how did Hailey get a hold of those keys?'

I stop myself from directly suggesting that one of the other Guards helped the prisoners escape. It'll be more convincing if Donnie joins those dots on his own. And at this point, turning the bad guys against each other is my only hope.

Silence.

'Donnie?' I try to blink the stinging mucus out of my eyes. The headlights are two bright patches. Everything else is dark. 'Are you still there?'

'Why didn't you escape with them?' Fred's voice this time. Donnie isn't alone. Fred sounds like he's thinking aloud.

I try to spread my arms wide, but with one missing, it probably just looks like I'm pointing to one side.

'I'm one of you,' I say. 'I've always been one of you.'

I hear the snick-clack of a slide being pulled back, a chamber checked for a bullet.

'If he was a cop, he would have left with the others,' Zara points out quietly.

'No, he would have stayed to arrest us,' Fred says.

'Look at him,' Donnie says. 'He's in no shape to arrest anybody.'

'To follow us, then, so he can turn us in later.'

'He doesn't look like he has a "later",' Cedric says.

I can sort of see the group, now. Four blurry shapes. Unclear who is who. Where's Kyle?

'What if he's not a cop?' Donnie sounds quietly horrified by the possibility that he cut off the arm of an innocent man.

My teeth are chattering. 'Can we discuss this in the van? I'm freezing to death out here.'

'Either way, we gotta get moving,' Cedric says.

'Who votes we take him with us?' Zara asks.

Three blurry shapes raise their hands. One doesn't.

That fourth shape is Samson's killer. It has to be. But I can't see who it is.

'All right,' Donnie says reluctantly. 'Get in the car, Lux.'

'Thanks, man.' I stagger towards the van, blinking away more tears and pepper spray. My surroundings are slowly coming into shape—including the house. I almost laugh. After what felt like hours of crawling, I'm still more or less where I started. My skin sizzles.

Fred—I think it's Fred—lifts up his phone.

'You gonna push the button?' Cedric asks.

'Yup. Should have done it five days ago.'

I look back at the house, remembering all the packages of ammonal crammed into the walls. Enough to turn the whole building inside out. Destroy all the evidence that a house was ever here.

I can see Penny at the attic window, watching us. My vision is still too blurred to make out her expression.

Fred pushes the button.

I cover one ear with my remaining hand.

Nothing happens.

'Okay.' Fred pockets the phone. 'Let's go.'

He opens the van door, and that's when I see Kyle's body inside.

CHAPTER 40

I wait for years, watching as you
gorge yourself, and then I hit you
where you love. What am I?

I scramble in and practically fall onto the corpse. And it *is* a corpse, already cold from the night air.

'Kyle!' I shake him. Slap his face. 'Kyle!'

No response. My vision is blurry, but I can tell that his flesh is pale.

'Help me!' I shout, like the Guards don't know what's happening. 'Kyle's dying!' I can't say the word *dead*. Can't even think it.

The others ignore me, hustling into the van and buckling their seatbelts. Fred is in the driver's seat. He releases the handbrake and starts us rolling down the gravel driveway.

I put my ear to Kyle's lips. Not breathing. A finger under his jaw. No pulse. I plant my hand on Kyle's ribs. I've seen enough open chest cavities to know where his heart is. I push down, over and over.

'Lux.' Cedric touches my arm gently. His eyes look hollow in the fluorescent light from the bulb overhead.

I shake him off. Keep pumping Kyle's chest, using every bit of my strength. Hitting him so hard that I might give *myself* a heart attack.

'He's dead,' Cedric says.

I keep pumping. These days they teach chest compressions only, not mouth to mouth. But Thistle kept me alive with CPR one time, and she used mouth to mouth. I put my lips over Kyle's and huff into him.

His chest rises partway, like a half-inflated bouncy castle, then sags immediately. I try again. The air won't stay in his lungs.

'Look.' Zara rolls Kyle's head sideways, so I can see the back of it. It's smashed in—a mess of blood and brain matter. As though someone clubbed him with a bowling ball.

'No!' I keep pumping, because I once met a woman who had survived a gunshot wound to the head. Impossible things happen. I can barely breathe. I'm choking. The son I only just met can't be gone already.

'There's no coming back from that,' Zara says.

I thump Kyle's chest over and over, tears and snot streaming down my face. Not just from the pepper spray anymore. I love him. I don't know why, but I do.

The van bounces as we reach the turn-off to the dirt road. My hand slips off Kyle's chest and I hit the floor. I try to get back onto my knees, but it's like my arm is made of rubber.

My airway is tight. 'Someone help him!'

No one does.

'Jesus, Lux. I'm sorry.' Donnie is hazy, but he sounds moved. He doesn't think I'm a cop anymore. A cop wouldn't care about a dead criminal.

I've convinced them that I'm on their side—but too late.

I lie next to Kyle and put my hand on his arm. Close my stinging eyes, like I can imagine him back to life.

You never told him, says the cruel voice in my head.

Shut up.

He died not knowing.

Shut up!

It's not just that he died not knowing who I was; it's that he died not knowing who *he* was. This boy from Ackerly never got the chance to become someone good.

Someone squeezes my shoulder as I cry.

•

Hours pass. Eventually streetlights start sweeping past the windows. Other cars cruise by. Sirens on the wind. We must be approaching Houston.

Lying on the cold floor, I don't intend to speak, or do anything, ever again. But eventually I hear my own voice: 'What happened? To Kyle?'

'He fucked up,' Fred says flatly from the driver's seat. If he has any feelings about leaving his mother behind, he's keeping them buried deep.

My voice cracks. 'What do you mean?'

'He left the slaughterhouse door unlocked. I've told him a million times to be careful about things like that.'

Fred's eyes must have been on the road this whole time. He hasn't sensed the mood shifting in the rest of the van. The others might not have cared about Kyle's death before— none of them seemed to like him while he was alive—but they care now. My grief is contagious. Plus, Donnie and Cedric don't think I'm a cop anymore, which might make them feel guilty about putting me through the grinder.

Guilt and grief are inward emotions. They make you ask uncomfortable questions of yourself. The easiest way to deal with those feelings is to turn them outwards. Transmute them into rage.

'The prisoners got out,' Fred continues, oblivious. 'I hit him. He tripped, bumped his head on a rock.' He sighs. 'Poor kid.'

I heard that punch. I was right there. I didn't even go back to check if Kyle was okay.

'Poor kid?' There's a dangerous tone in my voice. The others hear it and tense up.

Fred doesn't. 'It's a shame. He would have been willing to take the heat off us, as you know.'

A second ago I was burned out: physically, emotionally and intellectually exhausted. I haven't slept or eaten. But anger is an inexhaustible fuel source. It's like nuclear power—every time you think it's died away, it comes back to kill somebody.

I sit up.

'Lux,' Donnie warns.

'You killed him.' The words burn on the way up my throat, like vomit.

Fred glances at me in the rear-view mirror, eyes narrowing.

I launch myself at him, teeth bared. Donnie lunges at the same moment, trying to stop me. I claw at Fred's face, but he leans away and I miss, my hand digging into the head-rest of his seat.

'Christ, fuck!' Fred yells.

Donnie grabs me before I can try again. Pins me to the wall by my neck. 'Cool it, Lux.'

'You killed him!' I scream at Fred. 'Why would you do that?'

'I just explained that,' Fred says, looking annoyed. 'I—hey, what the hell?'

He stops the van. There's some kind of parade in front of us. No, not a parade. A protest. People are carrying tiki torches, waving cardboard signs that I can't read in the dim light. Some are carrying guns.

Fred puts the car into reverse, his gaze on the wing mirrors. I can hear sirens in the air. Shouts. Breaking glass.

'What's going on?' Cedric asks.

'Our escape plan is what's going on,' Fred says.

'Why here? Why not at the courthouse?'

'I don't know.' Fred swings the van around and drives into a side street.

Donnie still has me against the wall. 'Are you good?'

I glare at him.

'Lux,' he says, 'you gotta calm down, okay?'

After a pause, I nod, and he releases me.

I rub my throat. 'What's happening?'

'You remember Emmanuel Goldstein?' Cedric asks.

'Yeah.' The fictitious anti-mascot, designed to make people angry. He's a child molester, an abusive husband, an illegal immigrant, a racist cop who shot an unarmed Black teen, depending who you ask.

'He just got off on a technicality,' Cedric says. 'He's about to be released from the Herbert W. Gee Municipal Courthouse.'

I'm struggling to understand, and more than that, I'm struggling to care. 'I thought he wasn't real.'

'He's not.' Cedric licks his lips nervously. 'But when Fred pushed the button, hundreds of posts went live and thousands of messages went out. Hundreds of angry protestors should be converging on the courthouse right now. All the police will be there, a nice long way away from our escape route. At least, that was the plan.'

'Yeah.' Donnie stares through the windshield at the protest march in the distance. 'Why are they *here*?'

I shouldn't be surprised. Inciting a riot for personal gain is exactly the sort of thing these assholes would think of.

'Shit.' Fred has spotted a pair of police cars. He turns into a side alley to avoid them.

'Maybe it's not us,' Zara suggests. 'Could be an unrelated protest.'

'At exactly the same time?'

I don't care about this. Kyle is dead. Nothing matters except that. Fred has to pay.

But I'm outnumbered and unarmed. The only way to hurt him is with the truth. And the escape plan—start a riot to distract the police—is familiar. The last piece of the puzzle falls into place.

I clear my throat. 'Hey, Rick.'

Fred glances at me in the rear-view mirror.

'I thought so,' I say. 'Frederick is your full name, right? Frederick Allister. Your friends used to call you Rick. Before you shaved off the beard, and cut your hair short.'

Zara looks suddenly interested. She hadn't known this.

'So what?'

'You started hitting your ex-wife, Lynne, after she got pregnant. I think that's when she started to remind you of your own mother, the one who never loved you enough. Eventually Lynne left. And you tried to kill her. Shot at a bomb you'd planted under her car.'

I had assumed it was a coincidence, Fred filling the house

with the same explosive mixture Rick used. But it wasn't—Fred used that compound because he *is* Rick.

'Ex-wife?' Fred squints, feigning confusion.

'Whoa, Lux.' Cedric pats the air. 'Fred wouldn't do that.'

'Because of the bomb, you got classified as a terrorist,' I say. 'Suddenly the FBI were after you. So you worked out a way to distract them. You faked a Facebook post from a congresswoman threatening an assault weapon ban. The plan worked, maybe better than you could have hoped. Armed protestors turned out en masse in Hermann Park. There was chaos and violence. The feds were too busy to chase you. By the time the dust cleared, you were long gone.'

'What are you talking about?' Fred asks, still looking perplexed.

He knows what I'm talking about. But he can't shut me up without stopping the car. And if he does that, the protestors might catch up and block the road around us. Then the police might want to know why there's a dead body in the van.

The other three Guards are listening to me, still puzzled. Maybe wondering if I've lost my mind.

'But you hadn't realised your baby son was in the car. You nearly killed him by mistake. That rattled you. So you got some therapy. Anger management classes. You came out with a better understanding of anger—not just how to control it, but how to sell it. Rage to riches.'

'You were married?' Donnie asks Fred.

'No,' Fred says. 'He's full of shit.'

'Your idea was a website that gives subscribers the chance to vent their anger on criminals. But real criminals are hard to catch. So you grab regular people and exaggerate the bad things they've done. That's easier.'

'Those crimes really happened,' Fred objects. 'You can look them up.'

'No doubt,' I say. 'But your prisoners weren't the real perps.'

He's not trying to convince me; he's trying to convince the others. And it's not working. Cedric and Donnie and Zara are looking from me, to him, to each other, and back to me. No longer sure who to believe.

'There's no such person as Druznetski, is there?' I continue. 'He's just like Goldstein—you made him up. A fake source for all your information about the prisoners. To make them seem guilty, for the subscribers—and for the other Guards.'

'You're not thinking straight, Lux,' Donnie says, but he's starting to look uneasy.

'Those people weren't innocent,' Fred says, and I think he probably believes it. *No one's innocent.*

'Abbey Chapman was, when Lux abducted her.' I don't know if the others will notice that I'm referring to myself in the third person, and I'm too far gone to care. 'Lux sent you the videos, and you made up a story to go with them. That's why you told me to keep her background a secret from the other Guards. They needed to believe she was guilty of something. What about Reese Thistle? What did you say she had done?'

'She was a murderer,' Donnie says. 'She killed the kids she was supposed to be babysitting.' He looks at Fred for reassurance.

'Shut up, Lux,' Fred says instead. There's something I haven't seen on his face before—anger. The old Rick is coming back.

I don't shut up. 'But your site was *too* successful. The CIA noticed what you were up to.'

The other Guards look alarmed—especially Zara. She reaches into the front of her dress, where she keeps her gun. I don't know if it's just a threat or if she actually intends to shoot me before I expose her.

I talk faster: 'So a CIA agent shows up one night, and accidentally walks past one of your cameras. He has a dossier, which ends up in Samson's possession. It's full of profiles—not just of the Guards, but the prisoners, too.'

'This is all complete fantasy,' Fred says. But I can see that the others don't believe him.

The van is accelerating, the whine of the engine building to a crescendo.

'According to the dossier, all the prisoners are innocent. Samson doesn't trust any of the others, because it seems like one of them is a CIA spy. Not you, though, since you're the founder—you wouldn't infiltrate your own organisation. So early the next morning, he shows you what he found. He tells you Druznetski has been lying, and the prisoners aren't guilty.'

'But they were,' Donnie says to himself. 'They must have been.' He tortured innocent people. Murdered them. Put them through a meat grinder. He can't bear the thought of it.

'You ask Samson if he's showed the dossier to any of the others. He says no—he's not sure who to trust.' I meet Fred's gaze in the rear-view mirror. 'And you kill him.'

Donnie looks from me to Fred and back. He's like a casserole dish about to bubble over. Too soon to tell who'll get burned.

'Jesus Christ,' Cedric says. The anger has reached him, too. It's like an airborne pathogen, infecting everyone in the van.

'You made it look like a suicide,' I say. 'But you could tell I didn't believe it. You thought maybe I was the CIA contact. So you took me aside and asked me to investigate the murder. You tried to make me suspicious of everyone except you. Fed me some bullshit about seeing Samson on the cameras that morning—'

'Don't you remember?' Fred interrupts. Veins stand out in his forehead and neck. His jaw works back and forth. He's losing it. 'I was *with you* when Samson was shot.'

He must think I haven't figured that part out yet. He doesn't know about my backyard autopsy. The bullet I couldn't find—the bullet that had never existed.

'He wasn't shot.' I raise my voice, making sure Donnie and Cedric hear this part. The two men who both loved Samson. 'You stabbed him in the head with a screwdriver.'

'You son of a bitch!' Donnie snarls.

Zara whips out her gun and points it at Fred. 'Pull over.'

But Donnie is already in motion. It's like sharing the van with a charging rhino. He barges me aside on his way to the driver's seat. Fred lets go of the wheel, flapping both arms, trying to protect his head as Donnie reaches him. He only partly succeeds. Donnie's meaty fist glances off the top of Fred's skull. The van starts to veer sideways.

I don't even brace myself. I've done my job. I told the truth. We're all going to die, but Fred's going first.

Zara is out of her seat. She tries to grab the wheel. But Cedric tries to attack Fred at the same moment, and he accidentally backhands Zara. She grunts and stumbles backwards, tripping over my legs and landing on Kyle's corpse.

By accident or design, Fred's foot is still on the gas. The van zooms faster and faster through the streets of Houston. Streetlights strobe the interior. The wheels on the passenger side bump up onto the kerb. I can hear screaming from outside.

'You fuck! You sick fuck!' Donnie bellows, still trying to hit Fred.

Zara is on her feet again. She fires a deafening shot into the roof, trying to get everyone to freeze and shut up. It has the opposite effect. Cedric lunges for the gun, but Fred spins the wheel at the same time, trying to get Donnie away from him. Everyone hits the wall except Fred, who's still strapped in. The van drifts, tyres screaming, before it hits a bump in the road and rolls over—

The world spins, and for a split-second there's no gravity, all of us hanging in the air—

Then the side of the van hits the ground, and we come crashing down. As the metal grinds along the blacktop, I bounce off the roof, my arm covering my head, and then hit the floor—formerly a wall. Kyle thuds next to me, and Cedric lands next to him. A bone snaps. Not mine.

The van collides with something else and stops suddenly. I can't stand up. Can't even tell which way *up* is. It's like being inside a shipwreck, on the ocean floor.

Something gets jammed into the flesh under my jaw. A gun barrel. No—two fingers. Zara is checking my pulse.

I try to turn my head and look at the others, but she grabs my skull and twists it back to face her. 'Hold still.' My vision stabilises enough to see that her hair is all over the place and that blood has trickled into one of her eyes. It blooms pink around the retina—she's wearing a contact lens.

Finally she lets me go and I can look at the rest of the van. Donnie is retching on the floor, clutching his junk, his face pale and sweaty. Cedric isn't moving. His face seems to be on the wrong side of his head. Kyle is nearby, still dead, yet somehow looking healthier than all of us.

'This is Cassandra,' Zara is saying from somewhere nearby. 'I'm going to need extraction.'

Donnie mumbles something incoherent.

'No,' Zara says. 'He got away.'

I wipe my eyes on my bare forearm and look at the driver's seat.

Fred is gone.

CHAPTER 41

The roof of this war machine goes great
with your jeans. What am I?

I wrench the hammer off the wall and use my teeth to wrap the duct tape around my fist, holding it in place, just like the trick Fred showed me with the glove. I kick the rear doors open. The van is still on its side, so the top door flops right back down, almost hitting me in the face. But the bottom door crashes onto the blacktop and stays. I duck under the top door and stumble out onto the road.

Fred has to die. That's the only way this ends. I should have put this hammer through his head the moment I met him.

My crunching footsteps echo around the empty street. The van has crashed into a steel gate which blocks off a trash-filled alley between two apartment buildings. I try to work out if Fred could have climbed that gate and decide that he couldn't. There are spikes at the top and it's impossibly tall—or maybe it just seems that way because I'm concussed.

I can hear the riot we passed earlier, but I can't see it. Fred will head that way, hoping to blend in before Donnie recovers and comes after him, or Zara.

Where *is* Zara? I look back. No sign of her near the van. It doesn't matter. I shake my head like a dog, trying to get rid of the ringing in my ears and recover my sense of direction.

No need. The crowd comes to me. The first few runners emerge from a side street, drawn by the sound of the crash. All three wear dark clothes, baseball caps and sunglasses, and their mouths are covered by bandanas. I have no clue which angry mob they represent. The ones who think Goldstein was a racist cop? The ones who think he was a child molester?

They slow down as they approach the crashed van and see me, one-armed, shirtless and limping.

'Hey, man, you need help?' one of them asks. Then she sees the hammer and backs off.

I ignore her and stumble past them towards the street they came from. If that's where the rest of the crowd is, it's where Fred will be headed. Somewhere he can blend in, and hide from Donnie.

More people are jogging up the alley towards me. Some are wearing polo shirts, no logos but still with the feel of a uniform. Others are carrying assault rifles. A teenage girl with a cross around her neck is carrying a sign that says EVERY LIFE COUNTS. A young man with curly hair is wearing a sweater that says, THIS IS WHAT A FEMINIST LOOKS LIKE. A woman with a headscarf has a sheet of cardboard with BEHEAD THOSE WHO INSULT THE PROPHET in magic marker. These people aren't fighting each other, just running. Maybe they've realised Goldstein doesn't exist. Maybe the riot got too much for them and they're heading away from the action. Or maybe they're looking for more.

The crowd gets thicker. I walk against the flow. It's easy. People shrink back when they see me. With my swollen face, bleeding arm-stump and red-rimmed eyes, I probably look like a leper.

I can hear sirens now, whistles, screams, bottles exploding against riot shields, nightsticks cracking on skulls. Shouted slogans, all smearing over the top of one another. No gunfire yet, but it won't take long. One shot is all it will take to turn this into a bloodbath. Bullets beget bullets. I remember my dream: lying in the gutter as a river of blood flows past.

The side street opens out onto the chaos of a main road. Smashed windows. Burning trash cans. Stranded cars with slashed tyres. Thousands of people clumped together in their various factions, screaming abuse, tearing at each other's clothes. Throwing rocks and bottles and punches. Brandishing weapons. In the absence of Emmanuel Goldstein, it looks like the protesters have turned on one another. A smoke bomb sails overhead, spilling toxic fog. This is what hell will look like, when I get there.

The crowd is like a living thing, and the deep bass roar of angry voices uncoils something in my chest. A feeling both genetic and ancient. The sense that Godzilla is coming, or that the ship I'm on just hit an iceberg.

The cops fight to keep everyone separate. Both the FBI and the local police department are here in huge numbers—I don't know how they mobilised so quickly, or why they're here rather than at the courthouse where Goldstein was supposedly being released, or why the FBI showed up at all for what should be a local case. But it doesn't look like they're calming anybody down.

And some of them don't want to. A white cop with a can of pepper spray is advancing on a masked Black anarchist, apparently unarmed and looking the other way. Seeing this, a woman with a pro-choice banner hurls a water bottle at the cop. It misses him and instead hits a guy wearing goggles and army surplus gear. He draws a handgun and turns, trying to work out where the bottle came from. The cop spots him, and sprays him instead. He screams and drops the gun.

I spin around and around in the throng, scanning hundreds of faces, searching for Fred. The smoke and blood and anger blurs everything. Everyone looks the same.

In the end, I only spot Fred because he spots me. Even in a crowd of thousands, I somehow sense that I'm being watched. Among the jigsaw puzzle of screaming faces, about fifty feet away, there's a piece of stillness—a slice of Fred, his eyes widening and mouth falling open as he recognises me. Then he turns and disappears into the chaos.

I doubt he's scared of me. He probably thinks Donnie is nearby. I grip the hammer a little tighter with my duct-taped hand and give chase.

The going is tougher now. The crowd thicker, shoving me to and fro. Tear gas stings my throat. The road is slippery with booze, gasoline and blood. If I lose my footing, I'll be trampled to death.

A portly white man swings a star picket at a Latino guy in a cowboy hat, breaking half his teeth. The cowboy stumbles into me, moaning. I stay upright by grabbing the shoulder of a woman in an actual cape. She whirls around and tries to bring a sign down on my head, but her rage turns to disgust when she gets a better look at me, and that slows her swing down just enough for me to dodge the blow.

I get another glimpse of Fred. He's heading for an alley, but he's trapped between some cops with riot shields and a bunch of masked protesters throwing rocks. He's forced to backtrack.

'Fred!' The shout comes out wet, like I'm gargling blood.

He's close enough to hear, but he doesn't turn around. He sidesteps, trying to get out of the path of the riot police and circle around behind them.

'Grab him!' I shout to the police. 'Grab that guy!'

They have no reason to listen to me. I'm just one more screaming, bloodied lunatic in a sea of them. But the closest riot cop turns her head, her eyes lasering in on mine through the visor of her helmet.

'That guy!' I point the hammer at Fred like I'm trying to cast a spell on him. 'Get him!'

The cop looks, but it's clear she can't tell who I mean. Fred is weaving away through the crowd. I try to fight my way towards him, but a man with huge shoulders, a mullet and a blue tank top is unintentionally blocking my path.

'Stop him!' I roar, still gesturing wildly towards Fred. 'He's getting away!'

The cop seems to have lost interest, but the big guy in front of me can tell who I mean. He clasps my shoulder with a strong hand. 'Him right there?' he asks eagerly. 'White shirt, brown hair?'

'Yes! He's getting away!' I'm desperate for this man's help, although I have no idea why he would grant it.

He nods grimly and starts pushing through the crowd towards Fred. 'That's him!' he shouts.

Several other bulky men, all in blue tank tops, emerge from the crowd to accompany the big guy. He's here with a faction, although I have no clue which one.

'That's him!' Someone from a different group has picked up the chant—a white woman with a bandana and a leather jacket. She points at Fred. 'He's right there!' Several other people in bandanas follow her gaze.

With my head still spinning from the van crash, I can hardly keep up with what's happening. The big guy and his crew seem to think Fred is Goldstein. Meanwhile, the bandana group have overheard the shouts, and now they believe it, too. Fred is quickly becoming public enemy number one in the crowd, even though no one except me knows who he really is.

Fred, oblivious, has made it around the cops, but now the alley he's headed for is blocked by a group in grubby white robes, waving signs and chanting: 'God hates fags!' He turns to retreat, eyes widening as he sees the crowd bearing down on him, bloated by the righteous anger he impregnated them with. He backs away towards a shuttered grocery store, but the growing crowd fills the space before he can get to it. He spins around, confused and afraid, as people form concentric circles of hate around him.

'Fascist!' a woman screams at him.

'Commie scum!' someone else bellows.

'Jew!'

The outermost circle wobbles with confusion. They've noticed that Fred is being targeted by *everyone*. Therefore, he's the enemy of no one. That circle breaks up as the people in it forget about Fred and start hitting each other.

But the inner circles are too far gone. They're moving in on Fred, clutching bottles and rocks and planks. Fred makes eye contact with me for a split second, desperation all over his face, before he takes a baseball bat to the throat and goes down. I lose sight of him, but I hear him hit the ground, gagging. A white supremacist and a guy in a hoodie both start stomping on him, side by side. As I push through the crowd towards Fred, a biker barges past and ducks down, a switchblade gleaming in his hand. Fred makes a choked squeal, and the guy comes back up, the blade now red. Someone in a Klan robe holds up a bottle of lighter fluid and starts pouring about where Fred's face must be. After a second of spluttering, he goes silent.

I break through into the centre of the mob and raise the hammer, just as someone strikes a match.

CHAPTER 42

I visit every day, unseen by most.
I am beautiful, but if you touched
me, you would die. What am I?

I'm back at the van. I don't remember walking here. It's like waking up from a dream, and not knowing what's real for a while. The street is deserted. There's a faint glow from the horizon. I don't know where the rest of the night went. There's a cookout smell in my nostrils and my hand is scalded, like I was still trying to get to Fred even through the flames. The hammer is gone. For the first time since Monday, I'm not hungry.

Cedric's dead body is sprawled half on top of Kyle's. With the last of my strength I drag him off and collapse next to them both. No sign of Zara or Donnie. I take Kyle's hat off his head and crush it in my hand. He looks younger without it. His hair is a bit curly, like mine. I wonder why he always hid it.

I black out again, and then wake up with someone else's hands searching my pockets. As soon as I move, the person shouts: 'Argh! What the fuck?'

I try to sit up, but I'm still too weak.

'Sorry, man. Thought you were dead,' the voice says. 'My bad.'

By the time I've turned my head to look at him, the looter is already hurrying away.

The next time I wake, it's because of flashing lights. An ambulance is parked next to the crashed van. Two paramedics climb out, their faces drawn. It's been a long night.

My throat is too dry to call out. It doesn't matter. They come straight over to me. Maybe the looter called them, told them I was alive. A good Samaritan thief. Stranger things have happened.

One of the paramedics shines a light in my eyes. 'Can you hear me?'

'Yes,' I croak.

'What's your name?'

I give the question some thought. I'm aware it's Timothy Blake, but right now I don't remember who is allowed to know that. It feels like I've been Lux for a long time.

She's already given up on a response and is talking to her partner. 'Concussion, and signs of infection just here.' She touches my stump.

'I don't think a nurse dressed that wound,' the other paramedic says.

'No. I'm also seeing first-degree burns on his hand and around his mouth.'

The second paramedic shakes his head at my stupidity. 'Tried to eat something that was on fire, did you?' he asks me.

'Fred,' I say.

'Okay. Let's get you out of here, Fred.'

They roll me onto a gurney and then raise it up. I feel sorry for them. The rest of us hit each other, shoot each other, blow each other up, feed one another into meat grinders. Then we expect paramedics and nurses and doctors to repair us so we can do it all again.

As they slide me into the ambulance like it's a pizza oven, I raise my head for a last look at Kyle. I'll never find him again. I don't even know his last name. But the female paramedic pushes my forehead back down and says, 'Easy there.' Her hand is cool. She snaps a plastic mask down over my face. Oxygen flows into my mouth, around a foreign object. Something hard. A little piece of bone, but not a tooth. I swallow it.

•

The hospital is overflowing. It's all the same people from the riot, but they're not fighting anymore. Maybe they're too tired and sore. Maybe they've had their fill of violence. Or maybe, in their identical hospital gowns and bandages, they can't tell who they hate.

There's no point lying anymore, but with so many patients, the doctor doesn't have much time to quiz me. *Who am I?* Timothy Blake. *What happened?* Car crash. *And your arm?* Went into a meat grinder. *What about the burns?* I don't remember. She doesn't look surprised by any of this and asks no follow-up questions.

She unwinds the bandages and examines my stump while a nurse smears some antiseptic on my burns. A bag of someone else's blood arrives. It enters my body, this time through a vein rather than my mouth. The nurse gives me a juice box and some tepid pumpkin soup.

I watch TV. There's footage of the riot. Protestors screaming, punching, getting kicked. Apparently two hundred people were wounded and six are dead. I guess those six include Fred, Cedric and Kyle. It could have been a whole lot worse.

A commentator is badmouthing the protesters, calling them animals, saying the National Guard should have been summoned to control them. She says witnesses have described one protestor eating a corpse. The other talking heads look sceptical.

The director of the Houston FBI field office gives a press conference. She explains the riot was triggered by a torrent of fake news, distributed by terrorists. She says her cyber unit got on to it early thanks to intelligence sent by an undercover FBI agent within the terrorist cell. It takes me a while to realise who she means. I guess my package made it to Dr Norman after all, less than thirty-six hours after I mailed it. I'll never badmouth the USPS again.

Apparently one FBI team was dispatched to arrest the terrorists, while a second team set up roadblocks nearby so they couldn't escape. But locals noticed the police pres-ence, and soon rumours were spreading online that the barricades were for the protection of Emmanuel Goldstein. Instead of congregating at the courthouse as Fred intended, the protesters were drawn to the roadblocks, right in the middle of the Guards' escape route.

The director implies that this was a long-term operation rather than dumb luck. She doesn't admit how bad it could have been.

The same doctor comes back, looking even more haggard. Working a double shift, I guess. She gives me a script for

OxyContin and an antibiotic, and discharges me. I go downstairs to the pharmacy. The man behind the counter offers to send a bill to my residence instead of charging me on the spot. I give him a fake address and walk out.

It's too far to walk home, and I don't have any money. But the hospital is surrounded by drug addicts. I can tell them apart from the worried relatives by their hollow stares, the way they rub their thin arms through their coats. Some of them look a lot like Cedric. I wonder if he could have made OxyContin from his poppies.

I walk up to the most wealthy-looking addict, a woman in a knitted sweater and beanie. I sell her my painkillers and spend the cash on a bus fare home.

•

I can't tell if my house has been robbed. The lock on the door is broken, but maybe it was always like that. It feels like I've been gone for years. The fridge and the freezer are empty, except for some cash hidden inside a block of ice. The old TV is still there, but it might not have been worth stealing.

I sit on the battered couch and wait for Reese Thistle to come and arrest me.

But she doesn't.

No one does.

CHAPTER 43

What do you deep-fry to open a door?

Down in the editing room, screens were flickering. FBI agents appeared on more and more rectangles, bulked up by bulletproof vests and helmets. But the room was empty. No one was watching the feeds.

Six agents surrounded the slaughterhouse. Eight more crept around the outside of the main house. They saw the dog run, but no sign of any dogs.

The slaughterhouse door was still unlocked. Cautiously, one of the agents pulled it open. Inside she saw the sets, the chains, the cameras, the grinder. No people, just bad smells.

The front and back doors of the main house were locked. From a distance, the agent in charge counted to three. Others used battering tubes to smash in both doors at the same instant. The team swept through every room of the ground floor with flashlights, checking in closets and behind doorways for hostiles. There was no one.

Upstairs, they found a woman in her early sixties, holding a gun.

Fred had given it to her. Once he was clear, she was supposed to shoot it into the floor, igniting the ammonal and setting off the massive explosion that I had expected earlier. The fire would have consumed her and destroyed all the evidence of Fred's crimes.

She didn't, though. She kept the gun pointed at the floor as the agents shouted at her. She waited three, four, five seconds. Then, just as the FBI agents were about to open fire, she dropped the gun, having held it for long enough to prove that she *could* have killed everyone in the building. The agents wrestled her to the ground and dragged her downstairs so roughly that they didn't find out she couldn't walk until much later.

It was unclear why Fred expected her to die for him. Maybe he thought she owed him for all that time he spent growing up without her. Perhaps he thought she'd want to protect her son, despite everything he had done. Maybe he thought she would rather die than go back to prison. Or maybe he was just a bully, used to women doing what he told them. No one will ever know.

Penny was freed within days. She'd already served her time for Swaize's murder and had committed no crimes since then. She refused all interviews, and the media eventually lost interest in her. She couldn't be neatly categorised as a villain, a victim, a hero or a bystander, so there wasn't much reason to keep pursuing her.

Thistle also avoided the media. Ivy, too. The priest announced that he wanted to return to his congregation, but it turned out he had already been replaced. He had to fight to get his parish back, and even after he succeeded, his congregation shrank. Most people didn't really believe the accusations of paedophilia, but they left anyway. Better to be safe than sorry.

Hailey's show became the most downloaded podcast in America, a spot it held for almost a week.

Amar and his family had to move house because of all the harassment from people who believed he really was a terrorist.

Emily, being young, thin and blonde, was the one I saw on TV most often. It was always the same scrap of footage, her standing next to her father in front of their McMansion, dabbing a tear away from her mascara. The soundbite: 'It was like a nightmare.' Thousands of subscribers had watched her suffer in that slaughterhouse. Now she was on national television, where millions could enjoy it. Somehow, she's become the hero of the story, rather than Thistle. There's talk of Margot Robbie playing her in a Netflix series.

Donnie was later found crawling around the streets of Houston with a broken thigh from the crash. He had a knife, and slashed at anyone who came near him—the police subdued him with a taser. His prints matched those all over the house and the slaughterhouse. He's serving ninety-nine years in Huntsville, but his attorney is appealing. The judge sentenced Donnie as though he were a psychopath, the lawyer says. She failed to consider provocation—yes, the victims were innocent, but Donnie *believed* they were rapists and murderers. He has expressed remorse and can be rehabilitated. Legal experts say this defence is a long shot, but many columnists are on Donnie's side.

After Cedric was identified as one of the Guards, his book of poetry was reprinted and became a bestseller, popular among those who normally only read books like *Mein*

Kampf, On Guerrilla Warfare by Mao Tse-Tung and that romance novel by Saddam Hussein. Some avant-garde band put some of the poems to music. They were immediately condemned for profiting from Cedric's crimes. Protesters stormed a bar where the band was supposed to perform, trashing it. Nowhere else would book them after that, but the protest made them so famous that their streaming revenue went through the roof, and they were briefly rich before the publisher of the book sued them. The world kept turning.

Kyle was identified, too. I saw his mom crying on the TV. She said she didn't understand how this could have happened. She claimed he was a sweet boy, with a kind smile and a big laugh. She has his dimpled chin, his flat ears. He looked more like her than he did like me.

I could call her. But what would I say? Hi, I'm a stranger, and no, her boy wasn't sweet, he was an asshole—but I loved him anyway. I could have saved him, if I'd done a few things differently. Anyway, nice talking to you, goodbye.

My name doesn't appear in any of the news coverage. Maybe Thistle suppressed it somehow. Or perhaps Zara did. There's no mention of her, either.

•

I'm determined to stay on the sofa until someone arrests me, but pretty soon my hunger gets the better of me, as always.

I thaw out the cash from the freezer and take it to the mall, where I buy a whole roast chicken and some new clothes. By the time I'm halfway back to the house, I've eaten most of the chicken. I'm starving. It's like my body is trying to grow a new arm. I assume it can't do that, but I wonder why not. What's the medical reason that I can regrow skin, hair, flesh, bone and blood, but not a limb? A lizard can regrow its tail, after all.

When I get home, I have to put the bag of chicken on the ground so I can open the door one-handed. Then I have to pick up the chicken, take it inside and put it down again so I can close the door. I can't use a knife and fork at the same time, so I have to pick the bones clean using only my fingers and teeth.

By the time I've finished the chicken, I'm wondering other things. Like, what am I going to do if the police never come for me? What is the rest of my life supposed to look like? I have no friends, no family. No job, and no prospects of getting one.

Over the next few days I practise some things. Tying my shoes one-handed is too hard without a thumb, so I buy Velcro-fastening shoes from a thrift store. I buy a backpack so I can carry more than one thing at a time. I get rid of my shirt with the buttons, which are fiddly. I learn to pin objects down with my stump so I can manipulate them with my other hand. Mostly I just get used to life being a pain in the ass.

At night, I wake up screaming. The nightmares are about the grinder, but it's usually Thistle being fed into it, not me.

I'm too scared to call her. She knows my secret now. But I also saved her life. What does she think of me?

The throbbing from my stump fades as the antibiotics kill the infection. Every day I have a little more energy. I spend my time pacing around the house, asking myself the same questions over and over.

Eventually I do call Thistle. But her number has been disconnected. I can't even leave a message.

Kyle's hat is on the floor next to my mattress. One night I see that some of his hairs are still stuck to the rim. I close my eyes and sniff them. They don't smell of anything.

CHAPTER 44

What is good at the start
but sad at the end?

'I'm sorry, sir,' says the woman behind the counter. 'You need written permission.'

'I got a call to say the results were back,' I say.

'They are, but I can't give them to you.'

She's wearing a polyester polo shirt with her name embroidered on the lapel, too small for me to read. Thick glass separates me and her, as though someone might try to rob this place. There's a sign on the counter: CAUTION. SHUTTER RISES UPWARD.

'You need the legal guardian's permission when the subject of the test is underage,' she says.

'I can't get that. He's dead.'

'The legal guardian is dead?'

That's not what I meant, but I decide to roll with it. 'Right.'

'Then you'll need permission from the next-of-kin.'

'I don't know who the next-of-kin is,' I say. 'That's why I need the test.'

She looks at my empty sleeve, wet from the rain outside. Most people glance away quickly, act like they haven't noticed my missing arm, but her gaze lingers long enough for me to see some sympathy.

'IED,' I say. 'In Afghanistan.'

She nods sadly. 'I'll see what I can do for you, okay? But no promises. Wait over there.' She gestures to a plastic bench bolted to the wall of the corridor.

'Thank you,' I say, and sit down. The woman emerges from a door marked Staff Only and hurries away down the corridor, her black sneakers squeaking on the linoleum.

I look down at my own shoes, with the Velcro. Kyle's shoes had the same straps. Did no one ever teach him to tie his laces? I'm not good for much, but I could at least have done that for him.

After a minute, someone approaches, but not from the direction the woman went in. Maybe she called security on me. I keep my head bowed, hoping they'll walk right past.

'Blake.'

I look up. It's Thistle. Beautiful, strong, unbending. She's alone, in plain clothes, hair tied back, make-up on. I'm on my feet so quickly that she takes a step back.

'What are you doing here?' I ask.

'I went to your house,' Thistle says, 'but I didn't want to go in. And then you left, so I followed you.'

I don't ask why she didn't come in. There's no good answer to that question.

'Are you okay?' I ask.

'No permanent damage,' she says. 'You?'

'Yeah, me too.' My lie is more obvious than hers. I clear my throat. 'You look good.'

'You too.' She glances at my missing arm. 'Have you lost weight?'

'Ha.' I can't resist a smile.

'Listen,' she says. 'I—'

'Can you wait five minutes?' I don't want to get arrested before I get the results about Kyle.

'Sure.' She sits next to me. 'I can stick around.'

'Your roommate must be glad to have you back.'

'I'm not staying with her.'

'Oh?'

Thistle looks away.

'Oh,' I say.

'We're not getting back together or anything.' She sounds like she's trying to convince herself as much as me. 'He's just helping me get back on my feet.'

'Oh,' I say again.

'He's really not that bad.'

She doesn't say *compared to you*, but that has to be the reason. She thought her ex-husband was an asshole, until she fell in love with someone even worse.

Just as the silence is becoming awkward, the receptionist comes back and hands me a small cream-coloured envelope. 'Here you go, sir.' She notices Thistle. 'Your husband is so brave.'

'Mm-hm,' Thistle says, and raises an eyebrow at me as the woman walks away.

'She's not wrong about you,' Thistle adds, when the woman is gone. 'And yet I feel like she is, somehow.'

I look down at the envelope.

'Is that a paternity test?' she asks.

I nod, squeezing it as though that will help me work out what's inside. I don't want to open it in front of her. Don't want her to see my reaction, one way or the other.

'I don't think you should open it,' she says.

I look up sharply. 'Why?'

'Kyle wasn't your son. He can't have been. Think about it—the odds must be a million to one.'

'The odds of him ending up in that house with me were a million to one whether he was my son or not.'

There's a hole in my logic, but Thistle is kind enough not to point it out. 'Sometimes you think something will be okay until you're actually faced with it. And then it's too late.'

'I have to know,' I say.

She takes a deep breath. 'When I had the abortion, I was only nine weeks pregnant. The embryo wasn't even technically a fetus yet, so I only needed two pills. Like you'd use to get rid of a headache.'

I want to squeeze her hand, but I don't. She's sitting on the wrong side of me.

'The doctor said to take the second pill two days after the first,' she says. 'I managed to avoid thinking about the fetus in between. But I wasn't supposed to swallow the pill. I had to put it inside my cheek and wait for it to dissolve. It takes a long time. Long enough to name the baby. Long enough to plan out its whole life in my head.'

She doesn't look upset as she says this. It's ancient history to her. But not to me. I missed this whole chunk of her life. I wish I'd been there for her. My eyes burn.

'I've always been pro-choice. But when I was waiting for that second pill to work, it really felt like I was killing something. I wasn't,' she adds quickly. 'But it felt like it.'

I'm not sure why she's telling me this. 'You made the right call.'

'I know. But it was hard. Losing a potential child.'

She clears her throat. 'Either Kyle was your kid and he's gone, or he wasn't your kid and then you've lost him in a whole other way. Opening that envelope won't bring you any peace.'

I want to fight her. *What would you know?* But I don't.

'Do you think . . .' I almost can't finish the question. 'Do you think I would have been a good father?'

Thistle hesitates. Wanting to lie. Unable to. 'No. But I'm sorry you never got the chance to try.'

The tears come then, blotching the envelope in my hands. Thistle puts her hand on my back.

'Can I take this with me?' My voice wobbles. 'While I think about it?'

'Take it where?'

'To jail.'

'I'm not here to arrest you, Blake,' she says.

'You're not?'

She gestures at the corridor. 'Do you see a SWAT team?'

I'm flattered that she thinks it would take a SWAT team. 'I told you I'd come quietly.'

'I'm here to thank you for saving my life.'

'It's because of me that you were in danger in the first place.'

'Maybe,' Thistle says. 'But if not for you, the others would still be trapped, or dead. I can't see anyone else getting them out the way you did.'

Well, no. Escape plans based on self-mutilation are my specialty. 'You did most of the work,' I say. 'We make a good team.'

'Yeah. We did.' She looks at the floor. Takes a breath. 'I have to say goodbye.'

I don't know what to say. Does she mean right now, or forever?

'I'm sorry. I know it's not your fault that you're a—' she searches for the right word, or for a way to avoid saying it '—the way you are. But I can't do this.' She gestures back and forth between herself and me. 'Not with you.'

I knew this was coming, but it's still a gut punch.

I want to tell her that I can become a good man, someone safe for her to love, but we both know that I can't change.

'You could visit me in prison,' I say, knowing how desperate it sounds.

'I told you, you're not getting arrested.' Thistle forces a smile. 'As far as the FBI is concerned, you went to the house investigating Fred. When you found yourself outnumbered, you impersonated Lux. Then you got the prisoners out as fast as you could. I didn't tell anyone about the . . .' She hesitates. There's that word again.

'Why not?' I ask.

'Because I don't think you're a danger to anyone.' She gestures at my stump. 'And I think you have a good heart.'

Only when you're around, I want to say. *I'm nothing without you. Please don't go.*

'You should arrest me,' I say instead.

She looks sceptical and a bit pitying. 'You *want* to get arrested?'

'No,' I say, not sure what I'm feeling. 'But . . . you're an FBI agent. You have to.'

'Goodbye, Blake.' Thistle leans over and kisses me just in front of my ear. She doesn't steel herself or take a deep breath—she just does it.

I swallow the lump in my throat. 'Wait.'

'I'm sorry.' She gets up and walks away.

The air chills the saliva print on my cheek. I rise. Hesitate. I shouldn't follow her. It would be frightening, being chased by someone like me.

But I can't let her go. She needs to arrest me. Not because of who I am, but because of who she is. We had the same upbringing. We went through the same meat grinder, in a sense. But I turned out bad and she turned out good. She has to stay that way.

Thistle walks out the door without looking back.

I'm paralysed for a minute, knowing I have to let her go, knowing that I can't. Then something inside me breaks and I find myself running.

The door is hard to open one-handed, especially with the envelope pinched between my fingers. I discard it, twist the handle, barge the door with my shoulder and stumble out into the parking lot.

The wind blows the rain into my face. I shield my eyes with my hand and scan the lot. Thistle is already in the driver's seat of her Crown Vic, starting the engine.

'Arrest me!' If she doesn't, it will haunt both of us.

Thistle sees me, standing in a puddle. She waves, tears in her eyes, then reverses out onto the road. I don't know if she heard me or not. I watch the car zoom away.

Knowing everything I've done, she let me go.

I've corrupted the best person I ever met.

'Sir?' The receptionist is behind me. She falters when she sees the look on my face, but holds up the unopened envelope. 'You dropped this.'

I take it wordlessly. She scurries back inside. Once she's out of sight, I drop the envelope again. I watch the puddle slowly devour the paper, dark splotches of ink growing like tumours across the surface.

CHAPTER 45

Your rock-climbing clothes should go on which hanger?

When I get back, my house feels cold and empty. It's shabby, the rot barely concealed by the cheap paint. It suits me. Maybe I'll strip the paint away, so everyone can see what it's really like. Smash some windows. Let the whole world in.

Or maybe just burn the place to the ground. I can see the appeal in what Fred was trying to do. Let everything go up in flames. Erase your home to erase yourself. Turn inner pain outwards.

I kick the door closed behind me. My eyes still sting from the tears, the exhaustion and the after-effects of the pepper spray. Blinking and sniffling, I go to the bathroom and splash some cold water on my face.

'Is this a bad time?'

'What the fuck?' I whirl around, crashing against the towel rack. Zara is in my bathtub, neck deep in bubbles.

'I hope you don't mind,' she says. 'I let myself in.'

My heart is still racing. 'And ran a bath?'

Her hair has maroon streaks in it and she's wearing a darker shade of lipstick than before. Her eyes are lighter, roast turkey-gold, without the contact lenses. If she were wearing the right clothes, she might not even be recognisable as the empress of torture from the house in the woods.

She shrugs her perfect shoulders. 'You were gone a long time.'

I'm sick of deception and mind games. There's no reason not to just ask: 'Are you here to kill me, or seduce me, or what?'

Zara examines some bubbles on her fingertip. 'You cut off a valuable source of intelligence. My superiors are annoyed.' She purses her lips and blows the bubbles away.

'Well, I feel really bad about that.'

'They're also impressed.' Zara stretches out in the tub, putting a foot up on the rim. 'I was completely convinced that Samson's death was a suicide, and I'd been trying to work out Fred's real name for months. You did it in less than a week.'

I don't tell her that I'd technically been after Rick for years. 'You're welcome. I'm not going to tell anyone about you, if that's your concern.' I gesture at my empty, lifeless house. 'Who would I tell?'

'Hm.'

I wipe my face with a towel. By the time I can see again, Zara is standing up, naked in front of me. But the look in her eyes isn't alluring, at least not in the traditional sense. It's trusting.

'I'm not scared of you.' She spreads her arms wide. 'I won't run away like the FBI agent did.'

So she *is* here to seduce me.

403

'Not interested,' I say.

She steps out of the tub, dripping. Moves into my personal space, her face inches from mine. 'Wouldn't you rather have a partner who's more like you? Someone who respects your skills and isn't disgusted by your hobbies?'

'I'm not looking for a relationship right now.'

'I have a delicate situation at work,' she says.

The change of topic throws me. 'Work?'

'Right. It's another operation on US soil, so official support is hard to come by. I could use some unofficial help.'

It takes me a moment to realise what she means.

'You were wasted at the FBI, Blake.' She reaches past me, plucks my towel off the rack and winds it around her body. Smiles. 'How would you like to work for the CIA?'

ACKNOWLEDGEMENTS

Thanks so much to all the booksellers, librarians, reviewers and readers who have supported Blake in his journey. I'm more grateful than I can say. Without all you Hangman evangelists (hangfans? hangers-on?), he would be long gone.

Thank you to the hard-working and talented teams at Allen & Unwin, Bolinda Audio and Curtis Brown Australia for making *Hideout* possible. Special thanks to everyone who read drafts, provided encouragement and made suggestions, particularly Clare Forster, Angela Handley, Amy Jones, Ali Lavau, Sydney Liau, Sanchita McGregor, Venetia Major, Christa Munns, Jane Palfreyman, Benjamin Stevenson and Gareth Ward. If there was any justice in the world, all your names would be on the cover. (But there isn't.) Thanks to everyone else who volunteered to read the manuscript—don't worry, I'll be back to collect that favour on some future book.

Sincere thanks to everyone at Wardini Books, whose dedication to spreading the word about *Hangman* made me a minor celebrity in Havelock North, New Zealand.

Thanks to Jackie French for the quote about anger on the first page. She was quick to point out that she was paraphrasing someone else who had read *Hitler's Daughter*.

There's no cannibalism in that, but you should read it anyway.

Speaking of good books, thanks to the following journalists: Robert Evans (*It Could Happen Here**), Eileen Ormsby (*The Darkest Web*), John Safran (*Depends What You Mean By Extremist*) and Jon Ronson (*So You've Been Publicly Shamed*). Their work was valuable while writing *Hideout*. Views expressed are Blake's, not theirs (or mine).

Thanks to Lynne Allister, who donated $500 to #AuthorsForFireys and got a character named after her. I'm sorry your namesake was treated so poorly, but you did read the other books in the series, so you knew what you signed up for.

A lot happened during the development of *Hideout*. I moved house, twice. I became a father for the second time. There was the bushfire, and then the pandemic. Thank you to my family—Venetia, Redvers, Ash, Mum and Dad—for keeping me sane during a hard time . . . well, sane enough to write *Hideout*, anyway.

---

* Not technically a book, but still good.